I0573395

FLATTERED BY FLOWERS
THE ANTHOLOGY

HEMMED IN SILVER

CAPTURED ON FILM

BATHED IN MOONLIGHT

FLATTERED BY FLOWERS

TWINKLE PRESS

Songs of the Amaranthine
Flattered by Flowers: The Anthology

because there is always more to any story

TABLE OF CONTENTS

TABLE OF CONTENTS

CAPTURED
ON FILM

TABLE OF CONTENTS

BATHED IN MOONLIGHT

FLATTERED
BY FLOWERS

TABLE OF CONTENTS

ALSO AVAILABLE IN AUDIO
NARRATED BY TRAVIS BALDREE

HEMMED IN SILVER

because belonging is a kind of magic

*"This is new to me. What
are the cozy clans?"*

*"Gentle countryside clans
with a unique perspective
because they've always lived
close to humans. Mostly
rodents and small birds, but
many clans that watch over
animals domesticated by
humanity count themselves
among the cozies."*
*Dr. Bellamy was watching
her closely. "Their customs
are charming."*

TAMIKO AND THE TWO JANITORS

PLEA

"Is it important?" inquired Thrussel.

Wyn left off his fifth reread to blandly reply, "Most letters hand-delivered by heralds *are*. How did this even find me?"

"Discreet channels."

"Am *I* found, then?"

"No, Wyn. We songbirds have our *own* way of making sure letters reach their intended recipients." He touched Wyn's arm. "It was passed from dove to ptarmigan to warbler before arriving in our vicinity. Someone remembered Lord Alderney having a little place by the name, and I offered to see it delivered. None the wiser."

"Surprising, really." Wyn grimaced at the envelope, which bore scant postage and several notes in different hands suggesting possible locales. "Not much to go on."

Mister Godwyn Outler

Merritt House

"It *is* yours, though? You *are* the intended recipient?"

"Dismal day." He sighed. "We'll convene in the kitchen. Stay for tea, Thrussel. There'll have to be a reply."

"Too kind," murmured the herald.

Raising his voice, Wyn called, "Pennythwaite?"

His oldest friend stepped into the room, one finger in the ledger book he'd likely been updating. With a faint frown, Pennythwaite nodded a greeting in Thrussel's direction.

"Is Sonnet here?" asked Wyn.

"Close enough to summon."

Wyn rumpled his hair distractedly "May as well call Triggs and Beck, too. This affects all of us."

Lingering long enough to smooth Wyn's unruly thatch, Pennythwaite acknowledged his request. "The kitchen."

Wyn scanned the letter again. Sure, and it was trouble. He almost wished Thrussel had left it to gather dust in whatever bin they used to collect undeliverable letters. But the plea it contained brought back good memories of old vows. And a pact he couldn't ignore.

By the time he followed the pokey back hall to the kitchen, they were all assembled.

Pennythwaite, who counted him as a nestmate, despite the trouble it might cause if anyone of consequence found out.

Sonnet, a third-generation dog who liked to think of himself as a lone wolf.

Triggs, one of Lord Alderney's several sons, who was responsible for the dairy barn.

And Beck, the cheerful strutter in charge of their chicken coop and hatchery.

Wyn tossed the letter onto the table. "A boy wrote to me, thinking I'm his uncle."

"Are you?" asked Sonnet, his tail already wagging.

Reaching for the missive, Pennythwaite murmured, "You *do* realize how long Wyn's been here?"

Sonnet tapped a few fingers, then shrugged. "You're the mathy one."

"Technically, the boy isn't a blood relation, even though we share a name."

"Alfred Outler." Pennythwaite looked up sharply. "*And* Hazel Outler."

"They're newly orphaned, and the lad's desperate to find someone to take them in. If he can't sort it soon, they'll separate him from his sister."

Triggs folded his big hands together and quietly asked, "Why do you consider their problems your own?"

"He mentions names. I don't know his father, but I recognize his grandfather's name. Alfred is Darren's great-great-great-grandson. We vowed out together, swore a pact, and took the same surname." Spreading his hands wide, Wyn put it the only way he needed to. "They're what's left of my clan. My kin."

"When you say *children*, are we talking bottles and nappies?" asked Beck.

Pennythwaite passed him the letter. "Alfred is fourteen. His sister is four."

Sonnet crooned a sorrowful note. The softie.

"We keep to ourselves, but there's the rest of the cooperative to consider," said Triggs.

Wyn nodded. "If we can come to terms, I'll go to your father next. Or … I'll have to leave. At least until they've grown enough to make their own way."

"No," said Pennythwaite.

"This is your *home*," agreed Sonnet, looking anxiously from face to face.

Slowly, everyone in the room shifted into a cautiously receptive posture. Even Triggs, who usually wanted more time to consider before making big decisions.

"A pact is a pact," said Beck, already smiling again. "*Uncle* Wyn."

RISK

From his hilltop home, Northrop Hall, Tristan Alderney managed a cluster of secluded farms in Yoxall. He was known throughout the area as a fair-minded and levelheaded man. His tenants called him *lord*, though he wasn't a member of the peerage. Some out of respect. Some because they knew he owned the title as leader of his clan.

Lord Alderney listened to Wyn without comment, then held out his hand for the letter. "You intend to adopt?"

"I thought we could just take them in?" Wyn shrugged. "Can't we do it unofficially?"

"Abducting orphans?" He shook his head. "I know a solicitor who can smooth the way, but there *will* be paperwork. Your existence will become documented."

Something Wyn preferred to avoid. "Won't that cause trouble for the cooperative?"

After several moments, Lord Alderney said, "I think not. We disguise our differences and mingle freely with humans in the area. Bringing in two more could be considered … community enrichment."

Wyn was still worried. "There will be a paper trail connecting me to you. And I'm not supposed to have any contact with the Amaranthine."

"You aren't the only one bending rules. Our cooperative is unlisted and unaffiliated with the reaver community." Lord Alderney smiled tightly. "Most of us have one reason or another for avoiding notice."

Pennythwaite weighed in. "The risks are minimal. If the In-between was interested in you, Wyn, they wouldn't have let you go."

Triggs asked, "The children are unendowed?"

"Seems likely," said Wyn. "They're part of the general populace. Would there be anything left of Darren's bloodline after four generations?"

"We'll know once the dears are here," said Sonnet.

Beck chortled. "Harboring another unregistered reaver? No complaints here. My flock dotes on Wyn."

"Are you resolved?" asked Lord Alderney. "I'll put through a call."

"A pact is a pact." Turning to Thrussel, Wyn asked, "Will you carry a message?"

"Gladly," pledged the herald. "As many as you need."

Wyn kept it short.

We are farmers living a quiet life. Nothing fancy, but there's room. Once we sort the legal bits, bring your sister and make your home with us.

CHANGE

Wyn had always considered his study a peaceful place. A sanctuary filled with creature comforts. So it was unsettling to have Triggs and Sonnet stampede through, pointing out how many dangers to small children he kept around.

Matchboxes. Decanters. Even the chunk of crystal he used as a doorstop was called into question, since one of its edges was keen enough to cut.

Pennythwaite recommended adding doors to the lower bookcases in order to protect precious volumes. Wyn, who was getting more frazzled by the day, asked if they couldn't just put locks on their doors, keeping the little girl out until she was old enough to understand that certain rooms in the house were private.

Triggs took two days to install squat fences around the fireplaces in every room.

Beck stole every lamp and candle stand. Too tippy. Wall mounts and ceiling hooks were apparently safer.

"Dismal day," muttered Wyn. "How clumsy can one child be?"

"Better safe than sorry," Triggs said philosophically.

When Pennythwaite called them for dinner, he sounded strange. Strained.

Concerned, Wyn hurried to the kitchen, only to draw up short. Triggs showed up a moment later and with a surprised grunt, backed into the corner. Pennythwaite was clearly holding himself in check, a sure sign he was thoroughly flustered.

Beck sauntered in and swore. "Sonnet, what are you *doing*?"

"Getting ready for our children."

Gesturing widely, Beck squawked, "You're in a dress!"

"Well, I was thinking." Sonnet calmly slid a platter and a covered dish onto the table. "They're children. They'll need mothering."

Wyn couldn't have been more confused. Sonnet had traded his usual attire for a female's embroidered tunic, a full skirt, and an apron.

Beck weakly repeated, "You're in a dress."

"A little girl in a houseful of males? She'll need a chaperone. Someone to teach her how to be ladylike."

Triggs finally spoke. "I cannot deny you're the most qualified."

Sonnet beamed at him.

Nobody seemed willing to point out that Sonnet was still male under his skirt. Wyn shot a pleading look in Pennythwaite's direction. Normally, he would be the one to speak up. He had seniority.

Pennythwaite finally asked, "Can you do it?"

"I am quite set upon it." Sonnet gave a little shimmy as he adjusted some mysterious undergarment. "It's only for a decade or two. Five at most."

Wyn had to admit that for an Amaranthine, a few decades amounted to a short-term commitment.

"So be it." Pennythwaite indicated them each in turn. "Uncle Wyn is the head of this household. I am his man of business. Sonnet is our live-in cook. Triggs and Beck are hirelings, which is why you live separately."

To make room for the children, Triggs and Beck had cleared out, moving their belongings across the yard, into a tiny house surrounded by wizened apple trees. They would still share all their meals in Sonnet's kitchen, but living apart already felt strange.

"Cozy Cottage," said Sonnet. "We'll call it Cozy Cottage."

"Appropriate," conceded Pennythwaite.

Wyn thought it cutesy, but he could understand why it might appeal to his friends. Triggs and Beck belonged to clans whose animal counterparts had been domesticated. Always living in and around human communities, their histories intertwined—close, comfortable, cooperative.

Collectively, they were known as the cozy clans.

BRAVE

Alfie didn't like people pawing through his parents' belongings, deciding all on their own if something was worth keeping. Even though he couldn't bring himself to speak out, it wound him up inside. Already half-mad with missing, he was half-wild with fear when a reply to his letter finally arrived.

"Truly?" he whispered, though he shouldn't have expected a postie to know.

"Alfred, are you safe?" the man asked instead. "You and Hazel?"

"That lot." Alfie jutted his chin toward the back of the flat. "They're from the church. Trying to be helpful since we can't stay here. Good people, but ...."

"Not *your* people?" suggested the man.

Alfie hunched his shoulders and looked away.

"As long as you're safe?" Intent. Insistent.

"So far." Clutching the letter, Alfie asked, "This a good place?"

"Do you like the countryside?"

"Not sure. Never been."

"Well, this should prove an adventure." More quietly, the man asked, "May I pop around with reports? It might be odd hours, but you wouldn't need to let me in."

Alfie took a closer look. He was a wispy fellow, barely taller than himself, with reddish-brown hair and a dusting of freckles. Large, dark eyes were soft, as was his smile. Kind of pretty for a man, but he probably took after his mum or something. "You're not a postie, are you?"

"I *do* work for a kind of courier service, but I'm a friend of the family. My people are from Yoxall, same as your uncle." And with a genteel flourish, he said, "You may call me Thrussel."

"Alfie." He thrust out his hand. It was meant for a handshake, but maybe he just needed to make sure this messenger wasn't a figment of his imagination.

The hand that gripped his was solid and warm. As was the second hand that came up to double the clasp.

"What's my uncle like?" Alfie dared to ask.

"Like you, I should think." Thrussel gave his hand a small pat. "Brave."

COME

Thrussel always managed to appear when Alfie was alone. The messages were short, but they eased his mind. He could keep Hazel. That's all that mattered, really. The rest would sort itself out somehow.

A light rap on his window sent him hurrying to undo the latch.

More than once, Thrussel had turned up on the fire escape outside Alfie's window. Calm as you please, despite being three stories above a dingy alley. But usually after dark. It was mid-afternoon, and their minder had gone to the market.

"For you," said Thrussel, offering a fold of paper.

Like all of Uncle's messages, it was brief. **Not many can find Merritt House, but Thrussel knows the way. Come and be welcome.**

"Shall we?" asked Thrussel.

"Now?" Alfie asked in disbelief. "Just ... leave?"

"You finished packing, didn't you?"

He nodded.

"May I?" Thrussel eased between sash and sill. "Where is your sister?"

"Napping."

"I'll let in the porters. They'll take your trunks. Point out anything else you want to keep."

Alfie hesitated. "Can we do that? Go off without a word?"

"Why not? You're Wyn's now." Thrussel showed him another envelope. "We'll leave notice."

Twenty minutes later, Alfie, Hazel, and a modest collection of boxes, baggage, and furnishings were leaving London by lorry.

After a long day of driving, Alfie was more than a little confused when they turned into a lot in a nondescript village.

"This is a rental," explained Thrussel. "Help Triggs shift everything?"

So Alfie toted boxes to an honest-to-goodness ox cart, where one of the fellows who'd manhandled furniture down their apartment building's narrow stairwell was checking harnesses.

"I thought the lorry was yours," Alfie admitted.

"No. This rig is, though." He offered his hand palm-up. "Triggs. I'm one of the farmhands at your uncle's place."

Thrussel, who swept past with Hazel in his arms, slyly added, "He's too shy to say so, but Triggs is part of your new family."

"And you came for us." Alfie awkwardly shook hands and mumbled, "Thanks, sir."

"Just Triggs." His voice was deep and smooth, and his smile was lazy. "And these two are Riff and Raff. We're pleased to finally meet you."

While Thrussel showed off Hazel to a pair of gigantic bulls, Triggs taught Alfie how to tie the knots that would hold everything together for the last leg of their journey.

"Is it far?"

"Far and farther." Triggs smiled to himself and quietly added, "That's one of its charms."

ROOM

Between Thrussel and Triggs, Alfie had stopped mentally rehearsing all the terrible things that were meant to happen to orphans. The men were flat-out nice. Surely, they wouldn't be working for a wicked man. Still, when the ox cart rolled to a stop before a stone house with skinny windows and squat chimneys, Alfie had to own he was nervous.

A man stepped outside and lifted one hand in a weird gesture that turned into an awkward wave. "Alfie and Hazel," he said, searching their faces. "I'm your Uncle Wyn."

Alfie had sort of been expecting an old man. Why was that? Maybe because the papers had seemed old-fashioned.

The church people had gone through all the files, searching for any mention of relatives. A packet in the family safe had yielded the only possibility—Godwyn Outler. His name had been written alongside Darren Outler's, and that was their grandad's name. A postcard tucked between the pages had included the notation "in care of Merritt House."

It was all he'd had to go on.

It had worked.

Alfie had assumed Wyn was his dad's uncle, but the man before them looked younger than Dad had been. And nothing like him.

Thick waves of black hair. Pale skin and light eyes. Nothing like Alfie and Hazel, who'd inherited their dad's easy tan and straight hair.

Uncle Wyn also dressed strangely, in close-fitting pants, high boots, and a posh-looking tunic with fancy stitching around the collar. Was it a country fashion?

"Come inside," urged their new guardian. "Sonnet's been cooking since yesterday. I hope you're hungry."

Alfie was barely through the door when he was swept into a hug. It was embarrassing and confusing, but also reassuring. They were welcome.

"I'm Sonnet. I get to be the cook."

"Alfie," he managed.

She was quite tall for a woman, with an eager smile and unusual eyes. A brown so light, it was near to yellow. Gray streaked through Sonnet's pinned hair, but her face was unlined.

Leaning back to study his face, Sonnet announced, "I've read up on orphans. You haven't been oppressed, have you?"

"No, marm."

"What about aspirations? The ones with expectations usually fare a little better than the rest." Sonnet seemed eager to assist.

"Couldn't say, marm. I'm new to the whole orphan thing."

"Oh, you dear." She hugged him hard, sniffed his hair, and kissed his cheek. "I'm new to this myself. We'll muddle through together."

He found himself blushing under her gaze. "Thanks, marm."

"Sonnet," she insisted. "And what's this? Hazel, you're not a baby *at all*! Why, you're a big girl!"

Giggling at being swept up into Sonnet's arms, Hazel asked, "Auntie?"

"No, no. I'm all alone, you see. A loner. But you must *tell* me! What do you love to eat? I'm the cook, you know."

While Hazel happily listed puddings and jellies and biscuits, Wyn touched Alfie's elbow to get his attention. "Here is Pennythwaite."

This fellow looked respectable enough, with a pressed white shirt, black tie, and old-fashioned sleeve protectors that might've been borrowed from Bob Cratchit. His vest was a gentle golden color, lustrous like the metal, and spectacles perched precariously atop a hook nose.

"Welcome to Merritt House, Alfie." His voice was deep and sonorous, his enunciation precise.

Alfie suspected this man would be strict. He'd better look sharp and learn the rules of the house.

Only when the man turned to go did Alfie realize that Pennythwaite's pale brown hair hung in a thick plait almost to his knees. Odd, that.

Wyn had begun following Pennythwaite out, but stopped partway when he realized Alfie hadn't moved.

"Where did Thrussel go?" Alfie asked, unsettled that the most familiar face was gone.

"Back to his post." Uncle Wyn beckoned encouragingly. "I'll take you into Yoxall tomorrow, show you where to find him. He's a good friend to have."

Placated, Alfie followed his uncle and Pennythwaite upstairs and into a boxy bedroom with a mattress on the floor instead of on a bedframe. He'd always assumed that sleeping on the floor was a shabby sort of thing, but the blankets and pillows looked clean and soft. Even expensive, given the abundance of snowy white and shimmering gold.

"Not what you're used to," his uncle guessed. "But there's no way for your sister to fall out of bed. Or to wake up alone in a strange place. We can change things around later, but we thought that for now, it would be better for you to keep her close."

"It's good," he managed. "Thanks."

"Triggs will bring up your things. Help you arrange them."

Alfie could only nod and repeat himself.

Uncle Wyn looked up at Pennythwaite, who stood really close and really quiet. But with the slight inclination of his head, Uncle relaxed into a smile. "Anything you need, lad."

"We'll be fine," Alfie mumbled.

"You *will* be fine," Uncle Wyn asserted. "I'll see to it."

GRUEL

Alfie was getting along fairly well, all things considered. Hazel adored Sonnet, who seemed to expect to look after his sister. Which freed him up to pitch in. Triggs and Beck were decent about showing him around, explaining what needed doing. Alfie tried his hand at everything.

Dairy barn. Creamery.

Hen house. Hatchery.

The farm was big enough to keep everyone busy. Sonnet tended the door garden. Uncle and Beck handled fieldwork. Triggs walked the cows to and from their pasture and milked them, morning and evening. The work never stopped, but everything proceeded at an easy pace.

Alfie liked it. Even though things were … different.

There was no television, no automobile, no kitchen appliances. The house wasn't even wired for electricity. At least they had indoor plumbing, thanks in part to a well and a windmill.

Other things seemed a bit *off*, but Alfie couldn't be entirely sure. He was a city boy. What did he know about cows and chickens? Only he'd never known they could get so *big*. Some of Beck's hens were tall enough to pick Alfie's pockets. And the six milk cows Triggs devoted his time to were even bigger than Riff and Raff, who pulled their deliveries of milk, butter, and cheese into Yoxall.

There were other things. Littler than livestock, but just as strange.

Like Pennythwaite's obsession with bird feeders. Half of Uncle Wyn's trips into town seemed to be for the seed needed to keep the local songbirds happy.

Nights were full of strange noises, courtesy of all the owls in the forest beyond the fields. Their hooting kept Alfie awake the first few nights.

Sonnet had a second sense when it came to fire in the house. Alfie would have sworn that she knew the instant he struck a match, for she'd always pop in to check on him.

Actually, Sonnet may have been the strangest of strange things at Merritt House. She told queer stories at bedtime, like "The Sunshower and the Rainbow" or "The Angel and the Tump." And she kept mixing up the meaning of words, almost as if she'd never had anything to do with things Alfie would have considered ordinary.

Like at breakfast just this morning.

Same as always, Alfie had come down to find his uncle and Pennythwaite already at the table—both quiet, both comfortable.

"Good morning, Alfie." Sonnet ladled something into a bowl. "Come, eat your gruel!"

Uncle Wyn frowned. "Gruel?"

"Yes, yes! According to books, it's what orphans eat."

"You plan to raise them in the Dickensian style?" Pennythwaite inquired blandly.

"Well, not *exactly*," Sonnet countered huffily. "Only the good parts."

"Like ... gruel?" asked Uncle Wyn, his lips twitching.

Alfie wasn't sure where to look, there were so many glances darting about the room. None of them meant for him. He confined himself to a wary, "Thank you."

He knew a bit about gruel, though not from personal experience. It was meant to be miserly slop, thin and horrid. Poor sustenance for poor beggars. But the bowl Sonnet set before him was the farthest thing from meager.

Thick as custard. Spiced to a treat. Sonnet had romanticized gruel into a pudding. The stuff was lovely with strong tea. He paused long enough to mumble around mouthful. "I like it."

She was at his side in a twinkling, ladling more into his bowl. And he was glad to accept. Only … that's when he caught sight of it.

Alfie would swear upon the family Bible that something was swishing from under the hem of her full skirt. And that something was a tail—brown fur, tipped in gray. Plain as anything. And wagging.

Pennythwaite cleared his throat.

Sonnet backed away, flustered.

Uncle Wyn sloshed his tea and launched into a discourse on pumpkins, but there was an edge of nervousness to his voice. He trailed off, and the kitchen itself seemed to hold its breath.

That's when Alfie made up his mind.

This wasn't a normal sort of place, but it was a *good* place. Strange and silly and safe. He'd do anything to stay, even if it meant pretending. So he looked Uncle Wyn right in the eye and said, "You should try the gruel. It's good."

"Sure about that?" he managed faintly.

"Never had better." Alfie nodded to Sonnet and added, "Hazel will love it."

She brightened, and Uncle Wyn probably should have tried

a little harder to hide his relief. They were ready to pretend right along with him. Only Pennythwaite had a sharpish look in his eye. But the man of business simply inclined his head. And accepted a bowl of gruel.

HIDE

"Well?" asked Wyn. "I know you've been testing the waters. Are they deep?"

Pennythwaite set aside his book and beckoned. "Stop pacing. Sit down."

Just to be contrary, Wyn flopped onto the settee opposite Pennythwaite's.

Without comment, his friend stood, circled the low table with its orderly stacks of leaflets and communiques, and sat at Wyn's side. "Why are you out of sorts?"

Wyn stated the obvious. "He saw."

"He did."

"Was he frightened?"

Pennythwaite sighed. "Sonnet certainly was."

"Alfie, though." Wyn waved an arm in the general direction of the kitchen. "Have we lost trust before properly finding it?"

"You'll have to ask Sonnet about scents. He'll know."

"*She*'ll know," corrected Wyn. They needed to get used to referring to their friend as a female.

Pennythwaite inclined his head. "She will."

"Well?" All the uncertainties and unforeseen consequences had his insides in knots.

"Alfie's reserves are meager." He removed his glasses and a handkerchief from some inner pocket. Polishing the lenses, he calmly added, "With proper care, he might gain."

Wyn thought back. "We never were much. Darren ranked even lower than me."

"Did your friend have an aptitude?"

"Nothing to speak of. It's why we vowed out."

Pennythwaite peered at him with large, liquid black eyes. "A shame he wasn't cultivated by someone of superior patience and foresight."

Wyn's lips quirked. "Like yourself?"

"Like me." He resettled his glasses and carefully refolded the handkerchief. "You acquired no *official* classification, but surely there were preferences ... aspirations ... perhaps some inherent aptitude of lineage?"

"Darren found work in the Kith shelters because he loved animals."

"And you ...?"

Wyn laughed. "Just a farmer, same as now. But in daydreams, I was an ephemerologist."

Pennythwaite fussed with Wyn's hair. "Chasing fairy lights?" he teased.

It was an old joke. A fond memory. Wyn relaxed under the friendly fussing that both his unruly hair and Pennythwaite had always needed. "We applied together to several enclaves, but those places have minimum requirements. Hard workers aren't wanted if they'll only bring down the bloodlines."

"Statistics aren't everything."

Wyn knew that. Now.

Minutes passed before Pennythwaite quietly remarked, "There is the girl."

"Her name is Hazel."

"And she is lovely."

Something froze inside Wyn.

Pennythwaite went on. "I'll be asking Lord Alderney to ward our boundaries with greater care."

"Is she especially potent?"

"No, but she'll attract Ephemera."

Wyn couldn't help blurting, "Do I?"

Pennythwaite blinked down on him. "Are you asking me to compare you?"

"Not sure. Maybe." Wyn tried to be casual about it. "Is she more the thing?"

His oldest friend blinked some more. "Are you jealous?"

"Considering it."

Pennythwaite's tone was gently chiding. "She is a chick in the nest."

"A *lovely* one. Who will grow up."

"And until such time, she is in our care." In a rare show of affection, Pennythwaite kissed Wyn's forehead. "Hazel will flourish and fly away, and we will remain."

Reassured, he asked, "Will we need to ward her?"

"Sigils for now. Perhaps a necklace at Christmastide?"

Oh. He hadn't considered that. "We'll have to mark human holidays, won't we?"

"Sonnet will enjoy that."

"Can we leave that to him?" Wyn wondered aloud.

Pennythwaite hooted softly in amusement. "We can leave it to *her*."

MILK

Eighteen-year-old Alfie was halfway to Yoxall before he realized he'd walked away from his work without a word. But he needed to talk to someone, and *not* someone from Merritt House. That would be too awkward. And lead to certain admissions. Which left Thrussel.

Yoxall wasn't much of a town. Most of the shops did one thing and did it well—candles, bread, cloth, cheese. The fresh market operated according to rules that still baffled Alfie, since there was nothing like it in his old neighborhood. Best he could tell, the whole community treated it like their pantry, dropping off and picking up stuff without a single note or coin trading hands.

The biggest building along the square was mostly a tavern, but there was a counter just inside the door where people could collect letters and parcels.

Thrussel took one look at Alfie's face and lost his near-perpetual smile. Murmuring something to a co-worker, he left his post. "This is unexpected."

Alfie nodded.

"Did you walk?"

Another nod.

Thrussel reached for him but held back. "Something happen out your way?"

Now that he was here, Alfie had no idea what to say.

"Join me for a meal?" His friend indicated the tavern's dining area.

Alfie nodded again.

From a large pot that always seemed to be simmering on the

back of the stove, the taverner ladled two bowls of hearty stew. Loaves of bread. Fresh butter. Strong tea. Molasses biscuits. Alfie worked his way through most of it before mustering the courage to make a start.

"Do you know how long Sonnet's worked for my uncle?"

Thrussel slid his hands around his mug. "Seems like always."

"Is she from here?" Alfie was really only curious on this point. "Have family in the area?"

"Sonnet's always claimed to be a loner." Thrussel chuckled. "Sonnet may be the only person who *believes* that, but there's no harm in the notion."

Alfie smiled a little, but it faded fast.

"Did something happen, Alfie?"

"Yeah."

"And it's upset you?" Thrussel's gaze had gone soft with sympathy.

"Hazel has a new kitten. We're pretty sure she smuggled it from Lord Alderney's stables."

His friend hummed encouragingly.

Alfie said, "Sonnet seems … concerned?"

"What gave you that idea?"

"Earlier. Round back in the garden. I was close enough to hear. Sonnet was … scolding the kitten, I think. Talking like it could understand every word. And she was *growling*."

"You must have been downwind."

Alfie had to think on it. "Maybe. I didn't notice."

"Has Sonnet lost your trust?"

He slowly shook his head. "It's not *that*."

"What then?"

Alfie could feel color creeping into his face. "I was actually wondering if I should be worried about the cat. If Sonnet was *that* riled, do you suppose it's a threat?"

Thrussel's laughter was always nice. Musical.

Signaling the taverner for a fresh pot of tea, Thrussel eyed Alfie curiously. "You're worried about the *kitten*?"

"Yeah."

"Do you know if it's male or female?"

"Female. Hazel named her Milk."

"Because she has white fur?" guessed Thrussel.

"No. She's a ginger tabby." Alfie offered a half-smile. "According to Hazel, it's what she *wanted* to be called."

Thrussel reached across the table, placing his hand a little way from Alfie's. "I'm sure Sonnet and Milk were simply working out their differences. A matter of dominance, not danger."

"Oh." Alfie reached for another biscuit. "That's all right, then."

VIEW

On a swiftly-darkening October evening when Alfie was twenty, he caught a whiff of smoke from the direction of the barn. Sidetracked soon changed to stymied, for several of the cattle pens stood empty.

Merritt House kept as many as sixteen cows in the big barn, but Triggs doted on six in particular. His ladies. Their pens even boasted hand-painted name plaques—Bell, Star, Rose, Lass, Meek, and Mild.

Triggs was always chatting with them, and he absolutely hovered whenever one of them was close to calving. He'd allowed

Alfie in their pens from the start, teaching their city-boy how to curry and how to care for cloven hooves. On quiet afternoons, they'd shampoo tails, polish horns, and shine the bells that made the ladies' stroll to the far pasture so tuneful.

Where could they be at this hour? Cow-napping seemed unlikely. Or was it cattle rustling? Alfie checked the rest of the pens. All but a handful were vacant.

He was halfway to the door, intent on fetching Triggs, when he caught another whiff of the smoke that had first diverted him. Pipe tobacco? Alfie had only ever seen Uncle Wyn smoke in his study.

Climbing the ladder to the loft, Alfie stood for a moment, breathing in the sweetness of summer hay and waiting to be noticed. The upper doors had been thrown wide, and his uncle stood with a shoulder propped against their frame, a trickle of smoke slowly rising from the bowl of his pipe.

Wyn glanced his way. Acknowledgement.

Alfie said, "You're not supposed to bring any uncovered fire into the barn." Triggs was a stickler about it.

"I'm a careful man when it's called for."

Everyone in the house had tidy habits. It was one of the things Alfie liked about Merritt House. He ventured, "Where's Triggs?"

"Away. Which is the *only* reason I haven't been chastised and chased out."

Alfie eased closer. You could just see Cozy Cottage from this vantage, and there were no lights in the windows. Unusual in the extreme. "Where's he gone?"

"Not far."

"Did he take the cows?"

"He did." Uncle Wyn puffed softly. "They love to dance."

Alfie lowered his gaze and tried to come up with an excuse to leave.

His uncle spoke first. "Why do you never ask?"

It took a fair while for Alfie to compose an answer. "I wouldn't want to inconvenience anyone."

"Inconvenience?" Uncle Wyn echoed incredulously.

"Yes, sir," Alfie mumbled. "If I was too nosy or made trouble, I thought you might have to send us away. And I didn't want that. *Don't* want that."

"Very considerate of you." His uncle studied him for a few moments. "You *have* made things easier for us."

"Good to know."

"You're not afraid of our little secrets?"

"No, sir."

"And you're not curious?"

Alfie hesitated. He'd been pretending not to see, but he did sometimes wonder. Settling for a shrug, he said, "Not if it'll inconvenience you."

Uncle Wyn hummed. "You know, you're old enough to go off somewhere. Make your own way. I know Pennythwaite's offered to cover your tuition. More than once."

"If it's all the same to you, sir, I'll stay with Hazel."

"What about when she's grown?"

Alfie thought it should have been obvious. "I won't leave her. It's different if she wants to go."

"Say she does," posed Uncle Wyn. "*Then* what will you do?"

Ever since Alfie turned sixteen, Pennythwaite brought up boarding schools and universities exactly twice a year. Always at midsummer and midwinter. He and Uncle were incredibly generous, but Alfie always refused.

Uncle gently pressed, "Is there anything you want to do?"

"Yes, sir." He shuffled his feet. "I'd like to stay on."

His uncle was frowning. That might be a bad sign. Alfie's heart began to thud at the thought of being turned out.

Finally, Uncle Wyn asked, "Are you hoping to inherit this place? It's not ours, you know. Not really. We rent from Lord Alderney."

"I know that. It's nothing like that." Alfie hardly knew where to look. "It's just ... this is home."

"So you're staying," his uncle said, like it was settled. "Best take a look, then."

"Sir?"

Uncle Wyn pointed with the stem of his pipe. Out into the night. Out beyond fields full of ripening pumpkins. "Stand here, lad."

A heavy orange moon was lifting in the eastern sky, a lovely sight all on its own. But in the nearer distance, lights winked and wove. "What's that, then?"

"Some say they're fairy lights."

Sonnet certainly loved spinning fairy tales, but Uncle's tone suggested these weren't. Recalling his offhand comment, Alfie asked, "Is it a dance?"

"I've tried a few times to see firsthand, but the way in is well hidden. So I watch from here. It's best to keep to a safe distance, anyhow."

"Because it's dangerous?"

"Bah. Nothing like that." Uncle Wyn's smile was entirely fond. "It's because they're shy."

SCHOOL

Alfie was technically too old for lessons, but he still spent part of his afternoons sitting across from Hazel, reading whatever book Uncle Wyn had recommended while his sister applied herself to Pennythwaite's curriculum.

It was always intriguing, especially when Sonnet tried to be helpful. Between the two ladies of Merritt House, it was difficult to say which was more amusing.

"We have an *ice*box," exclaimed Hazel.

"We do." Sonnet paused at feeding the fire in their big iron stove, atop which an enamel kettle bubbled and steamed. "How *else* would we keep things cold?"

"But it's summer. There's no ice in summer."

Sonnet stood and brushed at her skirt. "We send for it, of course."

"From where?"

Alfie thought it was a good question. They lived so far from the nearest city, blocks of ice would surely melt before the oxen could amble their way to Yoxall. Now *he* was curious, as well.

"Well, I don't handle the orders. Pennythwaite takes care of those things for us." She pursed her lips and crossed to the squat box in the corner. Peering inside and sniffing, she nodded to herself. "Iceland, I should think."

Ice from Iceland. Alfie wasn't sure if she was making it up because she didn't know ... or if they really did get a twice-weekly shipment from some distant glacier.

Maybe Thrussel would know.

Maybe he shouldn't ask.

QUILL

Of all Hazel's many lessons, Alfie most enjoyed sitting across from her when she was working on her penmanship. Pennythwaite's lesson plans weren't always this antiquated, but Hazel had been so fascinated by his use of quill pens, he'd catered to her interest, elevating the girl's handwriting to an art form. Alfie doubted many fifteen-year-old girls routinely used dramatically flourished copperplate.

The faint scratch of her nib paused, and Alfie glanced up.

Hazel sat—her posture perfect—the tip of her pen resting on the lip of an ornate inkwell that had been a present from Uncle Wyn last Christmas.

"Sonnet?" she ventured. "Do you have a last name?"

Their cook bustled over with a fresh pot of tea. "Most everyone does."

Sonnet didn't seem perturbed, though she'd sidestepped the question. Alfie hoped this wasn't dangerous territory.

Hazel persisted. "Are you an Outler like us?"

"No, no. My people are from somewhere else."

This clearly intrigued Hazel, who enjoyed the books of maps that served as geography textbooks. "Are you foreign?"

"Not at all!" protested Sonnet. "This has been my home for a long while. Ever since I was your brother's age, more or less."

Hazel favored Alfie with a bright smile, but she wasn't finished. "What *is* your last name?"

"Oh! Well, now." Sonnet considered for a moment. "It would probably be … Cook. Since I'm the cook."

Satisfied with this entirely reasonable appellation, Hazel added

Sonnet's full name to her practice sheet. But Alfie was certain that Sonnet had made it up on the spot. What's more, he had to admit that he didn't know the surnames of anyone else in their immediate circle, either.

Not even Thrussel.

DISH

Somewhere along the way, Alfie had developed the vague idea that teenage girls were supposed to be a bother. Probably from school friends back in London. Or the telly. So he watched his sister for symptoms. It wasn't that he was *worried*, or anything. He was simply ... prepared. But Hazel passed her sixteenth and seventeenth birthdays without turning into a stranger.

Maybe other people in other places were terrorized by adolescent females.

Or maybe the men of Merritt House *were* being terrorized but didn't mind it so much.

"Where is the rosebud saucer, Sonnet?" Hazel called from inside the cupboard.

The cook ducked her head. Truth be told, Alfie also saw her tuck her tail. "Why not try a different one this evening? Or one of the tiny bowls?"

Hazel stopped clinking among the dishes to peer at the cook.

Sonnet wrung her apron. "Oh, Hazel. I'm sorry, love. I know it was your special favorite."

"It broke?" Hazel's whisper was tragic. "But they *prefer* the rosebuds."

"Who does?" Alfie interrupted. Sonnet looked in need of rescue.

"The fairies, of course." Hazel blinked, close to tears.

Encouraged by Sonnet's bedtime stories and nonsensical lore, Hazel had been taking care of fairies in the garden ever since she was small. It was a little girl game of make-believe. Harmless. Even cute. Alfie had always figured she'd outgrow it, but Hazel's faith in her imaginary friends had only grown along with her.

"There's other saucers," Alfie offered awkwardly.

"But we only had the one with rosebuds." Hazel's lip trembled. "They were yellow."

Sonnet, who looked close to tears herself, said, "Your uncle has gone up to Northrop Hall to see if his lordship has something similar."

Alfie was surprised Uncle Wyn would go that far over a bit of broken china. Then again, the man knew Hazel's little routines as well as any of them.

As the sun prepared to set, Hazel perched on a stool by the window facing the path to the manor house.

Pulling Sonnet aside, Alfie whispered, "Did Uncle break it?"

"Feels terrible, too." She sighed. "He'll try to make it right."

Alfie couldn't bring himself to scold Hazel. To say that she put too much stock in childish games. That it was only a dish, for pity's sake.

Twenty minutes passed in pensive silence before Hazel bounced to her feet and ran out the door, skirt flapping, ribbons flying. She was back moments later, leading their hangdog uncle and Lord Alderney himself.

Tristan Alderney was a sturdy man who overflowed with calm. If the men of Merritt House had become Hazel's honorary uncles, then Lord Alderney was her great uncle. And twice as doting.

"We did our best, child," he said, sliding a box onto the table.

"Lady Alderney sends these with her compliments. I even had the girls check the attic."

Hazel lifted each dainty dish out of the box. Soon the table was spread for a fairy-sized feast. Fine china. Cut glass. Subtle glazes. Shining facets. No two were alike, but none were a match for Hazel's lost treasure.

She hesitated over blue violets and yellow butterflies. "Will they mind, Sonnet?"

The cook hummed. "If we fill the dish with honey mead instead of cream, this once, I'm sure they'll take to the new pattern."

Alfie was surprised by that suggestion. He'd always rather assumed that the cream they put out was actually for Milk. Surely a cat would turn up their nose at an offering of liquor.

"Take the lot," suggested Lord Alderney. "Your wee friends may enjoy your little surprises."

"Even if the dish changes, you're the same," Uncle Wyn gruffly added. "It's *you* they visit, Hazel."

While the conversation roved from the virtues of tinted glass to the secret meanings of certain flowers, Pennythwaite emerged from Uncle's study and showed Alfie a catalog.

It was pretty obvious what the man had in mind. Honestly, Alfie was impressed. "That'd do. It's almost her birthday."

Pennythwaite inclined his head. "I will prepare the order form and payment. Would you be so good as to carry it into Yoxall in the morning?"

"First thing," promised Alfie.

Hazel was about due for a new passion. Why not a porcelain painting kit?

He'd tell Thrussel about it tomorrow. And see if his friend thought yellow rosebuds were a symptom of feminine terrorization.

CHILD

Alfie knew about high society and etiquette in the same way he knew about knights and chivalry. Fuzzy recollections of stories or shows. Allusions he ran across in books. He would have said such things were a far cry from farming, if not for Sonnet and Hazel.

Upon her eighteenth birthday, Hazel announced that she was a lady, and that meant they must all become gentlemen.

Sonnet agreed, and the two ladies put their heads together. Every few days, usually over mealtimes, they would make some new decree. The rules applied to all of them, and some of them were pure nonsense. Alfie was pretty sure they'd been cobbled together from Sonnet's stories, Uncle Wyn's books, and Hazel's own imagination.

Honestly, it was harmless. He didn't much mind the new rules.

Alfie had to shave before dinner, and Hazel now pinned up her hair.

Handkerchiefs were to be carried and dropped and offered.

Moving forward, they must always refer to the ox cart as their carriage.

Not all of it was about gentlemanly behavior, though. Hazel had rules about the pretty rocks she arranged on the windowsills, which were supposedly charms against the mischief of fairies. And she set chimes in the plum trees around Cozy Cottage, which had something to do with Beck's chickens. The phases of the moon were suddenly important, and there were rules for foggy mornings, for rainbows, for shooting stars.

She rearranged furniture so they'd have a breakfast room.

She begged Uncle Wyn to buy a pianoforte.

She began hinting to Lord Alderney about hosting a ball.

Most difficult was the whole thing about posture. Apparently, his was all wrong. There were different ways to stand, depending on your attitude. Or something. Alfie did try, but he botched the details or got them backward. Meanwhile, the rest of them made it look easy. Like the forms were natural.

"You'll catch on," promised Triggs.

"Watch and learn," Beck said with a wink.

The homebrewed etiquette was nothing more than an elaborate game, but Hazel took so much pleasure in it, Alfie did his best to please her. They all did.

But he noticed something.

The more Hazel insisted they treat her like a lady, the more childish she seemed.

Which was probably why everyone was so patient. Pennythwaite, Triggs, Beck, and even Uncle Wyn were unfailingly gentle with his sister because to them, she was only a child.

TRAY

Hazel tiptoed down the hall, quiet as a mouse in her continuing efforts to sneak up on the pitterhinds that were nesting in the shrubbery right up under the east window. They were too sweet for words, and she liked to wake early enough to watch them returning to roost after a long night.

Slipping the catch, she swung the circular pane out on silent hinges. Beck kept them well-oiled for this very reason. It was a pretty window, with golden glass along the edges and bevels to capture rainbows. When she was little, Sonnet had needed to lift her to see the pitterhind nest. Now, Hazel could lean right out for her first look at the day.

The sun wasn't far from rising, and fog hung in wisps over the low places. She could see Triggs ambling along the lane, returning from his morning stroll to the far pasture with his ladies.

He was empty-handed this morning, but that was all right. This being a Thursday, it was Uncle Wyn's turn to bring flowers.

That was one of their little traditions. Flowers on the tray that appeared at her bedside table every morning, courtesy of Sonnet.

The whistling flutter of wings drew Hazel's attention to the shrub, where two pitterhinds swung low for a landing. Even in the pre-dawn dim, she could see enough to tell the male and female apart as they scampered on clever paws toward their nest.

Pea green fur.

Tufted tails.

Tiny antlers.

Adorable.

She'd always wanted to catch and tame one. If only Pennythwaite didn't keep insisting he was allergic.

With a sigh and a smile, she latched the window and went to wash up.

By the time she returned to her room, Sonnet had been and gone.

The morning tray held its usual array of day-starters. A book recommendation from Uncle and a crossword puzzle from Alfie, who clipped them from the newspapers Thrussel collected. The tea she drank for her constitution. A teensy dish of sun cream, which kept her nose from burning and her cheeks from freckling. It smelled faintly of honeysuckle and was the only scent she was permitted to wear. Sonnet was choosy about such things. Then there was a list from Pennythwaite, who liked for her to rewrite them handsomely.

On any other morning, she would have arranged herself at her little writing desk to sip tea and open her inkwell.

But ... the flowers!

They were completely, awfully, dreadfully *wrong.*

Today was most certainly the third Thursday, which meant Uncle Wyn should have sent up the little blue bud vase with clusters of baby's breath. This was only proper, because the tiny white flowers meant that a pale moon was in the morning sky. But on her tray—jaunty and jarring as you please—was a speckled tin mug filled with purple asters.

And it was all wrong!

Oh, there would be words.

Uncle should *know* better!

Throwing a robe over her nightgown, Hazel seized the offending mug, holding it at arm's length as she marched it to the kitchen. But her righteous indignation faltered at the sight of someone new seated at the kitchen table.

His chair scraped, and he stood.

She could admit that was gentlemanly. But he didn't belong in the kitchen. Not at this hour. And she in her night clothes!

Her grip slipped, but Sonnet was there to catch the cup and murmur, "Good morning, love. I see you found Florent's flowers.

Wasn't that kind of him?"

"But it's *Thursday*," she countered, unable to tear her eyes from the stranger.

He was tanned, and he wore the same sort of clothes favored by Triggs and Beck. A worker, then? He was a youngish man, not much taller than she. Which was short. Indeed, he didn't even come up to Sonnet's shoulder when she hurried to place the mug of asters on the breakfast table. Right next to the blue bud vase of baby's breath.

"Found a wild thicket on the walk over," Sonnet went on in placating tones. "There aren't many flowers left this late in the season. They're a rare treat."

Hazel simply repeated, "But it's Thursday."

"So it is," Sonnet conceded. "I thought they'd be a celebratory touch. Since he's come all this way."

"What for?"

"Florent is the new farmhand," she happily announced. "He's moving into Cozy Cottage."

"But that's where Triggs and Beck live."

"They don't mind sharing." Sonnet turned to the newcomer and repeated, "This is Florent."

Hazel warily crossed to the table, which he still stood behind. At closer range, she could tell that his eyes were large and light, and his hair seemed to have gone prematurely gray. He was strange, and he wasn't supposed to be a part of Thursdays.

"I mind," she said stiffly, snatching up the proper vase of flowers. "I'm Hazel, and I mind."

He gazed at her stupidly.

Reminded of the state of her clothes, she turned on her heel and stalked away. "Nobody said anything about a new farmhand."

Sonnet, who always heard every little thing, called after her. "Didn't you see the note on your tray?"

A note? Who would notice such a thing with all those flowers distracting her?

"Send him home!" she called from the foot of the stairs.

"Oh, my dear." Sonnet must have been right behind her, she caught up so quickly. Cupping Hazel's cheeks in her big, warm hands, she gently chided, "He *is* home."

HIRE

Florent wasn't the biggest or best asset to an enclave, but his small knack for sigilcraft recommended him, especially when there was a festival in the offing. Shoring up gaps. Finessing finer details. He was especially good at camouflage, and he could pass himself off as human. Useful in places that didn't have ready access to a trickster's skills. But nothing special.

Ever since his attainment, he'd lived on the edges of cozy communities. Helping them hide their modest celebrations. Roving from circle to circle with little more than the contents of his pockets. A permanent place wasn't possible. Mostly because he shied away from questions about his past.

But a friend of a friend on the songbird circuit had discreetly passed along a name—Yoxall. An enclave of the unregistered variety. A place where nobody asked questions.

Lord Alderney had introduced him to Pennythwaite, whose

acceptance had been immediate ... if provisional. Florent could stay on if he could manage to live in human guise, at least until they finished raising the two human children currently residing at Merritt House.

Children.

Alfie Outler was a grown man. And someone really should have mentioned that Alfie's baby sister was a young woman. And that she was beautiful. And that her soul was singing to his with all the sweetness of a star.

"You go by Florent? Not Ren for short or anything?"

He dragged his attention to Alfie. "Florent," he said distractedly, because he was searching for ways in which the brother resembled the sister. "It's always been Florent."

Alfie was a man of middling height. Tanned from fieldwork and dressed in the breeches and tunic that were typical to the In-between. A fringe of bangs fell into shy brown eyes that held questions. But he didn't ask them. Pennythwaite had assured him the "lad" wasn't the type to pry.

Hazel had the same light brown hair and doe eyes. She'd descended upon the kitchen earlier with all the confidence of a queen, despite her rumpled braids and bare feet. Now, she was neatly dressed, and her abundant hair was pinned up in a fashion that fascinated him.

"It's impossible," she was saying. "I won't allow him to adorn my breakfast tray!"

"That's rather cutting of you." Sonnet's pleading gaze went unnoticed, for Hazel refused to look.

Wyn cleared his throat. "I'm sure you only want to spare him the extra effort. But won't Florent feel left out?"

He *would*. But he knew better than to say as much.

"If he *must* bring flowers, he can give them to Sonnet." Hazel leveled him with a challenging look. "For the breakfast table."

"Be reasonable," protested Wyn.

Florent finally found his voice. "I will. And happily."

Hazel inclined her head and focused on her bowl. Only to ask, "Why do we need another farmhand, anyhow?"

"*Not* to adorn your breakfast tray." Pennythwaite's crisp tone conveyed disapproval. "Florent will be working alongside Beck and your brother in the fields."

"And the meadow," Sonnet added helpfully.

Hazel's brows drew together. "What meadow?"

To Florent's amusement, Sonnet looked to *him* for help. But he was willing enough to distract the young woman. "Your uncle has already given me permission to cultivate some of the farm's little-used corners. Wildflower meadows are a hobby of mine."

Her eyes widened, and she whispered, "But that's *lovely*."

Around the table, everyone exchanged relieved glances. A good sign.

"Entirely," Florent agreed.

"And Sonnet shall benefit." Indicating the purple asters at the table's center, Uncle Wyn blandly added, "As shall we all."

LEAF

He was doing it wrong. Absolutely *wrong*. Because flowers belonged in vases. Surely that was universally understood? Yet Florent had commandeered Sonnet's soup tureen, and he'd filled it with *sticks*.

"The season is certainly turning." Sonnet eased a platter of griddlecakes onto the table. "Look at those colors!"

"We'll have a touch of frost within a fortnight," remarked Triggs.

Beck ladled spiced apples onto his plate. "Could be any day now. Better start covering your garden in the evenings."

"Oh, I do." With a squeeze for his shoulder, Sonnet added, "Florent's been helping me."

Alfie came in last, and when his eyes lit upon the ridiculous bouquet, they brightened … and Hazel's disgruntlement doubled. Of all things. Sticks.

The next day, it was a bowl of gourds. And the following morning, Florent contrived to bring in a tray of moss strewn with wee acorns. On the next, Florent *finally* used a vase, but Hazel was sure he was teasing her, because it held a bouquet of prickle burrs.

Then she came downstairs to find a single sunflower, big as a platter, resting in all its glory atop a shallow bowl between the curd and clotted cream.

They were for Sonnet.

Everyone knew that.

But Hazel had noticed a disturbing trend. Because while her loved ones faithfully adorned her morning tray with their usual bouquets, the flowers didn't give her the same old satisfaction. Indeed, she only gave them a fleeting touch, and she'd begun tucking away her puzzle and writing assignments for later. Because these days, Hazel was in a hurry to see what new strangeness Florent had foisted upon her family.

"What? What?" Hazel couldn't believe her eyes. Florent had brought in something very different from the usual twigs and sprigs. "How *could* you?"

Florent, who was helping Sonnet add an extra place at the table, chuckled. "They're fine. I'll release them after breakfast."

Beck took one look and snickered. "Above and beyond, friend. Above and beyond."

"Ah, I like them," said Triggs as he took his seat. "Been a lot of them lately."

Pennythwaite hummed. "They don't migrate anymore. They *congregate*."

"Can you blame them?" Sonnet bent to peer into the cage and whistled softly.

"Must be all those feeders you put out," said Uncle Wyn.

"*I* am not the source of their foolishness." Pennythwaite took his customary seat. "Rather, I will do what I can to make certain they don't suffer for their choices."

Uncle Wyn sat and elbowed Pennythwaite. "I'm sure they're as grateful as they can be."

"We could make a few brush piles among the trees," suggested Beck. "Winter shelter for laggers and loiterers."

"I'll help," Triggs said.

Hazel glanced at her brother. Usually, he was quick to volunteer.

Alfie was squinting at the little cage with a mystified expression. "Is there something in there?" he asked.

Pennythwaite sighed.

Uncle Wyn muttered, "Bah."

"There is," said Thrussel, who'd dropped by with letters for uncle, only to be invited to join them for the morning meal. Resting one hand on Alfie's shoulder, he pointed with the other. "See, now? They're easily overlooked."

Alfie blinked. "Oh. There they are."

"Dun nippets," said Uncle Wyn.

With a growing smile, Alfie looked to her. "No wonder you're gone on them. Cute little things."

Glad to see her brother so happy, she asked, "Can we keep them?"

Pennythwaite dryly pointed out, "You reprimanded Florent moments ago for caging them. Now, you want to prolong their captivity?"

Hazel blushed. "Maybe I could tame them?"

Thrussel spoke up. "Dun nippets are wild, but I've heard of people keeping coral nippets as pets. They have showier plumage."

"I had a friend who kept azure nippets by the dozen." Uncle Wyn chuckled at the memory. "He was in *so* much trouble when the mares found his flock."

"Mares?" asked Hazel.

Uncle smiled crookedly. "That's what we called the dorm mothers."

"You went to boarding school?" asked Alfie.

"Way back when." Uncle Wyn shrugged and smiled. "It was nothing special."

Hazel tried to imagine what he'd looked like as a little boy. But something else occurred to her then. She wondered why she'd never noticed before. Alfie was properly a man now, twenty-eight years old. And he looked the same age as Uncle Wyn.

WALTZ

"Lord Alderney would do it if I asked," Hazel argued.

"Oh, love. With everything else … well." Sonnet clung to her apron. "It's a busy time of year for him."

Hazel couldn't see how. The garden produce had been gathered in, along with every last bushel from the orchards. All that remained were the root vegetables and the vast pumpkin patch.

Alfie eyed her over the top of his book. "What put the notion of a ball into your head?"

"The chickens."

Her brother's mouth quirked. "And here I thought it was the cows who like to dance."

"They do. But the chickens would *so* enjoy the music!"

Alfie barely managed to keep a straight face. "Be sure to have Lord Alderney add them to his guest list."

"He would if I asked," Hazel repeated, although she was less sure on that score. "Would you dance with me?"

"You should know I've never danced." The teasing light was still in his gaze. "I know you haven't."

"I could learn!" Just then Triggs and Beck strolled in from outside, and Hazel pounced. "You know how to dance, don't you?"

The farmhands traded a look, and Beck answered, "Sure. I've

been to my share of dances."

Triggs nodded.

"Can you teach me?" Hazel abandoned her penmanship to face them both. "Something basic. I know! I want to learn to waltz."

"Waltz," Beck echoed vaguely.

"It's a dance," Sonnet whispered.

"Oooh, the dance. Right, then." Beck was nodding and shaking his head at the same time. "As long as it's something as basic as a waltz, we should be okay. Yeah, Triggs?"

"Alfie, too," said Hazel. "That way, we can all dance at Lord Alderney's ball."

Triggs looked increasingly perplexed. "Ball?"

"A festival," whispered Sonnet. "With fancy dress and dancing."

"*Someone* has been picking up on the excitement." Pennythwaite had appeared from the direction of the study. He fluttered his fingers at them. "Move the table aside so you can give our girl her lesson."

Permission! Hazel hurried to put away her things and help clear space.

Meanwhile, Triggs and Beck had their heads together with Sonnet.

"What about music?" asked Hazel.

"I will accommodate you." Pennythwaite positioned a chair in the corner, settled back with his long legs outstretched, and began to hum.

While he kept a steady rhythm, Beck showed Hazel how to hold on and where to put her feet. She was clumsy, but she was determined to learn. Grace would come.

When Pennythwaite migrated from *la-la-las* to singing words, she couldn't grasp their meaning. "Is that Welsh?"

Beck grinned. "Let's say it is."

Hazel wasn't doing very well. It helped that Alfie wasn't really doing any better, stiffly holding Sonnet, who was biting her lip to keep from laughing.

Triggs was the soul of patience, but Hazel kept stumbling. He and Beck even resorted to dancing with each other to show her how the footwork was supposed to go.

Round about then, Florent eased through the door. "I heard singing," he said.

Beck bowed. "We're teaching her to welsh."

"*Waltz*," corrected Triggs. "Here, Florent. Take my place. You're a better height for her."

"You know this one, yeah?" added Beck.

And before Hazel could so much as protest, they handed her off to a new partner.

ONCE

It had only been a week. Florent knew he was still an outsider in Hazel's eyes. On some level, he felt bad for trespassing on her safe corner of the world, but he'd resolved to be patient. If he left her be, eventually, she'd be ordering him around with the same breezy condescension with which she treated the other farmhands.

Yet here she was, about to step into his embrace.

Because she wanted to learn to dance.

Because she wanted to be treated like a lady.

But *not* by him.

Florent couldn't help smiling at her struggle. "Hazel," he tipped his head to catch her gaze. "You want to learn, and I can help. Be my partner this once?"

She edged forward, and he offered both palms.

Triggs had been right about their heights; he'd been stooping as he tried to guide Hazel through the dance patterns. Beck wasn't much better, being long in the leg. But Florent only had a scant handsbreadth advantage on Hazel. So as they came together, he had an excellent view of the blush rising in her cheeks.

Her scent didn't carry the usual snap of temper.

He tried not to let it go to his head, but it was nice to have his masculinity acknowledged by someone as lovely as she. Gently now. He was good at sheltering fragile things and encouraging them along. Surely, he could nurture her good opinion of him.

"This dance is easy as counting," he promised. "Slow enough to encourage chatting between partners, but with enough flourishes to keep it interesting."

Florent backed up, reviewing the steps Triggs had taught before flowing through the first transition.

"I can't," she whispered.

"No, look," he murmured. "Your foot chases mine, then mine will chase yours. It's just a friendly little game that two can play."

Hazel tried again. Success made her smile.

He counted off steps. "Do you know why there are so many twirls in the pattern?"

"Why?"

"So a lady can show off her festival attire." She was relaxing, so Florent kept talking. "In many places, a dance like this opens the evening. Ladies are led out by an uncle or a brother so that everyone can admire her."

Hazel asked, "Do you have a sister?"

Florent didn't like to speak of home, but he wouldn't withhold anything now. Not when Hazel was finally willing to talk to him. "I do have sisters, but I also have many brothers. *Older* brothers, so the privilege of first dances was theirs. I learned from watching."

She smiled again. At him this time.

As if liking and learning were linked, Hazel progressed.

"Come alongside," he coached. "Together. Just so. Flick your foot like this."

Hazel balked, for they'd missed a beat.

"Oh, don't worry about the timing. There's no hurry. Pennythwaite is enjoying the song too much to stop anytime soon." He knew for a fact there were dozens of verses to this old ballad. Pennythwaite's command of them was impressive. "Hold your arm here. Your partner's goes here. That's right. Now another spin. Are you dizzy? Lean on your partner if that happens. No one the wiser."

And she was leaning on him.

"Try it without looking down," he coaxed.

Hazel tried and floundered. "Where am I meant to look?"

"At me, I'm afraid." He laughed at her consternation. "While ignoring your partner would be rude, it's fine to look around. Chatting about what you see can give partners something to talk about. Take your brother, for instance."

Alfie was "waltzing" with Beck, now. Which was going to be

a disaster since both were attempting to lead. Meanwhile, Uncle Wyn was spinning Sonnet through the pattern with some degree of expertise.

Hazel giggled so much, they had to stop.

Florent kept hold until she caught her breath. "Shall we try it from the opening step?"

"Please!" she agreed. "I like this. It's fun."

He smiled his agreement and prepared to continue. He hadn't let go. He dared not.

To release Hazel was to end the dance, and to dance again would be irresponsible.

Once was fine. One dance wouldn't do any harm. But twice might cause some trouble. Because even if she didn't know his clan's customs, he did. Once was courteous, but twice was courting.

SIRE

Alfie woke to a faceful of fur and groaned. Lifting the cat with both hands, he muttered, "What is it, Milk?"

Her grumpy growl veered toward an alarming yowl. Was something wrong?

Abandoning his bed, Alfie hauled his breeches up under his nightshirt and padded after her. His bedroom door was ajar, and the house was still. It had to be the middle of the night. Downstairs, Milk stretched up to claw at the kitchen door. Alfie shoved bare feet into boots and eased it open. Only once he was outside did he catch the sound of voices. *Unfamiliar* voices.

"Help me understand, then." A deep voice, strangely accented.

"I shouldn't have to explain myself to you. I left the den centuries ago." Softer, sullen.

"Your mother wanted to know how you're faring. It worries her that you're alone."

A growl underlay the next words. "I'm a lone wolf, now. That's my choice!"

Milk crept forward on her belly to peer around the corner of the house. Alfie followed, trying to see who was in their yard.

"Haven't you had enough of this?" The stranger's face was in shadow, but his silhouette was imposing. Big as Triggs, but leaner. "Your responsibility to the clan ...!"

"I have responsibilities *here*!" growled the second figure, clad in loose pants and a light tunic.

This one's features were touched by moonlight, so Alfie had no trouble seeing. But he was having trouble understanding. He'd never seen Sonnet's hair down, nor heard her voice deepen or darken like this. But the faint tremor he knew very well. Their cook was on the verge of tears.

"I have children to raise!"

Alfie had heard enough. Rushing into the open, he placed himself between Sonnet and the stranger, fists balled. "Leave her alone!"

The stranger shifted, and his gaze darted around, landing on Milk. "The cat?"

"Oh, nooo," Sonnet moaned.

Alfie wasn't seeing much or well, but he caught how the stranger's head reared back. That heart-hammering growl returned. "He means *you*?"

"Yes," Sonnet sighed, sounding more like herself. "He's an orphan. He needed a mother."

There was an awkward silence. "That is … surprising."

Alfie backed toward Sonnet. "Are you all right?" he whispered.

"Oh, love. I'm so sorry. Have I ruined everything?"

He fumbled for her hand and gave it a squeeze.

The stranger cleared his throat and stiffly said, "Your mother safely delivered twins. She wanted you to know, in case you wanted them to get a whiff of you."

"Twins?"

"Sisters." He gruffly added, "They should know their brother."

Sonnet whimpered and tried to pull away, but Alfie tightened his hold.

"I thank you for your invitation," she said stiffly. "And I will thank you to leave."

The stranger muttered something, turned, and strode away.

Alfie didn't catch his words, but Sonnet snapped, "I know. I'll consider it."

Then she sagged to the ground, hugged her knees to her chest, and started to cry.

Glancing toward the dark house and toward Cozy Cottage, Alfie was surprised no one had turned up. "Should I bring help? Pennythwaite? Uncle Wyn?"

"No, he's away. Pennythwaite, that is. And Wyn's only human. Let him sleep."

He'd never been in a situation that made it impossible to pretend. So he wasn't sure how to proceed. "Sonnet, who was that?"

"My sire. He doesn't approve of my choices." Sonnet sniffled.

"But he worries twice as much as Mother."

Something moved, and Alfie quickly averted his eyes from the tail tucked against Sonnet's thigh.

"I'm sorry, Alfie. I'll go away if I must."

"What do you mean?"

"Are you very angry?" Sonnet asked huskily.

No, it was more than husky. Her voice had dropped an octave. Alfie dearly wished he'd brought a light. "I'm not angry with you. How could I be angry? I'm worried, is all."

"Don't worry. Please, don't worry. I only wanted you and Hazel to have a mother." Sonnet swiped at wet cheeks. "I've always loved you like my own."

Alfie guessed this was a confession. Which meant there was no pretending. "Sonnet, are you maybe … well. Are you a man?"

"Male." Sonnet was breathing oddly. Panicking.

"Do you want to tell me about it?" he offered, not entirely sure what he was about to learn.

Sonnet whined.

"Shh, shh. You don't have to." Alfie gently placed a hand on Sonnet's shoulder. "It's just a bit easier now … asking about your tail, I mean. Knowing we're both blokes."

An instant later, he was hauled into arms that had held him many, many times. And the person who'd been like a second mother to him gruffly declared, "My name is Sonnet Skybellow, and I'll tell you anything you want to know. But *please*, Alfie. Please, don't tell Hazel."

"I won't tell. Hazel still needs her mum." And because it was true, he shyly added, "We both do."

SULK

Hazel couldn't understand why the morning was so wretched. It wasn't the weather, even though low clouds threatened a chill rain. Sonnet was unusually quiet, which seemed to dampen everyone's mood. Except Alfie. Maybe because there was gruel for breakfast—his favorite. No, it had to be Florent's fault.

"Where is Florent?" she asked. "Did you fire him already?"

Uncle Wyn glanced up in surprise. "Nonsense. He must be somewhere hereabouts. See? He left his usual token for you."

Her gaze strayed to the center of the table, where a cascade of lantern flowers filled a milk bottle borrowed from their dairy. "They're for Sonnet," she said primly. "And its rude for him to skip mealtime with the family."

Pennythwaite favored her with one of those exceptionally dry looks that meant he was laughing somewhere inside. "A week ago, you protested his presence. Now, his absence offends you?"

"On principle."

She hoped the rain would catch him. Like in Sonnet's old bedtime story, "The Boy and the Thundercloud." Pour on him like a waterfall and chill him to the bone.

"I'll save back some breakfast," murmured Sonnet, who moved back to the stove.

Alfie caught her sleeve and shook his head. "Eat first."

Sonnet wavered, the strangest look on her face. Then she patted Alfie's shoulder and took her seat. Hazel couldn't understand it at all, and it was frustrating. Like everyone was having conversations around her, and she was excluded from them all.

She needed to do something. Something different. Something drastic.

"May I walk up to Northrop Hall this morning? I want to talk to Lord Alderney about the ball."

"What ball?" Pennythwaite was definitely hiding a smile behind his teacup.

"There will be a ball if I can talk to Lord Alderney about it. *He* is a gentleman."

Triggs said, "I'll walk with you."

"I know the way."

He smiled faintly. "A lady mustn't travel unescorted. It's your own rule, Hazel."

She couldn't deny it. But she didn't feel like acknowledging it, either.

Poking sulkily at the lantern flowers, she made up her mind that *somehow*, all of this was Florent's fault.

By midmorning, Hazel had to bring an extra pair of candles to the table to offset the gloom. Rain fell straight down with an endless drumming. The kitchen was stuffy, and everything was dull. This was the part of the morning she dedicated to letter-writing, although truth be told, she had no one with whom to correspond. A matter that troubled her sorely, since in books, young ladies were always faithful correspondents.

Usually, Pennythwaite or Sonnet let her rewrite their shopping lists, but the cook had retreated to her bedroom shortly after breakfast, murmuring about headaches. Even her brother had abandoned her, having gone into Yoxall on some errand for Pennythwaite. Hazel had been copying out a poem to add to Sonnet's collection of her namesakes, but even Shakespeare couldn't capture her interest today.

"Come along, Hazel." Uncle Wyn was wearing a cloak and carrying an umbrella. "Let's have a look around. Who knows what we might see?"

Gratefully, she snuffed the candles and found her own cloak, the plum-colored one that shed rain like a waterfowl. Donning her boots, she waded into the yard. Rain was a sharp rattle against the oversized umbrella Uncle Wyn held aloft.

It was an aimless, unhurried stroll.

The fresh air cleared Hazel's head, improved her mood.

She supposed Uncle Wyn's own daily routine had been overturned. After all, even *he* had his chores. Uncle and Pennythwaite were in charge of laundry, but there would be no pinning clothes on the lines in this wet.

They passed by Cozy Cottage, which was empty at this hour. Triggs in the dairy. Beck turning eggs in the hatchery or scattering feed.

As their meander continued along an outward curve, it occurred to Hazel that Uncle Wyn was checking up on Florent. "Where does the new farmhand work?"

"Have you forgotten his name since breakfast?" he teased.

She made a face.

"Are you sure you want to snub him? I think he'd be hurt."

He searched her face. "Dismal day, girl. He's been trying to make peace with you from the beginning."

Hazel wanted very much to change the subject. Casting about, she was quite surprised to spy something unfamiliar. "Oh! What's that?"

Her uncle followed her gaze but shook his head. "What now?"

"There are steps leading up and over that fence."

"A stile?" He squinted into the rain. "Show me where."

It was right in front of them, and she mutely pointed.

"Humor me." Uncle Wyn smiled apologetically. "Lead me to it. Place my hand upon it."

Mystified by his strange request, Hazel took his hand as if he were a blind man. "Just here. It doesn't look new. I wonder I never noticed it before."

Uncle grunted as if surprised. "There's a kind of boundary here. Off limits to us, I'm afraid."

"Why?" They weren't anywhere near their boundary line. "It looks like a pasture. Oh! Is this one of the meadows where Florent works?"

"I really couldn't say." Uncle Wyn took her arm and turned her toward the house. "Leave it alone, Hazel. We shouldn't trespass on the local lord's kindness."

He was being strange. Maybe even a bit silly.

Why would Lord Alderney care if they walked through a meadow?

Glancing back, Hazel could only admit that she was curious.

All thoughts—and plots—regarding the mysterious meadow vanished when Lord Alderney came to call. "I bring gifts!"

There was a net bag of strange fruit and another holding several kinds of nuts. Tins of oriental tea and a stack of foreign chocolates that brought a smile of pleasure to Sonnet's face. Especially for Hazel, Lord Alderney brought a set of plain porcelain bowls, which reminded her that she had two teacups that remained, as yet, unpainted. She might try adding lantern flowers to one of them. Or perhaps a flock of teensy dun nippets.

Lord Alderney interrupted her musings by taking her hands. With a benign smile, he said, "Your friends have spoken on your behalf. Something about a ball?"

"Oh! Oh, yes!" she gasped.

"Lady Alderney and I would be pleased to host a dance, but due to this and that, it must be soon. Would you be able to attend two nights from this one?" He lowered his voice to add, "I apologize for the suddenness."

"Oh, no. I mean, *yes*! I want to. Oh, can we?" She was thrilled into incoherency.

He chuckled. "We shall consider the date set."

Two days to practice her waltz and to choose a dress. She couldn't wait to begin!

Lord Alderney wasn't finished. "I am given to understand that such evenings are often arranged according to a theme."

"Are they?" She hadn't known. "But that's lovely!"

"The ladies settled on something seasonal—Frost on the Pumpkins." He smiled at the squeal she let slip. "Come at twilight. There will be lights in all the windows."

DRESS

Mister and Missus Partridge were clothiers who owned a small shop in Yoxall. Most people in the area relied upon them, so a trip into town was the first item on Hazel's agenda after breakfast.

As Alfie loitered beside shelves stocked with fabric bolts, it occurred to him that this couple was probably responsible for the unusual style of clothing people wore in these parts. While the garments Alfie remembered from his early years were sometimes mixed in, the Partridges' breeches and tunics were the standard. They felt normal now.

"A ball?" Missus Partridge asked. "Is it some kind of game?"

"A dance," said Sonnet. "So Hazel must have a new dress."

"You, too!" put in Hazel. "We're *all* going, so you must have something, too!"

Normally, Alfie would have left the ladies to their shopping and sought out Thrussel to catch up over a pint or a pot of tea. But he didn't feel right leaving Sonnet to weather this storm of fancywork and frippery, now that Alfie knew she wasn't a woman.

Maybe his solidarity wasn't necessary. But Alfie couldn't help wanting to be along and watching out for Sonnet. To thank her for being there for him and Hazel all along.

So what if their cook had a tail?

So what if their second mum was a wolf?

So what if Sonnet was actually male?

She was part of the family he'd needed with frightening desperation when his world fell apart. Sonnet practically defined the comfort and safety of home. She was the source of nonsense stories and hearty meals and steadying touches. He loved her like a son should. Always would. And if standing here, surrounded by ribbons and buttons and trimmings made that just a little clearer to her, then he wasn't going to walk away.

The chime over the front door jingled softly and Pennythwaite sauntered in, pulling Florent by the arm. "Missus Partridge," he said at his most officious. "This gentleman needs fitting out."

Mister Partridge hurried forward, tape measure fluttering.

Hazel, who had two lengths of cloth draped across each shoulder, followed just as quickly, eager to ask, "The azure? Or the coral?"

Pennythwaite's expression softened somewhat. "What are you, a nippet?"

Alfie chuckled over Hazel's triumph. She was the best at coaxing a smile onto Pennythwaite's stern face.

As if sensing Alfie's amusement, Pennythwaite's gaze sought him out. And with two words, sealed his fate. "Him, too."

PATCH

Florent had been busy in the pumpkin patch when Pennythwaite came swooping in with news that should have been delivered over breakfast ... if Florent hadn't been avoiding Hazel. Playing the part of a herald, Pennythwaite extended an invitation to a ball. With just enough of a show of dominance to make it clear that attendance was mandatory.

"She wouldn't miss me," he protested.

Pennythwaite blinked. "You were missed at breakfast. You

would be missed all the more at this ball of hers. Or did you fail to comprehend that *you* are her preferred dance partner."

Florent blushed under the other's gaze. "I would be a blot upon the evening, the poor country mouse in patched breeches tracking dirt into the manor house."

"If *that* is your only protest …!"

And so Florent found himself in Yoxall, in the hands of Pennythwaite's own tailor. With Hazel whisking forward, demanding his opinion on her appearance.

"Which?" she asked, turning this way and that before a mirror. "The azure or the coral?"

"I couldn't begin to guess," he confessed. "Far better if you help decide what your brother and I should wear."

The ploy diverted her. And divided her attention.

But Florent was no less flustered. Even with the amethyst pendant they'd used to ward her, she dazzled his senses and inspired vague hopes. And a pang that was becoming more and more difficult to dismiss.

Hazel Outler was lovely to look at, bliss to his parched soul, and eager to inspire devotion. A lady in need of a lord. A maiden ready to be courted.

He'd already paid his courtesies. Yet there was to be a ball. To dance again … could he? Surely, her family wouldn't be pushing them together if they knew how it was for mice. Florent would ask Pennythwaite to hear him out before events carried him—and his heart—into something irrevocable.

"What about the theme?" Hazel was saying. "Isn't this closer to pumpkin?"

Missus Partridge, who'd spun out enough ribbon to bind every bale of late straw in the far field, piped up, "May I make a suggestion?"

"Please!" exclaimed Sonnet. "We *rely* on you!"

"Since *both* colors call to you, you shall have both." With a roll of her hand, she indicated Florent. "He shall wear the blue with coral trim, and your gown will be coral with his blue for trim."

Florent protested, "She should match her brother, surely!"

The seamstress tutted. "Alfie has already chosen to wear Sonnet's colors."

Deep blue and amber cloth were piled together, and Sonnet was poking through a basket of buttons.

"Just as Wyn will array himself in Pennythwaite's colors," continued Missus Partridge, already rummaging for more ribbon.

"Is that how it works?" asked Hazel, clearly intrigued. "What about Triggs and Beck?"

"They will do honor to their family's crests." The seamstress recalled herself with an apologetic glance Sonnet's way. "Ah. It's a little like heraldry, Miss Hazel. A way to show familial pride."

"I'm not ..." tried Florent.

Sonnet interrupted amiably. "Anywise, partners should look well together."

Hazel's gaze flitted to Florent while Missus Partridge lowered her voice—a pretense of secrets in a room full of Amaranthine. "He will see the compliment, and you shall have his in exchange."

To Florent's amazement, Hazel seemed ... pleased.

Oh, this was not good for his heart. Did it already beat for her?

CHANGE

While the ladies returned to Merritt House, Alfie stayed back in Yoxall to speak with Thrussel. Safely ensconced in the tavern's far corner, Alfie searched his memories and came to a conclusion that seemed glaringly obvious. Now. "You haven't changed."

Thrussel reached for the bread. "Change isn't always obvious."

"I grew up, but you didn't grow older."

"Ah. That." Thrussel looked as if he'd hoped that wasn't what Alfie was talking about. "You've made great strides in a short time."

"It's not just you."

Thrussel simply inclined his head as he buttered.

"Nobody changes except me and Hazel."

"It's to be expected, Alfie. You're human."

Which was as good as saying that the others—including Thrussel himself—weren't. "What about my uncle?"

"Wyn is a … special case. Human, though. Much as you are."

"He doesn't age." It had happened so slowly, Alfie hadn't even noticed. At first. "We're practically the same age. Outwardly."

"Maybe you should ask *him* …?"

Alfie shook his head. "I don't want to put him on the spot."

"That's what friends are for?" Thrussel asked lightly.

"Really hoping so." Alfie could feel his face heating. "It's less embarrassing coming from you."

Thrussel tipped his head to one side. "Are you afraid of the answers?"

"I don't think so." That gave him pause. "Should I be?"

His friend laughed. From an inside pocket he produced a slender rod of translucent stone. Setting it on the table between them, Thrussel urged, "Place this on your palm."

It was pretty. Heavy for its size, too. Alfie was reminded of the stones Sonnet and Hazel used to decorate Merritt House's windowsills. To keep the fairies out.

"May I touch you?" Thrussel asked softly. "It works best if the crystal is clasped between our hands."

"If you say so." Alfie slid his hand closer, even though it was a little embarrassing for two adults to be holding hands like children. He glanced around the dining room, but nobody seemed to be paying them any attention.

"No one can overhear, now," said Thrussel in a normal tone. "We're mostly beyond notice, as well. Our secrets are safe with each other."

Taking him at his word, Alfie blurted, "Sonnet told me about being a wolf."

He didn't even bat an eye. "And …?"

"It was a surprise *to me*, but it's fine. Sonnet's my mum, no matter what."

"Good." Thrussel smiled. "And I'm your friend … no matter what?"

Alfie hunched his shoulders. "Rather counting on that. So … are there many wolves around?"

"Just the one." Thrussel chose his words carefully. "Please, understand. I cannot speak for others, but my choices are mine to make. Would you like a better introduction than I've dared give before?"

Here it was. Alfie tightened his grip. "If it won't get you in trouble …?"

"We brought you into our community. We knew there would

be consequences." Thrussel was so calm about this. "Compared to a wolf, the rest of us are hardly worth mentioning."

There was a strangely soothing sensation, as if Thrussel was sharing a little of his serenity. Alfie focused on that, wanting to keep hold of it.

"Oh!" Thrussel's laugh was a twittering thing. "*That* was unexpected. But not unpleasantly so."

"What was?"

"First things first." And cradling Alfie's hand between both his own, Thrussel spoke in a lilting tone. "Hear the secret I have been keeping. Many are the clans, and each has its merits. Mine was made for skies and meadows and sweet songs. My true name is Thrussel Morningswell, a thrush by birth, a herald by trade, and a friend, if you'll have me."

STILE

"Will Missus Partridge be able to finish all our orders before Lord Alderney's ball?" Hazel idled over a book, which was failing to hold her attention. "She wanted to embroider everything."

"Don't worry yourself over it," said Sonnet. "Her whole brood is quick with a needle. And I have no doubt that she and her mister will work through the night if necessary."

Hazel was reassured, but no less restless.

In the center of the table were this morning's "flowers." As usual, it wasn't a proper bouquet, although it made a pretty arrangement. A low tray of dirt held a triple row of mixed lettuces—green and red, ruffled and curled. One variety even had speckled leaves.

"Isn't it too late in the season for lettuce?" asked Hazel.

"Those are from the cold frame, my dear. It protects tender things."

Hazel trailed a finger along the edge of one leaf. "I think I'll go for a walk."

Sonnet paused. "Do you want company?"

"I'll bring Milk."

To her surprise, Sonnet accepted this without hesitation. As if a cat could be a proper escort.

Outside, she tried to decide which direction to walk. "Where do you suppose Florent will be?" she wondered aloud.

Milk offered a sage *mew* and strolled off. Hazel guessed she should follow and was soon glad she did. Events had conspired, and the forbidden stile had slipped her mind. Until Milk leapt to the top of the fence it straddled.

Three steps up, and three steps down. Hazel was over in a trifling.

Before her lay a large, circular meadow. It was neatly mown, without a spike of stubble to be seen. Yet at regular intervals, hewn stones had been set on their ends, a series of rugged plinths. Something sparkled atop the nearest, and she glanced carefully around, just in case Lord Alderney was pasturing a bull here. But no, this circle wasn't marred by hoofprints or dung.

Crossing to the stone, she discovered a large blue crystal.

No wonder this meadow felt safe. Hazel had always liked the blue ones.

She sat upon the grass, turned her face to the sun, and basked in the unusual fineness of the day. In her mind's eye, she pictured the meadow carpeted in flowers. Lovelier than any bouquet and too big for any breakfast table. Would Florent choose pink flowers?

Or red? Perhaps yellow? No. It should be blue, like the crystals. A meadow as blue as the tunic Florent would wear to the ball. Azure as the embellishments that would adorn her matching dress.

"Hazel?"

She opened her eyes, braced for a scolding that didn't come.

Florent crouched a short distance away, elbows on knees. "All right, there?"

"I was out for a walk."

He looked off toward the stile, then back at her. "Would you like to see something special-ish?"

"Only special-*ish*?"

"Rather depends on your fondness for pumpkins." He gestured with his chin. "I've been in the patch since early. Fancy a look?"

"I suppose." Hazel added, "If you'll escort me."

To her utter delight, Florent not only helped her to her feet, he offered his arm. Like a proper gentleman. He handed her back over the stile and into a field where Riff, Raff, and their carriage waited.

"I thought everything was harvested already," she admitted.

"Oh, we're waiting on the weather. We don't gather some things in until they're frost-kissed." He gave her a sidelong look. "It's said to make them sweeter."

Uncle Wyn dedicated an enormous field to the annual pumpkin harvest, and Hazel used to like to play in the vast patch, searching for baby pumpkins—small and summer-green—among the fuzzy leaves. But the vines that had run rampant were all wilted, revealing their cornucopia harvest.

"Lord Alderney placed an order for the ball," said Florent. "Will it spoil the surprise if I show you?"

"I want to see!"

He led her around the back of the ox cart, which was heaped with pumpkins. Although the field had been planted with every possible variety, Florent was only collecting white pumpkins. No, a few were pale green.

Florent said, "I thought we were in for an evening of orange, given the pumpkin theme. But it seems Lord and Lady Alderney are intent on frost."

"Have you seen the decorations?"

"Only these. But they're a good hint."

She nodded eagerly. "Are you excited for the ball?"

"Well ...." he said vaguely.

"I am. Now that I've learned how, I *love* to dance." She dared to suggest, "We could practice, if you want. So I don't forget the steps to the waltz."

Florent looked down, away, and finally back. With a small shrug, he said, "I can't, Hazel. Nearly all the dances I know count as courting dances, and I wouldn't want to presume."

"Even the waltz?"

His gaze was full of regrets. "Yes."

"But you danced with me *before*."

"Lessons are permissible. A courtesy offered to friends."

Hazel shook her head. "Then give me another lesson."

"You may certainly ask for lessons from other teachers. But if you were to dance again with me, it would be courting."

But this was *disastrous*. The ball would be spoiled if she couldn't dance with Florent. Why hadn't he spoken sooner?

He scuffed the toe of his boot in the soil and quietly admitted,

"There are loopholes, of course. Intended for couples who are confident in their choice."

Hazel knew that there were complexities to etiquette, especially surrounding a ball. She hadn't realized the rules extended to dancing in a pumpkin patch.

Florent squared off before her and presented his palms, though he didn't quite meet her gaze. Soft as secrets, he admitted, "I know a flirting dance."

SONG

Florent was so certain she'd refuse. This wasn't proper, and she was all about propriety. And he shouldn't be flirting, not when she didn't understand anything.

Hazel was certainly taken aback. "You want to flirt with me?"

"That is the purpose of the dance," he hedged, not wanting to frighten her with the truth.

"Even though you cannot be in love."

Oh, he couldn't let that go. Florent held her gaze long enough to ask, "Who says I can't?"

She drew herself up and retorted, "I don't like it! To *never* dance with you again?"

"The alternative is to dance with me always."

A standoff.

"Well ... what about this flirting dance?" she asked, her cheeks gone rosy.

Florent dredged up a small smile. "You'll probably enjoy it. Since it's dancing."

Hazel decided. "Right. Teach me."

"Side by side," he directed, taking his position. "This part is important, since traditionally, a gentleman who's courting takes his intended into his arms. I won't do that."

She nodded and asked, "What next?"

He showed her the complicated linking of arms, the press of palms. "No clasping of hands. Again, we require a touch that isn't holding."

Puzzlement puckered her brow. "We're just as close as when we're waltzing."

"Shh. Nobody splits whiskers over a little flirting." He shyly added, "It's only natural for couples to want to be close."

"Natural," she agreed, a smile tugging at her lips. "Yes, I think so, too."

Florent walked her through the steps, which became a sprightly rollick at full speed. Hops and switches, sweeping turns that were only possible if pressed close. They were locked together, and Hazel was alight with pleasure.

"If only we had music," she said. "Do you know the song Pennythwaite was singing?"

He glanced skyward, clan superstition in mind—*say the name; invoke the strike.* "That old thing? Wouldn't you rather learn a song in English?"

"Learn one?" She seemed intrigued, yet she hesitated. "It's just that the melody's been reeling through my mind ever since that day."

Florent doubted he could translate the ancient rhyme in its entirety, but surely he could work up something simple. Maybe repurpose the lyrics of a lullaby? Slowing to a stop, he asked, "Do you happen to have something I can write on?"

From her pocket, she brought a fold of paper and a fountain pen.

He tried not to gawk. "What *is* this?"

"Last week's grocery list," she said. "But there's room on the back. See?"

Turning the paper, he uncapped the pen. "Give me a moment to set something down." But his mind was oddly blank. He stole another look at her list. "This is artfully done, by the way."

She blushed prettily. "It's nothing."

But it wasn't. And she wasn't. And this wasn't.

"No. I must say, I'm impressed." Florent's heart was skipping. "When you wrote this out, did you know that you were composing a song?"

"What?" Hazel leaned in for a closer look. "It's a list for Alfie. Nothing more."

Florent tutted and made a few small notations, his writing neat and square among her looping extravagances. He hummed to himself, then laughed. "It works."

And so he began to sing.

Bring me cocoa and bring brown bread,

A beeswax candle and a twist of cherry thread,

Brown ink in a bottle, herring in a jar,

Hairpins for a coronet and wine to tempt a star.

Bring me sugar and bring cracked corn,

A cake of raisins and a wreath of fresh hawthorn,

Winesaps by the bushel, pippins by the peck,

Pickles in a dilly brine and half a stone of speck.

Bring me chestnuts and bring birch tea,
A yard of cheesecloth and a pot of quince confit,
Tobacco by the pouch, seed pearls on a strand,
Chalcedony for a ring to grace my lady's hand.

She leaned against him, and he basked in her laughter. Twice more, he sang it through, and she merrily joined him. Perhaps she absorbed the lyrics so quickly because she'd written the list herself.

"But what about that last part?" she asked. "The part about a ring?"

"I added that myself." Florent quietly admitted, "It's the sort of gift someone like me would give to the lady who will share all his dances."

"A betrothal gift?" she asked, suddenly serious.

He hummed. "A pledge to bind two lives."

"I've *heard* of engagement rings, you know."

"This is different. The giving and receiving of such a ring isn't a promise for the future. It signifies the wedding of two souls."

"Immediately? That *is* different. Not the way it is in books." Hazel surprised him by adding, "It's nicer."

"Such things are traditional where I came from."

"Are you a gypsy?"

He wondered how long she'd been holding onto that particular suspicion. "No. Although I have been a wanderer."

"Will you wander away again?"

Florent shook his head. "Pennythwaite offered me a home. I intended to stay even before I met you."

Oh, dear. Perhaps that was too much honesty.

Hazel let it pass, insisting that their new song must be accompanied by dance. So they linked arms and sang about nonsense, verse upon verse. And Florent was pleased with himself. And with Hazel, whose openness and interest made her a pleasant companion.

The sort he might choose for himself.

If such choices were his to make.

"What's chalcedony?" she asked.

"A pretty-ish stone. Pale blue."

"I'm glad you added a ring to our shopping list," remarked Hazel, all sidelong looks and secretive smiles. "Once you have one, you must show it to me."

PACT

After seeing Hazel safely home, Florent was humming his merry way back to work when a deep voice called, "A word, Florent?"

He flinched at Pennythwaite's sudden and silent arrival. His was one of the few owl clans that aligned themselves with certain human communities—barn owls. While cozies rarely made much of an impression, Pennythwaite was a daunting presence. Florent had his suspicions why.

"Hazel is in a bright mood," remarked Pennythwaite.

"Dancing seems to have that effect on her."

Pennythwaite hummed. "Everyone is relieved that there is peace between you."

Florent tensed.

With a small gesture, Pennythwaite asked why.

"There may be more than peace between us."

"A passing fancy, surely," said Pennythwaite in leading tones. "She is a child."

He looked off toward the largest barn, which had a heart-shaped *eulenloch* at every gable. "Maybe if I'd raised her from a nestling, as you did, I'd be blinded by fond memories."

Pennythwaite's eyes glittered behind his glasses. "I see more than you might realize."

Florent probably should have taken a submissive posture, but he firmed his stance instead. "Hazel is of an age to accept suitors."

"I am aware." Shifting into a neutral posture, Pennythwaite asked, "Are *you* aware of Wyn's status?"

"Only that I shouldn't mention his presence within your household."

Pennythwaite inclined his head. "Wyn and I share a pact, one that has proven mutually beneficial."

Florent's thoughts skittered in a tight circle. "He's your bondmate?"

"That is not the nature of our union, though we have woven a good nest ... and raised two chicks." His gaze strayed to the house. "I am willing to teach you."

"You want me to keep Hazel?"

Pennythwaite favored him with a withering look. "My opinion matters little. But Hazel's has never been difficult to comprehend. *She* wants you to keep her."

"But ... you have reservations?" Florent guessed.

"Yes."

His heart sank.

"Your suitability isn't in question. However, if there were to be a child, our girl might not withstand the bearing. Few do." Pennythwaite's voice softened. "I would rather spare Wyn—and all of us—that grief."

Florent hadn't expected *this* turn of events, but that didn't mean he was unprepared to face it. "Would you speak to Lord Alderney on my behalf?"

"With regards to Hazel?"

"No. That is between her and me." Florent drew himself up. "I am a preservationist."

"It was mentioned upon your arrival. An honored vocation."

"This is a good place. A safe place. I want you to ask Lord Alderney to lend his protection to a grove."

"I beg your pardon?"

Loosening his tunic ties, Florent brought out a warded chain, along with the items he always carried close to his heart. Spaced along its length were three silver lockets, each a hinged sphere, and a pale blue circlet carved from stone. The chalcedony ring that had come to him from his mother's mother.

"Ancients and angels!" Pennythwaite's eyes were wide. "Are those …?"

"If she will have me, if she wants them, I can give Hazel *three* children." Florent tapped each of the lockets. "They shall know a tree's blessing, even as she shall have mine."

LIT

Alfie had expected Hazel to be excited for her long-awaited ball. What he *hadn't* expected were the admiring glances she kept sending Florent's way. Or the farmhand's pensive gazing in Hazel's direction whenever she wasn't looking.

Sonnet tugged Alfie into the pantry on the flimsiest of pretenses. "To think. After all the fuss she made, she's gone and set her heart on Florent."

"Thought I was imagining things," Alfie muttered.

"Are you upset?"

"Uncomfortable …?" He didn't want to think of his sister with anyone.

Sonnet's searching look ended with a bit of sniffing. "Haven't you ever given thought to a bride?"

"Not really." Alfie felt justified in turning that around. "Haven't you?"

"I *have* given the matter thought." With a crooked smile, Sonnet whispered, "I can hardly go courting like this, now, can I? Perhaps another century or two hence."

"That's … a long time."

"More than enough," Sonnet agreed. "But you mustn't mind about Hazel. Mice are a good sort, and Florent's bond will give her that little extra something. Like Pennythwaite does for Wyn."

Alfie lifted a shaky hand to cover Sonnet's mouth. "You shouldn't be telling tales."

"Nonsense." She caught his hand and held it to her cheek. "How will you know *you* could share someone's years if I didn't say so?"

"You want me to marry … someone like you?"

"It's one way. Not the *only* way, of course. Wyn was about your age when he bonded with Pennythwaite, and he's still in his prime." Sonnet patted his shoulder encouragingly. "They're close as brothers, despite the differences between your kind and ours. *There's* an idea. Would you be opposed to trading your mother for a brother? You *do* look well in my clan's colors."

Alfie glanced down at his tunic, which the Partridges had embellished in the same style and colors as Sonnet's. "Maybe not," he managed. "I like being your son."

"Probably just as well. Since I'm a *lone* wolf." Sonnet quirked a knowing little smile. "And you seem better suited to songbirds."

By some unspoken agreement, Alfie was given the honor of escorting Hazel along the well-worn path between Merritt House and Northrop Hall. He supposed there was some sort of etiquette involved. Or maybe Sonnet had insisted because his sister's hand wouldn't be his to hold for much longer.

Whatever the reason, it was fun to watch Hazel's face as they rounded the bend and Lord Alderney's grand home came into view.

"What has he done?" she gasped.

"Thrown you a ball," Alfie replied. "Not one for skimping, is he?"

Every window on all three stories glowed, but not with the expected gold of firelight. Somehow, they'd contrived to change the light to silver and blue. Perhaps colored glass? It certainly was in keeping with the evening's frosty theme.

Alfie glanced toward the moon, which would surely be full tomorrow. The autumn air had a bite to it, the kind that promised frost.

Hazel was already in a whirl, all thrill and merriment. She clung to his arm but included everyone in the party in her remarks and speculations.

Triggs in pale green, his collar sprigged with clover.

Beck, whose cuffs were edged in needlework feathers.

Pennythwaite, resplendent in creams and harvest gold.

Wyn, who wore his best friend's colors, now that Alfie knew to notice.

He belonged with them. Possibly even belonged *to* them. And since that's all he'd really ever wanted, it'd always been enough. But Sonnet in her regal blues had spilled too many secrets. Alfie might not understand everything, but he couldn't help catching on. Probably because they were hoping he would.

Triggs, strong as an ox.

Beck, with his rooster strut.

Wise old Pennythwaite.

And *apparently*, a gentleman mouse in their midst.

Alfie found himself hoping that Thrussel Morningswell was on Lord Alderney's guest list. Because his head was filled with complicated questions. And Thrussel really was best when it came to simple answers.

TRAP

Florent spared the room and the dancers a glance. All Amaranthine, by his reckoning, and all swathed in festival finery. Clan colors were predominant. Crests on full display. The entire atmosphere was convivial, but he felt out-of-place. Usually, he didn't attend; he was otherwise occupied, piecing together the sigilcraft that kept such gatherings safe. Find the gaps. Shore them up. But this house was Lord Alderney's home, and its defenses were the product of centuries. Florent was extraneous.

From the edges of the newly dubbed "ballroom," he watched Hazel in her coral dress. She was already on the dance floor. Alfie led her out, then Wyn. Even Pennythwaite had his turn, as was expected. They were her protectors, her kin. After that, Triggs and Beck flanked her during a simple circle dance, which Hazel clearly enjoyed.

It occurred to Florent that he might not be missed.

Plenty of gentlefolk had gathered to give Hazel this gift, even though there were many last details to prepare before tomorrow night. The clothes, the banquet table, the paper lanterns, the punch bowl carved from ice, and even the musicians were all borrowed from their preparations for the morrow's Frost Festival. A foretaste.

He was giving serious thought to slipping out a side door when Sonnet was suddenly before him. "You must dance with the Partridges, as thanks for your festival clothes."

Which was only courteous.

Florent offered Missus Partridge his hand, just as Mister Partridge escorted Hazel onto the floor. Their smiles were pleased, even proud. But also coy in a way that should have tipped Florent off.

Dance was integral to avian courtship. And these two clearly approved of the match he longed to make. When the song reached its conclusion, a final turn placed Florent and Hazel face to face. The implication was simple—the next dance would be theirs to share. And with everyone looking on, how could he refuse?

Honor and honesty warred, and Hazel smiled through the stalemate.

Patting her chest, she laughed. "I am quite breathless. Florent, would you be so kind as to lead me to the refreshments?"

An out.

Gratefully tucking her arm through his, he ushered her to a table spread with traditional delicacies. Florent dipped a cup of punch and passed it to her, whispering, "Thank you."

"In all the fairy tales I know, only those with noble hearts ever make a lasting impression." She arched her brows. "I won't *trap* you into courting me."

He couldn't help smiling. Mice were susceptible to traps.

Neither did he wish to entrap Hazel. Not with so many truths untold.

But then the import of her remark struck him. "You *want* me to court you?"

"Aren't you in love with me?"

Florent matched her frankness. "More than a little."

"Do you want to court me?"

"Rather a lot."

Hazel tasted her punch before asking, "Why don't you?"

Leaving the nest as he had, Florent had forgone the usual rounds of matchmaking games. He had younger brothers more eager. He'd cherished his work and craved travel. Never once had it occurred to Florent that he'd want to settle. Nor that he might negotiate his own betrothal.

Grand-mere had known.

Many said she knew things others didn't. Because she saw

things differently. Because *she* was different. Touched by the starlight that silvered their clan's fur.

She'd blessed and pressed a ring upon him. *For someday*, she'd said.

And it seemed his *someday* had come.

Florent guided Hazel toward a quiet corner. Finding a curtained alcove, he gave her a questioning look.

Head held high, she preceded him inside.

Hands working in tandem, he plucked two sigils from the air and created a small pocket of privacy. Joining her, he echoed her question. "Why don't I? There is the suddenness to consider. Your family may object."

"*I* don't."

Florent gently countered, "You know very little about me."

She nodded once and ordered, "Fix that first."

"Very sensible." But where to begin?

Hazel took charge. "I have two requests. No, *three*."

"Let's hear them."

"I want to know your name."

"Florent."

"Your surname, silly. Since I'll be taking your name, I want to practice writing it."

His heart began a heavy beat. "My name is Florent Rimestead."

"Oh! But that's lovely."

Her admiration left him a little breathless. "Your next request, my lady?"

"Is there really a ring for me?"

"There is."

"May I see it?"

From under his tunic, he brought out his trove of priceless things. Slipping the chalcedony ring from the chain, he displayed it on the palm of his hand.

"It's not *set* with a stone. It's *made* of stone!" exclaimed Hazel.

"Yes."

She picked up the pale blue circlet, turning it this way and that, studying the narrow bands of white that rippled across its polished surface. "Are you giving this to me?"

Florent returned the rest of his necklace to its place while he decided how to answer. "Only my lady can wear my ring."

Immediately she offered it back.

Disappointment spiked, but he reclaimed the thing.

"Which finger do I wear it on?" she asked, switching her punch cup back and forth. "Aren't you supposed to put it on me?"

"So hasty," he chided, stealing away her cup and setting it aside.

"Feels like forever to me," she countered, offering both hands.

"This one." He tweaked the next to last finger on her left hand. "But it's too soon. When I place my ring on a lady's finger, the pledge is made and met. We would be wed."

"When is the ring usually given?"

"After a third dance." Florent basked in a growing sense of awe. She wasn't merely willing; she was insistent. "Once is courteous, twice is courting. Thrice is for always."

"Threes, is it?" Hazel arched her brows. "Don't forget. I'm making *three* requests."

His name.

His ring.

What next?

"Ask for anything." Florent knew he would give it.

"Dance with me *properly*." She bounced up onto tiptoe. "We cannot have a third dance until we've had a second."

TWICE

Hazel didn't think she was imagining the change in Florent. He held her differently.

It was subtle. The forms of the dance hadn't changed, but his posture had. The turn of his shoulder, the pressure of his hand. He angled his head as if listening with care, even when she was silent. And he had a certain *presence* about him.

She hadn't noticed at first. How could she have? Florent was so contrary. But maybe Uncle Wyn was right about him. He'd been trying to make peace with her from the beginning.

Florent and his ridiculous bouquets.

Florent and his shopping list lyrics.

"The fairies like you," she remarked. Because it was true.

"Fairies?" he echoed, questions in his gaze.

One of the things she liked best about Florent was his gentleness toward pitterhinds and welfhunds. She'd seen him in the door garden, kneeling among the herbs, smiling over their antics, making them welcome in his space.

Triggs acted like they were pests, puffing them away with gusty sighs. Beck was far less patient, flicking his fingers and clicking his tongue. Uncle Wyn and Sonnet banned them from inside the house with stones and signs.

But Florent brought her dun nippets.

Even now, he smiled at the manchette that must have stolen inside with the guests. Two of Lord Alderney's maids were trying to shoo it out a window.

He traded a look with her and laughed. "Fairies, are they? I suppose that fits as well as anything."

Hazel liked sharing something secret with him. She supposed she was finally, properly in love. Or maybe … *im*properly. That made her feel daring. And eager to dare more.

"I used to think I'd marry Alfie."

Florent confessed, "When I was tiny, I had a crush on my grand-mere."

"Was she wonderful?"

"Was and is and evermore shall be." His tone lilted along with the music.

Hazel wondered when he'd become so much easier to talk to, easier to admire. "Your hair looks blue in this light."

He glanced at the lanterns strung overhead. "My hair's always been this color. All of us Rimesteads are said to be frost-kissed."

"And sweeter for it?"

"I wonder." Florent smiled softly. "Nobody's ever suggested that before."

Right away, she wondered if *sweet* really was the right word for Florent. He was probably too disobedient to qualify. Still, he gave her that comfortable feeling that came when everything was gathered in before the first snow. All warm firesides and cozy chairs drawn close together, without a thought for the storms outside, even when the wind is whistling past the eaves and the windowpanes are etched by frost.

The dance continued, and she loved to dance. But Hazel liked that it gave her the chance to be close to Florent. To be foremost in his attention.

"Are you a fairy prince?" she asked, only half teasing. He felt magical.

"If so, I'm a younger son with no palace or prospects. But I do spend a lot of time creating … well, you'd probably call them fairy gardens." Florent guided her through a turn before adding, "My meadows are a little like Pennythwaite's bird feeders. They help me look after your fairies. Where I'm from, we call them Ephemera."

"Why?"

"Which part?"

"All the parts," she pleaded. "I want to know everything!"

"And you shall," he promised. The dance ended, but he didn't let go. "If I release you, the dance ends, and we must be done for today."

She whispered, "Oh, please. Not yet."

So Florent guided her into position for the next dance. Not letting go must have been one of those loopholes that couples had found to prolong the time they spent together.

"They're called Ephemera because there's so much variety. They borrow from every class, sometimes combining them in surprising ways." Florent spoke softly, his voice pitched for her ears only. "Many of them are useful to farmers because they're pollinators."

"Sonnet never told me that part."

"Well, your cook isn't a farmer."

"But she knows so many wonderful fairy tales!"

Florent nodded. "I grew up with similar stories. Do you have a favorite?"

So she chattered on about moonbeams and rainbows and whirlwinds. Florent's smile widened, and sometimes he chuckled. He listened as if bedtime stories mattered, and he contributed a few variations. All while guiding her through the steps of another waltz.

Hazel hoped it wasn't improper for her to dance with one partner for the rest of the night, because she didn't want to trade. Perhaps Florent felt the same, because he moved seamlessly from one dance to the next.

The same ballad Pennythwaite had sung began to play, and Hazel hummed along.

Florent wiggled his eyebrows and softly sang along, inserting their made-up lyrics.

She joined in as softly as she could, but they turned heads. It probably wasn't anything terribly improper. Otherwise, Pennythwaite wouldn't be trying so hard to hide his smile.

"You must be tired," Florent murmured.

"Not at all. I don't want this dance to end."

He gave the tiniest shake of his head. "If our second dance never ends, how will I lead you into a third?"

Which nearly startled her into stopping.

But he lifted and spun, and they didn't miss a beat.

"If this dance *must* end," she bargained. "Promise me it'll end well?"

Florent leaned closer. "What is it you want?"

"My first kiss."

Which startled him to a standstill.

Mercifully, the music ended a few measures later, and Florent led her off to one side, where potted palms were arranged before a wide window. Half-hidden by greenery, he faced her. "Not here. Not where anyone could see."

Hazel blushed. "I forgot anyone else was here."

Florent grew even more solemn. "That's ... flattering."

"It's not flattery. It's true."

He eased closer and pleaded, "Tomorrow?"

Disappointment was tempered by the shortness of the delay. "Why tomorrow?" she asked.

"Because tomorrow, there will be another dance."

FROST

When everyone parted ways after breakfast the following morning, Florent caught Alfie's sleeve and took a pleading stance. "Talk with me?"

The man's surprise faded into practiced neutrality. "If you want."

"I'd appreciate it."

Alfie nodded toward the field where they'd be working all day, and Florent fell in step beside him. They walked in a silence that grew awkward.

Finally, Florent asked, "Do you know about me?"

"I wouldn't say I *know* anything." Alfie cast a sidelong look in his direction. "Sonnet sometimes says too much. Is this about Hazel?"

"Yes." And he stalled out. He didn't want to apologize or make excuses to this man. Yet he couldn't think where to start.

Alfie helped things along. "I know about Sonnet, but Hazel

doesn't. Let her keep her mum."

"I won't meddle." Florent winced. "At least, not with Sonnet. Only … Hazel needs to know about me before I'd ever …."

"So she *doesn't* know."

"Enough to choose me, but not enough to have me." He could feel color rising in his face and felt ridiculously young, despite his years. "She was insistent, and I was willing. As of last night, we're courting."

"Sonnet was hoping so."

Florent tentatively added, "Pennythwaite approves."

Alfie nodded a few times. "Hazel is impulsive, but once she makes up her mind, she rarely changes it. You're an interesting exception."

"I know it's fast …."

"*That* doesn't bother me." Alfie stopped walking. "I knew from the first ten minutes I was here that it was a good place. Walked right into Sonnet's arms and knew we were safe."

"About Hazel. I do love her."

"That's all right, then." Shoving his hands into his pockets, Alfie eyed him thoughtfully. "Do you have a tail like Sonnet?"

"Not in speaking form."

"There's a different form?"

Florent realized that Alfie didn't really know much more than Hazel. His consternation must have been plain.

"Right. Maybe it's time I found out what makes my family so special."

He couldn't have phrased it any more kindly.

All the while they pulled the last of the pumpkins from

their withered patch, Florent explained about his people, their many clans, and how Uncle Wyn, Pennythwaite, and all of Yoxall were bending the rules. It was nearing noon when he finally came around to his clan and its customs.

"One more dance?" Alfie asked incredulously. "That's it, then? You'll be married?"

"In essence." Florent snagged his sleeve again. "I'll make that vow tonight, if you're willing."

"Me? It's up to Hazel if she wants you."

Holding fast to reinforce his plea, he said, "I'll sneak you into tonight's Frost Festival. Join the dance with your sister, and before the evening is done, hand her off to me."

"For keeps?"

Florent vowed, "She will have all my days, all my devotion."

"Will it be all right, though?" He gazed off toward the song circle as if he'd always known where it was. "Won't they mind?"

He really *didn't* know anything, but that would change once Alfie realized how gently the people of Yoxall held him and Hazel. Florent said, "They didn't mind last night, did they?"

Alfie's gaze darted to the hilltop hall.

"You're still in a good place, Alfie." Florent put a supporting hand under the man's elbow. "Surrounded by people who consider you one of their own."

STAY

The soft tap on Hazel's bedroom door was followed by her brother's usual call. "It's me."

She rushed to open up and hushed him with an upraised finger and urgent hiss.

"Sure, and I'll be quiet," he promised. "But there's not much need. The house is empty, except for us."

"Where've they gone?"

Alfie shrugged. "Come on. Florent's waiting."

Which flustered her enough that she forgot her shawl on the bed and had to run back for it.

Florent stood just beyond the door garden's gate, carrying a lantern to light the way. It was an unusually pretty creation. Hung from the end of a stick, it was shaped just like an oversized lantern flower, but this one glowed blue.

They wore their party clothes from the previous evening. Only with extra undergarments to counteract the crisp night. Alfie had added a cape, and she had her shawl. Somehow, Florent was getting along without the addition of a cloak.

He greeted them with a smile and said, "Worst first. There's something I need to show you before all the rest."

Hazel's heart fluttered, but not for fear. Anticipation hung in the air, stirring up the stars and fairies and putting an azure halo around the rising moon.

Passing the lantern to Alfie, Florent said, "Hold it high."

Its cool glow was sufficient to turn silver hair blue, and she still liked the effect.

"Not enough light?" He huffed and fished in a pocket, bringing out a handful of small stones—cornflower, periwinkle, lavender. As he touched each, they began to glow and rose into the air, suspended within a circle of luminous filigree.

"Why, that's lovely!" The crystals drifted in lazy circles, adding to the illumination.

Florent angled his head to one side and whispered, "Well?"

It took a moment for her to catch on. He was trying to show her his ears, which now came to elfin points.

"You really *are* a fairy prince!"

"No." His smile was cautious. "But this is how I really look. Will that change your mind?"

Hazel noticed that he was curling his hands to display a set of sharp-looking claws without pointing them at her. And the eyes that were pleading with her had changed. Not in color, but Florent's pupils had narrowed to fine lines.

"It's not too late to refuse a suitor for his strangeness," he said softly.

Hazel looked to Alfie, who seemed more interested in the hovering crystals than in strange suitors. But he spared her a small smile. "I *refuse* to offer an opinion on whether he's fanciable."

She couldn't help it. She giggled.

Florent immediately relaxed.

"I think *that's* the only refusal you'll get." Hazel decided Florent was even more fanciable than before. "Stay. We are *still* courting, Mister Rimestead."

His hands were warm. His touch was gentle.

Florent went so far as to kiss her cheek before tucking her arm through his. "Step lively and step light. This way to the song circle."

By the light of lantern, stars, moon, and crystals, he led them to the forbidden stile.

KIN

Alfie couldn't see the stile until Hazel set his hand on it. All at once, the air filled with fairy lights, and music drifted from the far side of the meadow, where dozens of people had gathered.

Florent plucked the blue crystal from midair and urged, "Put this in your pocket. It'll help."

Murmuring his thanks, Alfie clambered over the fence and was ready when Florent handed Hazel over.

"Lead her out, Alfie. Dance with as many as you wish, Hazel." Florent's gaze lingered on her face with traces of longing. "When you're satisfied, look for me. I'll be waiting."

It only took a moment for him to be lost in the crowd.

Alfie peered around and whispered, "This is all a bit magical."

She hugged his arm. "Has this always been here?"

"Probably." He turned so they were facing. "This is your wedding, Hazel. More or less. Are you happy?"

"I'd be happier if everyone could be here."

"I think they are, little sister."

"*Everyone* everyone?"

"Yes." He led her into line for the next dance. "I think all the people we care about are trusting us with their secrets."

He scanned the other revelers with growing confidence. There were antlers in evidence. And several sets of horns. Some of the costumes were liberally draped in feathers. To his amusement, there were animals mingling with their friends and neighbors. He recognized Riff and Raff. The chickens were harder to tell apart. Then he spotted an owl the size of an ox perched in a bowed pine.

"Are you sure you want to marry into magic?" he asked.

"You're not allowed to object."

Alfie focused on her face. "I wouldn't. I don't. I'm part of this, too, you know."

"Oh? Are you courting someone, as well?"

"Nothing like that." He *might* have been hoping for a glimpse of Thrussel, but he spotted someone else first. And drew up short.

"May I?" inquired one of their oldest friends.

Alfie yielded without a second thought. Though the horns got a second look.

Hazel knew it wasn't proper to stare, but she needed a few more moments to collect herself. "Triggs?"

"Good evening, Hazel," he replied, ever patient, ever pleasant.

Which banished the momentary strangeness. "You look well in clover. Are you here with your ladies?"

"They would not miss your bonding for anything."

"Is that what this is?"

Triggs smiled indulgently. "It's what this became."

With careful steps, much constrained by the differences in their size, he led her through the rest of the dance, answering her questions about the Frost Festival. And when the music stopped, he handed her off to Beck.

"You look very handsome," she decided aloud.

"*You* are the one turning heads," countered Beck. "You left your necklace off last night, too."

"It didn't match."

"It can't keep you safe if you don't wear it."

"Is that how it is?"

"And ever has been." He grinned in his usual way. "We knew you were special right from the start."

All through their dance, he talked about souls that could shine and the people—his people—who loved it when they were near. By the time the music ended, Hazel knew she was treasured. And that Florent understood that better than anyone. The musicians drew the dance to its conclusion, and with a bow, Beck handed her off to Pennythwaite.

"I've never seen your hair loose." So much rippling gold. He was eldritch and wild, and the change somehow suited him. "Everyone is so beautiful."

Brushing past her compliment, he announced, "We are making a present of Cozy Cottage. Triggs and Beck will move back into their old room. My only requirement is that you wait until Midwinter's Day to fully join with Florent."

"So you *do* disapprove ...?"

"Not in the least." Pennythwaite's expression softened. "You and your fine buck will need every minute to ready your new nest. And midwinter is an auspicious time. Give us a little longer to dote before we see our darling girl safely into her bondmate's arms."

"*Am* I your darling girl?" The notion was almost more surprising than the gold-tipped claws on Pennythwaite's hands.

"A chick in my nest, as dear as a daughter."

Twice, he danced with her, for he had much to say. About the past and the future. About him and Uncle Wyn. About a happy ending that would never end. It was straight out of one of Sonnet's fairy tales, and it was going to be hers.

The instruments strummed through the final chords of their ballad, and Pennythwaite kissed her forehead before turning her over to her uncle.

"How old are you really?" she dared to ask.

Wyn laughed and admitted, "I lose track."

"Guess?"

"I don't have to. Pennythwaite is meticulous about everything and reminded me just this morning." His smile went crooked. "I'm one hundred and sixty-four."

So he told her about the rules of reavers and his reasons for running away. About regrets and rough days. About chasing fairy lights on a night just like this, only to be captured and kept by a solitary owl with superior foresight.

Hazel thought it a wonderful story, but it made her a little sad. "We're not family?"

"We are," Wyn assured. "Always were, I suppose. You and Alfie just made it all the more obvious. Thank you for that."

Then Alfie was there and leading her by the hand. "Someone else wants a turn, but they're afraid to ask."

Hazel tried to think who else might want to dance with her. Lord Alderney? Thrussel? But the figure waiting at the far end of the meadow was as strange as they were familiar. Tall and bare-chested under a lavish fur vest, with beads at throat and ankle, standing barefoot in the moonlight. A tail flashed into a low sway.

"A wolf," she gasped. Straight out of Sonnet's stories.

"Don't think too hard, and don't ask questions. Please?" begged Alfie.

She wished she could see better, but they were away from the festival lights. "I only know how to waltz," she warned the wolf.

They danced in silence, with Alfie looking on.

Hazel didn't need to think hard or ask questions, for she'd have known Sonnet anywhere. It was perhaps the most wonderful transformation of the night, but she held her tongue. Because it was plain as the look on Alfie's face that he still needed a mum. So all she said was, "Stories about wolves have always been my favorite."

Sonnet hugged her close, all sniffle and sniffing. Another fairy tale come true.

Alfie asked, "All right, there?"

Hazel pulled back enough to kiss Sonnet's cheek. "*Completely* right. But where is Florent?"

"Here," came the ready reply. And Florent stepped from the shadows.

THRICE

Florent thought it was entirely fitting for someone whose clan was named for frost to make his pledge during a Frost Festival. He stepped forward to claim Hazel, and Alfie yielded her with a small nod. Her hand fit neatly into his own, and he drew her toward the center, where the lights and dancers moved in time to the music. On the way, they met Thrussel, who offered a courteous bow and continued along. Toward Alfie.

The matter of choosing was between him and Hazel, but it was a miracle from the Maker to have the entire cooperative's approval. One Florent wouldn't take for granted.

"I want to walk by your side." It was the beginning of pledges. It was also the truth.

"Like this?" she asked.

"Just like this." Florent laced his fingers with hers. "I want to sit with you."

"To get out of work?" she teased.

He wouldn't mind staying indoors all day if he had Hazel for company. "I want to build with you."

All at once, her presence brightened. "Are these your vows?"

"Yes."

Hazel stopped, and he stayed by her side. She asked, "Is it a long list?"

"A lifelong one." Florent touched her hair, her cheek. "Will you hear me out?"

"Am I allowed to say what I want, too?"

"Tell me," he urged.

"I want to dance."

"So hasty." Even so, he tucked her arm through his and walked her into the circle.

The others must have been awaiting this moment, for the musicians struck a familiar chord, and Pennythwaite began to sing.

Hazel's smile put a spring in Florent's step.

She caught his eye. "You want to build. What are we building?"

"A nest. A home." He added to his vows. "I want to hold you."

"Like this?"

"More than this." So much more. "I want to nestle with you. Share my years with you. Bask in the sweetness of your soul."

Hazel understood enough to blush.

"If you're willing, we'll welcome children into our nest, and they will thrive."

"Aren't you getting ahead of yourself?"

"A little." Florent would happily bide the weeks that lay between now and Dichotomy Day. "So ... what do you want from me, Hazel?"

"Everything."

"Yours," he pledged, a little surprised by how much that one word meant. For him. For her.

"Even if I want azure nippets?"

He laughed. "I will send for some."

"What if I asked for more verses to our shopping song? And flowers for the breakfast table?"

"Easily accomplished." Florent hadn't realized his little gestures meant so much. He would continue the tradition.

It was a long dance, that third dance. But Pennythwaite drew his ballad to a close, and people drifted toward the refreshment tables. Florent didn't release Hazel. Just stayed where they'd stopped, keeping her in the circle of his arms.

Hazel searched his face. He supposed his eyes were strange now.

Arching his brows, he encouraged, "Ask anything."

"A kiss?"

"Here?" he checked.

"It's my wedding," she reasoned. "In all the stories I know, the bride is kissed at the finish."

"Then first," said Florent, bringing the chalcedony ring from his pocket. Taking her left hand, he coaxed his ring onto her finger, not even surprised when it fit. Grand-mere had a gift for gifts.

Hazel admired it without a word. But he could tell how pleased she was. Indeed, every soul in the meadow had to feel her delight and know its meaning.

Her affections were his to savor, to nurture, to answer. All that remained was to gather her in—frost-kissed and sweeter for it.

Florent brushed his lips across Hazel's, nudging her into alignment before adding a firmer press. He tugged, and she came closer, a fine fit. The tip of his tongue against her bottom lip earned him a startled look. Gently now. Little by little, he'd lead her along.

Drawing back, he asked, "Satisfied?"

Hazel bit her lip and shook her head.

"This part's easy." He pressed his cheek to hers and spoke into her ear. "I'll chase you, then you'll chase me. It's the kind of game that lovers play, and I am yours."

He kissed her earlobe, her eyebrow, her nose. Teasing her a little.

She thrust out her lip, and he kissed her pout away.

Adjusting his hold, he started the pattern from the beginning—brush, press, flick.

Quick as ever, she answered in kind, and when he hummed appreciatively, she swayed into him. Reached for him in intangible ways. Found him waiting and willing. And thoroughly awash.

"If you're dizzy, lean on me." Her arms around his waist were definitely keeping him upright. With a playful twinkle, she added, "None the wiser."

He laughed, and she joined him.

For all his dances. For all his days.

THE END

CAPTURED ON FILM

because unlooked-for things can be treasures

*"On the popular television
series* Dare Together, *what
famous cryptid did brothers
Caleb and Josheb Dare
bring out of hiding
for an interview?"*

TAMIKO AND THE TWO JANITORS

DARE YOU

A clatter of knocks on Caleb's door startled him so that he nearly lost his balance. Teetering on the next-to-top rung of a six-foot stepladder, he sourly muttered, "Rude."

He hated ill-mannered people. And inconsiderate behavior.

Staying home was supposed to spare him from such things.

Nessie shot from the plush cushion that took up most of the space under Caleb's computer desk and scrabbled on bare planks until she found purchase on the Turkish rug. Bouncing as high as she could, her baying drowned out Caleb's grumbling as he worked his way back to the floor.

The pummeling of his door didn't cease, only changed tempo.

Couldn't be a courier. Groceries had been sent up earlier, and he wasn't anticipating any further deliveries until after the weekend. But really, Caleb already knew who it had to be. This wasn't Nessie's stranger-danger bark. And her tail was whipping fast enough to stiffen egg whites.

Doggie bliss on this level only meant one thing.

Caleb grudgingly released all his locks in order to face the grinning fool whose battered boots were firmly planted in the center of his pristine door mat. Which had been chosen because it did *not* say "welcome."

"Hey, bro!"

Caleb barely recognized his younger brother. Too much hair. Too much beard. He warily returned the greeting. "Josheb."

Squatting to rough up Nessie's fur and tug at her long ears, Josheb laughed. "Well, *somebody's* glad to see me! Aren'tcha, girl?"

That was fair. Caleb wasn't exactly glad to see his brother. Maybe a little relieved. Josheb was always off on some adventure, usually in some godforsaken off-the-grid thicket of wilderness. Doing things that required survival training. And surviving in general.

Josheb's smile had gone lopsided. "Is that for me?"

Caleb glanced at the lightbulb in his hand. "I was in the middle of something."

"Need help?" Nodding past him, he cheerfully added, "Heights are more my thing, right?"

Silently stepping back, Caleb invited his brother inside with the sweep of an arm.

Josheb tossed a mammoth duffle through the door first. It landed with a *clang*. He eyed Caleb critically. "You stopped growing."

"Lose the boots."

With the glint of challenge in his blue eyes, Josheb ditched the footwear and stood tall. Preening. As if a couple of inches mattered in the long run. Competitive much?

Caleb shut the door but hesitated over the locks. Maybe Josheb wasn't staying?

His brother was already halfway up the ladder, hand outstretched. Deciding to let the idiot put his extra inches to good use, Caleb passed along the lightbulb.

Completely at ease at the tippy-top, Josheb screwed it back in place.

"I need the one next to it," said Caleb.

Josheb extracted it and held it up to the nearby skylight. "I don't think this one's burnt out."

"Neither was the last one."

That earned him a stare. Josheb finally asked, "What? You rotate them like tires, or something?"

Caleb produced the microfiber cloth tucked in his back pocket. "They don't need to be changed out. I'm dusting them."

Josheb looked around Caleb's apartment like he was seeing it for the first time. "You've got nothing better to do than dust lightbulbs?"

"I have a maintenance schedule," he retorted stiffly. It wasn't like his loft needed a lot of upkeep, but he was diligent, even with details. Changing the subject, he asked, "What are you doing here?"

His brother ran a hand over a dark blond beard. "Hear me out."

Okay, this was already bringing back bad memories. "No."

"I came to invite you."

"No."

"Remember how Dad would take us camping?"

Caleb held up a hand. "Invite Dad. He'd be thrilled."

Josheb's eyes narrowed. "I'm making this official. I dare you, Caleb Dare."

"You can't."

"Can, too. Just did." From his doubly superior height, Josheb smirked. "Live up to the name, or live down the shame. You *know* what's riding on this."

He did.

As one, they both looked to Nessie, whose tail thumped the floor.

GUILT TRIP

"I'll walk Nessie."

Caleb scrambled to get between his brother and the door. "Not without me."

Sporting a knowing smile, Josheb asked, "Afraid she'll run away with me?"

"You're not a … a fit parent." Which sounded stupid, so he tried again. "You're not stable enough to take care of her."

Josheb reached past him for the leash that hung on its peg beside the door. "We chose a bloodhound so we could track down adventures. Remember?"

"That was a long time ago," Caleb grumbled.

Dropping to one knee to clip the lead onto Nessie's collar, Josheb grabbed her face. "What do you say, old girl? Want to run a little wild? Put your nose somewhere new?"

"I hate camping," muttered Caleb. Ever since the last time, when he'd been plagued by all the tiny creatures that were supposedly figments of his imagination.

There were *reasons* he lived on the twenty-second floor of an urban highrise. His loft was as far from grassroots as he could get.

"You're the one I need," said Josheb. "I can't do this without you."

"*This*." Caleb wasn't ready to give in just yet. "Define *this*."

"A tip came in at the paper I've been working for. Editor in charge gave me first right of refusal, and I jumped at the chance. If this pans out, it'll be the story of the century!"

Caleb cringed inwardly. His brother didn't write for any sort of reputable paper. He wrote largely speculative articles about bizarre happenings and unidentified creatures.

"Don't look so skeptical!" Josheb promised, "This time, it's the real deal. And it'll be a good chance for us to hang out. Maybe work through some stuff."

He closed his eyes. "Please, don't make this about brotherhood and bonding."

"At this point, it's about your good name."

Thinking fast, Caleb said, "No swamps." Never again.

"Scouts honor."

"No crossing international lines."

Josheb laughed awkwardly. "Couple of state lines. Half a dozen, tops."

"I want the whole story."

"Done."

"I want the map."

His brother's shoulders went limp with relief. "You got it."

"I need a week to prepare."

"Hey, now! We've gotta follow up before the trail gets cold."

Caleb wasn't going to get caught up in his brother's reckless pace. "If I'm going, I will go prepared. It takes time to plan and pack. And I need to put my affairs in order."

Okay, that sounded more ominous than he'd intended.

Josheb looked ready to argue, but he shut his mouth and tugged at his beard. "Three days?"

"Five."

Desperation crackled in his final bid. "Four days."

It was enough. "Done. But I won't do the thing."

The look on Josheb's face said it all. This wasn't about brotherly bonding or old times. This was about the right tool for the job. And Caleb wasn't a fan of being used.

"What if it's … absolutely necessary?" asked Josheb.

Caleb knew he might not have a choice. Even so, he grimly repeated, "I'm not doing the thing."

ASPEN HOLLOW

The next morning, Caleb found a tent pitched in his living room, its poles firmly lodged in his Turkish rug. But Josheb was gone, as was Nessie. With little else to do, Caleb started the coffee pot and the computer and settled in to work.

An hour and a half later, the apartment door opened, bringing in a damp, outdoorsy smell. He looked up in surprise. Sure enough, raindrops showed on the skylight. Even more surprising, Josheb held Nessie on the doormat until he could wipe her paws.

Like a civilized person.

Caleb nodded his thanks. Nice to know Josheb could be gracious in victory.

Turning her loose, his brother shook a bakery bag invitingly before retreating into the galley kitchen to help himself to coffee.

Caleb caught the sound of the toaster oven timer grinding down and logged out of TOS. He'd met his daily goal and shored up his accounts. A couple of weeks away wouldn't do any harm.

Josheb was leaning against the counter. Waving his bagel toward the bag, he said, "Got some of those blintzes you like, too."

A rare treat. These days, he never went that far from home. As if six blocks was a major journey.

"Where's the map?" Caleb asked.

"I'll grab it."

They spent breakfast crowded over a big topographical map that flopped over the edges of Caleb's tiny kitchen table. He pored over the lines, concentrating on every detail. His recall was nearly perfect once he studied a thing.

"We'll start from here." Josheb tapped a dot labeled Aspen Hollow. "It's remote. The road we'll be taking at first used to be a lumber trail."

At first?

Caleb flicked some of his brother's crumbs off the map and onto the floor. Much to Nessie's delight

Josheb traced a line to a river. "We turn off here. Follow it upstream to Quaking Creek. Then it's trail blazes for a while. I reserved a cabin near here, a place called Red Stag Spring."

"There's a rental cabin? Way out there?"

"Sure. They get hikers like us. Or there's hunting and fishing. Guy I talked to said the last group through there was into battle games, like with paint balls and pellet guns. They left early. Spooked."

"By ...?"

Josheb waggled his eyebrows. "Bigfoot."

COURSE CORRECTION

Caleb could tell his brother was making an effort. Staying out of the way. Keeping quiet. Tidying up after himself. Caleb tried not to find it suspicious. Unfortunately, he knew better.

He'd just finished suspending all the deliveries that would have come during the next couple of weeks and logged onto the USPS website to hold his mail. They wanted specific dates.

"Two weeks, right?" he asked.

Josheb sat very still, eyes averted.

Giving the matter some thought, Caleb wilted inside. "You *said* a couple of weeks."

"Well, there are a lot of variables."

"Josheb," he warned. "How long?"

"It'll probably take us a week to hike in. Once we get to Aspen Hollow."

Which was already a lengthy cross-country drive.

"How. Long."

"Six weeks." Josheb's stare was rebellious.

Caleb swiftly recalculated and grimly said, "I need another day."

His brother sheepishly muttered, "Done."

"What *is* all this?" Josheb asked incredulously.

Caleb slid another two cans into an already bulging duffle. "Nessie's food."

"You *can't* be serious."

"She has a strictly regulated diet."

Josheb made a rapid tally and shook his head. "We can't pack in this much dogfood. You'll break your back. And mine."

"She needs to eat." Caleb kept right on stacking cans.

"What's this other crap?"

He glanced over and bristled. Josheb was pulling ration packets out of his second duffle. "Those are for *me*," snapped Caleb.

Without so much as a by your leave, Josheb ripped open one of the crinkling silver, astronaut-approved meal pouches and took a whiff. "No." His whole demeanor shifted into disdain. "This is a no-go, bro. Absolutely not."

"I have to eat."

For just a moment, Josheb looked hurt. But all he said was, "I won't let you go hungry."

SADDLE SORE

By driving in shifts, they made it to Aspen Hollow early on the third day.

Caleb was more than happy to abandon Josheb's sorry excuse for a vehicle. Four-wheel drive may have been a plus on the rutted road that pulled them up slopes thick with the miniscule town's namesake trees, but Caleb preferred cars with doors. Not zippers. The rumbling rust bucket was far from airtight and not quite weatherproof. And Nessie had been carsick. Five times.

She bailed out right behind him, nose to the ground, zigzagging through a search pattern.

He watched her dazedly, wondering what kinds of scents she was finding, when Josheb hustled to get in front of her. Clipping a long lead onto her collar, he roughed up her fur and gruffly said, "Careful, girl. These aren't safe parts for small fry. Don't wander off. Either of you."

Ice trickled through Caleb's veins. He couldn't afford to be careless here. What if she'd shot off after some new scent? Lost in these woods could mean landing on some predator's menu.

Josheb handed him the end of her leash. "I called ahead. Everything's set. We'll get breakfast over there, then hit the trail."

There looked more like a pole barn than a restaurant.

Once inside, Caleb decided it was more of a bar. But the owner had no issues with frying up half a dozen thick hamburgers at seven in the morning. At least Caleb was pretty sure they were hamburgers. Maybe beef tasted different in this part of the country? He added extra mustard and tried not to think too hard about it.

Afterward, he loitered with Nessie outside the rental office.

Josheb emerged grinning and jingling a couple of keys. "You love me."

He rolled his eyes. "Family obligation."

"You love me, and I'll prove it!"

Josheb jogged away, disappearing behind the building. A moment later, an engine roared, and Caleb dared to hope it was coincidental. But his brother swerved into view on a four-wheeler, a cart rattling along behind it. Braking beside him, Josheb waggled his eyebrows. "Confess your deep and abiding love."

"We don't have to walk the whole way?"

"The cabin comes with transport. It'll save us a twelve-mile hike." He radiated smug.

Caleb, who never went twelve blocks, let alone twelve miles, was relieved enough to gruffly answer, "May brotherly affection abound."

Josheb laughed and handed him a helmet.

NATURE CALLS

"I hate you."

"So fickle!" Josheb managed to sound cheerful, even when out-shouting an engine.

Caleb grunted as they hit another bone-jarring bump. It was his own fault that he was stuck in the cart with the dog. Nessie was enjoying this experience far more than the car ride, her nose to the wind. Josheb had even lured her into one of their howling contests, something she wasn't allowed to do in urban lofts. Caleb was feeling both left out and put-upon. A proper pity party.

The metal of the cart was cold and unforgiving.

The road—this was a generous term—was littered with tiny pitfalls.

The air was thick with enough gasoline fumes to choke a forlorn day trader.

And the worst part, the part he *wouldn't* mention, was the uptick in interest he was drawing from things Josheb could neither see nor dissuade.

Regrets. Caleb had them. "I want to go home!"

"Can't hear you!" Josheb sang out.

But after the next switchback, he slowed to a stop and cut the engine. Swinging from the four-wheeler's seat, he stretched as he smiled toward the sun. "This is great. Pure awesome."

"A little help?" grumbled Caleb.

One good thing about Josheb. He was quick to act. Lifting Nessie down, he clipped her leash to the trailer hitch before hopping up onto the side of the cart. They locked wrists, and Josheb hauled back. With the extra leverage, he managed to unwedge Caleb.

"Any hope for a bathroom?"

"Shovel's clipped to my backpack," Josheb replied with a wink.

Caleb knew the drill. Didn't mean he had to like it. "I'm going to stretch my legs."

His brother waved him off. "No rush. We're making great time."

Stepping off the road felt like slipping into a different world. Far from home, yet familiar. How often had Dad taken them camping? Seemed like every weekend, though it was probably more like once a month. When they weren't on a trip like this, they were planning the next one.

Last year's leaves rustled under his boots while this year's batch quaked overhead. Caleb aimed for a pine whose drooping boughs would shield him from view. Nature's call dealt with, he turned back toward the road, but a shimmer in the shadows caught his attention.

Strange.

Caleb probably should have turned right around and walked away, but ... he couldn't. Even though he was reluctant to go any nearer, he couldn't help himself. He did try to be careful about it. Edging along with slow, soft steps, he waited breathlessly for something to happen.

The stone column was roughly four feet high and etched with lines that glittered. A trick of the light? No. Couldn't be. The delicate patterns appeared to be lit from within. Once he was closer, he could see that a crystal had been mounted onto the column—big as his fist and pale green. Was that what was calling to him?

Wait.

No.

He wasn't like Josheb, prone to whimsical notions. Rocks didn't call out. Right?

"Rocks will cry out, and trees will clap their hands," he whispered, slowly reaching out until his fingertips rested against cool crystal. "Hello?"

Did the light pulse? Maybe. Just a flicker, really.

Was that a hum? He could almost feel something. Not a buzz like appliances gave off, not a machine hum. This was more like music. A sustained note.

This couldn't be natural.

But it felt … right.

His camera was back with the rest of his gear, but Caleb fumbled for his phone and snapped one picture. Partly to prove to himself that he wasn't imagining things. Column and crystal were right there on his screen, looking like they'd been lifted from the set of a fantasy film. But the glowing lines hadn't picked up. They were fine as threads. He could still see them.

Zooming in he tried again.

No luck. Which probably put them in the figment category. In other words, stuff he couldn't explain or prove. Figments had only ever caused him trouble. So Caleb whispered a firm, "Goodbye." And walked away.

TWELVE MILES

"Ride up with me for the last leg," Josheb offered.

"But Nessie …!"

"… was *fine*. She's having the time of her life."

Which Caleb couldn't deny. "All right."

Josheb pulled a canteen out of his bag and passed it along. "Getting hungry?"

"Too rattled to think about food."

But his brother was eyeing him closely. "What's got you rattled?"

Caleb dropped his gaze and kicked at the rutted road. "Maybe you should ride in the trailer for the last leg. See how *you* enjoy off-roading without suspension."

Josheb snorted and swung a leg over, scooting forward to make room. Caleb settled in behind him. "No touching," he gruffly ordered.

"Oh, you'll want to hang on."

"You know what I mean."

With a brief look that was hard to read, Josheb started the engine, pointedly slapped his palms onto the handlebars, and didn't let go.

Twenty minutes later, he shouted, "This is Quaking Creek."

Caleb only grunted. But mentally, he plotted their position on the map he'd memorized. They were two-thirds of the way there.

They crossed more streams and runnels that somehow

merited names. Slaughter Creek. Broken Bend. Shrill Creek. Clanless Spillover. Lost River. "Is it just me, or are all these names unnecessarily ominous."

Josheb grinned. "What? Like *stranger beware*?"

"Shrill, broken, quaking, lost? Come on. They're horrible names."

With a shrug, his brother changed the subject. "What do you want for dinner?"

"Actual food. I refuse to eat grubs and roots and … and bitter herbs."

"How 'bout a plate of shrimp. Maybe a side of mashed potatoes? Some of that fancy-schmancy kale?"

Caleb grit his teeth. "It's not the same!"

"It's not that different. But you're safe for today, brother dear. I packed your favorite."

That stumped him. "Which favorite would that be?"

"Guess."

For the remaining few miles, Caleb made increasingly implausible guesses. The road ended in front of a small cabin tucked under a grove of cedars, almost as if the entire trail had been one long driveway.

"Twelve miles to the mailbox," he remarked.

Josheb stood and scanned their surroundings. "Right. Everything inside, including Nessie."

"It's not as if I'd leave her out in the cold. Figuratively speaking."

"Me, either. Too many bear tracks."

Caleb glanced at the ground. The afternoon was getting on, but there was plenty of light to see by. Even so, he didn't see tracks. "Are you trying to scare me?"

Jumping to the ground, Josheb strolled along one side of the cabin, disappearing briefly behind it before circling around the far side. "Elk, deer, squirrel, mouse, and any number of birds. Bear's the only one I'm worried about, for Nessie's sake. Though a skunk or porcupine would be a nasty surprise."

The cabin wasn't locked.

One room. Four bunks built into the walls. A cast iron stove and its pipe, both of which had been painted a smoky blue. Kindling in a crate. Canned goods on shelves over a sink that had an honest-to-goodness hand pump. The calendar on the wall beside the door was almost sixty years out of date.

"Seems about right," Caleb muttered.

The windows were small and smeared with grit. Nothing he couldn't fix with some water and a paper towel. But otherwise, the place seemed straightforward, snug, and so much better than a tent.

"This won't be so bad," he remarked.

Josheb opened the front of the stove and grabbed kindling. "Don't get too attached. We're not staying."

A sobering reminder that this wasn't their destination. More like the starting line.

LONGSTANDING RIVALRY

"Canned ravioli?" Caleb was surprised into a chuckle. "We're not *nine*, you know."

Josheb arched a brow. "That's why we each get our own can."

"I thought we weren't packing in a bunch of stuff."

"We're not. But I'm not opposed to the occasional treat." With a smirk, Josheb added, "Starting tomorrow, you're at my mercy."

Caleb and Josheb were a scant year apart. Close enough in age and looks to have been confused as twins for most of their lives. Back before Josheb entered his grizzly phase.

"Doesn't all that hair get in the way?"

"Nope." Amusement glinted in Josheb's eyes. "Is that follicle envy I detect?"

"Nope." Caleb accepted an open can of ravioli and a fork.

Digging into his own dinner, Josheb pointed between them. "Think of it as a lazy man's attempt to distinguish himself. I got tired of being called Caleb just because I'm taller than you."

It was only a slight edge. Hardly worth mentioning.

"And once it got to a certain point, it seemed a shame to submit to the shearers." Josheb chewed ruminatively before adding, "Girls like the hair."

"And the patriarchal beard?"

"Not so much. But *I* like not shaving." He cheekily added, "For the right girl, maybe I'll buy a razor again."

Caleb supposed they had that in common.

While Josheb had always been friendly with girls, even dated a few, he wasn't the sort to settle down to any one thing. Always on the move. Always moving on.

For Caleb, it was a weird mix of awkwardness and lack of opportunity. It was hard to meet girls when you never left your apartment. Or made an effort to strike up conversations. Or make eye contact, for that matter.

Nessie was the only female in either of their lives. And in a way, they were rivals for her affection.

Caleb gave her ear an affectionate tug.

Josheb fed her a ravioli. From his fork.

Probably a point in his favor, as far as Nessie was concerned, but ... *eww*.

SOME WEATHER

Getting to sleep was as hard as Caleb's allotted bed. The bunk was a veritable slab. His sleeping bag's zipper jingled faintly every time he moved. Summer nights were chilly at this elevation. And Nessie had abandoned him in favor of curling up with Josheb.

When he finally did drift off, Caleb was caught up in a confusing dream. He was a star trapped in a stone. Then a bee in amber. Or was he a moth?

The *click* of the cabin door woke him, and he struggled against his prison, only to realize it was just his sleeping bag. Josheb was coming in, bringing a gust of damp air and Nessie, whose claws clicked on the wood floor.

It was morning. Barely.

"How soon can you be ready to go?" Josheb asked softly.

Caleb wasn't all that comfortable in this cabin, but he was suddenly reluctant to leave its safety. A roof and a door and a stove had to be safer than a tent, especially when facing nature's unknowns. Still, he said, "Fifteen minutes, more or less."

"I want to get as far as we can."

Something in the way he said it put Caleb's back up. "Why?"

"Fresh tracks."

"What kind?"

"Bear."

Caleb frowned. "You think those guys who were spooked just saw a bear?"

"Guess there's a chance, but … this isn't where they saw it." Josheb started rolling up his sleeping bag. "We have a long hike to the site. And we might run into some weather."

Caleb knew the map. And the number of miles they could hike on a good day.

But nature didn't conform to anything resembling a schedule, which is why he begged for mercy barely a third of the way to their first campsite.

"I can't do this," he muttered. Then louder, to be heard over the rain, "Josheb, I can't."

"Giving up already?" Josheb's teasing tone grated against Caleb's nerves. "It's just a little rain."

He white-knuckled Nessie's leash. Rain wasn't the problem. He could have put up with a little rain.

"Something wrong?" Josheb backtracked to where Caleb stood. "Hey. Bro?"

Yeah, something was wrong. The light rain had stirred up hundreds of tiny figments. They were kind of a cross between a newt and an insect, silvery and slippery, with powerful back legs. Every step Caleb took, they sprang up like a field full of grasshoppers all around him, trailing light that burned into his retinas. He blinked dazzled eyes, barely able to see.

"What's with you?" Closer, softer, Josheb asked, "See something?"

Caleb flinched away from his brother's hand. "I'm not doing the thing for you."

Josheb's eyes narrowed. "But you're seeing stuff anyhow?"

"Oh, for the love of ...! If I could stop, I would!"

His brother gaped at him. "It's always on?"

Eyes shut. Teeth gritted. "Constantly."

"Are you okay?"

"Far from it." Caleb had lied so much about the things he could see. It was something of a relief to tell the truth.

Josheb was the only person who'd ever believed Caleb. Because if they were touching, Josheb would glimpse the same things. Maybe that was why the idiot believed in so much other nonsense. It was Caleb's fault. He never should have told his brother about the figments. Never should have started "the thing."

The secret they'd shared had become the wedge that drove them apart. Because Caleb had learned to resent Josheb, who only came to him in order to see something beyond him. Treating his own brother like one of his fine-tuned instruments for paranormal detection.

One brother believing in all the things he couldn't see.

One brother wishing he was blind to unbelievable things.

BETTER TOGETHER

"Show me?" begged Josheb, offering both hands.

Caleb glared for all he was worth, but he already knew he'd give in. He didn't want to be alone in the strangeness, so he seized his brother's wrist.

"Ow!" Josheb protested. "Ease up a little ... whoa!"

Tightening his grip, Caleb held his breath and waited for Josheb to say something. Anything.

"Are you kidding me?" Josheb swore softly and stepped closer to him. "They're like ... creepy little comets. The afterimages are killer. How long've you been putting up with this?"

"All my life." Through gritted teeth, he begged, "Get them off."

"Aw, geez. You never did like bugs. Hang on." And Josheb, who'd never minded anything, started picking figments like fleas. "On second thought, I think they're amphibians. But you don't really like *any* of the creepy-crawlies, so moot point."

"Very moot." As his brother casually tossed aside figments like it was nothing, Caleb began to relax.

"Don't let go." Josheb sheepishly added, "Please."

"Because you want to see."

"Hell, yeah. But also because we're better together. Don't you think?"

Caleb muttered, "I hate this."

"Yeah, I know. Man, I hate you." His tone held no rancor. In fact, his eyes were as bright as his smile. "Want me to pitch the tent?"

"Yeah. Away from them."

Josheb scanned the area with a critical eye. With a little

twist, he adjusted his hand so he could grip Caleb's wrist. Locked together, they scrambled uphill, away from the worst of the silver springers. Within ten minutes of Josheb choosing a campsite, Caleb was inside their tent, burrowed down in his sleeping bag.

"Hang out in here while I look for dinner."

"Don't you mean *hide out* in here?"

Reaching inside to touch Caleb's forehead, Josheb peered around their campsite, which was arranged beside a narrow stream. Polecat Creek, if memory served. "Nothing to hide from, yeah? So rest up, warm up, and work up an appetite."

Zipped inside, Caleb curled on his side and listened to raindrops ping off the top of their tent. It was a different color than the one they'd used as kids, but it still brought back memories. The sounds, the smells. The feel of the ground under his body—uneven and unyielding.

Somewhere along the way, he'd lost his taste for roughing it. Sure, he liked his creature comforts, but away from home, there were actual creatures to consider. At first, he hadn't realized he was seeing things. How was he supposed to know? It wasn't as if any of the stuff he saw was *scary*. But "imaginative" descriptions of strange animals were only cute when you were little. After that, you earned strange looks, a reputation for lying, and appointments with therapists.

Caleb was dozing when Josheb next checked on him. "Hungry?"

"Depends. What's on the menu?" He could smell smoke and something savory.

"Fresh fish. Come on. Rain's stopped."

The fire was tiny, but it did the job. They ate standing up, and Caleb offered to fish for seconds. Josheb produced a couple of beers, which he'd chilled in the creek. Caleb wanted to call him out for packing non-essentials, but he was too grateful to be petty. By the time they'd eaten their fill, the day was dimming.

"Early bedtime," decreed Josheb. "We'll try to make up for lost miles tomorrow."

They sprawled in the tent, Nessie between them, and Josheb poking his nose out the partially unzipped flap. Caleb grumbled when his brother touched his arm.

"Don't be stingy," Josheb whispered, his eyes fixed on something outside. "You live in a beautiful world."

Beautiful? Caleb snorted. "I don't want to look."

"I do." His brother spared him a wink. "I'll keep watch."

A surprisingly comforting sentiment. Maybe—just maybe—the Dare brothers *were* better together.

CREDIBILITY ISSUES

"I've been wondering," Caleb said over breakfast the next morning. "What are we supposed to do if we find this thing?"

"Take pictures."

"Won't people assume you shopped them?"

Josheb cradled a blue-speckled enamel coffee cup against his beard, breathing in the steam. "Co-witness testimony?"

"They'll assume we're in it together."

"Because we *are*. But you come off more trustworthy."

Caleb inhaled his own faceful of steam before taking a cautious sip. "They'll dig up files from that year Mom made me go to counseling. Undermine my credibility."

Josheb grunted. "You're good with a camera. Take pictures for me. Document the whole hike. Ever snap any figments?"

"Never tried." He'd been too busy wishing he could unsee the things to consider confirming their existence.

"Try." Josheb scratched and yawned. "Maybe science-y folks will perk up if you bring back pics of an undiscovered species. They'll name it after you. Claim to fame."

He liked taking pictures. It'd give him something to do while they hiked. And it was worth considering … what if bigfoot was elusive because he couldn't be seen by just anyone? Getting a picture would be impossible if the photographer didn't know where to point and click.

Which reminded him. Pulling out his phone, Caleb brought up the snapshot he'd taken the day before. "Ever seen anything like this?"

"Never. Where'd you see it?"

"Here." Caleb gestured vaguely at the trail behind them. "Yesterday. When I was stretching my legs."

Josheb was wide awake now. And annoyed. "Why didn't you tell me?"

"Because … it was weird."

"I *live* for weird!" He crowded next to Caleb on the lichen-encrusted stone that had been his choice of seating for breakfast. Zooming in, studying details, he asked, "Could you find it again?"

"Probably. It was glowing."

Josheb dropped his scowl. "Where? Which part?"

"Camera didn't pick it up. There were glowing lines all along the column."

His brother lit up in his own way. "Damn. There really is something here!"

Caleb didn't like to point out that mystic columns weren't part of bigfoot's aesthetic, so he only offered a vague, "Maybe. Be careful, in any event."

"And take more pictures. Tag them, date and time. Starting today." Tossing back the last of his coffee, he added, "Be thorough. It'll be important. I can feel it in my bones!"

BLUE BLAZES

The next two days were almost fun. Yes, Caleb was still trudging through the middle of nowhere, but with intent. Instead of just marching far enough to meet Josheb's milage quota for the day, Caleb was looking for landmarks. He snapped unusual trees, rotting logs, rocky outcroppings, and every one of the blue trail blazes that confirmed their course.

Documentation. He was good at this stuff.

"Why did those war games guys bother to go this far?" Caleb asked. "Plenty of woods between here and Aspen Hollow."

"We're moving slower than they did." Josheb had taken charge of Nessie. "You know how it is. Buncha guys trying to outdo each other. They probably double-timed it the whole way—*hut, hut, hut.*"

They *were* taking it slow, and not just for Nessie's sake. Rain had hampered progress the first day, and they were further delayed by Josheb's on-the-spot decision to keep careful records. Caleb created a field journal, logging date and time, location and direction. At each waterway, Josheb held up scraps of paper with creek names while cheesing for the camera.

Caleb was confident that his charts were so thorough, anyone could retrace their steps.

Josheb insisted that he not hide behind the camera the whole time. After some convincing, Caleb posed with Nessie. And they took a few duo selfies. Mostly to send to their parents once they returned to civilization.

"Anybody else queuing up to get their picture taken?" asked Josheb.

The figments. Caleb shrugged. "Can't say I've noticed."

"Nothing to lose, right?"

"Maybe with a digital camera, since we can delete duds." He cradled an old-school camera protectively.

"What if they only show up on actual film?"

Caleb hadn't considered that. Was he being too stingy because their supplies were limited?

Josheb suggested, "Wait to take a shot you've already lined up until something slides into the frame. We can check later. See if anything develops."

He snorted. But he also lifted his phone and snapped a picture of Josheb.

His brother threw his arms wide. "I'm hardly a figment."

"Josheb Dare, my imaginary younger brother?" Caleb suggested blandly. "I'm not *that* crazy. But you must have crumbs in your beard."

Eyes crossing as he looked down, Josheb mock-whispered, "Tell me I don't have one of those baby krakens on me."

Josheb had taken exception to the tiny airborne figments with tentacles. Caleb was fairly sure the miniature jellyfish were harmless, but they gave Josheb a case of the shudders.

"Birds," he quickly assured, wanting to put him at ease.

Josheb glanced around. There were birds everywhere. "How do you know they're figments?"

"You can't see them," Caleb reasoned. "And they're too tiny to be anything but figments."

"How tiny?"

He made a circle with his thumb and forefinger. "And they're purple."

"No way."

Caleb rolled his eyes. Then checked his phone. With a crooked smile, he said, "See for yourself."

Josheb squinted at the display, zoomed in, and muttered, "What in …? How are those *birds*? They look like tiny pom-poms."

"Easier to tell when they're flying." It was silly, defending the goofy little puffballs. But they were one kind he didn't mind so much, possibly because they weren't an amalgam of anything.

"It's out-of-focus, but I definitely see something." Brushing idly at his beard, Josheb ordered, "Keep trying."

EASY PACE

Although Caleb had initially focused on the downsides of camping, he was remembering parts he *did* like.

The quiet.

The simplicity.

The pace.

And in a way, he liked having Josheb to himself. With little else to do but talk, they were slowly but surely catching up. Filling in the gaps left by months apart. Reminiscing about camping trips past. And speculating about what they'd find tomorrow, when they reached the previous group's base camp.

Caleb asked, "When you say the last people up here were spooked, what do you mean?"

"Something scared them off."

"But ... what exactly? Are we talking giant footprints or actual sightings? Strange sounds, strange spoor?" Caleb tried to come up with plausible explanations. "Could a rival group have been messing with them? Or is there some chance they encountered someone with reasons to run them off?"

"Interesting theories." Josheb flashed a smile. "You're taking this seriously."

"I wouldn't say *that*. I mean, come on. Bigfoot?"

Josheb lifted a finger and wisely said, "Every legend has some truth to it."

"Says who?"

"Me." As if that's all it took to make myths materialize. "Can you make it six more miles?"

Caleb snorted. "I have nothing better to do."

"Not true!" Twirling a finger at the camera, Josheb said, "Take more pictures. Catch a figment on film."

They passed more landmarks—Black Squirrel Spring, Washboard Ford, and an overlook with a view of Turnabout Creek. As the long summer twilight took hold of the woods, Caleb remembered another detail that he liked about camping.

"Hear that?" he asked.

Josheb glanced up and around. "Which part? The leaves? The crickets?"

"They're birds, I think."

His brother sat still, ear cocked as he listened. "By any chance, do you hear things as well as see them?"

"Oh." That hadn't really occurred to him. It had to be possible. "Maybe?"

Coming to sit next to him, Josheb offered a hand as if to shake. "Put 'er here."

The clasp must have taken immediate effect because his brother began looking about, trying to pinpoint a new sound. Caleb asked, "Which one couldn't you hear before?"

"That pip-pip-pipping. Might be birds, but it could just as easily be tree frogs. Or even those little jumping streakers from before."

Caleb sent up a fervent prayer that it wouldn't rain. He couldn't handle another plague. "Why me?" he sighed.

"And why *not* me?" countered Josheb.

"I'd trade if I could." Although Caleb wasn't sure he meant it. At least this way, his brother still included him.

NIGHT NOISES

Caleb woke without understanding why his heart was hammering. He listened closely for several moments before he caught an odd snuffling sound. His breath caught when a deep grumble joined the party.

Nessie woke with a snort and set to barking.

Whatever was outside growled with enough authority to shake

the very tentpoles, and Nessie immediately switched to fearful baying. Caleb wished for his noise canceling headphones. She was worse than the alarm system in their apartment building, which was murder on anyone's ears.

Somewhere in the middle of everything, Josheb shucked out of his sleeping bag. "Bear," he muttered. "It's just a bear. Nothing to worry about."

As if running into a predator on that scale was no different than a passing thundershower.

Leaving the relative safety of the tent, Josheb soon set up a racket outside, banging their cookware together and shouting. "Go on! Git! Get outta here, ya big mooch! Nothing to see! Move it along!"

Caleb went to peek out the tent flap, and Nessie shot through. "Wait!" he yelped.

But she only went to Josheb, cowering between his legs as she added her own insults.

Bending to catch her collar, Josheb encouraged her. "That's right. You tell 'em. Make his ears ring." He dragged her to the end of the leash they'd anchored earlier and clipped her collar.

"*Was* it a bear?" Caleb asked.

Josheb dragged his hands wearily through his hair. "Definitely a bear."

"What are we going to do?"

"What do you expect me to do?" He scratched his stomach and looked off in the direction the beast had apparently run. "I'm not really equipped to hunt bear. You're not *that* hungry, are you?"

Caleb's incredulity melted into a weak laugh. "That may have been the farthest thing from my mind."

Josheb set to work calming Nessie, whose fur stood out in ways Caleb could sympathize with.

"I'm not sure I can sleep," Caleb admitted. "I don't feel safe."

"Want me to set you up with a hammock?" Josheb squinted into the darkness. "Ten feet up ought to do it. Though if you go higher, you'll have a better view of the stars."

"So my only options are a bear mauling or plunging to my death?"

Josheb snorted. "I'd strap you in."

"I am *so* reassured." Which was close to true.

Josheb's confidence was as catching as a cold in season, and Caleb recognized the symptoms. Lack of caution. Baseless optimism. And a niggling suspicion that it was far too late to turn back.

BASE CAMP

They reached the previous group's base camp before the sun was high.

"Looks like they left in a hurry," remarked Josheb.

That was an understatement. Four tents sagged from their poles, and a fifth looked to have been trampled. A heavy pot hung from a tripod over a firepit, and the clearing was strewn with everything from clothing to cooking utensils.

"How many guys were up here?"

"Sixteen."

"And these were shoot-first, war games types?"

"Tough as nails." Josheb tipped an open cooler onto its side with his foot. "The critters have been into everything. Probably not much hope I'll find tracks, but I'll try."

"Want me to gather this up? We could bring it back with us. Offer to return it."

Josheb snapped his fingers. "In exchange for interviews! I like how you think!"

Actually, Caleb had been tallying up the cost of all this gear. Most of it looked expensive. Surely some of those men had to regret the loss.

"Stick to the plan! Before you move anything, take pictures. Map the site on a grid. That sort of thing."

Caleb paced off one edge of the clearing and started taking notes.

Meanwhile, Josheb began at the firepit and slowly circled his way outward, reporting whenever he found tracks. "Squirrel. Deer. Pheasant. Ah, here's our friend the bear again."

"It's the same one?"

"We're probably in his territory."

"Or hers?"

When Josheb didn't answer right away, Caleb turned from his task. His brother was hunkered down, comparing the length of his hand to something on the ground.

"Don't know if we're any closer to finding what I'm looking for, but the squirrels sure do have big feet."

"How big?"

Josheb tugged at his beard and shook his head. "Must be something else. Can't think *what*, but this isn't right."

"Why not?" Caleb pressed.

"I mean … if these were squirrel tracks, those suckers would be as big as Nessie. Bigger, even."

"We're tracking giant squirrels?"

"No. We're tracking bigfoot." Josheb grinned. "The squirrels are incidental."

He was laughing it off. Maybe even dismissing it. But he made Caleb snap some pictures so he could compare the tracks to a field guide later.

Which got Caleb to thinking. How big could a figment get?

STOMPING GROUNDS

"Find anything?"

"Not really. Foraged some things for dinner." Josheb shook a fistful of greens and patted a bulging pocket. "Just need to see what the creek has to offer in the way of protein."

"Need me to fish?" offered Caleb.

"That'd be great." Josheb gestured toward the woods. "There's a good spot not far. Stone's throw. You can't miss it."

Caleb gathered the gear and checked his compass. Eastward trail. Downhill. It didn't take long for him to pick up the sound of running water. But he was catching something else, too. A scent.

Sort of sweet, but also sour. A little like flowers, but with a heavy, sticky quality. Honey? Yes, it was possible they were close to a honey tree.

Closing his eyes, Caleb listened for the telltale hum of bees.

He was still standing quietly, sifting through sounds, when Josheb ambled over with his arms stacked with kindling. "Why are you zoning out? The fish don't catch themselves."

"Do you smell that?"

"I just got the campfire going."

"Not smoke. It's sort of sweet. A ripe smell, I guess?"

Josheb inhaled slowly, took a few steps away and breathed in again. "You're right. Smells like a distillery to me."

"Liquor?" Caleb frowned thoughtfully. "As in moonshiners?"

"Well, we're not on the right continent to score some monkey wine. Which is too bad."

"You out of beer?"

"Didn't say that. Just wouldn't mind sampling something from a wild reserve. But honestly, this could be a combination of a couple of different smells. Some flowers have a special stink for luring in the pollinators, and I'm thinking some of your figments would qualify."

Stinky flowers. Caleb nodded. "Makes more sense than someone running a microbrewery way out here."

"If you were serious about studying those things, you could probably chart a whole new ecosystem."

"Why don't *you* do it?"

"Not me." Josheb waggled his eyebrows. "I'm here for the apex predators. Much more interesting than streaking crickets and boozy bees."

Caleb couldn't help being skeptical. His brother wanted bigfoot to be real, so he believed they'd entered his stomping grounds. By the same token, Josheb didn't find insects and amphibians all that interesting, so their activities were easily dismissed.

But what if boozy bees—or whatever these new figments might

be—were the clue they needed to figure out what in the world had happened up here?

SHUTTER BUG

All of the following morning, Caleb kept busy setting up photographs. His goal was capturing figments on film, but he had to figure out how to get them into the frame. Since he'd spent most of his life ignoring and avoiding them, attracting them was a new concept.

Luring them in wasn't working, which meant Caleb had to go where they were. So for the first time since his youngest years, he sat back and watched them.

Gradually, patterns emerged.

The whispery tendrils liked drifting through sunlit places, aimless and eerie. Types that mostly looked like rodents or amphibians lurked in shade. He spent twenty minutes on his belly in the moss, waiting for an antlered mouse thingie to decide he wasn't a threat.

The instant the shutter snapped, it was gone in a flurry of wings.

Cute little weirdo. He almost felt bad for scaring it off.

Near noon, there was a shift in the air. Caleb wasn't sure what else to call it, but something definitely changed. Suddenly, all the figments were moving toward the north. Was something luring them in that direction? Or were they moving away from some unseen threat?

Caleb sat up and scanned the vicinity.

He stood, brushing off his pants. Yes, they were on the move.

But where were they going? He wanted to find out. Because if they were congregating somewhere, he might be able to snap a much better picture.

Taking small, careful steps, Caleb cut through the undergrowth. He paused to check his compass, marking his direction. It would be truly mortifying to lose his way so close to camp.

Wait.

Why was he so certain they weren't going far?

Although Caleb couldn't come up with a logical reason for the impression, it stuck. Moving with the mini migration, he waved a hand to discourage passengers while looking for signs that the previous campers had come this way.

Tracking was more Josheb's thing.

Caleb had a vague idea about footprints, broken twigs, and bent grasses, but that was mostly gleaned from old movies and bore no resemblance to the uninterrupted carpet of leaves and needles that made up the forest floor.

Focused on the movement of airborne figments, Caleb nearly stepped off an embankment.

A river lay below, sliding by with hardly a ripple. And on the opposite bank, shored in by rocks, stood a low plinth. Lines shimmered against stone. A faint note seemed to reach for him, emanating from a pale blue crystal.

He had no idea what to do.

Just then, something rustled in the bushes. Caleb held his breath, deathly afraid that he was about to meet an apex predator. But it was only a deer. The young doe high-stepped through the ferns, her ears swiveling. All very dainty and lovely and harmless.

Except that she wore a collar. Knotted cords hung with beads. No, they were crystals. And her rump was branded by a pattern that gleamed against her pelt.

While he watched, she browsed her way unhurriedly toward the plinth.

Suddenly the air fizzed as if charged by a power source, and a scent wafted his way. The same he'd picked up earlier, but stronger now—thick and ripe and boozy.

The sun slipped behind a cloud.

The air filled with an ominous tension.

The doe took another step. And vanished.

ONTO SOMETHING

"You've got to see this."

Josheb followed, asking, "How far did you go?"

"Not far." Caleb waved a hand. "Alongside the river."

"Really? I was all through this area. Never saw a thing."

Caleb offered a rambling description of the movement of figments, ending with the disappearance of the doe. To his own ears, it sounded implausible, but his brother's eyes took on a shine.

"Didn't you follow?" Josheb demanded.

"Isn't that your job?"

"Every time. So how much farther?"

Caleb waved at the low column. "We're here."

"Where?"

Edging closer to the relic, he pointed, his finger mere inches from its surface. "This. Here. Is it invisible?"

"Not exactly." Josheb narrowed his eyes. "I see a shrub."

"Give me your hand."

Switching Nessie's leash to his other hand, Josheb grabbed hold. "Still shrubbery," he reported.

Caleb was confused enough to reach for the plinth, which was reassuringly solid under his hand—cool, rough, and responsive. It thrummed, almost like a purring cat. Grabbing Josheb's wrist, he pulled his brother into contact.

"Whoa. I see a shrub, but I'm touching stone. This is brain-breaking. Possibly also breaking news." Josheb passed along the leash and explored the column, eyes shut. "Talk about effective camouflage. Is it the same as the one you took pictures of before?"

"Almost exactly. The color of the crystal is different, but it has the same glowing lines."

"Is it just me, or is there a wall here?"

"Is there?" Caleb couldn't see one, but when he reached for the area Josheb was pushing against, his hand passed through something odd. There was definitely some resistance. It clung strangely to his skin, so he quickly pulled back. But not before Josheb noticed the difference in their rate of success.

"Mystical barrier, confirmed. So who put it here?"

Caleb supposed that was the big question. "Can't be the figments."

"Maybe all those itty-bitty figments have bigger, badder buddies." Josheb shot him a gleeful look. "Hey, maybe ...!"

"*Please*, don't say aliens."

Josheb grinned. "I'm not saying it out loud, but I'm pretty sure this isn't our technology."

"What about magic?"

"And you're a wizard?" teased Josheb.

"How else are we going to explain this?"

"For starters, we need more facts. Is there a way past this?"

"Haven't tired." Caleb was already cringing, because he knew what his brother was about to say.

Josheb met every expectation with one word. "Try!"

YOU FIRST

"What do you think?" Caleb asked Nessie.

She had been snuffling and sneezing among the stones at the base of the pillar, as if intrigued by the scents she'd found there. With a tug of her leash, Caleb tried to guide her past the column, but she balked, sitting flat on her rump and refusing to budge.

"You'll have to go in." Josheb fished in his pockets, coming out with a ball of string.

"What are you, a boy scout?" It was a weak attempt at diversion. It didn't work.

"This has come in handy for more things than you can imagine." Pulling a length free, he tied the end around Caleb's ankle.

"You know, they used to do this with priests before they entered the Holy of Holies."

Josheb shot him an amused look.

"A rope and bells," he clarified, setting aside his camera.

"Because if the bells stopped, they'd know it was time to pull out the body."

"The moral of the story: don't mess with God on holy ground. You going in barefoot?"

Caleb muttered, "I'd rather not go in, at all."

"Easy does it, bro. The bush isn't burning. It isn't even a bush." Patting the column, Josheb added, "Take a quick look, then peace on out of there."

"Trade you?"

Josheb's expression turned wry. "Any day of the week. But we're working with what we've got."

"Come with me?"

"We can try." Josheb knotted Nessie's leash around the column, stood, and they locked wrists. "You first. Pull me through if you can."

Caleb brushed his fingers against the barrier, then pushed through. It was a little like water, but without any temperature difference. He turned sideways and eased his whole arm through, thinking he could poke his nose through for a quick peek. But the barrier didn't cooperate with that plan. As if to prevent dawdling, it pushed out and engulfed him, although it stopped short at Josheb's hand.

Pulling didn't change the barrier's mind.

With a small squeeze, Josheb loosened his hold.

Caleb didn't let him slip free, though the barrier fizzed unhappily around the breech. His gaze darted around skittishly, half expecting to find himself face-to-face with a monster. But the forward view wasn't much different from the forest that lay at his back. Same trees. Same river. Same hush. The only thing that stood out was another stone. It was different from the crystal-topped columns: larger, rounded, with holes pocking its mossy surface. But glowing lines traced patterns all over the thing. So it had to be special. Somehow.

Josheb's hand shifted. He was checking Caleb's pulse.

Nothing in this new clearing seemed dangerous, so Caleb scraped together the gumption to give a goodbye squeeze and slip free. With every step, he felt string tugging at his ankle. It was embarrassing to find it so reassuring.

He used his phone to snap a couple of pictures of the new rock.

The glowing lines didn't pick up. If only he'd brought his field journal. He thought he could replicate the patterns on paper, given enough time.

A faint whirr of wings caught his attention, and an insect circled his head a few times. He ducked and tried to wave it away, and it dropped onto the stone. Against the rich green of the moss, the bug mostly looked like a shaggy white bee. Pollen clung to its paws, and its faceted eyes sparkled like gems that were the same starry blue as the stripes along its back.

Figment. Definitely a figment. It looked at him, feelers twitching, before scurrying into one of the nearest holes. A heartbeat later, a hum started somewhere inside the stone. Was it hollow?

All at once, they began streaming from every orifice. Bee thingies spiraled up, and a high-pitched chirping emanated from the swarm.

Caleb backed away, stepped on the string, and landed on his rump.

The din rose in pitch and urgency, and the figments dove. The first one struck his chest. Another hit his shoulder. Something landed in his hair. Scrambling onto his knees, Caleb found his feet and bolted. He burst through the barrier, narrowly avoiding Josheb, but they followed, funneling through the barrier as if his passage had left an opening. It *was* decreasing in size, but not quickly enough to stop the sparkling swarm from following.

"What happened?" called Josheb.

"Bugs!" Caleb ran for it, but he reached the end of his tether. The string at his ankle sent him sprawling.

"I can't see anything!" complained Josheb, when he caught up. "How am I supposed to help if I can't ... *dang.*"

Caleb writhed miserably under the swarm's onslaught. "Get them off," he moaned.

Josheb swore. Hauling Caleb to his feet, he all but dragged him through the woods.

FEELS BAD

Caleb wasn't the kind of guy to jump from *any* height. Especially into strange waters that could be too shallow or hiding dangerous rocks. But when Josheb hustled him to the verge, Caleb grabbed his nose and stepped off.

Staying under, Caleb flicked his hands through his hair and along his limbs, urgent to rid himself of passengers. When he surfaced, Josheb was already there, swiping water from his face.

"Are you stung?" he asked urgently. "Bitten?"

"Don't think so." Caleb's feet touched, but he stayed low in the water, one wary eye on the sky.

Grabbing him by the shoulders, Josheb made his own reconnoiter, then steered Caleb closer to the steep bank they'd plunged from. "Stay put until they're gone. Then head to camp and get dry. I'll go back for Nessie."

They'd left her? What kind of person abandoned their pet in bear territory? "Sorry," he said glumly. "Poor Nessie. Please, hurry?"

"As long as you're good …?"

"Yeah. Fine. Really. Go." Caleb sank to his chin in the water while his brother sloshed up the bank and disappeared from view. His heart still hammered, but good sense was returning. The figments hadn't harmed him. None ever had, for all their oddness. Yet he'd panicked, and now there were consequences.

Josheb had to be unimpressed.

Their clothes and boots were soaked.

Nessie probably felt abandoned.

With a groan of regret, he extracted his phone from his back pocket. Would he be able to retrieve the pictures he'd taken so far? With one last long look, he left the cool river water and squelched uphill. "Why me?" he sighed.

Staggering into camp, he dragged off sodden clothes.

Holy ground or no, he was barefoot now. And a complete tenderfoot.

Finger-combing his hair, he gave up on the day, crawled into the tent, and curled up under both sleeping bags to wait for Josheb's return.

A hand gripped his shoulder. "Caleb. Hey. Wake up."

He hadn't expected to fall asleep. Was it dark already? "Why'd you let me sleep?" he mumbled.

"She's gone."

"Huh?"

"I'm sorry." There was a rigidity to Josheb's posture, a directness to his gaze. He'd always been the kind of guy who owned up to his mistakes. "I'm really sorry, and I need your help. She's always liked you better. Maybe if she hears *you* calling ...?"

"Nessie's gone?"

"Yeah. I've been trying to track her, but it's getting too dark."

Caleb was thinking more clearly now, and he didn't like their options. Nessie was important, but so was his brother. Josheb looked exhausted. Pressing his hand to clammy skin, Caleb snapped, "You're freezing!"

Josheb only grunted.

"Get out of those wet clothes. I'll get the fire going again."

His younger brother quietly reminded, "I can't find Nessie."

As if Caleb didn't know what that could mean. But they had to go about this the right way. "If you get sick, we're sunk. What kind of survivalist wanders around in wet clothes? Even I know that's bad news."

"But ...!"

"I want to find Nessie, too. But not without dry clothes. And you probably need to eat. We skipped lunch."

"You're right." Josheb was shamefaced.

"Yes, I'm right." Caleb fished in his own bag for something to wear. "It's strange, though. Usually, Nessie finds me no matter where I am. I mean … she's a bloodhound."

Josheb tossed his wet shirt outside. "Your camera was gone, too."

"What?" Caleb remembered putting it down. He'd been worried the barrier would mess with his film.

"Your camera was gone, and I think whoever took it took Nessie." For once, Josheb looked troubled rather than tantalized. "We're not alone out here."

STAY PUT

"Is it smart to try this at night?" asked Caleb.

"No."

"Do you want to wait for daylight?"

Josheb twisted his hair into a knot atop his head before shoving a stocking cap over it. "No."

Caleb pulled on a heavy hoodie. It might be summer, but the damp and their drenching had chilled them both. Which was all the more noticeable because the winds were whipping up. "Is it going to rain?"

Light flickered along the edges of clouds, and an ominous rumble echoed in the distance. Josheb's jaw clenched. "It's going to storm."

"Got it." Caleb moved to get the fire restarted. "I'm boiling water before it does."

"I'll add a tarp."

Caleb fed kindling to the fire to hurry along the big kettle, which he refused to watch lest it never boil. Instead, he kept an eye on Josheb, who checked tent pegs and stretched a sloping tarp to divert the worst of the rainfall.

He was just topping off Josheb's thermos when the first raindrops hissed into the embers of his fire. Focusing determinedly on his task, Caleb tipped in powdered orange drink before securing the cap. It was one of Josheb's favorites—or used to be—and his brother needed the vitamin boost. And the sugar.

Back inside the tent, Caleb handed it over. "Drink it all."

Josheb breathed in the steam, smiled ruefully, and took a careful sip. "How's your phone?" he asked.

"Dead. Yours?"

"Fine. Mine's waterproof. What about the field journal?"

For once, Caleb's caution would be appreciated. "Left it under my pillow. I've been updating it from notecards. Seemed safer."

"Turns out you're right." Josheb quietly added, "Sorry."

"I thought you'd be more excited, given the things we've found." Hugging his thermos, he asked, "Isn't this what you were after?"

"No! Well, yes. But ... aren't you mad at me?"

Caleb had been afraid, was *still* afraid, at least for Nessie's sake. Usually, his brother was the one to brazen through the scrapes they found themselves in. But for the first time, Josheb seemed afraid. Of Caleb.

"I'm not blaming you," he said gruffly. "I'm worried. And

embarrassed. All the work we did has been undone. But maybe that was the point."

Josheb's expression went blank, then sharpened. "You think it was intentional?"

Caleb doubted anyone could have planned for him blundering past a barrier. It wasn't as if they'd sprung a trap. "I think someone could have seized an opportunity. And our evidence."

"And Nessie."

Thunder crashed, and rain rattled against the tent with every gust of wind. Caleb's heart sank, but it was useless to search for their dog on such a night. He was the responsible brother. The one who used his head. He needed to give Josheb permission to give up. For now. "We'll get her back tomorrow. Together."

SMALL COMFORT

Caleb couldn't get to sleep. Partly because he could tell that Josheb wasn't. And there was a distinct possibility that if Caleb dropped off, his brother would sneak out. So he had no choice but to keep watch. Not for bigfoot, or whatever threat awaited them. But over Josheb, who loved Nessie more than he liked to let on.

Rolling onto his other side, Caleb said, "You didn't find anything bad." He was comforting himself as much as his brother. "No blood? No signs of a scuffle?"

"Yeah. Nothing like that." Josheb's next words came slowly. "I'd fastened her leash around that column. Someone unclipped it and led her away."

"Someone that the others mistook for bigfoot?"

Josheb snorted.

"If anything's possible, and you do tend to believe in anything, then you have to admit that it's possible that Nessie's fine."

"I thought you'd be frantic."

"You've got it covered."

Josheb punched his shoulder.

Caleb asked, "When will it be light enough?"

"Four, if the storm passes."

"Two more hours. Let's catch a nap, then do what we have to do."

"Can't sleep," Josheb grumbled.

"It's easy." And because he knew it would help more than it would embarrass him, Caleb said, "Want to know my secret?"

"I know your secret."

"You know the big one. I have little ones."

After a long beat, Josheb asked, "Yeah?"

He sounded so hopeful. He sounded gullible. But while Caleb often refrained from mentioning things to his brother, he'd never lied to Josheb. "There's a reason I live in the highest loft I could find."

"Distancing yourself from nature?"

"No." Caleb could feel a blush coming on. "I was trying to close a distance. The higher I am, the better I can hear them."

"Figments?"

"Nooo. At least, I don't think so. Figments have tiny voices."

Josheb fumbled in the dark, and Caleb reached back. His brother's hand was too cold.

After a few moments, Josheb whispered, "I don't hear anything but rain."

"Listening with your ears doesn't work." This was so hard to explain. "They're singing, and I can hear them."

"But not with your ears."

"It's more like ... umm ...." He trailed off, feeling vulnerable. The songs had always been his secret, too precious to share. "Look, I don't know how it works."

Scooting closer to lock arms, Josheb said, "Doesn't matter, as long as it works."

Talk about a childlike faith.

"Okay." Caleb cleared his throat. "Sometimes, I think they know I'm listening. And then they sing for me. Maybe if I'm listening for you, it'll carry over ...?"

"Someone sings for you? Are we talking *angel chorus*, here?"

"That makes as much sense as anything." He sheepishly added, "I guess I've always imagined it's the stars."

Caleb focused on the melodies he'd learned to love. The voices were closer than usual, which may have had something to do with the elevation. Or maybe the stars that shone more brightly away from city lights also sang more sweetly.

It wasn't hearing so much as feeling. Like the song was aimed for his heart instead of his ears. Caleb found most figments to be pests, but this ... *this* had always been his personal proof that humans must have a soul.

Just a little. Let me share this.

If that counted as a prayer, it was answered. He knew the moment his brother figured out how to listen.

Josheb offered a breathless, "Oh."

Caleb relaxed and whispered, "Yeah."

FIRST LIGHT

A hand shook Caleb's shoulder, dragging him from dreams.

"Storm's passed," said Josheb. "Come with me?"

He grunted and fumbled for another layer. Everything felt damp, especially his boots, but it hardly mattered. Soft pattering beyond the tent walls suggested a lingering drizzle. At the very least, the trees were still dripping. Unless the sun broke through, there wasn't much hope of drying out.

Caleb emerged from the tent, immediately at odd ends, since the first thing he usually did in the morning was walk Nessie. It felt wrong, standing there without a leash in his hand. Crossing to her food dish, he tipped out the previous night's rainwater. Then stuffed it in the top of his backpack, along with a packet of emergency kibble. "She might be hungry."

"Good thinking," said Josheb. And they trudged toward the river.

The ground underfoot was a misery of mud. Caleb gave up on the trail, which had been reduced to a slick rut, filled with standing water. Fallen leaves were nearly as slippery, so he picked his way through stands of fern and other scrubby brush. It was steadier underfoot, but the leaves wet his pantlegs below the knees so thoroughly, he might as well be wading through water.

"Try whistling?" suggested Josheb.

Caleb used his *come along* whistle, which didn't really carry far. But even the breathy tweeting between his teeth seemed loud. The woods were too quiet, and the hush he felt put him on edge. "Hey, Josheb?"

His brother turned.

"Something's not right."

"How so?"

"Do the woods feel *empty* to you?"

Josheb peered around, a frown on his face. Backtracking, he took hold of Caleb's wrist and gave the surrounding woods a longer look. "Let's call it a good sign," he finally muttered.

"What kind of sign?"

With a roll of his eyes, Josheb quietly answered, "This would be an *apex predator* kind of sign."

"I was afraid of that."

As they trudged onward, the drips turned to drizzle, further dampening Caleb's spirits. He didn't want to meet an apex figment. Unless it was one of those singing stars. Were they around by day, hanging out behind the blue of the sky or these persistent clouds?

I could use a song right about now.

His weak whistling couldn't compare.

Something bright flashed in his peripheral vision, and Caleb paused to look. Lightning? If so, no thunder followed.

"Caleb." Josheb beckoned urgently.

On the riverbank below, something had changed. A shadowy bulk dominated the area near the spot where the stone column should have been. In the dim light, it was impossible to tell what it was. However, Caleb could feel its presence. Big. Dark. Aware.

"That's alive," he whispered urgently.

Josheb, who'd already taken a step toward it, skidded several feet down the muddy slope. Turning back, he hissed, "What?"

Caleb's heart lurched as the misshapen lump shifted and turned, revealing itself to be an enormous bear. Were they supposed to get this big? Surely even a grizzly wouldn't rival an elephant. "B-bear!" Voice snapping under the strain of sudden terror, he flung an arm toward his brother. "Come back! Quick!"

With an oath, Josheb scrambled uphill, and they took off together along the embankment. Crashing through underbrush, hardly daring to look back, Caleb begged, "What do we do? Where do we go?"

"Stay close!" ordered Josheb. "Keep up."

Caleb struggled to orient himself on the map he'd memorized. Had there been any shelter they could reach before they were outrun? The bear bellowed, and Caleb's knees went weak. Stumbling, he grabbed at a tree to keep from slipping, but the tree tilted toward him. Everything was confusing, then, because the ground underfoot was crumbling away in a sloppy blunder.

Balance lost, he tried to step back from the edge. Rocks and trees were tumbling, and he was caught up in their momentum.

The last thing Caleb saw clearly was Josheb lunging for him, hand outstretched.

But they failed to connect.

NATURAL DISASTER

Caleb groaned into awareness—cold, wet, and confused.

Someone loomed over him, blocking the raindrops. Focusing was difficult, but a hand patted his cheek, and words rumbled, deep as thunder and just as impossible to interpret. Squinting, he made out a worried face. Warm hands smoothed the hair out of his eyes.

He was a large man with a broad face. His skin was brown, and his eyes were dark. When he spoke again, the words were foreign. But he spoke slowly, and his tone was apologetic.

"Not your fault," Caleb mumbled. "So much rain."

With a crooning sound and a sigh, those big hands began scooping earth and straightening Caleb's limbs. He kept up a steady stream of words, probably an explanation or reassurances, but it was no use. The guy had no English.

Teeth chattering, Caleb tried to sit up, only to be scolded. It was all in the tone. *Don't move.*

But Caleb was alert enough to want to know where Josheb was. "My brother," he croaked, trying to look around. "Where's my brother?"

Another voice snarled nearby, and as Caleb's rescuer turned to answer, more features came to light. Woven cloth. Tasseled sash. Pointed ears. Clawed hands.

Caleb whimpered.

The man gestured with both hands and offered soft words.

He worked steadily to shift the clinging earth and jabbing stones.

The grumpy voice came nearer, and Caleb turned to see a shaggy mountain lumbering closer. It had to be bigfoot. Which was alarming on several levels. Caleb may have whimpered again.

But then light streaked near, and a face hovered above his—elfin, luminous, and stern. It rested a finger against its lips.

Hush?

Caleb was completely ready to give in to fear when this glowing person carefully rested a hand against his cheek. A voice filled the space where songs belonged. Caleb heard it, but not with his ears.

"Peace, friend. You are safe."

Caleb managed a small nod.

This thing, this person—they weren't human. Josheb would love this. Where was Josheb? Caleb tried to crane his neck to see.

Concerned sounds were coming from the big guy again, who seemed to be arguing with bigfoot. Caleb hoped vaguely that *his* rescuer won the debate.

"*Sleep,*" urged the radiant one, whose smile held sympathy. "*Andor does not want you to know the path to his den. This is his right.*"

Caleb realized why the voice was so calming. He'd heard such voices before … and treasured them. "Sing me a lullaby?"

Their lips curved into a lovely smile, and somewhere far overhead, a playful cascade of notes joined the raindrops as, with alarming speed, Caleb sank into slumber once more.

CAVE DWELLER

When Caleb next opened his eyes, he was indoors. Probably. Light from a pair of candles on a table showed walls that appeared to be shingled. And the ceiling overhead was all irregular shapes and shadows. Like bare stone. Was he in a cave?

As far as he could tell, he was alone. Not so much as a figment in sight. Shifting under the weight of too many blankets, he realized several things at once. His clothes were missing. He was clean, even his hair, so someone had washed him. And he'd been bandaged.

The bed was strange. A pad of thick fur beneath. Very ticklish. The blankets he pushed aside were a variety of fabrics and textures. Some woven. Some fine enough to pass for silk. All clean and smelling of sunshine.

Caleb swung his feet to the floor and found more fur. An unsettlingly animalistic touch. But he had more urgent things on his mind. Like locating a place to relieve himself.

Finding his feet, he tottered forward and leaned against the table. Yeah, he was definitely hurt. But only bumps and bruises. And maybe some scrapes, given the uncomfortable stickiness under his bandages. Unfamiliar herbaceous smells suggested a home remedy had been smeared here and there.

He really wanted a bath. But first a bathroom. Provided this cave had plumbing. Maybe he should just go outside? Hauling one of the blankets around his shoulders, Caleb shuffled into a dim hallway. Which way was out? All he could do was guess.

The first room he encountered was a dead end lined with large barrels.

Three similarly equipped chambers later, he figured he was in someone's wine cellar.

Rounding a corner, he found his way barred by the shaggy, scowling person who might not *be* bigfoot, but had probably been mistaken for him by the last group of campers.

Caleb took a step back.

Two steps later, he hit a wall.

Mister Big huffed and grumbled something unintelligible.

Upright and up close, it was easier for Caleb to tell that he resembled the man who'd pulled him from the landslide. He was similarly burly and brown, but he was vastly more unkempt. A furry coat hung open, revealing a dark gold tunic, and several necklaces lay against the nubbled cloth. Caleb caught the glint of crystals, but one necklace looked to be entirely made of teeth.

Most imposing was Mister Big's hair, a mess of thick dreadlocks that hung to his hips.

"I'm lost. I need a toilet."

Dark eyes narrowed.

Caleb bit his lip and made what he hoped was a universal gesture.

Mister Big grunted and turned. His words, while strange, sounded like a command.

Following, Caleb found himself back where he'd started. Moving to the corner, the big man hooked his foot around a squat, lidded clay pot that had been mostly lost in shadows. Dragging it into the open, he made a gesture that did indeed translate universally.

"Chamber pot. Got it." Caleb self-consciously adjusted the drape of his blanket. "Can you tell me where my brother is?"

With another grunt, Mister Big left.

Caleb had mixed feelings about the chamber pot, but beggars couldn't be choosers. He was missing all kinds of things now—toilet paper, hand soap, underpants. But all of that ceased to matter when the click of claws announced Mister Big's return. And he wasn't alone.

"Nessie!" Dropping to his knees, Caleb threw his arms around her and accepted an enthusiastic face-washing.

She was *fine*.

A length of knotted cord had been looped through her collar; it was the same golden hue as Mister Big's tunic. Nessie's belly was rounded by a good meal. Caleb pet and apologized to her, too relieved to be self-conscious.

One gruff word.

Caleb turned.

Mister Big pointed to the bed and spoke again.

It wasn't hard to understand. Caleb perched on the bed's edge. Nessie clambered up to join him. Mister Big loomed large, and for a moment, Caleb was afraid he'd toss her back to the floor. But he simply untied the cord from her collar.

"Thanks," Caleb said.

But then the guy dropped to one knee and caught Caleb's heel. Pulling back didn't help. Mister Big knotted the cord around his ankle, then tied the other end to the bed frame. Definitely a bad sign.

"I'm a prisoner?"

With a grunt, the shaggy man walked out.

"What about my brother?" Caleb called.

He didn't get an answer.

LANGUAGE BARRIER

Even though very little changed in Caleb's environment, he was able to keep track of the passage of time because meals arrived at regular intervals. While he ate, Mister Big took Nessie out and returned her.

It was pointless, given the language barrier, but Caleb asked more and more questions.

"Where is my brother?"

"Can I have my clothes back?"

"Any chance of a bath?"

"Do you have a name?"

"Why can't I hear the stars anymore?"

"Please. Is Josheb okay?"

He was pretty sure two full days had passed before the pattern changed. Voices carried in the hallway—male and female. And then the first man was back, the one who'd rescued Caleb. Less wild, less gruff. But was he any less a captor?

Dark eyes snagged on Caleb's leash, and his eyebrows shot up. With a torrent of words, he bent to untie the cord. He sounded irritated.

Caleb stole a look at the woman, who'd remained just inside the door. She gave off the same vibe as the other two. Quite tall. Athletic build. Strong features. But this lady's hair was short, and her pointed ears were pierced. Caleb registered the lipstick first, since she was smirking. By the time he took in her yellow hightops, he dared to hope.

"Hi," he managed.

"Hi, yourself." Her smile widened. "Oaken brought me here to translate."

"Oaken?"

She indicated the man kneeling beside the bed, petting a delighted Nessie. "He says he's sorry for Andor's lack of manners. Are you in pain?"

"A little sore." He rubbed at his forehead. "Mostly confused."

More words flowed past as they talked over him.

She said, "He'll brew a tea to help with the headache."

With a gentle pat to his shoulder, Oaken excused himself.

"I'm Hesper Merryvale, by the way. Oaken is my mother's uncle, more or less. He applied to us for help. You're a long way from civilization."

Caleb begged, "Where's Josheb?"

"Your partner? You don't know?" She made a crooning noise in the back of her throat. "I call that cruel. Follow me."

Trailing his blanket shroud, Caleb shuffled after her. Why did she say cruel? Had they hidden Josheb's death from him? Was he going to have to identify the body or something equally gruesome?

But Hesper led him into a room not unlike Caleb's. Mister Big, whose name hadn't really stuck with Caleb, was hunched over a narrow pallet, spoon in hand. He was dribbling its contents little by little between Josheb's parted lips, grumbling all the while. It was an oddly soothing tone. And relief caused Caleb's eyes to sting.

"He's your kin?" asked Hesper.

"My younger brother." Caleb swallowed hard. "He's okay?"

"Oaken set his leg before leaving to fetch me." She nudged him closer to the bed, rattling off something to Mister Big. He answered, and she sighed. "It was a bad break. Andor has been keeping him under. He's essentially drugged."

Caleb wanted to make sure. Stealing closer, he knelt beside the bed, edging perilously close to the big guy in order to reach. He took Josheb's hand, which was reassuringly warm.

Hesper growled something at Mister Big, who huffed. A heavy hand settled on Caleb's shoulder long enough to deliver a squeeze. It felt like an apology.

Caleb embarrassed himself with a sniffle. And accepted it with a nod.

HONEY MEAD

They weren't human.

Somehow, that little detail had temporarily escaped Caleb. But it was sinking in, and it was surreal. Really, it should have scared him more. Because … *they weren't human*. And that couldn't be good. Except it wasn't bad, either.

These people were decidedly strange, and they were definitely intimidating. But there was a courteousness in their treatment of him, and their cooking was excellent. A good meal was a serious mood enhancer.

Having a translator didn't hurt, either. "Can you ask about my clothes?"

Hesper chuckled and went to speak with the other two. It took long enough for Caleb to imagine several terrible fates for his missing boxer briefs … and his dignity. Walking around in a blanket was inconvenient, even after he rigged it into a sort of toga.

She returned with a solution, though not the one he'd hoped for.

"Oaken says your things still aren't fit to wear. He's loaning you these."

"We're hardly the same size." But these garments weren't tailored on Andor's or Oaken's scale. On closer inspection, Caleb was forced to admit, "They should work. But why does he have clothing in my size?"

"I didn't ask." Hesper offered a casual shrug. "I don't like to be nosey. Those two are pretty private. In fact, I should be thanking you for giving me an in. Do you *know* how much any sow would give to be where I am now?"

Caleb was sure he'd misheard. "Any … sow?"

"Female." Hesper's eyes took on a teasing shine. "*Ladies*, then. My sisters are sooo jealous. My first cub will be *sturdy*. Seriously. Thanks for that."

"Cub," he echoed uncertainly.

She rolled her eyes and leaned in. "You didn't hear it from me, but we're bear clan, okay? Boars and Sows. Sleuth or sloth. Litters and cubs."

Bear clan? Was that a Native American thing? Hesper didn't really look the part. He'd have guessed mixed heritage, since her features didn't slot neatly into any of the people groups he was familiar with. Then again … *they weren't human.*

So he simply parroted her words, hoping for more. "Bear clan?"

"Andor is a legend, one of the first to remember how to take speaking form. Some even call him First of Bears, at least on this continent. He and his son Oaken look after the bears in these mountains."

Caleb hummed in what he hoped was an interested way. He needed more information, and Hesper seemed willing enough to fill him in.

"Of course, Andor and Oaken are *most* famous for their wine. My clan are vintners, too, but our claim to fame is honey mead."

"I've never heard of it."

"Merryvale's mead is world-famous. Even little reavers take nips on festival days." She studied him with a faint smirk. "You have reaver blood. Did you know that?"

"Pardon?"

"You're probably an offshoot or a throwback. And it probably saved your life." Lifting her jaw toward the others beyond this room, she cheerfully revealed, "You made Andor very, *very* angry. But you're surprisingly sweet, and bears have a weakness for your sort of soul."

Caleb shook his head, trusting his face to communicate the enormity of his bewilderment.

"You have reavers in your pedigree, and your inheritance is lovely. I wouldn't be surprised if you've been pestered by Ephemera all your life." She pointed at him, giving her finger a little twirl. "Untrained reavers let it all hang out, and it can be … alluring."

"I'm not the only one who sees things?"

Hesper's expression gentled. "No. You're not alone. The world is full of reavers, and my people cherish humans with the qualities you possess."

It occurred to him that this was a rather large secret. Warning flags were waving. "Should you be telling me this?"

"Not under ordinary circumstances, but I'm providing context. You may as well understand your place."

"Which is?" asked Caleb.

"Here." Hesper didn't mince words. "You saw too much. You know too much. You're not leaving."

BORROWED CLOTHES

Once he was alone, Caleb inspected the clothes Hesper had brought. He seriously doubted they were readymade. No label to hint at the size or country of origin, let alone the fabric content. He was no expert, but he was pretty sure the seams hadn't been machine stitched. So who was the tailor?

Unlike the rough-looking tunics that Andor and Oaken wore, this one looked expensive. The cloth slipped over his head and settled against his skin like silk. Caleb didn't think he was imagining the faint luminescence that was a dead giveaway that he was dealing with a figment. Had these people harvested thread from the figment-equivalent of the silkworm?

That in itself was plausible enough, but he couldn't imagine someone as scruffy as Andor handling such a delicate task. But maybe he should investigate the rooms, see if he found anything resembling a loom.

The color, a pale gold, did adhere to the trend in Andor's and Oaken's wardrobes. Did they like the color on a personal level? Was the dye a local product? Or were all these honey hues important for another reason?

"Are you kidding me?" he muttered. No undergarments had been provided. Still, this was a far sight better than dragging around in a blanket.

His pants were a warm golden-brown, and the fit reminded him of athletic wear—stretchy and snug. But the cloth was far from flimsy. He scratched and prodded at it, curious what gave it so much toughness. Was it hide? Was it synthetic?

"Dressed?" Hesper leaned past the curtain that served as his door.

"More or less." Caleb was grateful that the tunic fell to mid-thigh, preserving his modesty. Even so, he was highly self-conscious.

Hesper didn't help. Giving him a long once-over, she said, "The tunic looks well with your hair."

"It's out of control," he muttered, scratching at hair that was getting unruly.

She startled him by brushing her knuckles against the scruff that was an inevitable consequence of camping. "You usually shave?"

Caleb hadn't really registered how tall Hesper was. He had to look up. "Y-yes."

"Want me to clean you up?" She arched her brows. "My family's last cover was a barber shop. I doubt I've lost my touch."

"I thought you made mead."

"We do. Privately." Hesper shrugged. "We've always operated some kind of shop in our neighborhood."

That surprised him on several levels. "You pass yourself off as human?"

"We have a few tricks to hide the most obvious differences. But yes, and we're invested in our community." She patted his cheek before stepping back. "I'm the sort of person who has lots of friends and knows all her neighbors."

"I'm not." He desperately missed his tiny, tidy apartment and the privacy it guaranteed. "Maybe just loan me a razor?"

"Ever shave with a straight edge?"

Caleb's shoulders sagged in defeat.

Hesper took a coaxing tone. "We bears are big, and we can be formidable, but we've a light touch. I'll be careful, and you'll feel more yourself. Am I right?"

She was.

"We can wait until your brother's awake. Moral support." Hesper chuckled. "Set a good example, too. He's shaggier than the hind-end of a yak."

"All right. I'll let you." It would be a relief. Give him back something lost. Glancing around, he asked, "What about shoes?"

Hesper grimaced faintly. "You won't be allowed any."

He was about to protest, since he wouldn't get far if he was barefoot. But at the same time, he realized that this was undoubtedly the point.

They may as well have shackled him.

ANSWER ME

"Maybe you should go on back," said Hesper.

"If they won't give me shoes, then I'll just have to toughen my feet." Caleb, now cleanshaven, stubbornly picked his way along a path that was barely wide enough for rabbits. Nessie didn't mind, though. If her tail-wagging was any indicator, she approved of both the trail and its most recent occupants.

"I'm one of them, you know. Are you sure you should be confiding in me?"

"Don't make light of this," he muttered. "It's … it's captivity!"

"You made all this trouble for yourself. What are you even doing in our territory?"

Caleb stepped on something and paused to brush at the bottom of his foot. Irritation sharpened his tone. "Looking for bigfoot."

"What? You?" Hesper snorted. "No."

"What can I say? My brother's a true believer. Or something. That's the whole point of this … this expedition."

Mouth twisted to keep from laughing, she glanced back toward the crevice that apparently served as the den's doggie door. "Speaking of your brother …."

"*Caleb*! Are you hearing me?" bellowed Josheb from somewhere inside. "*Caleb*!"

Sucking in a lungful of air, he hollered, "Here! I'm here!" And because she would get there faster, Caleb unfastened Nessie's leash. "Go on, girl. Get to Josheb. Find Josheb."

She bayed and bounded toward his voice, which hadn't stopped.

"Caleb! Tell me you're safe!"

"Coming!"

Heedless of the path, Caleb stumbled back the way he'd come, bruising his soles in the process. By the time he reached Josheb, his brother was sitting up in bed, eyes wide, using Nessie as a shield against Andor, who'd moved to the far corner.

Hesper jostled past Caleb, quicker than he would have expected. She had a hand on Andor's arm, and she was talking in a low voice. Probably translating.

Limping a little, Caleb closed the distance and dropped to a seat beside his brother. "I'm here. We're safe."

"We found him!" Josheb hissed, pointing at Andor. "Bigfoot's *real*."

Everything was suddenly too much to explain. "Yeah. Congrats."

"You okay?" Josheb was gripping his side. He was too pale, and a sheen of sweat had risen on his forehead.

Caleb dredged up a smile. "Don't worry about me. You're the one who took on a landslide and lost."

His brother grimaced. "Broken leg. Bruised ribs. But that's not important right now. I have questions. I mean, this is *huge*."

"Bigger than both of us," Caleb acknowledged. "Seems like there's a whole society living in hiding. It boggles the mind."

Josheb's jaw dropped. "You understand them?"

"Not the guys, no. But they brought in a translator."

Hesper waved. "Wait your turn, scruff-bucket."

When she addressed Andor again, Caleb seized his opportunity. "We're safe, but I think we're in trouble. They won't let us leave."

"But that's perfect!" Far from concerned, Josheb rallied a smile. "If they don't kick us out, I can get the whole story."

"It's not a big scoop if you never get to tell it." Caleb pushed his brother back onto his pillows. "We're prisoners."

Josheb waved that off. "We're *here*. Hard part done. Leave the rest to me!"

Caleb wanted to argue. A real shout-and-throttle tiff. But he forced himself onto a more reasonable course. Even if he and Josheb had seen eye-to-eye, they were effectively stranded by bruised ribs, a broken leg, and bare feet.

Turning his brother's order around, Caleb said, "Rest. We can talk about leaving later."

RECLUSE CODE

Caleb was beginning to feel invisible.

As usual, Josheb was at the center of everything, monopolizing Hesper as he asked questions … and asked her to ask questions for him. Andor wasn't the most cooperative interviewee; in fact, he disappeared for hours on end.

After one such absence, the big guy returned with a bundle containing their abandoned gear. Caleb's heart sank. It was the only clue to their location, *if* anyone bothered to come looking for them. With a grumble Andor held out Caleb's field journal.

"I left it under my pillow," he said reaching for it.

Andor pressed a thick finger to the open page, where Caleb had sketched one of the pom-pom birds. Mister Big spoke at considerable length—for him—but it wasn't any use.

"They follow me." He shrugged uncertainly. "Figments usually do. Not lately, though."

His captor grimaced, sighed, and surrendered the book.

Giving up was apparently preferable to interrupting Josheb's cheery inquisition in order to borrow their translator. With little else to do, Caleb located his pencils and settled in to bring his journal up to date.

It's what he was there for.

Documentation.

Hours passed before the smell of cooking distracted Caleb from his task. Tucking the journal under his pillow, he padded along the passage to Josheb's room, where a table had been set up. Apparently, shared mealtimes were important to Hesper, who assumed that Caleb would want to be with Josheb. She wasn't wrong.

More surprising was Andor's arrival. Josheb had to be thrilled, sharing a family-style meal with bigfoot.

Caleb focused on taking one bite at a time. And slipping tidbits to Nessie under the table.

Suddenly, Hesper waved a hand in his face, then jerked her thumb at Josheb, who was propped up in bed, eating off a tray. "You're being paged."

"Hey, what's up with you?" Josheb asked. "You seem down."

Down. Talk about understatement. "Somewhat," he said through clenched teeth.

"Gonna tell me why?"

Caleb swiftly edited his possible rant down to a single statement of fact. "I can't hear the stars anymore."

"Why?" asked Josheb. "Did something change while I was out?"

"I don't know," he said, barely clinging to a polite tone. "I haven't had the chance to *ask.*"

Josheb looked between Caleb and Andor, then at Hesper. "Oh, whoops. My bad. You're up, bro. Ask away!"

Since he'd already stated his problem, Caleb looked expectantly to Hesper. Only to be met by a blank stare.

"The stars," he repeated. "Why can't I hear them from here? Is something interfering?"

Her eyebrows slowly arched, but she turned to Andor and spoke a few words.

He simply grunted.

"I met one. Right after the landslide." At Hesper's expression, Caleb muttered, "I'm not crazy. Oaken was right there. Ask him."

"Oaken's gone."

"I thought you said these guys never leave?" It was part of the recluse's code. Caleb was in a position to know.

"There was a message. A summons," said Hesper. "He didn't have a choice."

Josheb blurted, "You get mail up here? How?"

"Don't ask," snapped Hesper. Like she'd said it a hundred times already. "And don't ask me to ask. So help me, I'm staying on this guy's good side."

But she did say *something* to Andor.

Who only grunted, again.

SECOND MOON

Night fell, but Josheb and Hesper kept right on laughing and chatting. Caleb was about to steal back to his own room when Andor's posture shifted in a way that drew Caleb's eye. They might not have had a word in common, but Andor rolled his eyes toward the two chatterboxes, then lifted his chin toward the door.

An invitation to escape.

Caleb nodded cautiously.

Andor stole outside.

When he followed, Caleb hesitated at the limits of the lanternlight. "I can't see a thing."

A big hand found his.

He was about to protest that he didn't want to hold hands when matters worsened. Andor lifted him right off his feet. And tucked him up against his chest so Caleb was perched on his forearm. Like a toddler.

Which was equal parts disorienting and humiliating.

But Andor was already striding into the woods.

Searching for handholds, Caleb found the ropy mess of Andor's hair. Mister Big didn't growl when he grabbed hold, so Caleb wrapped a dreadlock around his fist and held on for dear life.

Away from the den, his eyes gradually adjusted. Picking out trees became easier because they were thinning. Then Andor stepped out of the forest. There was a steep drop, with more woods below. Mentally, Caleb was plotting their location. Probably Boar Ridge, which meant that base camp had been practically on bigfoot's doorstep.

Bad luck. Or dumb luck. Either way, at least the other guys had gotten away.

Andor pushed something into Caleb's chest and grunted.

It was a flask. Unscrewing the top, he sniffed. Whatever it was, it was alcoholic. "May I?" he checked.

A grunt.

A sip. Quickly followed by a deeper slug.

"This is good." Caleb was already shaking his head. "No, this is *excellent.*"

Another grunt. And pleased by the sound of it.

Caleb caught on. "You made this?"

Andor nodded toward something farther along the ridge. Trees grew right up to the edge, and the moon shone between the branches of the tallest. Except ... it was in the wrong part of the sky. And then the second moon began to descend, climbing down, branch by branch, to drop the last few feet to the ground.

TIPSY STAR

It was her! Or wait, maybe *him*? As the star person moved closer, Caleb couldn't be certain, and he wasn't sure if preferred pronouns was really where he wanted to start a conversation. Either way, they were *not* a figment of his imagination. And a different mystery was solved, because they were dressed in the same style as he'd been.

"These clothes," he touched his chest, then pointed to the oncoming star. "You borrowed these from them?"

Andor spoke, but the words weren't meant for Caleb.

The other sped up, practically skipping the rest of the way, and was scooped up to perch on Andor's other arm. Face-to-face, there was little doubt that they were dressed to match.

"I didn't dream you up." And feeling foolish, Caleb asked, "What should I call you?"

As before, the radiant one carefully placed a hand against Caleb's now-smooth cheek. *"You may call me Eri, for that is my name."*

"Eri," he echoed, glancing at Andor, whose expression had gone all soft and indulgent. "Are you an angel?"

"Not I. My descent was an accident." With the air of a confession, Eri revealed, *"I was tipsy and slipped, and Andor caught me. Now, I am a vintner."*

A winemaker. The distillery scent and rows of barrels all supported their story. Caleb glanced at the flask in his hand and asked, "You made this?"

"I helped." Eri touched the flask with one finger. *"May I?"*

They took a long swallow and sighed, *"Aaah, me. Is there anything nicer?"*

"I was trying to tell Andor it's excellent."

"This he knows full well." Eyes alight with mischief, they added, *"Do you want to know why?"*

"I'm probably interested in anything you care to share." It

might be all that was left to him.

"*Caleb,*" Eri chided. "*Do not sound so resigned. The songs are culminating, and their resolution may surprise you. Pleasantly.*"

"I can't hear them anymore," he muttered. "The songs stopped."

Eri looked startled, and their gaze slid toward Andor, whose blank expression quickly shifted. It was pretty clear that Mister Big was being scolded by his starry friend.

Andor adjusted his hold and grumbled something, then Eri was guiding Caleb's hand to the ring upon Andor's first finger. "*Touch the stone. Unlock the sky.*"

All at once, a chorus of lilting, laughing notes spilled into Caleb.

Tipping his face skyward, he let himself be relieved. Maybe even a little happy.

A faint whine startled him.

Had the piteous sound come from Andor?

"*He did not mean to deprive you.*"

Caleb wasn't sure what to say. Or what to do. He, who'd protested hand-holding minutes earlier now clung to Andor's fingers, keeping contact with his ring. To let go was to lose touch with something he wanted badly enough, it might be a need. But clinging to his captor smacked of some kind of syndrome.

With great reluctance, Caleb took back his hand.

Eri claimed it instead. "*We must stay close, or my words will not reach you.*"

Averting his gaze, he asked, "Are you a prisoner, too?"

"*Too?*"

"You said he caught you."

They lifted a palm and mimed pulling something to their chest.

"He rescued me when I tumbled down. Was it not the same for you?"

Fresh fear pierced Caleb as memories resurfaced—the raging bear, the reckless path, the crumbling riverbank. Did Andor's rescue count if he was the reason they'd needed one? Maybe Eri was happy here. Even Josheb treated his captivity as a stroke of good luck. But Caleb whispered, "It's *not* the same."

STAR WINE

Caleb could tell Eri was speaking with Andor because of the range of fidgets and grimaces that were the latter's response. Mister Big was clearly frustrated, but Caleb didn't have the context to understand why.

He needed facts. He wanted answers.

Touching Eri's arm—in part to see if they were real—Caleb asked, "Why didn't Hesper know about you?"

"I am a very great secret. And a good one." Eri's hand settled over Caleb's. *"Few know that there is truth in the old stories of the clans of sky and stone and wood."*

"You're a myth?"

"I am the truth behind the ancient tales." Pressing the flask into Caleb's palm, they added, *"I am a foretaste of an unfolding future. Share it with me."*

Caleb took one mouthful and then another. The liquor was mellowing his mood and sharpening his senses. The stars were braver and brighter, and their songs rang clearer than ever. "I told Josheb. Maybe I shouldn't have. Maybe it won't matter."

Nobody took Josheb's wild speculations seriously.

More to the point, nobody would hear them.

"Do you want to know why star wine is superlative to all others?"

Caleb smiled bitterly. He already knew too much. What was one more secret? "It's unlike anything I've ever tasted. Not that I'm any kind of aficionado."

"In long ago days, when the stars were young and the mountains were unclimbed and whole forests stood empty, a curious star found a cleft in a rock and dipped in a finger."

Eri waited expectantly, so Caleb asked, "Was anything there?"

"The contented purring of celestia bumbers, fat upon the rarest of pollens, and the sweetest of delicacies, for the star's curiosity was rewarded by a taste of their nectar."

Caleb stole a glance at Andor. "Is that important?"

"For one curious star, a defining *moment."* Eri touched their chest. *"Have you reasoned out the purpose I found?"*

"You said you're a vintner. And Hesper mentioned honey mead." Caleb drew the obvious conclusion. "Was the honey you found an ingredient?"

"Merryvale's mead takes its sweetness from the sun—golden bees and golden honey. Star wine is another matter, and Andor knows the secret."

"Because you shared it with him?"

Eri plucked the flask from Caleb's hand and drained it. *"Celestia bumbers and their silvery nectar are precious to the heart of the one whose wine defies comparison."*

Caleb's heart was sinking. "Are they rare, these bumbers?"

"Increasingly so."

With another sidelong look, he asked, "Do they look like fuzzy white bees with blue eyes?"

Eri placed a hand over Andor's heart. *"He was dismayed over their loss."*

Hesper had said something about angering the First of Bears.

"They swarmed me." Caleb bit back all the excuses he could have hidden behind. "I apologize. I didn't mean to deprive you."

Andor huffed and spoke to Eri, who broke into a hopeful smile.

"Will the curious man who found a cleft in a rock call home the flock he scattered?"

Caleb hesitated. "He needs my help?"

"Reluctant as Andor is to admit it." Eri's tone turned wry. *"You are their only hope."*

MISSING PIECES

Caleb couldn't exactly remember how he found his way back to bed, but nothing seemed amiss. Judging by the height of the candle glowing in the corner, it was morning. Was he actually getting used to measuring time in candle wax? That was an unhappy thought, so Caleb pushed it aside. Because he felt good. Better than he should have, given how much star wine he'd consumed the night before.

What was this lingering sensation?

He felt … elation? Was it hope? Maybe it was a little more like anticipation. But what did cave-dwelling captives have to look forward to?

Eri's words rang in his memory. *The songs are culminating, and their resolution may surprise you.*

With a sudden and desperate need to *not* think, Caleb pushed that aside, too. Instead, he tackled the slapdash bundle of gear Andor had harvested from their campsite. Unpacking everything, he set about organizing and inventorying, from Nessie's flea and tick ointment to Josheb's remaining stash of canned ravioli.

Almost by accident, he realized something was missing. His driver's license.

Heart hammering, he located his brother's wallet and thumbed through its contents. Josheb's ID was gone, too. Which brought up a bunch of questions.

Could these people be running some kind of background check?

Was somebody reporting them missing or found ... or found dead?

Oaken must have them. Since when? And who had summoned Oaken? Because if he'd left with their driver's licenses in hand, then he'd probably been called in about them. Which begged a whole bunch of other questions.

"Caleb?"

He jumped and turned to find Hesper standing in the entrance. "Umm. Yeah?"

"Andor's asking for you."

"Is it about the bees?"

Hesper's eyebrows rose. "That's right. He needs your help getting them back to their nest."

"Be right there," he said distractedly. Should he change into his own clothes? Or keep borrowing Eri's?

"Caleb?"

He hadn't realized she was still there. "Yeah?"

"How did you know about the bumbers?"

Oh. Right.

I am a very great secret. And a good one.

Without a word, Caleb crossed to the bed, pulled his field journal from under the pillow, and opened it and added a quick sketch of a bumber. "Pictures and gestures can go a long way toward understanding."

Hesper hummed. It was a skeptical hum, but she didn't challenge him further.

"You're up?"

Josheb was out of bed and in a chair at the table in what passed for the kitchen. Patting a rustic crutch leaning at his side, he quipped, "You can't keep a Dare down!"

Caleb thought he was missing the point. "*Should* you be up?"

"Yes, I should." His brother's eyes narrowed slightly. "Don't go off having adventures without me. Better together, right?"

Which meant Caleb didn't have to do this alone. He claimed a chair, and relief must have shown on his face, because Josheb's smile widened.

He asked, "So what are we doing?"

Caleb toyed with his spoon. "I'm supposed to bring back those figments that chased us. It seems Andor is a little like a beekeeper, and he's pretty upset that I scattered his flock."

"Big Bo Peep has lost his sheep?" asked Josheb.

Hesper snorted into her cup. "They're Ephemera. Rare and irreplaceable celestia bumbers."

"Leave them alone and they will come home …?" suggested Josheb.

"But they *haven't*," countered Hesper. "And that's been troubling him."

"So how's Caleb supposed to bring them back?"

Caleb could only shrug. Nobody'd covered that part.

Hesper leaned forward. "I'll tell you a little secret, scruffbucket. Your brother's the attractive one."

Josheb pulled bemusedly at his beard. "We look alike. And when it comes to personality …."

Caleb jumped in to confirm, "He's the popular one. Always has been. Always will be."

"Not where I come from. Not here and now." Hesper turned a look on Caleb that was decidedly flattering. "No contest."

With a put-upon whine in his tone, Josheb extended a hand. "Nessie, *you* still love me? Dontcha, girl?"

She immediately went to him, delighted as ever to have his attention. But Caleb could tell it was small consolation. With a sudden shifting of paradigms, he saw Josheb from Hesper's point of view. He wasn't plagued by figments, and he didn't hear the songs of stars. That didn't make Josheb reassuringly normal. For someone like her, it meant that he was missing something.

A missing piece that had always belonged to Caleb.

Making him attractive to a potentially dangerous set.

POPULARITY CONTEST

Andor picked up Caleb. Not exactly unexpected, given the events of last night. But when Hesper plucked Josheb off his feet, his brother yelped. "Whoa! Hey, now! What're you ...?"

"Stop flailing!" snapped Hesper. She had him in a cradle hold, and he was helpless to resist.

But that didn't stop him from protesting. "I call this undignified."

"It's a *long* walk, gimpy. Calm your ego and enjoy the ride."

He did quiet down. Briefly. "You're not even straining."

"Would you prefer I was inconvenienced?"

"How strong *are* you?" Josheb asked.

"Stronger than a dainty fellow like you."

Oh, Josheb wouldn't like that. He'd always been above average in height, strength, and athleticism. And he'd gone straight from sports to survival training to thrill seeking. All physically demanding. All a point of pride.

But Josheb didn't bristle. "Give me *numbers*. How much can you bench press?"

"No idea."

"How can you *not* know?"

Hesper laughed. "Why would I go drawing attention to myself by showing off at a gym."

"Because you *can*?"

Andor lengthened his stride. Caleb suspected that Mister Big wasn't used to the noise and was distancing himself. He could sympathize. Maybe Hesper could, too. She was letting him get away.

Even Nessie hung back, dogging Hesper's steps, keeping Josheb in sight.

For a while, Caleb searched for landmarks. Maybe if he could plot their position on his internal map, he could … what? Escape? His chances were slim if not none, and time was getting away from them. If they were still here when snow struck, they'd be stranded until spring.

"I don't know what you expect me to do," Caleb said softly.

Andor eyed him briefly, grunted, and … patted his back.

"You should know, I don't like bugs." This was pointless, but he needed to be heard. "Most figments scare me on some level. And you're the biggest one of all."

A baffled gaze. A worried frown.

Caleb knew the words weren't getting through, so he tried for the right tone, the right expression. Could he get the gist across?

"Some are cute. I'll grant you that. I don't mind them so much. Or the ones who leave me alone. But your bees, your bumbers, they came after me, and they clung to me. I'm not hurt, but it felt like an attack. I don't want to go through that again."

Andor grumbled, adjusted his hold, and gave Caleb his hand.

More specifically, he was giving Caleb access to his ring.

Whether it was just to get him to shut up or because he thought this was what Caleb was trying to ask for, he was glad for the chance to study the stone in daylight.

A roughhewn crystal had been set into a wide metal band etched with dozens of tiny symbols. While they didn't shine, the stone gave that impression. Was it actually glowing? No, it had to be a trick of the light, which seemed to collect within. The stone was clear. Or nearly so. Angling his head to one side, Caleb located a blush of pink near its center, like a frozen flower petal.

He touched it. Or it touched him. It was difficult to say which.

And the veil was swept aside. He could hear the stars. Not singing *per se*, but chattering and laughing, as if they were swapping tales somewhere in the wings. No one voice stood out, and Caleb couldn't understand a word of it. But the tones were pleasant, and eavesdropping gave him something to do while Andor covered several more miles.

"Put me with him," ordered Josheb. "There's room."

Caleb perched atop the bumber nest, with its riddling of holes. Silent now, and somehow colder.

"Barely," protested Hesper.

"It's a rock," pointed out Josheb. "We're not going to break it."

She said something to Andor, who grunted and waved. Caleb wondered if he'd need to learn Andor's language. Oaken might be patient enough to teach him, once he returned. Or maybe Eri? Was there any point, though, if Andor stuck to nonverbals?

Josheb crowded close. "Make room."

"If I move over any further, I'll fall off," said Caleb.

"I'm your counterweight." Josheb wrapped an arm around his waist and leaned away, as if daring gravity to take either of them. "So this is a hive?"

"Nest," Hesper corrected. "And Caleb is going to be a little like a homing signal. As they say, a lure that works once can work twice."

"Who exactly says that?" Josheb asked.

Hesper smirked and sidestepped the question by addressing Andor. Again, Caleb paid more attention to the tone than the foreign syllables. She was so much more polite than she was with him or Josheb. Respectful.

Andor's answer barely counted as an explanation. His words were few, but his actions were plain. From the bag at his hip, he withdrew another stone. Much larger than the crystal in his ring, this one was as big as his fist and winking with pale green facets.

"Looks like some kind of beryl, maybe," murmured Josheb. "Is it just a mineral? Precious? Semi-precious?"

"It's a remnant, and it's rare enough," said Hesper. "Treat it with care. Crack it at your peril."

Josheb was blatantly delighted. "How menacing."

Andor offered the crystal to Caleb, who needed both hands. It was heavy, and it was humming. "Hello," he muttered.

"Are you talking to a rock?" Josheb leaned closer. "You've never mentioned that before."

"I never noticed before this trip. And I don't know what it means."

"Interesting." Josheb turned to Hesper. "What's the deal? You called it a remnant. As in a leftover scrap? Or one of the last of its kind?"

Hesper rolled her eyes. "We'll save such stories for when the work is over. Caleb needs to call the flock."

"How?" asked Caleb, looking to Andor.

When he spoke, it was with slow words and many gestures.

Hesper nodded and translated. "Tune your heart to the stone, and it will amplify your hopes."

Caleb was incredulous. "Still waiting for the *how*."

Josheb, who'd never been good about the 'no touching' rule, traced a fingertip over the stone's winking facets. He quietly asked, "Am I imagining the hum?"

They were touching.

They were doing the thing.

"No," replied Caleb. "It's almost like the stone's alive."

"More like there's a little bit of life hidden in the stone," Hesper corrected in reverent tones. "A memory. A prophecy. The remnant of a song."

Josheb considered that for a moment. "So you're asking Caleb to sing with it?"

"I don't sing," Caleb protested.

"We're not putting you on the spot for a solo." Hesper reached out and tapped his chest. "Think happy thoughts, and include the bumbers, if you can."

Happy thoughts and figments didn't often go together. "I'm not sure ...."

Andor suggested something, and Hesper translated. "To call them home, think of home."

"That's a long way from here."

"But home has a feeling, doesn't it?" countered Hesper.

Josheb tightened his hold. "Can't hurt to try."

Which was true. So Caleb focused on the big crystal in his hands, rubbing his thumb along rough edges as he listened. It was a little like hearing stars. In fact, he thought he could hear their voices, though they were muffled. Caleb wasn't touching Andor's ring, but he knew right where it was, and when he focused on it, everything came clearer.

"That's the way," murmured Hesper. "You've got the right idea."

Andor grunted, then offered a remark.

Josheb whispered, "What did he say?"

"You don't want to know, scruff-bucket." Hesper's voice was huskier than usual. "Only make you jealous."

COME HOME

Why was it working? Caleb hadn't even given a thought to home yet.

He cradled the stone to his heart and tuned out Josheb and Hesper. What was it, now? He'd been listening to the stone and thinking of stars. But they weren't part of his home. *Home* was his orderly loft, high above the city. Where he kept a window cracked, even on frigid nights, so he wouldn't miss the distant melodies of the stars.

Stars like Eri.

The hum in the crystal became a clear note as Caleb's thoughts dwelt on a second moon and a shining face, the taste of star wine and the sharing of secrets.

"Oooh, yes. Hesper hummed appreciatively. "Settle into that groove. Andor's banishing the barrier."

Josheb wriggled and shifted, and then his jacked dropped over Caleb. "Keep your head down. And keep up the good work."

Humming wings came closer, and Caleb was grateful for his brother's forethought. He didn't want to be plastered with homesick bugs, clinging and crawling in their eagerness to touch him. Turning his face into Josheb's shoulder, he wished for peace and wine and songs with everything he had.

"Help me keep them off," snapped Josheb. "He doesn't like bugs, all right?"

Hesper spoke.

Andor growled.

Nessie whined.

Suddenly, Caleb could smell something sweet on the air, and another weight dropped over him—thick and stifling, heavy with spice and musk. He struggled to push it off.

"Leave it," Josheb ordered. "It's Andor's coat, and it's shielding you pretty well. Only a few stragglers, now. Hang in there, bro."

More words.

A husky chuckle.

Josheb exclaimed, "They purr? Dang, that's almost cute."

But Caleb kept his head down and his eyes clamped shut. Because one voice was carrying more clearly than all the rest. And he was sure it was Eri's, because the song was in English. Were they singing for Caleb's sake?

It seemed important. He wanted to know.

Caleb focused harder, reaching for Eri.

A voice reached back. *"Sing with me."*

Caleb shook his head.

Eri said, *"Accompany me."*

As if Caleb had an instrument. Again, he balked.

"Not with harp or lute or pipes." There was a gentleness to Eri's merriment. *"Accompany me in the manner of friends. Hear my song and learn of me. Let my song become part of you."*

Caleb wanted to ask what would happen if he did.

And somehow, Eri understood his question and answered. *"I will become your treasure."*

Josheb's arm was tight and tighter, and his voice was sharp against Caleb's ears, but Caleb wasn't listening with his ears anymore. It was so easy to let everything else slip away. His world was a crystal and a star and a startling song that could only be true.

LONG SLEEP

Caleb lost three days.

At least, that's what Josheb told him when he woke. His younger brother had moved into his room, sitting with his injured leg propped across the entrance, the missing camera in his hands.

"You got it back," Caleb said, voice rusty.

"I reasoned with them. They had a change of heart."

He didn't believe that for a second. "No, really?"

"Made a pest of myself. Assured them this would shut me up." Josheb grinned. "Between you and me, bigfoot's a pushover."

"I know."

Josheb levered himself up and passed Caleb a cup. "They've been keeping you going on this stuff. Don't ask me how they feed it to you."

"You don't know?"

"You don't want to know." Josheb smiled crookedly. "I'm not the only one who's been worried. Where'd you go, anyhow?"

It was an interesting way to phrase it. "Something like a dream, I guess. Three days, though?"

He waved his phone. "Checked on you every three hours."

Caleb took a long swig of water, which wasn't just water. There was a sweet aftertaste, reminiscent of honey. He peered into the cup, trying to place the flavor. Could it be one of the ingredients for star wine? Either the nectar or … was there pollen involved?

Pulling his field journal from under the pillow, he made a careful note of the date and scratched at his cheek. He'd been shaved. Recently. Strange to think he'd been so out of it.

"You had a smile on your face the whole time," Josheb announced casually.

"It was a nice dream."

"They put away your singing rock. I wouldn't be surprised if Andor buried it." Coming to sit on the bed, he lightly punched Caleb's shoulder. "I thought we agreed that we'd head into adventures together."

"I'm right here." Caleb jotted a few details from Eri's lyrics. He'd have to add more later, when Josheb wasn't hovering. "And we're definitely in all of this together."

"Three days," he said softly. "You were as good as gone for three days."

"You leave for months on end," Caleb pointed out.

Josheb pulled at his beard, messed up his hair, and promised, "Not anymore."

"Not anymore," he agreed. Because he knew it was true. But he couldn't explain why. "How long until breakfast?"

Checking his phone, Josheb said, "Sun won't be up for a while, but I'm beginning to think our cohorts don't sleep. Like, at all."

Cohorts. It was nicer than captors.

And if Eri was right, it was true.

Josheb elbowed him and asked, "In the mood for ravioli?"

With a nod and a smile, Caleb replied, "Set me up."

SHOW DOG

"It's September." Caleb marked his place with his pencil before tucking the field journal under his pillow.

"I can tell," said Josheb, who was going through his morning workout. "Days are getting shorter. Nights are getting colder."

"Leaves are starting to change. Early gold in the aspens."

"I didn't realize you were still keeping track."

"It's my job. Documentation, remember?" Josheb's phone battery had given up days ago, so Caleb was down to analog methods of timekeeping.

"We might be stuck here a while."

Caleb snorted. "I've been trying to tell you that since we got here."

"Yeah, well … you're the smart one."

"Breakfast?" suggested Caleb.

"Smells good enough to eat."

They followed their noses to the kitchen and drew up short. Andor and Hesper were at the table, and Oaken was at the hearth, stirring the morning stew.

"He's back," whispered Josheb.

Caleb elbowed his brother and said, "Welcome back, Oaken."

He turned from his task and smiled a greeting.

"Uhh … he's not alone." Josheb pointed to the shaggy rug before the fire. A big dog with reddish fur sprawled beside Nessie, tongue lolling, tail wagging. "Hey, Oaken. You went and bought a dog?"

Hesper translated his question, then relayed, "Oaken says, 'he followed me home.'"

They went back and forth like this, with Hesper stuck in the middle.

"Why'd he follow you?"

"Curiosity."

"Is he a wolf?"

"A dog."

Josheb wasn't giving up. "What's his name?"

"He doesn't want to say. Call him whatever you want."

Caleb dropped onto his usual chair. He thought a better question might have been … *who* didn't want to say. Because Hesper said it in a way that gave him the distinct impression that she meant the dog. Not Oaken.

"He's a beaut," remarked Josheb. "A regular show dog. What should we call him?"

Hesper raised both hands. "Nuh-uh. I'm out."

"You *always* have an opinion," countered Josheb. "Why the change of heart?"

While they lapsed into their usual banter, the animal in question heaved to his feet and ambled to the table, ducking underneath. A moment later, Caleb had a long muzzle prodding him in vulnerable places.

Copper eyes peered up at Caleb with startling intelligence, and he quickly slipped him a chunk of mystery meat from his bowl. It was graciously received, and the dog stayed put, with his head resting against Caleb's thigh.

While he didn't normally encourage begging at the table, it

seemed wise to befriend an animal of this size, so he offered another tidbit. The dog took it carefully, looking more amused than adoring. In fact, Caleb got the idea that the dog wasn't begging so much as daring him to continue.

Three bowls of stew later, the edge was finally off Caleb's hunger, and he'd made a fast friend. In fact, when he went outside to stretch his legs, the dog remained by his side. Caleb found a seat on an upturned log beside the firepit that he thought of as Andor's grill.

Roughing up the dog's fur, he admired its rich hue. Dark auburn was striking enough, but the eyes really put this dog in a class all his own. The copper had an almost metallic sheen, and the pupils were narrow. More like a cat's than a canine's.

"I guess I shouldn't be surprised." With a sidelong look in the direction of the den's entrance, Caleb softly confided, "The stars were singing about a newcomer."

Peaked ears snapped forward. Like he was interested.

"I don't think it could be you, though." He scruffed and scratched, earning a lick to the chin. "Close, but not quite. Unless I misheard or misremembered."

Those eyes searched his with an intensity that called for more.

And since it had always been easy for Caleb to confide in dogs, he confessed, "I could have sworn they were talking about a cat."

ON TIPTOE

The dog—whom Josheb dubbed Sasquatch—stuck so close, Caleb was tripping over him all throughout the day. And the night. And the next day, as well. After a week, Sasquatch's dedication was becoming embarrassing.

He tagged along for barefoot walks with Nessie.

He watched Hesper give Caleb his shaves.

He ate exclusively off of Caleb's plate.

He posed when Josheb decided Sasquatch needed documenting.

He kept an eye on Caleb while he bathed.

He looked on while he updated his field journal.

He lay with his head resting over Caleb's heart every night.

Which was comforting in a way, but also troubling, since Sasquatch made a point of staying between Caleb and Andor at all times. Like a bodyguard with a mission. Not so long ago, Caleb might have appreciated having an over-achieving guard dog between him and his captors.

But no contact with Andor meant other things, too.

Caleb couldn't touch his ring, so he couldn't hear the stars. And there were no more opportunities for Andor to pass along his flask. Caleb craved the taste of star wine. Even one mouthful would have been welcome.

But how did one sneak away from a dog who never relaxed his guard?

"Stay." Caleb tried for a no-nonsense tone, but it was difficult to deepen a whisper. "Stay, Sasquatch."

Only, when he tried to sneak out, the dog padded after him.

"Stay," he insisted, pointing to his bed. "Wait here. Please?"

Sasquatch edged closer, tail wagging.

"You're an excellent watchdog, so I'm going to give you an important job." Caleb was desperate enough to try anything.

"Watch over Josheb for me. Keep my brother safe while I'm away."

Sasquatch's attention shifted to the other brother.

"Stay. Protect Josheb."

The dog whined softly, but he went to lie on the floor beside Josheb's bed, muzzle on his paws, gaze mournful.

Caleb slipped out and tiptoed down the passage. He wasn't surprised to find a candle lit in the kitchen or Andor seated beside the hearth—feet propped, frown firmly in place as he stared into the embers. Until Caleb stepped into the open.

Andor's eyes widened, then shifted to the passage, as if expecting Sasquatch to appear.

Swallowing his pride, Caleb pantomimed drinking. "Is there any wine? I was hoping ...?"

With a hesitant tone, Andor asked something. But then he curled his fingers, beckoning Caleb closer.

"I really need to learn a few words. Maybe Eri could teach me?" Pointing to the door, he practically begged, "Can I visit Eri? I was actually, really hoping ... you know?"

With another long look at the inner passage, Andor wrestled briefly with the ring on his finger and extended it.

It wasn't exactly what he wanted. But they were closer to an understanding.

Caleb strode forward and closed Andor's fingers over the ring, then plucked at his sleeve and pointed at the door. "Eri. Please? Will you take me to see the stars?"

All of Andor's hesitation vanished, replaced by the same kind of pleased look he'd shown when Caleb complimented his wine. With slow movements, he took Caleb by the wrist, pressed his ring against his palm, and closed Caleb's fingers around the crystal. Working his jaw, he spoke a single word. In English. "Peace."

"Peace," Caleb readily agreed, elated that Andor was making an effort.

With a grunt, Andor swept him off his feet and smuggled him out the door.

They stopped in a different cave long enough for Andor to pass him three cups and to shoulder a squat cask. It was all very secretive and celebratory, like the stars were welcoming Caleb home. He was jittery with anticipation. Or maybe it was just the cold.

"Should have brought a jacket," he mumbled. "And we need to have a serious discussion about socks and shoes."

Andor grunted.

He might have been smiling.

Caleb wished he knew why.

Then again, not everything in life needed to be documented.

COMPLAINTS FILED

Hours later, Andor tucked Caleb back into his own bed. The blankets were bliss. Everything was. Possibly thanks to the star wine. How much had he consumed? Andor had topped off his cup every few sips, so it was difficult to guess. Caleb was beyond buzzed and happy to have pulled off something daring.

"Lived up to my name," he mumbled to Sasquatch.

The dog grumbled and snuffled and sniffed and sneezed.

Then a hand was stroking his hair, and two voices rumbled overhead. Gruff, but not angry. Andor bent over him, his expression troubled. But he touched Caleb's shoulder and said, "Peace."

Happiness washed over Caleb. He'd befriended bigfoot.

Andor blinked, and he looked embarrassed. But he kept his promise and handed over his flask before hurrying away. Caleb curled around it, pleased with his prize. He could share it with Josheb tomorrow.

It took a few moments to register that someone was still petting his hair. He turned, squinting into the dim. Candlelight wasn't much to go by. "Whossat?"

"Sasquatch."

"Oooh." He caught the faint sheen of copper, which corroborated the claim. "That's all right, then."

"You are thoroughly drunk, dear boy." Even in an undertone, it was a big voice.

Caleb didn't know the face, but he liked the smile. And something even more important. "You speak English."

"As it happens, I do." Sasquatch gravely added, "I can hear you out, if you have any complaints about your treatment here."

So easy. He definitely had one. "Warm socks, please."

"That can be arranged."

"Mmm ... more star wine?" He hugged the flask to his chest. "Ever tasted it?"

"It's an especial favorite of mine." Sasquatch leaned closer and his voice took on a sing-song quality. "To drink star wine is to remember the scent of ancient trees and the kiss of starlight and to hope for a paradise where remnant songs are sung in full."

"Yasss," Caleb agreed, clumsily patting Sasquatch's arm. "Just like that, only better. The best."

"It is." Sasquatch's gaze was so full of concern. "Have you been mistreated in any way? Even in … intangible ways?"

"Is *that* what you think?" Caleb was a little offended.

"No." Sasquatch smiled. "You clearly trust Andor. And he is careful with you."

"Not at first." Looking back, it was easier to see it now. "Mmm … guess we worried him almost as much as he worried me."

"You made peace with the First of Bears. Not many do. He isn't what I'd call *safe*. Too close to the old ways."

"Didja know he's bigfoot?"

"Bigfoot is a myth."

Caleb's eyelids were growing heavy. "So's Sasquatch, but here *you* are."

"You're a long way from home, Caleb Dare. Why come here, of all places?"

"Map. Tip. Star. Trip. And Josheb is Josheb." He was the reason for most of the trouble Caleb found himself in. "My brother was looking for bigfoot. Funny, huh?"

"Not really."

And because it was the direction his thoughts had been taking, Caleb added, "I wasn't looking, but I found something, too."

Sasquatch, who'd been sniffing the air, patted his cheek, keeping him awake. "What did you find?"

"Where I belong."

"That's unexpected. You want to stay?"

Caleb snorted. "I want to *go*. With Josheb. We'll go and go and go. Josheb will love it."

Shaggy eyebrows furrowed. "So you *do* want to go home?"

"I *am* home." He shook his finger at Sasquatch. "I'm home wherever I can hear the stars. Mine most of all. See?"

Big hands cupped his face, angling him toward the softness of candlelight. With a low chuckle, Sasquatch said, "Maker bless. It's slyly done, but it's done."

"Oh, that?" Caleb rubbed his forehead. "They kissed me."

"Say no more. I know a thing or two about souls who've been marked by stars."

And Sasquatch said no more himself. Just went back to being a show dog. And since everything was quieter that way, Caleb could finally drift off to sleep.

CLINK CUPS

"Okay ...? What's this?" Josheb asked in an undertone.

"Star wine."

"And why did we have to come *this far* to taste it?"

They were about half a mile from the nearest entrance to Andor's den. Far enough to guarantee a smidgen of privacy.

Caleb wrestled with the flimsy can opener from their camping kit. "Because ... I don't know. Does there have to be a reason?"

"Gimme." Josheb expertly opened two servings of ravioli.

"I just wanted you to get a share." Caleb handed his brother a fork.

"Because someone shared it with you?"

"Yeah. This is Andor's flask. You were almost right about the distillery. He's a wine-maker."

"And his special reserve pairs well with Italian?" Josheb munched cold pasta.

Caleb angled his shoulder to keep Sasquatch's nose out of his mid-morning snack "There wasn't much else to work with."

"Here, boy." Josheb offered the dog a ravioli, chuckling when Sasquatch delicately slid it from the tines. "I mean, I knew there was booze. Hard to miss the barrels. And I asked Hesper about it, but she only knows the basics about Skypact business dealings. Mostly by reputation. This is her first time here, and honey mead is her branch of the family's stock and trade."

"Wait. Did you say ... Skypact?"

"Apparently, it's stamped on every blessed barrel. It's Andor's surname. Well, they call it their *clan* name. Andor Skypact. Oaken, too. He's Andor's son. Their wine's in high demand, but they're a two-man operation. Except it's more properly *males*. Or more specifically, boars. Since they're bear clan."

Caleb sort of wished he'd brought along his field journal. "You know a lot."

"Been asking a lot of questions." Josheb offered Nessie a ravioli. "Interviews—it's what I do. Investigative journalist, remember?"

"You're actually doing your job? Even though they'll never let you publish the story?"

"Not much else *to* do." Josheb chewed thoughtfully. "We're really in deep this time. Not sure we're actually in trouble, but it's like you said at the start—*bigger than both of us.*"

Skypact. That had to refer to Andor and Eri, didn't it? People knew about star wine. It might even be world-famous. But did anybody else know that the father and son brewers had a silent partner?

Josheb offered Sasquatch another ravioli, but the dog turned up his nose. "More for you, sweetheart," he said, passing it to Nessie instead.

Caleb suddenly remembered something of the night before. "I think Sasquatch is holding out for the star wine."

"Big drinker, is he?"

Oh, yes. It was all coming back to him. "Star wine is one of his favorites."

"And how would you know that little detail?"

Caleb stared at his too-cold toes and quietly admitted, "He told me so."

Josheb hummed. And when Caleb stole a glance, his brother asked, "Just now?"

"Last night. I was a little drunk."

Sasquatch cocked his head to one side, and he sniffed in the direction of the flask.

"I might have been *very* drunk," Caleb offered lamely.

"No, I think you're onto something. I mean … he's smarter than your average dog—no offense Nessie, darling—and there's more clans than bear. Hesper says those giant squirrel tracks I spotted were from some local boys."

"There are others living out here?"

Josheb listed, "Squirrel, deer, pheasant—sound familiar?"

Caleb looked to Sasquatch and asked, "Is there a dog clan?"

Copper eyes held laughter as he offered a paw.

"Maybe he's not allowed to say? It could be a secret," suggested Caleb.

"I got Hesper to show me. She's a shifter." Josheb's brows lifted. "That giant bear we saw? It was Andor."

Caleb admitted, "I wasn't sure."

"Honestly, I think it's great. Shifters are trendy." Josheb picked up one of the camp cups and jiggled it toward the flask. "Great hook for an epic story, if we ever get around to telling it."

With less ceremony than the wine probably deserved, Caleb tipped a little into his own cup, then filled Josheb's to the brim. "I already had some. This is your share."

"Not gonna argue, not gonna complain." Josheb clinked their cups together and took a small sip, then a whole mouthful. His eyes slid shut as he gave the wine his full attention.

Meanwhile, Sasquatch sidled closer and snuffled hopefully at Caleb's cup. Without really thinking about it, Caleb flicked his nose.

The dog's rump hit the ground, and they stared at each other for several moments.

Clearing his throat, Caleb said, "Please tell me I didn't just biff the King of Dogs."

"Could be." Josheb sounded supremely unconcerned. And duly impressed. "Kind of sweet, like dessert wine. And there's some fizz. At least, it tingles against my tongue. Wish I could see it in a flute. Does it have a color? Hey, if there's *star* in the name, does it shine?"

"Not sure." Caleb peered into the enamel cup. "Guess this is lacking in presentation. Since when are you into wine?"

"Learned some stuff from a friend of a friend." He tugged at his beard and smiled lopsidedly. "I usually just grab a beer, though."

Caleb admitted, "I'm a little hooked on this stuff."

"Wonder if Hesper's honey mead is just as good?"

Sasquatch huffed.

Was he offering an opinion?

But then Hesper's voice carried from close at hand. "*Here* you are! Oaken, they're over here!"

"Tattle tale," accused Josheb, who raised his cup. "Come to crash our party?"

She eyed their impromptu picnic without much enthusiasm. "You're being summoned. And you're in luck. Andor's about to open a fresh cask of his finest. Shares for all."

"What's the occasion?" asked Josheb.

"Guests." With a long look at Sasquatch, she added, "High-ranking guests."

The dog paused long enough to lick Caleb's cheek before sprinting away.

Josheb snickered. "Thirsty boy?"

Hesper hauled him to his feet and helped him balance while Oaken and Caleb collected their things.

Caleb ventured, "What kind of guests?"

"You'll see for yourself in a minute."

"Give us a hint!" Josheb had always been the persistent type. "What clan?"

"Clans. Two." Hesper didn't seem worried by the incursion. If anything, she seemed … impressed. "Care to guess?"

Josheb blurted, "Dog!"

Equally sure that he was right, Caleb answered, "Cat."

WARMING WELCOME

Oaken and Hesper carried them right into the kitchen, where two chairs waited before the hearth, each with a large, foamy basin set before it. Steam carried a pleasant scent, but Caleb hesitated to plunge his cold feet into hot water.

Josheb dipped in a toe. "Are we in some kind of hot seat? Or is it spa day?"

"You want a mani-pedi?" Hesper asked lightly. "I'll do it if you let me unbeard you."

"Not a chance." And with a roll of his eyes toward the other end of the room, he quietly asked, "You thinking what I'm thinking?"

Caleb, who was already sizing up the newcomer, could only nod.

A big guy with long, auburn hair stood chatting with Andor, who had a tall glass poised below the spout of one of the mid-sized wine casks. Stray thoughts flitted through Caleb's mind. Like ... it was a lot of wine for six people. And that Sasquatch was well-named, since he looked larger than life. His height rivaled Andor's, and while his build was more lean, that didn't diminish him a speck. Indeed, his presence dominated the room to such a degree, Andor came off modest and retiring by comparison.

Turning slightly, Sasquatch raised his glass.

His easy smile was the same Caleb remembered.

"You're *totally* Sasquatch," accused Josheb.

"And you're not bothered?" His nostrils flared, and his smile widened. "Are you pleased to meet me, or simply pleased to be correct?"

Josheb laughed. "Guessing right hardly counts. The hints you dropped were bigger than Andor's barrels. Why the subterfuge?"

"Curiosity, at first. And necessary caution." Indicating Nessie, he added, "I needed to stick close, and you seemed the sort to be accepting of dogs. In truest form, I am somewhat less alarming."

Hesper snorted. "In truest form, but not at truest size."

Sasquatch's copper eyes sparkled. "The past several days *have* been an exercise in restraint. But what else could I do until my good friend arrived?"

Caleb sheepishly glanced around. Not six people. One more made seven.

"I am here." The new arrival quietly stepped into the center of attention. "Is the water too hot?"

Josheb dropped both feet in and asked, "Do you guys have names, or do I get to pick one for you, too?"

The new guy, who was dressed in gray, gestured gracefully to Sasquatch.

"My name is Harmonious Starmark, and I speak for the dog clans."

"Speak for?" interrupted Josheb. "As in … their leader?"

"More of a representative."

Turning to Caleb, Josheb gleefully accused, "You totally biffed the King of Dogs."

Harmonious chuckled. "That's hardly worth mentioning."

Oaken conferred briefly with Hesper, who now held her own tall glass of star wine. She reported, "Harmonious is firstborn son and heir to the First of Dogs. Show a little respect."

"No kidding?" Josheb's smile turned sly. "So what's the Crown Prince of Dogs doing way out here, begging food under the table."

With a slightly pained glance in his companion's direction,

Harmonious gruffly answered, "I was … in-character. And I couldn't very well proceed until Hisoka arrived. There's a balance to these things."

"Which means …?" prompted Josheb.

"Equal parts," replied Harmonious. "Two of us, two of them, two of you."

"The water." The gray-clad male knelt before Caleb and dipped his fingers into the basin. Still in an undertone, he urged, "Do not let it go to waste."

Caleb slid his feet into water that was not too hot and not too cold. All at once, he felt like Goldilocks. "There are three bears," he mumbled.

Head down, hands kneading, the newcomer proceeded to wash Caleb's feet. "Word reached us that Andor and Oaken had captured two hikers. Hesper is not part of the complaint. Indeed, I am pleased to find her here. I can have you provided with a human translator as well."

Josheb asked, "Why? Hesper's been great."

Harmonious dropped to a seat in front of Josheb and grabbed his ankle. "For balance, of course. You'll be wanting a reaver's perspective."

"One from my cortege is on his way." And raising eyes that were a startling shade of orange, he said, "My name is Hisoka Twineshaft, and I speak for the Amaranthine clans."

"All of them?" asked Josheb.

"Yes."

"But which one's yours?" he pressed.

"Cat."

Offering his fist for Caleb to bump, Josheb whispered, "Nailed it!"

Caleb had no idea how his brother could be so relaxed. Oaken and Hesper were standing back, watching in overt fascination. Everything about their body language made it clear that important guys like these didn't normally wash the feet of humans.

"Why are you doing this?" Caleb managed weakly. "You don't have to do this. I can take care of it."

Josheb jumped in. "Is this some kind of ritual?"

Hisoka said, "Perhaps we should call it an apology."

"For what?"

"Cold feet." He sought Caleb's gaze. "I understand it was one of your two grievances."

Harmonious boasted, "I arranged for socks. And shoes."

Oaken added more hot water to the basins, and the swirl of heat felt good. Caleb had never experienced anything like this, and he was more than a little embarrassed. Everything felt backwards. These people were important. He was the trespasser in their territory.

Suddenly, Josheb made a garbled sound. "That tickles!"

"Is that so?" Harmonious didn't show a lick of repentance. "Was it here?"

Caleb looked on in increasing bewilderment as Josheb dissolved into giggles, then fought back with much sloshing of water and hairpulling.

"Oh for the love of …!" And reaching over, he flicked the nose of the Crown Prince of Dogs. Again.

Harmonious Starmark's attention swung to him, and his grin widened, revealing an entirely daunting set of fangs. "I *like* you boys. If Andor wasn't exerting prior claim, I'd gladly add you to the Starmark pack."

Caleb spied Andor watching moodily from the corner.

"You can't just go around claiming people willy-nilly ... can you?" quizzed Josheb.

"Well, no." Harmonious was mopping at the floor with the towels Hesper brought over. "It's usually considered a gift."

"Sort of an honorary member of the family?"

"Nooo." Shaggy brows furrowed. "You *would* be pack. Nothing honorary about it."

Caleb asked, "Can the gift be refused?"

Harmonious looked entirely baffled. "Why would anyone do that?"

Oaken and Hesper whisked away the basins. Warmed feet were further warmed by the friction of toweling. Then there were thick socks and fur-lined shoes with heavy soles, reminiscent of moccasins. Caleb's feet were comfortable for the first time in weeks. "Thank you."

When the two remained on the floor before the Dare brothers' chairs, Caleb wondered if they were waiting for something along the lines of ... *apology accepted*. Even though he still didn't think he was owed one. This whole trip had been disorienting and frightening and awkward as hell, but they'd found a way past their differences. With a little help from a guiding star.

"Caleb Jonathan Dare." Hisoka offered a card with both hands.

For a moment, Caleb thought it was a business card, but it turned out to be his driver's license.

"Josheb Benjamin Dare." Hisoka repeated the process with his brother.

Harmonious cleared his throat. "We have to be so careful. We checked into you a little, and we were surprised by what we learned."

"Good surprised or bad surprised?" asked Josheb.

"Good," Harmonious quickly assured. "*Very* good, given everything that's culminating. I hardly know where to start, there's so much to explain. Hisoka …?"

"Caleb. Josheb." With a whisper of a smile to offset the gravity of the moment, Hisoka Twineshaft said, "We have a proposition for you both."

AT HOME

"Does returning seem weird for you?" asked Caleb, staring up at his building.

"Every time." Josheb stabbed the button for the crosswalk a few times, then shrugged. "You'll get used to it."

"I suppose I will. If I keep this place."

"You're thinking of moving?"

"Might have to, once everything goes down. For security reasons." Caleb had committed the timetable to memory. "Besides, if it's both of us, we'll need more room."

"You sure?"

"About our paparazzi potential? I'd love to be wrong."

Josheb tugged at his beard. "About living together."

"I'll make it an official dare, if necessary."

Opening the building's front door with a doorman's flourish, Josheb asked, "Better together?"

"Wherever we go," agreed Caleb. And so one bloodhound and two men in fur-lined moccasins scuffed across the foyer to wait for the elevator.

After months away, they were back where they'd started. However, this part of Caleb's life felt like a distant memory. He and Josheb had accepted the terms posed by Hisoka Twineshaft on behalf of the clans. To serve on a committee that was paving the way for the Amaranthine people to step out of hiding. To take an active role in informing the world about their not-so-new neighbors.

The elevator opened on the twenty-second floor.

Nessie tugged on her leash, aiming straight for their door.

Caleb had his key ready, but he hesitated.

"Been a while, huh?" Josheb mimed insertion and a twist. "Give it a few days. It'll feel normal again in no time."

"It's just ... different."

"Nah. Not really. *You're* the one who's changed." And with a wink, his brother whispered, "Lots of changes ahead."

Understatement.

Caleb opened the door, eased out of his shoes, and stepped inside. Everything was hushed and stale and dusty. He probably should have been worried about the mail and the state of his portfolio. He even felt a little guilty for not giving past priorities their former place.

He had a new job. One that involved film crews and interviews and documentation. One that put a permanent smile on Josheb's face, since he'd be delivering the scoop of the century on a weekly basis. Because the Amaranthine clans were their myths and legends come to life.

"Den sweet den," quipped Josheb. He unclipped Nessie's leash, and she trotted into her former domain, nose to the rug. "I'll crack a window."

"Do me a favor?" Caleb pointed toward the loft. "There's a skylight up there, above the bed. See if it opens?"

Josheb shucked out of his own slippers, offered a jaunty salute, and hopped to it. "Gonna sleep under the stars tonight?" he called from the utility closet.

"Not sure we can see them from here."

"But you're hoping to *hear* them."

"Yeah." Caleb could admit that much. "Yeah, we'll listen for them again tonight."

It was cold. March was too soon to be sleeping under an open skylight. But Caleb and Josheb unrolled a thick pad woven from fur—a parting gift from Oaken—and piled every blanket in the house on top. With Nessie sprawled between them, it was almost homey. And when Josheb grabbed Caleb's wrist, it was even closer to normal.

But there was no *pip-pip-pipping* of figments, and no flicker of firelight. "I'm going to buy a candle tomorrow," muttered Caleb.

"Cell phone, too. Hesper wants us *both* to text." After a lengthy pause, Josheb asked, "Getting anything?"

"Not really." Compared to the mountains, the stars were dim and distant.

But as soon as Josheb retreated into sleep, a trickle of music touched Caleb's soul. As if the stars had been waiting for a private word.

They sang of all that had happened, and they sang of things to come. Of dogs and dragons and foxes. Of embassies and treaties and pacts. Of long-held promises and unfolding plans. And of seemingly insignificant moments with consequences that would culminate in surprising ways.

DARE TOGETHER

"This the place?" asked Josheb, pulling into an open space across the street.

The house was a century old, at least. One of those big, sprawling historical homes just a block off the main drag. The kind with a wrap-around porch and three colors of paint on its filigree trim.

Caleb had memorized the map, but the neighborhood was nothing like he'd expected. "It's so … normal."

"Well, sure. They're shooting for normal." Josheb hopped down and opened the back door to let Nessie out. "Hesper says they're using Vale for a surname right now."

"I remember."

"Wouldn't be so bad, moving someplace like this. Hesper would have our backs. Drive for an hour or two, and we'd be up a mountain. You'd be okay, yeah?"

Caleb did pay an embarrassing amount of attention to his current elevation. He hadn't realized Josheb noticed. He simply nodded and peered around.

Hesper's hometown wasn't a big city by any stretch, but they weren't far from a more major metropolis. Close enough for this to count as a suburb. Plenty of people probably commuted from here to there.

Every house on the block had deep front yards with towering trees. Most had several cars lining their driveways, but this *had* to be Hesper's place. Bunches of yellow and gold helium balloons bobbed above the mailbox and along the porch railings, where two handmade banners boldly declared:

BETTER TOGETHER

and

DARE TO BELIEVE

"You made it!" Hesper strolled toward them, smiling broadly. "It wouldn't be much of a viewing party without the guests of honor."

Caleb checked his watch. "We still have a couple of hours before showtime."

"But proper greetings take time." She quirked a brow. "You should know that by now."

Josheb quietly admitted, "There was a little trouble in the paparazzi department."

Hesper's gaze snapped briefly to the street. "Were you harassed?"

"No," Caleb quickly assured. "But *he* can't say no to his admirers. He was signing autographs and posing for group selfies for nearly an hour."

"Free promotion!" argued Josheb. "And that's good for everyone, yeah?"

"In the long view," Hesper conceded. "So, how's it feel, getting your international debut?"

Tonight, one of the big networks was kicking off their summer lineup with a special two-hour premiere of *Dare Together*, a new television series starring Josheb and Caleb Dare. Multiple simulcasts would broadcast the show worldwide.

"I'll probably cringe my way through it," admitted Josheb. "I was such a newb when we filmed. My posture will probably be as appalling as my pronunciation. Caleb kept having to correct me, and now we're basically typecast."

Caleb had stepped easily into his televised persona—meticulous, informed, diplomatic, polished. As the straight man of their duo, they often played up his discomfort in the face of all things rugged or reckless. By contrast, Josheb was being portrayed as a garrulous thrill-seeker—fearless, eager, chatty, and enthusiastic. Again, not too far from the truth. Just exaggerated a bit, to make their series more entertaining.

Just then, a stir on the steps drew their attention to half a dozen young women ogling them. The resemblance was strong enough for Caleb to assume they were part of Hesper's family, and he raised his hand in a basic Amaranthine greeting.

"Friends of yours?" inquired Josheb.

"My sisters." Hesper lowered her voice. "We have a betting pool going. See which of us can get you into the barber's chair and make a respectable man of you."

"Not a chance." Josheb smoothed a protective hand over his lengthening beard. "This is part of my image."

"Oh, yes," she drawled. "Very iconic. So what other myths and monsters have you been chasing?"

Caleb hung back, letting Josheb do all the talking.

Tonight, they were airing a heavily revised version of their real-life encounter with bigfoot. Caleb's photographs and drawings had been used, along with reenactments of the earlier campers' panicked retreat and the Dare brothers' investigation. Josheb did most of the on-screen interaction, interviewing Andor with the help of an interpreter. Bringing in Hisoka Twineshaft for that role had been a stroke of genius. Caleb did all the voice-over narration.

"Hey, Caleb!" Hesper had stopped just before the porch steps, waiting for him to catch up. "You won't want to lag. We have two casks of star wine on tap. They were hand-delivered."

"Oaken's here?" asked Josheb.

"I wish." She smoothed a hand over the slight swell of her belly. "The whole clan's in a tizzy, trying to catch the eye of your *other* co-star. After all, it wouldn't be much of a viewing party without bigfoot ... am I right?"

Caleb couldn't believe it. "He left the woods? But he'd never leave the woods. He's a total recluse."

"So were you, once upon a time," teased Josheb.

"Every sow for miles around is angling for his eye, but we're not the reason he's here." Hesper gently nudged Caleb toward the stairs. "You gonna keep him waiting?"

It had been weeks—no, *months*—since they'd filmed the interview that was part of tonight's special. Since then, the brothers Dare had been whisked from place to place, usually with a film crew in tow. Always to some new destination with an air of mystery and a connection to the clans.

So it had been months since Caleb's last taste of star wine.

Weeks and weeks since he'd seen the one who considered him kin.

And more days than he cared to count since he'd felt a star's touch.

"Andor?" And louder, "Andor!"

Before Caleb could draw another breath, he was yanked against a familiar wall of grumbling, growling fur. All of his lessons in Old Amaranthine escaped him. So much for impressing the First of Bears with his studies. But he could be glad. Soaringly, daringly glad.

With a mutter, Andor hooked a claw around the pendant Caleb had been given. It was a personal ward, intended to mask his presence from figments and Amaranthine alike. Andor dragged it over Caleb's head, eyed the stone with obvious disdain, and chucked it over his shoulder.

Caleb leaned to the side to follow its arc and heard the soft thud as it landed in the grass. Because everything else was suddenly as still as a forest when an apex predator was on the prowl.

Nessie trotted over, tail wagging, to retrieve the pendant from the lawn.

But then Andor was dropping a different necklace over Caleb's head. One that incorporated two crystals.

"I know you," Caleb murmured to the clear one with its blushing heart. "But … your ring?"

Andor lifted his hand. He still wore a ring, but the stone was different—pale blue with a decided twinkle. A match in color to the smaller stone on his necklace.

"That's an impressive upgrade." With an admiring look, Hesper added, "It's *very* well done. He's had it tuned to you."

"What's that mean?" asked Josheb.

Hesper was talking, so she must have been answering, but Caleb didn't catch anything she said. Because another voice was nearer, filling the place where songs belonged.

"Andor has been fretful. This will give him some peace."

"Eri?" he whispered.

"Here I am. Here I will always be."

Caleb often knew that Eri was close. Sometimes he even picked out their voice in the nightly chorus. But lullabies and dreams weren't enough. How much he missed the one who'd promised to be his home.

Searching Andor's face, Caleb touched the pendant. "You'll have to explain."

"The pink is for our sake. Touch the stone. Unlock the sky." Eri did try to make their meaning more clear. *"If I sing with this stone in mind, my voice will reach you."*

"We can talk?"

"Call, and I will answer."

Including Andor in his smile, Caleb asked, "And the blue?"

"Tuned to the stone in Andor's ring. He wishes you to know that he can find you, no matter what path you have taken."

A tracer of sorts? Andor's expression was hard to interpret, but his posture was tense. Even rigid.

"This gives you peace?" Caleb checked.

Andor grumbled something and looked away.

"Call, and he will find you. Lost or injured or lonesome, he will reach you with all speed."

"That's a big promise."

"We call it a pact."

Caleb understood enough to ask, "What's my share? There has to be balance."

Eri's laughter was effervescent as star wine. *"Andor was half sure you would flee and certain you would refuse."*

Closing his hand around the pendant, Caleb said, "I live up to my name every once in a while."

Andor offered a satisfied grunt

"What's this? Is our name at stake again? Dares will derring do!" Josheb hooked his arm through Caleb's and greeted Andor before asking, "Are the rumors of star wine on these premises true? I feel certain we should thoroughly investigate the matter!"

Hesper laughed and rattled off a smiling translation.

Andor beckoned them to the house, striding through like he owned the place.

Josheb, who still had Caleb by the arm, leaned in to relay, "Hot tip from another guest about the true identity of Nessie's namesake. Let's add it to the schedule!"

Caleb paused just outside the door to make a note in his field journal, but he did so distractedly. He was honestly more intrigued by the weight of his new pendant and the terms of his new pact. "Are you close?"

"As can be." Eri sounded pleased.

"We'll talk later?"

"Long into the night."

"Will I *see* you?" Caleb wanted to see Eri's face almost as much as he craved star wine. "I was half sure you were a figment of my imagination."

"I am true," promised Eri. *"And I, too, can live up to my name."*

STAR POTENTIAL

Caleb was rarely far from his brother for the rest of the evening, but in some ways, they were worlds apart. When it came down to it, Josheb was still a people person, and Caleb was still a hermit. So while one brother was learning names and coaxing interesting tidbits out of everyone, the other was retreating into corners, hoping for some quiet, ready to go home.

A hazy memory stirred, and his own words came back to him. *"I'm home wherever I can hear the stars."*

With an envious glance at Nessie, who was somehow able to sleep through the din, Caleb found the nearest door and escaped into a warm June night. The wrap-around porch was nearly as crowded as it had been inside, with the Vale family and their friends—all part of the same enclave—milling and mingling.

Caleb was feeling just a tiny bit desperate when Andor caught up to him.

In a familiar gesture, the bear clansman rolled his eyes at the entire doings and lifted his chin toward the lawn.

Nodding gratefully, Caleb shadowed his steps, but hesitated once they were beyond the reach of the party lights. With a sense of déjà vu, he called, "I can't see a thing."

"I will light your way."

"Eri?"

Andor hoisted Caleb up and pointed, presumably into the heights of one of the enormous trees that dominated a lawn that must have taken hours to mow and manicure. Blinking, Caleb tried looking a little to the side. The trick worked. In his periphery, he caught a faint glow, like figment light. "In the tree?" whispered Caleb.

Placing a finger over Caleb's mouth, Andor ... jumped.

It was over too quickly for Caleb to work up a holler. Instead, he swore softly and asked, "How high are we?"

Hands framed his face, and Eri smiled for him. *"Not as high as I like. But higher than you hope."*

"How ...?"

"Save such revelations for a later verse." Eri softly added, *"More time and trust are needed."*

Caleb had to ask. "But you can fly?"

"Not I, who left the sky and cannot return." Eri's wistful tone turned hopeful. *"Unless Andor carries me."*

Andor plucked Eri from their lofty perch and like a second moon, they rose.

"Won't we be seen?" Caleb asked. "You really are lighting our way."

"Hide me."

With a little rearranging, Eri crowded into the cover offered by Andor's vest. Cramped and precarious, they drifted higher. It was quiet, blessedly so after the constant crowding and congratulations. For the first time in his life, Caleb was both out of his comfort zone and comfortable.

"Is it awful that I don't want to tell Josheb about any of this?"

"Is it?"

"We're brothers. We're roommates. We're business partners." Caleb toyed with the crystals on his pendant. "He'd probably keep our secret if I asked him."

"You would rather keep it with him than keep it from him?"

Caleb slowly shook his head. Hadn't Eri said that their friendship would be Caleb's to treasure?

"You wish to remain distinct."

"Yeah." In much the same way Josheb avoided razors in order to keep from being mistaken for his older brother, Caleb wanted to distinguish himself. But in a much more intangible way.

Andor produced his flask. His jaw worked, and he carefully pronounced, "Caleb Jonathan Dare."

"Yes?"

The bear clansman muttered something in Amaranthine.

"Trade with us in the manner of friends. Become part of our balance." Eri's lilting delivery gave their words a certain formality.

We will reveal our hearts because you hide nothing.
We will make our vows because you want peace.
We will tune our song to your soul because it is sweet.
We will accept your path because you chose it.
We will heed your call because you will need us.

Every song his star ever sang had only ever come true, so Caleb believed Eri and accepted Andor. "All right. Yes, please. I'll share your pact."

A pact with the sky. A home close to the stars. A secret worth keeping.

Andor rumbled in a pleased way, looked toward the heavens, and shouted something in his own language.

"He declares his vow before the Maker," Eri reported in reverent tones. *"It is finished. It is done."*

They passed the flask until no drop remained, then Andor bumped Caleb's forehead with his lips and bestowed a final gift. One that was widely considered an honor. One that no human would even think of refusing. Slow and solemn, but also proudly, Andor gave him a secret name.

"Caleb Jonathan Skypact Dare."

THE END

BATHED IN MOONLIGHT

because it can be good to give in to awe

*Juuyu skimmed the listing.
"Seven score. The packs
actually mark time via
140 unique moons?"*

*"It's actually 144 if you
add in the migrating moons.
But who's counting?"*

FUMIKO AND THE FINICKY NESTMATE

LITTLE GIRL LOST

The woods were dark and strange, but they were less frightening than the creaking wagon in which she'd been kept. How she hated the hands that reached through the gaps in the woven cage—pinching her skin and pulling her hair. Strange words had grumbled and groaned on every side, and no matter how she cried, her captors had laughed at her fear and licked it from her skin.

Some knew her words, but that was no comfort. All their promises were terrible. All their whispers were warnings. All they wanted was everything, for they nibbled at her edges and fed her despair.

The farm was gone. Da and Mam were gone. The monsters had left the buildings in flames before taking to the woods … and taking her along.

But tonight, the wind had changed, and the stars whispered. A sly shaft of moonlight crept across the musty furs that were her bed and over the pot they'd provided for her mess, angling until it illuminated her prison door. Had they somehow forgotten to set the latch?

She jiggled and pushed, tumbling free of her cage with a whimper.

But nobody heard, for they were all asleep, probably wrapped in greedy dreams. Nobody followed when she ran into the woods, but they could stir and snarl and sniff her out again.

The moonlight danced ahead of her, silvering a path.

Sometimes, she thought she saw a smiling face.

Once, she was sure a hand pointed the way.

Her bare feet hurt, but she trudged after the moonbeam until—all of a sudden—she broke into the open and stepped into a creek. Cool water slipped around her ankles, soothing her feet and reminding her how thirsty she was.

Every handful she scooped sparkled as she drank.

Light drew her onward, and she stepped onto pine needles, thick as a mat. A little way further, her moonbeam shone upon a stump that was stout as a barrel and just as hollow. Curling up inside, she hid … and hoped.

Maybe it was her imagination, but a lacework of glowing lines twirled through the air, prettier than fireflies and singing softly.

Eyes heavy, soul weary, she slumped against dusty wood and into a beckoning dream.

THE LONE CEDAR

She didn't wake until the sun was high enough to banish every moonbeam. Even hers. But while she slept, she'd dreamed, and in her dream, she'd followed the creek to a branching and continued upstream.

The dream proved true, for it guided her to the smooth, round lake, then along a creek, through a series of linked meadows, to a place where a lone tree stood, bigger around than the strange cottage at its base and tall as the sky itself.

Was it safe?

Should she get closer?

Dare she knock?

She was picking her way across a wide meadow, gaping up at the impossible tree, when she nearly bumped into a man who hadn't been there a moment before. He was terribly tall and strangely dressed, with a crown of tiny pinecones on his head.

"Are you lost, leafling?"

He seemed concerned, and he reached for her.

She hugged herself and stepped back.

"You're hurt. You need help. I can tell." Beckoning with both hands, he backed toward the tree. "This way. Follow me …?"

She held her ground.

He wrung his hands and gentled his tone. "Come, little sprig. I want to show you to my sister. She'll know what to do."

What should she do? She needed help, and he was offering it. The dream had been good, so maybe the tall man was also good? He didn't seem mean. He wasn't trying to touch her. No pinching or plucking. And he didn't seem hungry. They'd all been so hungry.

If anything, he radiated a deep contentment, the kind that came from a full belly.

She shuffled forward.

He looked grateful.

Chatting and coaxing, he lured her closer to the spindly stone cottage, which was at least three, maybe four stories tall. Smoke threaded from a chimney, and a shifting wind carried the half-forgotten scent of bread. Her stomach rumbled.

"Are you hungry?" The man seemed delighted to know it. "My sister loves to bake. She will feed you, leafling. Come, meet Moss."

MEETING MOTHER MOSS

To her despair, the man's sister looked very much like her captors. Pointed ears and strange eyes, with claws like an animal's. But Moss's abundant hair was richly red, just like Mam's, and that hint of home was enough to keep her from bolting straight back out the open door.

"What have you found, Cedar?" Tall and spare, the red-haired lady's eyebrows arched toward a swirled mark that sparkled like a gem at the center of her forehead.

"A girl. She's lost, and she's hungry," said the man. "Could we give her something to eat?"

"What a good idea!" She pulled a chair from the table. "I'll fill a bowl and find a spoon. Sit, girl-child. Rest your feet and calm your heart. You've found your way to a safe place."

Once the lady moved toward the enormous hearth, where a lone kettle steamed over a tiny bit of fire, the girl clambered awkwardly onto the lofty chair. She stayed on her knees, the better to reach the tabletop, and peered around. The house was small, but the ceilings were high and the furnishings were big.

"May I join you?" The tall man tapped his chest. "I'm Cedar. She's Moss."

She nodded. With Cedar close by, she felt safer than she had since ... a long time ago. But what about the lady? Bare feet peeped from under her skirts, and there were claws upon her toes. Moss was like the monsters, but she didn't feel hungry. Like Cedar, she felt like someone who was full of good things.

The lady stirred the contents of a copper kettle and fished muffins from a cloth-covered basket.

A dim memory surfaced. About mealtimes and manners. Mam would've been miffed by how dirty her hands were. "May I wash?" she whispered.

The words barely carried, but the lady heard. "Show her where to go, Cedar."

He stood, backing and beckoning anew, leading her to a large room with deep sinks and water that fell in an endless sluice.

The girl dug her nails into a fat bar of soap and stared all around. Wide windows let in the summer air, which rippled through laundry hanging near the rafters. Corded wood lined one wall, and a female turkey wandered through an open door, scratching and pecking her way across the floor.

Outside was more of that big, wide meadow, with grasses cropped short. She had a vague memory of pastures and spotted horses, but the only thing grazing under the giant tree was a cow.

"She's called Best," said Cedar. "She's very gentle."

"What about her?" she asked, pointing at the turkey.

"Calliope." He quietly pointed out, "All of us have names, here."

She nodded and held her hands under the small waterfall in the corner.

"Even the stream," Cedar continued. "It's known as the Queen's Footpath."

She nodded again and checked her hands. They were better. Good enough.

"What about you?" asked Cedar. "Do you have a name?"

"I don't remember." The monsters hadn't been the sort to tell her things or to give her things. They were taking, taking, always taking. And their word for her wasn't anything like a name. It was a sneer and a slight and a threat all wrapped into one, yet it was the only thing she could offer. "They just called me Morsel."

SEVEN SCORE MOONS

"That's … not nice," said Cedar, who looked ready to cry.

She made up her mind then, not to tell. This tall man was too good for bad things. She could keep him safe. So she walked right up to him and showed her hands. "Am I clean enough?"

With tentative fingertips, he touched her palms. "Are you hungry?"

From the other room, Moss called, "She's starving, Brother. Help me feed her."

This time, *she* led the way, beckoning for Cedar to follow.

He did, though he went to Moss first and hugged her close. "Did you hear?"

"I did, indeed. And we must do something about it." Wriggling free, the lady set a steaming mug next to the bowl already waiting at the table. "A good meal is a good place to begin, I always say."

Returning to his chair, Cedar confided, "She really *does* say that. I think it must be true."

The girl slowly reached for the spoon waiting beside her bowl.

How long since she ate with anything other than fingers?

"Go ahead and eat your fill, my sweet," said the lady. "Don't mind me. I'll just be mixing a bit of this and that over here."

Cedar pushed the little plate of muffins closer to her. Then the butter crock.

Reassured on both fronts, she scooped until she'd scraped the bowl clean.

"More?" he asked.

Moss promised, "Plenty more."

So she ate another bowlful and felt heavy and sleepy and safe.

The lady crossed to the far wall, which seemed to be a strange sort of cabinet full of drawers, every one of them a little square. And in the center of each square, there was a round knob. Not one knob looked the same as its neighbors, except that they were all perfectly round, about the size of a walnut. They caught the light, shining or sparkling or glowing in a range of subtle colors.

Touching one, Moss asked, "Henloo-dex is near, is she not?"

"Near enough."

"I'll fetch her nearer, and we'll see what she makes of the trail. But I'm thinking our girl needs a name."

Our girl? That had a nice sound to it.

Cedar asked, "If we name her, do we get to keep her?"

"I don't think she belongs to us, but I do think she belongs here." Folding her hands over an apron that had eleven pockets, Moss nodded to herself. "What do you say, Brother? Shall we let the moon name her?"

"That *is* how it's done in these parts." He inclined his head to the girl and promised, "It really is, and it's very nice."

"The moon gives names?" she asked, remembering the guiding dance of moonlight through the forest.

"It's more that the packs take their names from the moon. Wolves, my sweet. They do love her and her many maidens."

The monsters had sometimes been grasping people, but sometimes they'd change into scrabbling animals. She didn't remember a wolf among their number, but she had a vague idea—from before—that wolves were to be feared.

Although she wasn't sure she wanted to know, she asked, "Are you a wolf?"

"No, but they're our friends and our protectors. This place is sacred to them, so they keep it safe. And so *you* are safe."

Cedar leaned closer to confide, "Sister is a squirrel, and I am her tree."

She glanced at the lady, who gravely curtsied. "That's the way of things in places such as this. Now! Do you know the name of the moon that is currently on the rise?"

"Oh," murmured Cedar, who clearly knew the answer. And liked it.

"Moons have names?"

"They do in wolvish." Gesturing to her cabinet, Moss explained, "This is our calendar of the Seven Score Moons. Each has a name, and every wolf knows them and sings them true. And *sometimes*, they are named for them."

She was confused, but in an interested way. "How many are there?"

"One-hundred forty is the usual reckoning, but there are a fair few special moons—migrating and maiden and blue. All of them are accounted for here—the Grand Cycle." Moss touched a stone knob here and there, seemingly at random, yet she gave each a name. "Marrow. Tinder. Portent. Fallow."

"You know all their names?"

"I learned them from our friends, and I can teach them to you." Tapping a pinkish stone, Moss said, "You could take the name of this month's moon. I daresay it suits you."

She didn't mind. Mostly. *Anything* would be better than Morsel, but she didn't think she wanted a name like Portent or Marrow. But Cedar was smiling and nodding and enormously pleased, so she simply asked, "What's my name?"

"Pippin."

THERE'S ONLY ME

Pippin hadn't realized she'd fallen asleep on Cedar's lap until he was patting her cheek and calling her softly by her moon name.

"Sister is back," he said. "She brought Henloo."

Another lady was in the room, crouched by the door, showing her palms and swishing a luxuriant tail. Her sun-browned face was stern, and her hair—and fur—were a dark gold.

Moss said, "Henloo is one of the wolves who keeps us safe. She's a friend."

"Hello," Pippin offered, since it seemed to be expected.

The wolf's features softened, and she asked, "May I approach?"

Pippin leaned more firmly into Cedar, but she nodded.

When Henloo stood, she was easily as tall as Cedar. Pippin might have been afraid, if not for Moss's calm and Cedar's cradling embrace. The wolf lady dropped to one knee, making it much easier for Pippin to see the orange stones and polished bones that were knotted into her many necklaces.

"I am Henloo-dex Deepnight, and I was born on a summer evening while the Candle Moon waxed toward full. In wolvish, my name means 'lantern festival,' for my pack celebrated my arrival for ten full nights afterward."

"Deepnights do tend toward merriment," Moss said in teasing tones.

Henloo chuckled. "Call us *rowdy* and be done. It's only the truth."

Cedar softly repeated, "She's a friend. Our friend."

The lady wolf inclined her head, then asked, "May I know your name, pretty one?"

And because Henloo's name had come with a story, Pippin decided to tell hers. "The wind woke me, and the moon set me free and guided me here. My name got lost, so Mother Moss let the moon choose a new one. I'm Pippin now."

The adults traded looks, and Henloo sighed. "May I touch, Pippin?"

"Wh-why?"

Tucking her hands behind her back, the wolf said, "At the very least, may I learn the scents you carry?"

"Why?" she repeated in an even smaller voice.

"I'm a tracker, and your captors shall be my prey. Were there others like you?"

Pippin wasn't sure if she meant in the cage ... or before. Either way, there was no one left to rescue. "Only me."

"That's a mercy, I suppose." Her gaze was old, her voice gentle. "Can you tell me anything about them?"

There was much she could tell.

Henloo expanded on her question. "How they looked? What they said? How many of them there were?"

Pippin clung to her resolve. "I don't want Uncle Cedar to hear."

"What if we were to speak privately. You and I?" Henloo placed a hand over her heart. "I was born in the dark, and I am strong enough to face its secrets."

"How about this?" Mother Moss brought a shining stone from one of her apron pockets. "This is a stone for secrets. If you hold it between your hands, nothing can be overheard. Even by Cedar."

Moss coaxed her brother to come away, leaving Pippin in Henloo's company. The wolf lady didn't curl her clawed fingers around Pippin's small, pale hand. Instead she cradled it—and the crystal—between both her own.

"Give shape to my understanding. Give purpose to my hunt."

So Pippin unburdened herself. All the things she'd seen. All the things done. Sometimes, she would shy away from something that was hard to say, but Henloo seemed to know. Her questions grew simpler, so that Pippin only needed to nod or shake her head. And when the worst was out and the crying began, Henloo gathered her close and gave her a promise.

"My pack will find the scoundrels who wronged you. We'll make certain no other bright soul is caught and kept. And if you like, we can try to get word to your kin …?"

But Pippin shook her head. "There's only me. And this is where I want to be."

DOWN THE DRAIN

After the wolf sniffed her thoroughly and promised to return with a report, Mother Moss decreed it time for a proper bath. As it happened, the big sinks in her kitchen were plenty large enough for a girl Pippin's size.

While the lady squirrel stole the pitiful rags that were Pippin's only clothes, there was a fair amount of sniffing. "Are you a tracker, too?"

"Trickster, my sweet." With a faint smile, Mother Moss said, "You make me several kinds of curious."

"I do?"

"Nobody is supposed to be able to find this Circle. Or Cedar for that matter. Yet you strolled past all our little safeguards, easy as you please."

"A lady made of moonlight showed me in a dream."

"Did she now? I like her more and more." Mother Moss sounded like she believed her. "Do you know how many years you have?"

"Seven ...?" Had her birthday come and gone since she was taken? "Could be eight, by now."

Mother Moss hummed and handed her a lathered square of cloth. "Let me find a soft brush for your feet."

There was much soaking and scrubbing, while Cedar hovered on the periphery, trying to watch over them without looking. And jumping to do any of the little tasks Mother Moss asked of him. Twice, they changed the water. It was good, watching the filth drain away.

Under the grime, Pippin found freckles on her arms. Hers were lighter than those strewn across Mother Moss's skin, but they weren't all that different. Red hair and freckles had always meant family.

"Will you let Cedar wash your hair?" Mother Moss casually spread her fingers, bringing attention to her claws. "His nails are less sharp, and he'll be pleased to be asked."

"Uncle Cedar?" Pippin called.

He brightened. "You don't mind? I'll be gentle."

"We need you," Mother Moss assured, handing over a wide-toothed comb carved from wood. "You're more patient with tangles."

"Sister does not get them so much anymore, but I remember what to do."

Pippin sank to her shoulders in the water, watching Mother Moss bustle about the kitchen while Cedar coaxed the comb through her matted mess.

"Your hair is almost the same color as Sister's," Cedar remarked, all admiring. And to Moss, "We look like a family, don't we?"

It was so close to what Pippin had been thinking. It was so nice to hear.

"Oh! Oh, leafling," murmured Cedar. "Oh, fronds!"

Moss stopped what she was doing, covered in flour right to her elbows. "What is it, Brother?"

He gently patted Pippin's head and said, "She *smiled*."

It had taken many, many basins of rinse water and a few strategic snips of Mother Moss's scissors before a comb could pass smoothly through Pippin's clean hair. She hardly recognized herself. A borrowed tunic for a dress. Thick socks to protect her freshly bandaged feet. Yet she felt more like herself.

Cedar carried her outside to meet the turkeys and the cow. In the afternoon sun, Pippin's damp ringlets slowly dried and tightened into curls, and Cedar coaxed them into a soft billow that floated around Pippin's shoulders.

Peering up at the tree, she asked, "What is that? Way up there?"

"Did you see an owl?" he asked.

"No. It looks like a box."

"Oh! That's a *room*. I have many rooms." He proudly revealed, "Sister runs an inn."

GOLDEN CEDAR CONE

They watched the sky turn colors and the evening stars shine faintly through the blue. Pippin was clean and full and safe and sleepy.

She was grateful that she didn't have to ascend the vast tree in order to find a bed. Mother Moss had readied a snug room in the little house, right at the top, up under the eaves. One whole wall was made from chimney stones. On the opposite wall, the shutters swung wide on an east-facing window.

Mother Moss tucked her in.

Uncle Cedar held her hand.

Pippin asked, "Will I learn the names of every moon?"

"We can teach you," Moss promised.

"Us and the wolves," Cedar added. "They're often here."

Mother Moss told a bedtime story about a redheaded girl who ran away from everyone she knew, carrying nothing but a golden cone in her hand. She was brave, but also foolish. Prone to tangled hair and fond of muffins. And when she was sure that she'd scampered farther than any squirrel ever had before, she stumbled into trouble and had to be rescued by wolves.

"Was the girl frightened?" Pippin asked.

"She was only afraid to be alone, so she was glad to have found friends among the packs."

"Did they bring her to this tree?"

"No." Mother Moss smiled softly at her brother. "They brought her to this Circle, which was empty then. And at its very center, she planted her golden cone."

"And he grew tall and straight, and she named him Cedar," said Cedar.

"A brother for a sister, and a sister for a brother," said Mother Moss. "They grew together in a safe place, where another runaway girl would find them."

Cedar asked, "Did she have red hair, too?"

"Red as little red apples," confirmed Mother Moss.

"And freckles?" he asked.

"Like a thousand golden kisses upon her face."

"And ... she wasn't alone anymore?"

"A brother for an uncle, and a sister for a mother," said Mother Moss. "A new name, and every reason to be brave."

Pippin winked and blinked sleepily. "But no golden cone?"

Mother Moss dipped into an apron pocket and brought out the same shining stone from before. It was dark amber and almost the same size as the cones in Cedar's crown. With a wink and a waving of hands, Mother Moss turned it into a golden cone.

"You changed it?"

"I reimagined it. Just one of my little tricks." She placed the stone in Pippin's hand. "Perhaps during the next Song Circle, I can find an artisan to give your crystal this shape."

"*My* crystal?" Pippin asked shyly.

"My girl?" countered Mother Moss, just as softly.

Pippin nodded, and it felt as if they'd made a good trade.

EAST FACING WINDOW

When Pippin woke in the night, Cedar was no longer in the chair beside her bed. She'd fallen asleep holding his hand. To keep away bad dreams, he'd said. She lay for a little while, listening to the crickets, their summer song carried on the warm breezes puffing though the open window. But an unusual amount of light shone into her little room, pale and pretty.

Turning her head, she saw the lady from her dream.

Pippin sat up and passed a hand across her eyes. "Am I dreaming again?" she mumbled.

The lady laughed softly and beckoned with curling fingers.

Sliding from under her coverlet, Pippin tiptoed to the window and reached past the sill, wanting to see if her lady was real.

Her skin was luminous, and she was mostly bare, with a misty sort of light wreathing her body, as if she were draped in moonbeams. Silver hair rippled to her hips, and her eyes were silvery as well.

A slim hand reached back, and their fingers hooked together.

"Are you the moon?" Pippin whispered.

Soft and smooth, the lady replied, "What if I am?"

"I would believe you." And because it really needed to be said, Pippin added, "You're very beautiful."

The lady drew closer and caressed Pippin's red curls. "And you are entirely captivating."

"Did you save me?"

"I meddled a little." She put a finger to her lips and whispered, "I am not supposed to, but I could not leave you in danger."

"Thank you."

The lady folded her hands over her heart. "I am grateful to find you safe. This place is a far better setting for a soul such as yours."

Pippin showed off her new stone, which Mother Moss had promised to string upon a ribbon for her to wear. "I have a family again."

"Tell me."

Shining hands folded around hers, and Pippin wondered if that meant her stone was keeping their secrets. She told about Uncle Cedar and about Mother Moss. About the wolves and the turkeys and about the big kitchen with its deep sinks and about the tall tree that was also an inn.

The lady smiled. "Will you stay?"

"I want to. I will." Pippin asked, "Do you want to stay, too? Uncle Cedar says there are lots of rooms."

"I cannot stay, but … may I be selfish?"

Pippin was sure she owed this lovely person her life. "What do you want?"

She glanced over her shoulder, up into the sky. Then she whispered, "Do not forget me?"

Such a thing seemed impossible. But maybe this was the sort of memory that could fade if you let it. Like a dream that grows fuzzy at the edges. Pippin said, "I can't forget you if you visit."

The lady's eyes widened a little, then softened a lot. "Would you welcome my return?"

"Yes."

"Shall the midsummer moon be our marker?"

Pippin wasn't sure. "I only started to learn about moons. They called me Pippin for this one."

"Is that so?" And mostly to herself, she repeated, "Pippin."

"Will you only come once a year?" That wasn't very often, but it would give her time to learn the names of all the moons.

"I will grant you a full cycle of moons, with this circle and this stone for witnesses. Will you watch for my coming?"

"Midsummer," Pippin repeated.

"And will you keep my coming a secret?"

"Even from Mother Moss and Uncle Cedar?" Pippin didn't want to lie to her new family.

The lady smiled a secretive smile. "They will know that you are mine."

"How?"

"There are ways," she replied, looking Pippin up and down.

"Like what?"

"Like this." And the silvery woman took Pippin's other hand, turned it, and placed a kiss upon her palm.

TWELVE YEARS LATER

Rinloo-dex Highwind finished his pad around the perimeter and spiraled back toward the borrowed den where the greater share of their allotment had gone deep. The sun was lowering. It'd soon be his turn to watch over the sleepers, freeing Ninook from his post.

Though they'd only arrived a scant handful of days ago, this was familiar territory for most of them. Every dex on this continent learned this Song Circle's territory and served as its guard from time to time. Well ... every *wolvish* dex.

Ninook-dex Trebellaire was an old hand at this. Although he had the years, he'd ceded the lead to Rinloo. A sensible decision, should there be trouble. Rin's boldness and aptitude with blades outstripped those of his companions, with the possible exception of young Laud. Rin was glad of the lad's solemn presence, even though it'd meant bending a few rules to smuggle him in.

Cedar came into view, and Rin breathed deeply.

This was only his third visit to the Queen's Circle, and he hoped he'd never lose his sense of awe. This place was rare beyond knowing, graced as it was by a fabled tree. Cedar was enormous, a veritable pillar of the world, and such a grateful host. All who'd met palms with the gentle Impression would have fought to keep him safe.

Truth be told, Rin would gladly take on an entire horde if it meant keeping Moss's bread oven intact. Her penchant for pastry was both a treasure and a trap. Rin would have stayed on indefinitely if it meant a never-ending supply of her baking.

On a whim, Rin took the stairs that spiraled their way up Cedar's considerable girth. They hadn't been here the first time he'd pulled guard service, and there had been other additions since his last visit.

Platforms.

Porches.

Ladders.

Walkways.

All built for the sake of Cedar's and Moss's fosterling.

Rin climbed to the room Beloor had taken for a den. This high up, the air was cooler and the sky wider, giving a fine view of its expanse. Ninook sat just outside a fur-draped door, a soft smile on his face as he gazed at the sky.

"Ready for a romp?"

Ninook's light brown tail thumped. "Welcome back. Anything?"

"Peace abounds," he assured. "The only thing getting past Moss's barriers are Ephemera, and that is surely by design."

Standing and stretching, Ninook's tail swayed in a peaceful arc. "All is as it should be. Provided you ate …?"

"I'd hardly hunt these woods. Most of the critters hereabouts are probably pets."

It wasn't a lie. It wasn't the whole truth.

Alas, Ninook was wretchedly wise. Perhaps it came with being a parent? Unlike most dex, the Trebellaire tribute had become bondmate to a she-wolf of the Elderbough pack. Ninook doted on their cubs with understandable delight.

"I'll hunt for you, if you need the meat," offered Ninook.

Rin grimaced. "I'll keep that in mind."

Stepping closer, Ninook softly challenged, "I can't match my provision to your preferences if you don't make them clear."

He huffed and admitted, "Ever since my first taste, I've always craved Moss's cooking."

It was embarrassing for a wolf of his stature and skills to favor such *tame* food. Yet he rarely hunted anymore. Might have even lost the taste for killing. He hated the tang of fear on the air, hated inspiring it.

All Ninook said before dropping away was, "I'll ask Moss to send up a tray."

Rin stood with head bowed and tail tucked.

"Sister's food is good." Cedar pulled him into a gentle embrace. "Pippin is almost here, and you must eat. I know you're hungry."

"Is there bread?" Rin asked.

"Two fat loaves. And a pie," promised the tree.

He could already smell it and smiled. "I love it here."

"Stay."

Rinloo laughed and wished it were that easy. But none of the duties given to tributes involved lolling in hammocks and taking dinner on trays. "I'm glad to know I'd be welcome."

"Here's my girl," crooned Cedar.

Turning, Rin blinked. It had only been six years, but humans skimmed through their adolescence with a speed that still startled him. "Is that you, Pippin?"

"Welcome back, Rinloo. Uncle Cedar, could you fetch the basin? I couldn't carry both."

The tree vanished, only to pop back with a basin of steaming water. "This one?"

"Yes, please. Set it on the stand in front of the window."

While Cedar complied, Rin asked, "Why not let him carry all the trays? It would spare you the climb."

"Oh, I'm used to it." The young woman's cheeks were pink, but she wasn't out of breath. "And how else would I check in on our guests?"

"You wanted to see me?"

"Don't sound so surprised." Her blue eyes sparkled. "How else am I supposed to get any news."

He stole the tray from her and settled cross-legged on the room's shallow porch. "So any guest will do, provided they've time to chat?"

"You and Ninook are the only ones who are here early … and awake."

Realizing Cedar was taking his sweet time, Rin leaned back and poked his head past the door covering. "Cedar's gone," he reported.

"Mother Moss has him running all sorts of errands. Both for the Queen's Festival and for your friends. Uncle Cedar says they'll be waking soon, so Mother Moss is preparing a feast."

Rin hummed around a huge bite of a pie that involved custard and crumble. Dessert first. It was a way of life he could only embrace here.

"Will you sleep next?"

"That's the idea." Truth be told, once his belly was full, it'd be hard to stay awake. "Gotta be fresh for the festival."

That's when something caught his eye.

Setting aside his pastry, Rin beckoned. "Show me your hands."

She only hesitated a moment before presenting her palms, as if in greeting. "Not everyone can see them," she mumbled.

He could.

During his last visit, he'd remarked upon the silvery filigree on her right palm, only to confuse everyone else in his group. Now, Pippin had a complementary mark on the left palm, more delicate and varied than any sigil he'd ever seen.

"A matched set?" he asked.

"Yes." Her tone didn't invite more in the way of curiosity.

Rin asked anyhow. "Still a secret?"

"Part of a vow."

He raised his hands. Tributes knew all about vows, and in a place like this, there was little wonder that Pippin had found her way into some kind of pledge.

"Are you okay alone?" Pippin asked.

It took him a moment to recall what they'd been talking about. "For my long sleep? Certainly. I'm a lone wolf, sweetest of pips."

She wrinkled her freckled nose. "You *want* to be alone?"

Rinloo smiled so she wouldn't worry and gently promised, "I'm alone by choice. Or some will say … set apart for a different purpose. It doesn't mean I'm lonesome."

"Are you, umm, waiting for someone?" she asked.

He wasn't—not really—even though Ninook and Beloor were prime examples that a dex *could* become someone's choice. But Rin rarely trod the kinds of paths that might bring him to a she-wolf's attention. And he wasn't likely to be singled out to foster a cub.

Too carefree. Too casual.

Too much a drifter. Too fond of humans.

Too tame.

"Rinloo?" Pippin asked, calling his attention back.

With a small shake of his head, Rin said, "I've taken a different path than most choose. Who can say if another will ever walk it with me?"

She nodded thoughtfully and said, "This month is a maiden moon, you know."

"I did know." It was the primary reason he and the other dexes were here. "This is one of the rarest festivals. Wolves will come from all over."

Pippin waved that off as if it were inconsequential. "Why don't *you* take part?"

"I'm part of the boundary patrol. If I sing for the maiden moon, it'll be in snatches, mostly under my breath, and at a great distance from the Song Circle."

"Maybe so, but they get around."

He shook his head.

"Moon maidens," she clarified. "You're *nice* Rinloo. Maybe one will want you to keep her."

THE UNHAPPY MAID

Bad luck was to blame. Or perhaps the Moon was being petty? Tripping the latch on the midivar cage had been an accident. And it was only natural that the Ephemera scattered. Who'd want to be stuck in a cage? Their spiraling escape had glittered like a thousand rare stones, a sight to behold. A sight that had been intended for the finale of the Queen's Festival.

So when the lots were cast and Char's name was called, the demotion was no surprise to anyone in the Luminous Court.

Maid.

Char hadn't thought it possible to sink any lower than drudging with the gardeners. How many phases had seen him toting water and tipping prescribed measures onto the roots of every serenity vine and rillberry bush?

But this? This was worse.

It wasn't that the work was difficult. For the most part, maids handled dusting, sweeping, scrubbing, and polishing. Endlessly. But a gardener's duties were all outside, surrounded by blooming things and diverting creatures, while maids were closed up indoors. As far as Char was concerned, he'd been confined to a cage.

A pair of maids passed below the stone staircase he'd been assigned to wipe.

Heads together, they were twittering over the lots for the Queen's Festival. And what sort of wolves they'd try to attract, given half a chance. Char couldn't understand the appeal, though he'd tried for his sister's sake. Seela had loved the whole idea of them.

Wolves were always heroic in maiden tales. So loyal, so devoted, so amazed to catch glimpses that were rare by design. Only on certain moons, the agreed upon ones, did the gates between their lands open. The wolves honored the Seven Score Moons and gathered for high moons and migrating moons and the maiden-tempting moons, always raising their plaintive songs.

Music appreciation wasn't Char's strong point. He liked wolfsong as much as the next moonbeam, for it pulled at the soul. But a wolf could have botched their inflections and skipped a phrase or two, and Char couldn't have cared less.

Other things were more important. For him, there were three—blue pebbles, sweet foods, and most especially dancing. As far as Char was concerned, moonlight was made to dance upon water.

That had been the only part of being a gardener that he'd cared about, dancing upon the rippling surface of the water, deep in the well, where there were just enough shadows to encourage a little sparkle. But he'd been scolded for playing. And banished indoors.

Granted, there were more shadows here, but there wasn't much room to dance in a bucket. And soap bubbles were the worst kind of dampener.

Yes, this was the worst, and Seela would have agreed with him. Seela who had loved wolves for being big and strong and dark and wild. Seela who had always been far luckier with lots. Seela who was no longer part of the Queen's court.

Shining tears struck the stone where Char knelt, clutching a rag, missing his sister.

TEMPTED BY TARTS

Char was getting more used to his duties and knew which ones to save for last. The porches were long and wide and deep, and sweeping them took ages, but they were outside … and they overlooked the kitchen garden where the Luminous Court's wolf was kept.

Seyroo-nim was much adored, for he was tall and broad and brown, which was a truly shocking color until you got used to it.

Not that Char planned to.

Except that Seyroo spent so much time with another of the court's oddities. Theodora was a human of uncertain years who'd been carried away from the Widelands by a bold moonbeam whose match was so admirable, the Queen had granted him a princedom.

Seela had been in awe of Theodora, who baked the most miraculous foods. Sweet cakes with soft crumbs. Creamy tarts with honeyed fruit. Small loaves of warm bread to dip in bumber nectar. Char knew, for he'd peeped through the kitchen door often enough. Seela had lingered there until Theodora gave her an official post, washing dishes while the baker kneaded and chatted and laughed.

Theodora had shine, and most of it was for her prince. But Char thought a little of it went into her baking. Why else would it be so difficult to resist? If he could find a human woman half so lovely, he might try carrying her home. Maybe then, the Moon would look on him with more favor. Or even make him a prince.

Some did go questing. At least, that's what the stories said.

Those who had nothing—and Char qualified there—would go in search of courting gifts. He was a bit vague on what those were meant to be. Perhaps blue pebbles? But if keeping a girl meant giving up hard-won pebbles, Char thought he might rather keep his bits of blue.

Maybe instead of questing for a princedom, Char should search for his sister. Seela, who'd earned a spot in the Queen's entourage. Seela, who'd attended a maiden-tempting festival. Seela, who must have been wooed by songs and drawn into some wolf's shadow.

"That you, Char?" hailed a voice from below.

He flinched at Seyroo's call and ducked out of sight.

Feet landed lightly on the wide porch railing. "You all right? Seems so. Don't be shy, little lad."

This was yet another reason Char didn't like wolves. If you weren't a friend, they were all raised hackles and low growls, but if they decided to be friendly, they were impossible. Seyroo had been fond of Seela, and now that she was gone, he was fussing over Char instead.

And ... it hurt.

Seyroo with his pitying gaze. Seyroo with his swishing tail. Seyroo who had tempted a moonbeam.

Long ago, this big, brown wolf had taken part in a festival and won the heart of a maiden from the Luminous Court. To test the wolf's resolve, the Moon had imposed a difficult task. To leave the packs, becoming a lone wolf. All so he would understand the loneliness he would ask of the maiden he favored.

So romantic. Or so the maidens claimed.

So noble. Because giving something up had always been a part of getting something new.

Everyone said that Seyroo had accepted the Moon's demands and become a wanderer in the Widelands. He'd brought gifts and given pledges at the appointed times, and all his songs were for her. And when the cycle of moons was complete, the Moon was satisfied. But instead of whisking his beloved from the sky, Seyroo had offered to take to it. He'd been a part—albeit a strange part—of the Luminous Court ever since.

Seyroo was all right. He was quite famous through all the districts, and he was probably part of the reason all the moon maidens swooned at the idea of binding their soul to a wolf. They *didn't* of course, or the courts would stand empty. Char thought the maidens were silly to wish themselves away. What if Seyroo was the only truly good wolf that ever was? Whoever had taken Seela hadn't undergone any courtship Char had ever heard about.

Even so, the maidens always wanted to see the Wideland wolves for themselves. Lots were cast, and those chosen joined the Queen's entourage. They'd leave the Luminous Court in order to see a wolvish festival. Most simply came home again. Seela had not.

Not for the first time, Char wished that whatever wolf had carried her off had been less selfish. If they'd been more like Seyroo—if they'd left the Widelands as he'd done—then Char would be less lonesome.

"Char. Are you listening?"

He looked up and shook his head.

Seyroo huffed and reached for him.

Char ducked away from his clawed hand.

"All right, all right." The wolf gestured his surrender. "But listen up, lad. Because I've got to get back. A friend of mine is here for a visit. Come, hear his tales. And have an extra share of these."

The wolf pointed.

Char rose enough to peep over the rail's edge. A single, perfect rillberry tart glistened upon a plate. The same blue plate Theodora always gave him when slipping Seela and Char treats at her table.

Somehow, Char managed a protest. "I do not like wolves."

"Yes, you *do* enjoy making a point of that. But not all of my friends are wolves." Shaggy eyebrows wiggled. "This one's a dragon."

ACCORDING TO TRADITION

Char peeked through the arched entrance into Theodora's kitchen. He'd followed Seyroo this far, but he wasn't sure he should go any further. Not when there were so many lofty personages gathered in her domain.

Theodora's prince was there, as soft-eyed as ever where she was concerned.

And Seyroo's bondmate had been invited, all slight and silvery and smiling.

Which meant the other person at the table was the dragon. He blended in rather well, though his hair was pearly white instead of silver, and his pale skin was rosy with star wine instead of bright with it. Also, he was draped in more cloth than a moonbeam ever wore, even at this phase of the turning.

Theodora, whose voluminous apron covered a simple gown that shimmered with her prince's own affection, came to speak to Char. "I'm glad Seyroo found you. Isn't this exciting?"

Char supposed a dragon's visit was unusual. There were stories about dragons, but as far as he knew, they only ever bothered about winds. So there was probably nothing to fear. Seyroo wouldn't have brought Char into danger. Knowingly. And ... the wolf had called this dragon a friend.

"He asked for you," Theodora murmured.

"Who did?"

"Our guest."

That was strange. "Why me?"

"I wonder." The woman's dimple showed. Like she knew but wasn't telling.

"How would a dragon know about *me*?"

"Oh, I can think of a way or two. But I've always been told I have an active imagination. You should ask him."

Char scowled. He should just go. He'd be scolded again if he didn't finish sweeping. But then he had a daring idea. What if somebody had sent the dragon to check on him? What if it had been Seela? And what if there was a message?

Desperate to find out, Char shuffled out of hiding.

All attention swung his way.

The dragon's eyes were a very pretty blue. "*This* one?" he asked. "Are you quite sure?"

"Who else could your star mean?" asked Seyroo.

"But he's clearly manifesting as male."

"Does that matter?" posed the wolf.

The prince raised a hand. "What were the *exact* words of the lyric?"

"The unhappiest maid in the realm of moons," quoted the dragon.

Seyroo tapped his nose. "It's him. *Definitely* him."

Char was so confused. "Star? What about a star?"

"Where are my manners?" Seyroo beckoned him closer. "Char, this good dragon is Opulence Windlore, widely known as Opal the Sage, a tale-bringer and lore-singer in high demand throughout the Widelands."

"Charmed," said the dragon, whose smile was winsome and wily.

Seyroo went on, "He bore witness to my courtship and sings its story still, which pleased the Moon so much, Opal was given an honorary place in the Luminous Court."

The dragon blinked his pretty eyes and wiggled a bejeweled hand Char's way. "Do not be afraid."

As if he ever would be. Char could be courageous when he wanted.

"Come to me, brave light."

And even though Char had already decided to keep his distance from everybody and everything, he set his hand upon Opal's and blushed.

"Will you sit with us?"

Someone brought a stool, and they crowded Char between the wolf and the dragon. The former kept sliding tarts onto his plate, while the latter launched into a story.

"When Time was young and the Amaranthine were new, before the circles were dreamed of, let alone prepared, the Moon and her entourage never descended into the Widelands. But little by little, the songs of wolves compelled them, and they were drawn into darkness. There, the moonbeams shone brightly. There, they danced upon willing winds. There, they flirted with the sons and daughters of the First Pack."

The dragon's voice was pleasant, and listening was the only thing Char really wanted to do. Aside from eating tarts.

"In season and out, the Moon and her maidens would array themselves in light and linger wherever the songs were sweetest. All knew they must return before dawn, for once the Luminous Gate closed, the way home would vanish.

"Yet it came to pass, on a certain night, that a young maid who had never been brave enough to explore the Wideland skies, let alone dance through them, made a hasty descent. Her pet pitterhind had wandered through the open gate, and she gave chase, even though dawn would soon arrive."

This was news to Char. And distressing. Pitterhinds were popular as pets. Seela had always wanted one, but Char had never been able to catch one for her. He felt bad for the maiden in the story, and he worried for her pet.

"Her chase drew the notice of a fine wolf with copper eyes, who tracked the pitterhind and returned it to her hand. But though his deed was good and well-meant, it was too late. The sky turned pink, and the way home closed."

"Is daylight terrible?" blurted Char. "Does it hurt?"

Opal shook his head. "Daytime was only frightening to the maid because it was new. But her trembling drove the wolf to try to protect her. Coaxing her into his arms, he carried her to his den. And in offering her the customary comforts of the packs, he inadvertently robbed her of the sky."

"Descent," murmured Seyroo.

Char shivered and pitied the moonbeam who'd lost her way home.

"Indeed. By the time the Moon came looking for her missing maid, her descent was accomplished. The copper-eyed wolf vowed to keep her safe, but the Moon fretted and lingered, night after night. The pack tried to make her welcome, and so the first Song Circle was established.

"But by and by, the Moon's worries faded, for the noble wolf took the moon maiden for a bondmate, and she flourished in his den. All the children she carried were born with white fur and copper eyes.

"This turn of events pleased the Moon so much, she prepared a second blessing. To celebrate the happenstance that led to so much happiness, twelve of every kind of Ephemera were gathered up and released into the Widelands. Which is why, to this day, a maiden's descent is accompanied by the release of a fresh bounty of Ephemera."

It was a nice story, and it had lasted until the last tart vanished from the platter. What more could anyone ask? Char was satisfied. And ready to leave. But a staying hand dropped to his shoulder.

Seyroo said, "A fine story, Opal. But wasn't there a point?"

"Hmm? Ah. Yes. There *was* a point." The dragon gazed thoughtfully into his empty glass, then blinked benignly down at Char. "Did you catch it, maid-boy?"

"Keep your pitterhind on a leash?"

"Not … quite."

"Avoid the wolves that roam the Widelands?"

The dragon's brows knit. "Nooo."

"Pink skies are a bad omen?" Char guessed.

Seyroo chuckled. "Even I'm not sure of the point anymore. Spell it out, Sage of Stories."

Opal pouted a little, but he gave an answer. One Char never would have been able to guess. "You *also* released an entire bounty of Ephemera into the Widelands. Or so the stars do say."

Char blushed. "That was an accident."

"Yet according to tradition, a considerable blessing has been bestowed." Opal cheerfully announced, "By rights, you could go fetch yourself a bride."

DRAWN INTO DARKNESS

Char half-expected someone to notice he was shirking his duties and call him back. But whenever anyone looked their way, Opal would cheerfully say, "Don't mind us."

And they lost interest.

Leaving Char alone.

With a dragon.

Opal glanced over his shoulder and called, "Come along, maid-boy."

Char didn't like the nickname any more than he liked Opal's pushiness. He'd already lumped dragons into the same category as Widelands wolves. Clearly, they were trouble, yet Char trailed moodily after this one. "Where are we going?"

"The gates."

Was he supposed to see Opal off? That courtesy should have belonged to Seyroo. "Why?" he asked.

"Because they are *open*."

As the gates to the Luminous Court loomed large, Char could see that they *were* open. Whatever lay beyond them was lost in shadow. It must be night—or nearly so—in the Widelands.

"I cannot compel you to go." Star wine had left Opal in high spirits. "Well. I could, but this choice is yours to make."

"A choice?"

"Yes. A very simple one." And then Opal, who definitely liked to talk, winged off on another lesson. "Are you aware that these gates are a marvel? While they always connect to the Widelands, they do not always open onto the same place. That is why they must remain open for the duration of a festival."

Char nodded. He knew that much. It's how the gate had always been. Linking the Moon and her maidens to the festivals they chose to attend.

"Isn't it early?" The phase wasn't right, Char was sure.

"Shockingly so. Though convenient for my purposes." Opal twirled on the threshold, almost like he was dancing. "I could not have visited otherwise."

"Did you open the gates?"

"I did not."

"Was it Seyroo?"

"Again, no." Opal's eyes sparkled. "Not many have the authority to swing wide these gates."

Char thought that over and shrugged. "It's the Queen's Gate. I thought she was the only one with a key."

"And so *her* choice gives *you* one."

Char glanced suspiciously between the dragon and the gate. "A choice?" he repeated.

"Will you go back? Or will you go forward?"

He was appalled. "You want me to go into the Widelands?"

"Far better to ask, do *you* want to go into the Widelands?"

"Why would I?"

The dragon countered, "Why wouldn't you?"

"There might be wolves."

Opal smiled. "Oh, there will certainly be wolves."

"And I have nothing to offer a bride, even if I wanted one," he reasoned.

"You have yourself." The dragon's tone took on a lilt. "Many find moonbeams alluring."

Char blushed and stared at his feet. "Is Seela in the Widelands?"

"Who might that be?"

"My sister. She went." Char softly added, "She did not return."

"I see." Far gentler than before, Opal said, "I could only guess, and that is no kind of answer."

"Could I trade for *her*? Instead of a bride?"

The dragon blinked and murmured, "Is *that* what this is about?"

Char had no answer.

Opal gazed off, head cocked as if listening to something far away. He seemed troubled, but then his lips quirked. "I have one more thing to impart, maid-boy. If you choose to go forward, I can show you the way to a pretty little lake."

"What is a lake?"

The dragon asked, "You like water, yes?"

"To dance upon it," he admitted.

"A lake is like a basin of water, big as a courtyard. Bigger, even."

Char tiptoed to the verge and whispered, "Where?"

ONE LAST LAP

Rinloo's senses were dragging, but he'd find rest more easily if he pushed himself to the edge of exhaustion. One last lap around the lake. Then he'd rejoin his allotment and let them take their turn watching over his sleep.

He'd always liked this lake, which was located a little above and away from Cedar's circle. It was of similar size and as round as the moon at her fullest, situated as it was in the hollow of a hilltop. On calm nights, like this one, it looked like a chalice of stars.

Which brought star wine to mind. He hoped Moss would set aside a cask for them. She wasn't one to stint, but preparations for the Queen's Festival were consuming all her time and attention. Perhaps if he put a word in with Pippin?

Rin leapt lightly over a tangle of roots, glanced out over the water, and stumbled to a standstill. Had his weariness caught up with him? Because this was the stuff of dreams.

Someone was dancing on the lake. Or ... over it, for their feet never disturbed the surface of the water.

A moonbeam.

She was early.

Which was perhaps the most mundane thought he could have had.

Here was a moon maiden. Something every hot-blooded

young wolf hoped to spy, longed to pursue, wished to keep. Yet many still thought them fables. They were *that* rare.

Slowly crossing to the base of a tree that overhung the lake's edge, Rin wearily lowered himself to the ground, rested his chin on his fist, and gave in to awe.

She was even lovelier than the ballads let on. Dainty and graceful. Wreathed in wisps of light.

Rin allowed himself to pretend that the moonbeam danced for him, which was a foolish notion, really. She wasn't dancing for an audience. Anyone with sense could see that she danced for the joy of it. Because she was made for such things.

The lake sparkled.

The hour lengthened.

The wolf sighed and slipped away, hoping his dreams would be filled with moonlight.

PEEKING IN WINDOWS

Even though it was too soon, Pippin's heart leapt when she caught a bit of shine out of the corner of her eye. So silly. She was still in the kitchen, and these windows looked south. Her lady only ever visited at the east-facing window up in her room. And only during the fullness of the midsummer moon.

But when Pippin turned back to her task, that sparkle returned. And when she glanced up, a shining someone was peeping at her over the sill.

"Good evening," she offered in a quiet voice. Cedar attracted all sorts of Impressions, and most of them were shy.

Silver eyes widened, but the newcomer lingered.

"Are you curious?" she asked. "I don't mind questions."

A slim hand touched the sill. "You are human?"

"Mm-hmm. Are you a star?"

A pert nose wrinkled. "Nothing like that."

"I suppose stars have a bit more gold in their complexion." Pippin went right back to lifting custard cups from their cooling bath, carefully drying them before lining them up on trays that were bound for the icebox. "What then?"

A put-upon sigh.

A second hand upon the sill.

But before the shining boy—she was quite sure he was a boy— could say anything more, he was interrupted.

"This is a moonbeam, leafling," said Cedar. And to the boy, "Would you like a spoon? You look hungry."

The boy squeaked in alarm.

In soothing tones, Cedar said, "Pippin, bring a spoon. I believe he wants a custard."

"Wh-where did you come from?" quavered the moonbeam. "You were *not* here a moment ago."

"I've been here for *ages*. See? You're sheltering under me, even now."

"My name is Pippin. He's Uncle Cedar." She set a custard cup on the sill and offered the boy a dainty silver spoon. "Do you have a name?"

He looked warily between them, then plucked the spoon from her fingers and claimed his treat. "Char."

"Are you here for the Queen's Festival?"

Seated in midair, the boy sniffed at his pudding. "I came for the lake."

"Is there something special about our lake?" Pippin asked.

"It is *perfect*," asserted Char, whose first tiny taste was followed by a bigger spoonful.

"And what makes it perfect?" she prompted.

He hesitated, sucking at the spoon. "Me?"

Pippin smiled at that. She'd chatted with other imps—mostly stars or northern lights, the odd fog, and once a rainbow. They were always so sure of their own prettiness. It was one of their charms.

"Are you still hungry?" Cedar asked solicitously. The custard cup was empty.

Char peered around the kitchen and asked, "What smells nice?"

Pippin didn't mind feeding moonbeams at windowsills, but it hardly seemed hospitable. "Do you want to come inside?"

"Are you trying to lure me into a den?" He looked between them suspiciously. "I thought only wolves did that."

"We wouldn't do that," Pippin promised. "I only thought you might be interested. Mother Moss has been turning out the loveliest pastries."

"Show him," urged Cedar.

So she served him a slice of nut tart, a scone studded with candied fruit, and a plate of shortbread. Char nibbled and crooned and mumbled over everything. Not one crumb was left behind.

Pippin giggled. "Don't eat so much that you sink."

He tucked his knees up to this chest and peered warily at the grass. "Opal says if I touch the ground, I will be trapped."

"True," said Cedar. "No ground and no floors, but my branches are safe for resting."

"Maybe later." Char stacked each small plate and the empty custard cup, then carefully balanced his spoon atop them. "But only maybe."

"A friend is always welcome," Pippin replied breezily.

"Friend?" he echoed, clearly perplexed.

Pippin liked this pretty, shining, contrary boy. "We're friends now, aren't we?"

"Maybe." He was frowning as he drifted backward, then turned toward the lake. "But only maybe!"

BASIN OF WATER

Char was dancing when Opal found him again.

"Have you been here all this while?"

"I looked around a little." And because the notion appealed to him, Char asked, "Can the lake be mine? I would choose it."

"Ambitious," the dragon said with a chuckle. "If cool, as brides go."

"But it is *perfect*." Char spun to demonstrate the way light scattered across its surface.

"Alas, I know of no way to abscond with an entire lake." Gesturing back from where he'd come, Opal said, "If you find you need shelter, there is a tree in that direction ...."

"I know. I saw." Char bragged, "He fed me."

The dragon covered his eyes. "You ate from the tree?"

"I ate from the *windowsill*." He proudly added, "With a spoon."

"Well, that is somewhat less disastrous. So you met Cedar?"

"And Pippin."

"Oho? So you *did* find a potential bride."

"Nooo," Char said patiently. "I found a lake."

With a bemused glance at the stars above, Opal said, "I only wanted to warn you that there will be a great many wolves arriving over the next few days. The Queen's Festival is nigh, and I am one of the performers."

"I do not like wolves."

"Yes, I did recall that little detail. Should you plan to linger, I will be hereabouts for the duration of the festival. Find me if you need anything."

Char frowned suspiciously. "Are you trying to make friends?"

"Would that please you?" Opal inquired lightly.

"Maybe," he muttered. "But only maybe."

When the sky began to lighten, Char gave up on dancing in order to watch the water turn silver, then peach and gold, then pale blue. Really, it was too bad that he couldn't keep this lake. He was quite sure he could love it.

Whisking back to the tall tree, Char flitted about its top, then spiraled lower, searching for a place to hide from the sun.

Branches were safe.

Cedar had promised.

But there were other things hidden among the tree's limbs. Boxes and platforms and stairs and nets, most of them empty. The topmost box wasn't. He noticed because there was a basin of water sitting on a table just under a window. It tempted him close enough to see what else was in the room.

A wolf in speaking form sprawled upon a bed of furs.

Char held very still. So did the wolf. Was he asleep?

Slowly, he eased through the window, pausing to dance above the water basin, since it would have been a shame not to.

Still, the wolf slept, and feeling rather daring, Char drifted closer. He panicked when the wolf suddenly breathed more deeply. It might be bad to let a predator catch his scent. But the wolf didn't leap up or snatch at him. If anything, his expression grew more peaceful.

Bolder now, Char reached down and set the tip of one finger upon brown skin.

Warm.

There was a sudden clamor of impressions—dark and wild and strange. Snatching back his hand, Char scowled at the wolf for being so wolvish. He still didn't see the appeal. But then ... a smooth blue stone caught his eye. And another. And *more*!

They were the most wonderful color and polished to a treat. They caught the shine of his happiness, which doubled until the wolf was bathed in moonlight. Yet he didn't stir. Only deepened each breath, as if trying to fill his lungs with shine.

Although he knew he shouldn't, Char lightly touched each stone, hoping to find a loose one. But all of them were bored and looped and knotted into the wolf's decorations. Still, he touched each one again, for they were the nicest blue pebbles he'd ever seen.

Were such things common in the Widelands?

Maybe he should search for some of his own. Ones that weren't attached to a wolf.

ONCE A YEAR

Pippin was often told that when you did something year after year, you gained expertise. That's why Mother Moss's pie crusts were always flakiest and why her custard never curdled. But even after twelve years, Pippin found she was no better at waiting than she'd ever been.

Her moonbeam had kept her promise, returning each year at midsummer, always with some token from her travels. The sky was boundless, and moonlight could fall on any part of the world. And in those far-off places, she found gifts for Pippin.

A silver whistle to call the wind.

A pale stone sphere sparked by rainbow flecks.

A seashell locket in which she'd placed a curl of silver hair.

A cup as small and delicate as an eggshell.

A crystal with a whisper of lavender at its heart.

A droplet of silvered glass suspended on a chain.

Year by year, Pippin stored up each small token. They were her treasures. And year by year, her lady placed another kiss somewhere on Pippin. And with each, she left behind another subtle reminder of her visits. A whisper of silvery filigree, faint upon freckled skin.

A cycle of moons. That was what her lady had promised.

Pippin had accepted it without second thought when she was little, but she'd learned quite a bit about wolves and moons since then. Names. Customs. Songs. Which is why *this* midsummer had her a tiny bit worried. Because it would be the twelfth. And with the twelfth, the cycle of moons would be complete.

One full cycle was all she'd been promised.

It could all be over, yet she didn't want it to end.

The visits. The gifts. The kisses.

Pippin was also worried about the Queen's Festival, for Mother Moss figured they'd be overrun. How was her moonlit friend supposed to reach the east-facing window if Uncle Cedar was surrounded by packs of keen-eyed wolves? What if some eager whelp snatched Pippin's moonbeam for himself?

"Let me take that from you."

Pulled from her thoughts, Pippin smiled at the silver-eyed wolf who leapt to her side. Beloor and his Kith were regular guests and guards.

"Let one of us fetch these up," he gently chided, relieving her of her tray. "Especially since Rinloo chose the highest possible den."

"You're kind to offer." Pippin waved to Beloor's son Joonta, who perched with Laud outside Ninook's room. Joonta looked to be around her own age, though he had to have two centuries, at least. He'd recently come into his attainment and would be recognized during the Queen's Festival. For the occasion, he'd somehow found a way to smuggle in his best friend, even though Laud Starmark was from a dog clan and not a wolf at all.

"I'm looking forward to hearing your songs," she called.

They grinned shyly and dipped their heads. Laud may have been blushing.

She looked to Beloor and whispered, "I've heard them practicing. They'll be a tribute to your den."

"I have every confidence in them," he returned warmly.

Nodding toward the warded den that was higher up the stair, she asked, "Is all well?"

"Rinloo sleeps with a smile."

"And dreams of moonbeams?" she asked. It was an old joke and appropriate to the oncoming festival.

Beloor chuckled, "It is said that those who linger longest in dreams are dancing with moon maidens. If Rinloo sleeps past his due days, we shall tease him for chasing fancies."

"Moon maidens are real, you know."

"So the songs say." With a half-smile, Beloor nodded toward Joonta and Laud, who sat shoulder-to-shoulder. "According to the traditions of the Ambervelte pack, there you see proof."

Pippin shifted her posture to one of puzzlement.

"White wolves," he said, as if that explained everything.

Beloor was a friendly sort, and he'd shared a little about his son, who resembled his bondmate, and about Laud, who'd come to him for training. The boys were kin to each other and looked it. Both had snow-white hair and copper eyes.

"It is said that white wolves have moonlight in their pedigree." He radiated paternal pride. "Those two are a tribute to their dens, to their Maker, and to the fables that fuel our songs."

Pippin wasn't sure if he was trying to keep secrets … or if he really didn't know. But as she descended the long and winding stairs, she whispered the truth to herself. "Moon maidens are real. And moon boys, too."

NIBBLING AT PASTRIES

Char hadn't exactly planned to revisit the girl whose face was kissed by moonlight and freckles. But she reminded him a little of

Theodora, and she was just as generous. And ... there was a silver spoon waiting on her windowsill. Not that he'd been checking. It just happened to catch his eye. Because when he was near enough, it gleamed with a bit of his shine in the twilight.

He stole a peek inside. She was there, and she seemed to be alone. "Is this for me?"

"You came back!"

She carried over a wonderous domed confection that was thick, rich, and honey-sweet. Theodora never made these, and he wondered why not. It was blissful.

"Do moonbeams sing?" asked Pippen.

"I *dance*," he corrected.

"You were humming just now. It was a happy sound."

Char knew this was impossible and scowled for all he was worth. "I am not happy."

She nodded, but it was a dutiful sort of nod. Like she was agreeing to be polite. He had half a mind to tell her that his unhappiness had been foretold by stars to a dragon. Or something.

All of a sudden, someone else burst into the kitchen, arms weighed down by woven sacks. With barely a glance his way, she asked, "Who's this, hanging about, my sweet?"

Char may have been trying to hide behind his spoon.

"My new friend." Pippin blithely added, "Char loves your baking, Mother Moss."

"You have excellent taste in friends." Sliding her burden onto the worktable, the lady dusted her hands before showing them to Char. "Consider yourself at home for as long as you linger."

She had claws. She might be a wolf!

"You will not chase me?" he challenged.

Moss asked, "Why would I do that?"

"Because I shine …?" Thinking back to what Opal had said, he added, "I have allure."

"You are definitely a bright spot in my evening, but I have Pippin, who shines in her own way." Rolling her eyes toward the door, Moss said, "And I have Cedar. Much as he has me."

Right then, Cedar rambled into the room, leading a familiar figure. "Look, Sister. Here is our old friend Opal."

Char blurted, "They know you?"

The dragon struck a pose. "That is what it means to be *famous*."

"They know *me*," he mumbled.

"A fair beginning," Opal assured, before turning his attention to Pippin. "And a fair lady …?"

Quickly bored with all their niceties, Char darted up and away, for he wanted to dance across the lake again, before the festival wolves spoiled things.

That thought reminded him of the sleeping wolf high in Cedar's branches. Changing course, he wove his way higher.

The window remained open, and Char flitted inside with more confidence this time. Staying close to the ceiling, he considered the wolf, who was a little like Seyroo. The brown of him and the big of him. But this wolf's hair and fur were shockingly black.

"I do not like wolves," he announced quietly. "And you are a wolf."

No response. This wolf was certainly a deep sleeper.

"I do like blue pebbles. Where did you find so many?"

A little lower. A little closer.

"I tried to find one, but rocks are tricky. They are almost always on the ground, which I am not supposed to touch. Floors, too. Cedar said so."

Char let his arm hang down. He let one fingertip touch the wolf's cheek. Then two. Then his whole hand. The impressions were back, though the wildness had a sleepy feel to it. It wasn't scary at all.

"Maidens say that love can tame a wolf." He sternly informed this one, "I would much rather tame a pitterhind."

It was nice to have someone to talk to. Seela had been gone so long.

"Have you ever seen one? Pitterhinds are cute, but they are so hard to catch." Char eased a little closer, spoke a little softer. "If I had a wolf, I would make him catch one for Seela."

Not a bad plan, really. But there was a hitch.

"Maybe Seela chose a wolf because he brought her a pitterhind?"

Which gave Char another idea. A daring one.

"If I tamed a wolf like you, could you find Seela for me?" He wondered if it was even possible. "I might like a wolf who could do that. Maybe."

A teardrop landed on the sleeping wolf's cheek. Char quickly, guiltily smoothed it away.

The wolf sniffed and made a soft sound. Was he waking?

Char guessed it was time to leave, in case the wolf suddenly opened his eyes. But he hesitated, because he kind of wanted to know what color the wolf's eyes were. If he'd only stop sleeping all the time, then Char would know.

Without any further warning, the wolf turned his face into Char's palm and breathed deeply.

He snatched his hand back. But waited. Just in case.

However, the wolf slept on. The only change was a small furrow between his shaggy eyebrows.

"I said *maybe*," reminded Char. "Only maybe."

Using a cautious fingertip, he tried to pet away that crease.

"You might be terrible." And because he'd wanted to say it for so long, he added, "I hope whoever took Seela is not terrible. I would not mind being unhappy so much if I knew she was happy."

PLAY OF LIGHT

Rinloo breathed deeply, trying to place a scent, but it wasn't much use. He could tell it was new. It was also lively and close enough to touch. Or had it touched him? Opening his eyes, he blinked at the ceiling, where reflected light played like ripples on water.

The basin under the window must be catching moonlight.

Turning his head to confirm his suspicion, Rin's breath caught.

A slender figure pirouetted over the basin's surface, scattering silvered light. That posture. That abandon. It was *his* moonbeam.

So close, it was possible to make out more details. Chin-length hair, sleek and straight and silver. Delicate points to the ears, and an added shimmer across a pert nose, like luminous freckles.

Nearness brought another detail into unforeseen focus. His moonbeam was male.

Feeling both fortunate and foolish, Rin chuckled.

The moonbeam flailed on the verge of falling, then whirled to face him, silver eyes wide with fear.

"What a lovely way to wake," Rin murmured.

"I almost fell!"

"My apologies, beauty. I didn't mean to interrupt. Continue, if you like."

Rinloo hadn't been aware that moonbeams could glare.

The boy pointed a warning finger. "I will not let you touch me!"

"Peace, beauty. I have no need of moonbeams."

"You will not try to trap me?"

"I won't." Tucking his hands behind his head, Rin solemnly added, "I promise."

The moonbeam took him at his word. Which probably meant they were *both* foolish … and fortunate. Rin had no objections to spending more time in the presence of such miracles.

"Your eyes." The moonbeam drifted closer. "They are silver."

"Is that important?"

He seemed the sort to argue every little point. "It is … familiar."

Rin nodded. "*Your* eyes are silver."

"It is the color eyes are meant to be."

Though he'd never given much thought to appearances before, if the color of his eyes made him trustworthy in an imp's opinion, he was glad. Rin suggested, "Maybe I have moonbeams in my bloodline?"

"But you are a wolf."

"True. But according to many a tale, wolves and moonbeams can find happiness together."

The boy came closer, within arm's reach. "Where did you get your blue stones?"

Rin angled his head to peer at his small collection of necklaces. "These? Different places. Do you like them?"

"They are *perfect*," he breathed.

"Would you like one?"

The moonbeam's scowl was back. "I will not let you trick me."

"I'm the least tricky soul you'll ever meet," promised Rin. "As simple as they come."

"Promise?"

"I already gave my word. How many more times do I have to promise before you believe me?"

He grumpily demanded, "How am I supposed to know? Is there a tradition for it?"

"There are traditions for everything," Rin conceded with increasing amusement. "Come here. I can give some of these to you, and if you hold still, I can do it without touching you."

Rinloo slowly unclasped his hands and sat up, then picked at the knot holding one of his bracelets.

His moonbeam nudged closer, all his attention on the promised treasure.

"Hold out your arm," Rin urged.

With great care, he looped and reknotted the bracelet around a slender wrist. Hooking it with his claw, Rin spun it. "There, now. Five blue stones to call your own."

The boy hugged his arm to his chest and warned, "I will not give them back."

"They're a gift. Entirely yours."

He sighed, eyes soft as he considered his prize. He smiled, though Rinloo didn't think he realized it at all. He brightened, which seemed further proof of the moonbeam's pleasure. And then he remembered Rin.

With a decidedly sulky look and mumbled thanks, he darted out the window without a backward glance.

Rin shook his head and rubbed bemusedly at his cheek, because somewhere between the scowl and the retreat, the little fool had kissed him there. Just a peck. Barely friendly. It probably shouldn't count, even if it *was* really very traditional.

DIFFERENT THAN BEFORE

Pippin was milking Best when a soft tap drew her attention to the window. She'd expected it to be Char, but to her amazement, her lady was at the window.

"You're early!" she managed weakly. And fumbling for anything else to say, she added, "This isn't our usual window."

"True." Her moonbeam's manner was solemn.

"Is something the matter?"

"There is a … a small matter." And with the barest of pouts, she explained, "I made so many plans, only to have them come to nothing. And the only one who can set things right has vanished."

Pippin wasn't sure what was going on. She'd gained fleeting impressions that a moonbeam's life wasn't all flitting through forests and shining through windowpanes. At the very least, she could sympathize with her lady's obvious disappointment. "Sounds like trouble."

"It is! My final gift—*phases* in the making—has scattered to the winds, and I am without recourse."

"A gift?" Pippin dared to ask, "For me?"

"*Yes*, for you. Is this not the twelfth moon?"

"It is." Carefully, she added, "I don't need a present, you know. It's you I look forward to seeing."

With a haughty tilt to her chin, her lady retorted, "There are traditions to uphold. I will not skimp."

"We've made our own traditions, haven't we?"

Her moonbeam reached out, and Pippin hurried to the window, leaning over the sill. She smiled for her lady, hoping to reassure her. Gifts were lovely, and she treasured every one, but she wanted more time together. It would have been nice if the traditions that moonbeams adhered to allowed for more unscheduled moments. Like this one.

Pippin tugged their secret-keeping stone from under her tunic and held it out on her palm. Her lady beckoned, and so she slipped it from around her neck. This was a fairly new trick, and she was curious where the moonbeam had learned it. But their conversations were so brief, and her lady could be so evasive when it came to explanations.

With a kiss, her moonbeam set the crystal aglow, then lofted it so that it spun just over their heads, trailing ribbon ties as it cast its warm light over them.

"Will you tell me your name?" Pippin asked. It was at the top of her list of questions for this year. In part because the exchange of names was considered a bond, and she wanted stronger ones.

Her moonbeam dimpled. "Will you give me one?"

That hadn't occurred to Pippin. "Am I meant to?"

"What do you call me in your heart?"

"Lady." Pippin considered for a moment. "My moonbeam."

"A title. A fact. These are not names."

"I suppose not. I was named for the moon during which I arrived."

"A good moon," her lady murmured, patting Pippin's curls and stroking her cheek.

"I met you during the same moon. We can't both be Pippin."

Her lady hummed in agreement. "We are two who met and do still meet, since my gifts are accepted."

Pippin would have liked to point out that between those brief meetings, they spent far too much time apart. But she'd lived with Amaranthine long enough to know that time flowed differently for them. Maybe her lady didn't notice the months like Pippin did.

As was her custom, the moonbeam began searching out the marks left by past kisses, as if to reassure herself that they remained. They always seemed to shine more brightly when she was near.

Like usual, Pippin stole a lock of moon-pale hair and wound it around her fingers, as if she could tie her lady down, make her stay. But Pippin wouldn't complain. She had too many reasons to be grateful. "So I'll be seeing you twice this year. Maybe more?"

"That is my hope. If I can track down the source of my troubles, we may yet complete our final exchange."

Final. Pippin couldn't be happy about that. She ventured, "There are so many wolves already. Be careful?"

Her lady blinked. "Why?"

"This is a maiden moon. Young wolves will be looking to attract moonbeams like you."

A low laugh. A fond smile. "They might aspire to me, but they cannot acquire me. Have you been worried?"

"Maybe a little." Pippin quietly admitted, "I'd hate for them to take you from me."

Slender arms settled around Pippin's shoulders, and her moonbeam whispered, "Do you know which moon will be in our sky for midsummer?"

Pippin knew the Seven Score Moons by name, but the maiden and migratory moons often earned special nicknames. Nobody had mentioned this one's. "I've only heard it referred to as the midsummer, maiden, or festival moon."

"I named it Tryst." With a light kiss upon Pippin's cheek, the moonbeam slipped free and drifted away. "I may see you sooner and again. Wish me luck."

Even though she was dreading what might be the finish of her connection to this lovely lady, Pippin raised her hand to catch her stone, to wave goodbye. And she softly called, "Good luck!"

UNDER MY PROTECTION

Rinloo couldn't decide which of the whelps looked more uncomfortable. Joonta was like a child on the eve of a festival, all eager fidgets and hopeful glances. Laud was somewhat more stoic, but if he'd had a tail, it would have been puffed double.

"Well?" Rin didn't quite manage to keep the laughter out of his tone. "Did you have something you wanted to ask?"

Joonta blurted, "We think we saw a moon maiden!"

Any urge to smile faded. "Planning to give chase?"

Both boys quickly shifted into submissive stances. "Not really," whined Joonta. "Not when you have ... well, you know ... prior claim?"

Laud bluntly said, "She seems more interested in you."

"I may have met a moonbeam," Rin admitted.

"She was in your den." Joonta's eyes goggled over the importance of this detail.

Rinloo snorted. "I haven't seduced any moon maidens, if that's what you're thinking. He seemed curious. We talked a little. That's all."

"*He*? A male?" Joonta's tail took a disappointed tuck. "*Are* there males?"

Laud shrugged.

"Yes, the moonbeam I met is a young male. I don't think he's a child exactly, but he brims with innocence." Rin casually added, "I'd rather you didn't chase him off."

"Do you mean Char?"

The whelps hurried to relieve Pippin of her burden, but Rin was more interested in the possibility that the young woman knew his moonbeam. "Char?"

"Are you the one who gave him a bracelet? I hope you know how much he treasures it."

Rin was glad to hear it. "You're friends, then?"

"Are *you* giving chase?" blurted Joonta, looking to Rinloo for answers. "She could, couldn't she?"

"Not every moonbeam craves pursuit," muttered Rin.

Pippin laughed. "Char and I are friends. Which is why I was going to put this in the last empty room. Mother Moss agreed not to let it to anyone else, but if you and Char are already friends, maybe ... could I put this in yours, Rinloo?"

"What is this?" asked Joonta.

"My bathtub." Pippin propped her hands on her hips. "Would you be willing to fill it? It would take me several trips …."

"We will!" Joonta promised, dropping away.

"Yes," agreed Laud, following his friend.

Turning to Rin, Pippin asked, "My idea was to give Char a safe haven, since the woods will quickly fill."

He adopted a receptive posture. "I'm willing. If he is."

Pippin raised her voice. "Uncle Cedar, could you let Char know?"

"He knows." The tree was simply there, standing with them on the platform. Cedar pointed toward his trunk. While it wasn't nearly as thick at this height as it was at the base, the girth was more than sufficient to hide the shy shine of a moonbeam in daylight. "Come out," coaxed Cedar.

Char peeked into view. "*Are* we friends? Nobody told me."

Rinloo showed his palms. "We may not have traded names, but you were there when I woke. When a wolf sleeps safely in the presence of another, it's considered a bond."

The moonbeam scowled. "It was a trap?"

"No, beauty. It was trust." Rin rested a hand on his sword hilt and straightened into a dominant posture. "I may be a paltry wolf at best, but my strength is sufficient to keep one churlish moonbeam safe. You may consider yourself under my protection."

SEEING TO COMFORTS

Char hid. And he hated it. Even though the room was open and airy and supplied with a tiny round lake—called a bath—it was like being cooped up in the Queen's castle all over again. Except this time, there were no chores to keep him busy. And … no company. The wolf who'd pledged so boldly to keep him safe was always gone, running wild with the rest of his kind.

"I do not like their noise," he grumbled. "I cannot dance to noise."

"Sister can help." Cedar visited from time to time, usually with a plate of something interesting from the kitchen. "Will you let sister help?"

Dipping a toe into cool water and giving it a swirl, Char muttered, "Maybe."

Moments later, Cedar's sister bustled in, dropping a bundle of cords in the corner and sliding a fresh plate onto the windowsill. "Poor dear," she sighed. "Speak up if you need more than what's been provided."

"I did not ask for anything," he grumbled.

"Yet it is my solemn duty to make sure a guest is as comfortable as they can be."

Char's gaze remained fixed on the little green plate, which held something bread-ish and buttery.

The redhaired lady began plucking at the air, spinning threads of light into pretty patterns that thrummed with startling power. She asked, "Do you like savories as well as sweets?"

"Maybe." Char hugged his knees to his chest. "What are you doing?"

"Giving you some more privacy." She flashed a reassuring smile. "I already made the way to Rinloo's door impossible for any other wolf to find. Now, I'll turn down their racket, as well."

Char shook his head. "Rinloo?"

"Your wolf."

"He is not *mine*."

"The wolf you trust is named Rinloo-dex Highwind. Didn't he introduce himself?"

"He said he is a paltry wolf."

She laughed. "Rinloo is too humble by far. He's different, to be sure, but in pleasant ways. You chose well."

Char thought that was going too far. He mumbled, "I did not choose."

"Better?" she countered.

All at once, Char realized that he could no longer hear the endless din of speech and swell of wolfsong coming from below. "Did you banish the wolves?"

"I used sigilcraft to push away the sounds you do not like."

He listened. And into the relative silence a bit of melody slipped. "I hear a wolf."

"Is that so?" She smiled broadly. "Good. I'm satisfied with a job well done."

Char pointed in the direction of the noise. "But there is a ... a humming sort of noise coming from that way."

"I didn't think you'd mind keeping track of your wolf. That's Rinloo." She moved to the odd bundle she'd brought and announced, "One last amendment. I've never heard of imps needing sleep, but even Cedar rests from time to time."

Still distracted by the snatches of melody carried on the wind, Char watched the lady shake out a net of woven cords. She found rings set into the wall, and after much tugging and tightening, she secured knots on a soft sort of ... baskety thing.

"You shouldn't risk the floor unless you wish to remain with us indefinitely." Patting the swaying mesh, she explained, "This is a hammock. I daresay it'll make a safe and comfortable perch."

Char found that difficult to believe.

She spread one of the wolf's shaggy blankets over the ropes, pushing and tucking. "Eat your scones. I'll send Cedar along with a fresh treat, by and by. Pippin is making more of those puddings you like so well."

"Promise?" he ventured.

The lady's gaze softened. "It shall be done."

Once he was sure she'd gone, Char abandoned his little lake in order to explore her gifts. The buttery breadstuffs were gone too soon, and he licked every crumb from his fingertips before approaching the hammock. He tested ropes and touched fur, which was dense and black and tempting.

Char listened closely, reassuring himself that his wolvish protector was still far from the den, then balanced on hands and knees atop the hammock. It rocked unsteadily.

Slowly, he slid down, trusting more of his weight to the swaying bed. He had been dancing so much. Rest felt nice. How long had it been? Winding his fingers into the thick shag, he hid his face and went limp. Did Seela know these same luxuries, wherever she was?

He curled on his side and listened for the distant song of the wolf who might be his.

Was the song good or bad? Char couldn't tell. It wasn't the sort of music that made him want to dance, but the humming was undeniably … cheerful.

Char nuzzled deeper into the fur. Mostly to hide his smile.

ELEVEN SHINE TRUE

Pippin was under Moss's and Cedar's protection, and the packs respected their bond. The wolves held her in high regard, but they also kept her at arm's length. With a few notable exceptions.

Henloo-dex Deepnight was like family. Not quite a second mother. More like a big sister. And as the passing years brought Pippin closer in relative age, a confidante.

Swept into a twirling embrace, Pippin laughed. "I didn't know you were coming!"

"*Every* Deepnight is here," countered the she-wolf. "Ours will surely be the loudest voices in the chorus."

Pippin kissed her cheek and turned to offer a hand to Henloo's much quieter companion. "Welcome back, Kyloora."

"Peace, friend," murmured the other she-wolf, whose yellow eyes caught on Pippin's palm. Kyloora-soh Elderbough was another who could see the marks left by moonbeam kisses on Pippin's skin. But Kyloora rarely said all she could.

Still, Henloo seemed to understand. Turning to Mother Moss, she asked, "May we watch over Pippin's sleep?"

"By which you mean keep her up half the night with gossip?"

Henloo cradled Pippin close. "Such are the rites of sisterhood."

Moss laughed and flicked her fingers toward the stairs. "You hardly need my permission any longer. She's grown enough to have her own wants and wishes, wouldn't you say?"

"I would." Henloo's eyes sparkled. "Warn Cedar away?"

"He can be discreet. And Pippin has her ways."

Pippin lifted her carved crystal on its ribbon.

So the she-wolves carried her aloft, pleased with their prize.

Kyloora spread furs she'd brought special, and Henloo set Pippin's crystal glowing, along with a handful of her own. Only after they'd found a comfortable arrangement for everyone's limbs—and tails—did the girl talk begin in earnest.

"Is your moonbeam still stealing kisses?" asked Henloo.

"Mm-hmm. But I don't think she's stealing. They feel more like gifts."

"Eleven marks shine true," reported Kyloora.

"Interesting!" murmured Henloo, who began sniffing about.

Pippin asked, "Why is *that* interesting."

"Two reasons, I suppose." Henloo tugged one of Pippin's long red curls. "Did you know that an imp's mark fades along with the affections of its recipient?"

"Mine haven't faded."

"Yes."

Kyloora jumped in. "These are proof of your moonbeam's resolve, but they are also proof of you undimming attachment. You are loved, and she knows you love her in return."

"Oh!" Nobody had mentioned that part before. "That's good, then. She knows."

Henloo said, "Another reason this is interesting is that there are eleven. One more will complete a full cycle."

"Mm-hmm. I know. Doesn't that mean she ... she has no reason to visit anymore?"

"That is undeniably true," Henloo said gently. "But only because you will be at her side henceforth."

"I will?"

"That *is* the usual outcome. And it's time you were told."

Kyloora helpfully added, "We think you're being courted."

ROOM FOR TWO

The moon had just crested and spirits were as high as the stars when Ninook insisted that Rin take a break.

"My bondmate wants to run the boundaries with me. Together, we are enough." With a significant nod toward Cedar, he quietly added, "And you are not entirely alone."

Rin sighed. "Have those whelps been telling tales?"

"Spinning fantasies," Ninook easily agreed. "According to all the lore I know, moonbeams are not as solitary as stars. Be certain yours hasn't grown lonesome."

"If you insist."

Ninook bussed his cheek and strolled in Adoona-soh's direction, tail flagging. He was such a romantic. Rin wondered if Ninook would be half so optimistic if he met the snippy little moonbeam for himself. Still, Rin took the shortest path to his den, tail high and heart light.

After so long an absence, he expected to find Char in a sulk, squatting over the bath and glaring.

Instead, he found his moonbeam in a languid sprawl upon his furs.

Poking the bed with a slim finger, Char announced, "*This* is called a hammock."

"I've heard rumors of their existence," Rin returned blandly.

"Do you approve?"

"Maaaybe."

"If you're uncertain, I'll just have to see for myself. Budge over." Rin wasn't surprised when the skittish moonbeam evacuated to the far corner of the ceiling. Even so, Rin stretched out on the hammock, giving a push with his foot to set it swaying.

His moonbeam glared furiously. "I was there first."

"Plenty of room for two. Come back."

"You are too big! It is full."

"Do pardon this one's excessive bulk." Rin folded his arms behind his head and shut his eyes. "But if you don't mind my saying so, you are a dainty bit of impishness. I'd wager we'll fit."

To his utter amazement, Char returned. Not to the hammock, exactly. He hovered above Rin, laid out above him, close enough to catch. And as before, his interest was fixed upon Rin's accessories.

Rin asked, "Did you need a necklace, as well? Which did you fancy?"

"You would give me more of your stones?"

"They please you," Rin reasoned. "And that pleases me."

Char reached down to touch one of the larger stones. "This?"

Rin moved slowly, finding the correct cord and freeing its knot. "Will you let me tie this on you? You'll need to come closer."

His foolish moonbeam surprised him all over again, slipping down to sit on his chest. "Can you reach now?"

"Much better, thank you."

"I am not caught," Char warned.

"You are free to come and go as you please," agreed Rin. "But stay if you like."

Tilting his head to one side, his moonbeam asked, "Do you want me to stay?"

"Honestly?"

Char primly insisted, "You should not lie."

Rin didn't need a lie to avoid the truth. "Did you know that some are saying I have a pet moonbeam? And the rest are saying I have become a moonbeam's pet?"

"Moonbeams are not pets."

"Neither are wolves." Rin carefully knotted his necklace so its blue stone rested over Char's heart. "They tease because they're envious that your shine fills my den."

Char folded his new stone between his hands and glanced around. "Dens are small, with close walls and low ceilings."

For once, Rin thought his moonbeam's distaste wasn't just for show. "You don't like to be inside?"

"I was not made for dens."

"I suppose not."

Char poked Rin's chest. "I thought wolves ran wild. Why do you want dens?"

"Mmm. Running makes me want to rest, and resting makes me want to run."

"I dance."

"That you do," Rin agreed. "Are there other things you like?"

"Blue stones and black fur. And … when I touch you."

"Like now?"

"Like *before*."

Rin asked, "What happened before?"

Char's gaze drifted out of focus, and he didn't exactly answer.

"You are all the things I am afraid of."

"I know you're not afraid of me." He didn't want to be feared. Not by this stray imp. "Though I don't think we like the same things."

That inspired a frown. "You have blue stones and black fur."

"I'll grant you that," Rin laughed. "But what if I told you that what *I'd* like is to hold you?"

"Why?"

"It would make you seem more real … I suppose?"

Char poked him again. "I *am* real."

"You're so certain. I'd like to be certain, as well."

Hesitantly, the moonbeam asked, "Will it be like before?"

Rin patted the spot at his side. "Let's find out."

PINK MOON RISING

Pippin couldn't think of a thing to say.

Henloo nudged her. "Show Kyloora the gifts your lady has bestowed."

"Souvenirs from her travels," Pippin explained, leaving their bed to fetch the little box that held her treasures. "She brings one every year, during the midsummer moon."

She felt shy about showing them, but Kyloora listened with a respect that slowly morphed into wonderment. "Pippin," she said in reverent tones. "These are courting gifts."

"That's what I said!" exclaimed Henloo. "All the elements are here. A moon. A meeting place. A gift. A kiss."

"Who is the witness?" asked Kyloora.

"You have to ask? As Moss did say, 'Cedar can be discreet.'"

Pippin looked from her gifts to her friends and asked, "Mother Moss and Uncle Cedar ... know?"

"How could they not?" Henloo tapped Pippin's nose. "I was here that night. An imp of considerable influence whispered you past every barrier and placed her mark on you in order to see you safe. In essence, she allowed Moss and Cedar to foster you."

"Isn't that strange, though? Courting a child?"

"Let's call it foresight," suggested Henloo. "There's no denying your soul has always held appeal."

"You *are* a rare beauty," agreed Kyloora.

"And since then, you've only gained luster. Cedar has been generous." Henloo nudged her companion. "Show her yours."

Kyloora brought out a necklace that had been tucked inside her fur vest. Braided cords were knotted with wishes and promises, and small items—very familiar items—were secured at intervals along its length.

A droplet stone.

A tiny cup.

A silver whistle.

They weren't *exactly* the same, but they were similar enough to suggest significance. "Are these traditional gifts?"

"They are." Kyloora touched a blue bead. "Customs vary from place to place, but all of the packs adhere to key points from lore."

"The Deepnight pack chooses gifts that invite the blessings of the twelve angels." She tapped a few on the necklace Kyloora displayed. "Auriel ... Cadmiel ... Kestriel ... Mondriel. You know their stories?"

"Of course!" The moon and stars shared the night, and tales of the sky clans often wove together. Suddenly, it occurred to Pippin to ask Kyloora, "Who gave you this necklace?"

"I did," Henloo said warmly. She made the sign for secrecy. "I am bending the tradition to suit myself, but my gifts have been welcomed so far."

Kyloora simply smiled and tucked away her own treasures.

"Does this mean my moonbeam is waiting for me to answer … somehow?" Pippin asked.

Henloo hummed. "Have you ever called to her? She might like an invitation to visit."

"It *is* a trysting moon," agreed Kyloora.

"Pink as a maiden's blush, and on the rise."

Pippin cautiously asked, "Isn't trysting for sweethearts and lovers?"

"It is for you and for the one whose song weaves well with yours." Henloo shared a look with Kyloora. "You know our traditional phrase—*you make me glad our paths crossed*?"

"Yes, of course."

"Some in this life find another they are so glad to have met, they no longer wish to part. Better together, they choose to run the same path."

"What if …?" Pippin began, looking from face to face. "What if the one I want to stay with goes places I can't follow?"

Henloo propped her chin on her fist. "If I were in your place, I would choose my witness—or witnesses—with care. They could serve as your attendants, making clear every nuance of the traditions that surround a bonding. They could sing for your sake. And you could trust them to carry you to the very gates of the Luminous Court, if that was where you wished to be."

HAPPENING TO SOMEONE

Char bit his lip. "If I let you, will you let me go, after?"

"You are free to come and go as you please," the wolf repeated. "And if you're as curious about me as I am about you, that's fine. I'm not shy. You can touch."

"Wolves are not pets, but they like to be petted?"

Rinloo flashed a smile. "Admittedly true."

Char poked once, tapped twice, then spread his hand over the wolf's heart. Its beat never wavered, nor did his wolf's gaze. Nothing about Rin's request sounded wise, but maybe that's why Char felt so daring. He grumbled, "Make room."

Hands closed around his ribs and lifted, and when the tilting and tucking stopped, Char was nestled in a wolf's embrace. His nose was pressed to smooth, brown skin. And there was a hand sliding up the back of his neck into his hair.

"Well, what do you know," the wolf said huskily. "You give every impression of being real."

"I told you so."

"I should have listened. But I'm glad I didn't, or I would have missed this."

Char's hair was being petted, and he wanted to remind this wolf that he wasn't a pet. But it wasn't unpleasant. At least the wolf was being gentle.

"Are you afraid?"

"Not me." It was hard to be afraid of a wolf who didn't growl and snatch and snap his teeth.

"Then try to relax."

A large hand kneaded its way down Char's back, pulling him more firmly into Rinloo. A low vibration began, which was unsettling, and the deep darkness that lurked inside the wolf threatened to pull Char into unfamiliar territory. He shivered.

"Are you cold?"

Before Char could answer, the wolf leaned back and away, and the whole hammock swayed. Char scrabbled for a handhold, but he wasn't sure where to grab. Then, the wolf dragged another of the furry blankets over them both.

"Is this better?"

The wolf seemed to disappear into the darkness. The only light Rinloo gave off was borrowed shine reflecting in silver eyes. Char could see himself there. He reached up, illuminating more of the wolf's expression. Rinloo leaned into his touch, blinked slowly, and smiled.

It was a nice sort of smile.

Char petted his wolf.

The vibration deepened.

"Are you growling at me?"

"No." He went back to fussing with Char's hair. "Surely you can tell I'm not angry."

Yes, he supposed he could. "Are you ... happy?"

"In this moment? Yes." The wolf inhaled deeply and exhaled on a sigh. "You are the most beautiful thing ever to happen to me."

That was an interesting idea. *Happening* to someone.

Char dared to ask, "What if I needed a wolf?"

"You could always try catching one."

"Are ... are you caught?"

"Entirely."

Puzzling that through, Char asked, "How would I keep you?"

"Oooh, there are traditions for that sort of thing. I never really looked into the particulars."

He was so relaxed. Not at all how a trapped animal should behave. Maybe Rinloo was an uncommon wolf. That brought another important question to mind. Char ventured, "Are you a *noble* wolf?"

"If so, nobody's ever mentioned it before." With a small lift of shaggy eyebrows, he asked, "Why do you have need of a wolf?"

Char squirmed up in order to whisper in Rinloo's ear. "I lost someone. Can you find her?"

ALL YOU ASK

Rinloo asked all sorts of questions then. Good ones. The kind no one else had bothered to ask before, let alone tried to answer. The conversation took a long time, but it was good to talk about Seela, good to be angry, good to cry, good to be held.

His wolf took to growling, and Char could tell he was angry.

"Not at *you*, beauty," he promised. "*For* you. How could your people leave you wondering? That isn't how pack works."

"You have a pack?"

"Every wolf since our emerging was born into a pack. Even a lone wolf like me."

"You are alone?" Char knew what that was like. He'd been alone since Seela went away.

"Not at the moment." Rinloo curved around Char as if trying to surround him.

"Me, too. Maybe."

"Only maybe?" teased his wolf.

Char grumbled without words and pretended to pay more attention to Rinloo's remaining necklaces than to him.

Nothing more was said for a while. Everything was close and dark and crowded, which should have been terrible. But his wolf kept nudging and nuzzling, and there were gentle touches. Char went back to loving hammocks and luxuriating in the tickle of fur.

Maybe he should keep this wolf.

Maybe Opal knew the traditions involved.

Traditions were difficult. They'd only given Char trouble. Although … Opal had told him he could choose a Widelands bride. Peering up into Rinloo's face, Char asked, "Do you like being a lone wolf?"

"Why do you ask?"

Char frowned. "I did not like being a maid."

"Mmm, yes. I liked that part of your story."

"That was the *worst* part!" he protested. Except that there were no lakes in the Luminous Court. And the Queen was upset about her missing midivar.

Rinloo chuckled. "I mistook you for a maiden the first time I saw you."

"I am male!"

"So you are. But I didn't know about male moonbeams or luminous maids until you set me straight. I am a wiser wolf, thanks to your patience."

Char grumbled, "I am not patient."

His wolf warmly returned, "I find I do not mind, little churlish one."

For a while, Char sulked. But then he remembered why he needed Rinloo and asked, "Can you find my sister?"

"I can try. With so many wolves here, someone may know where Seela settled."

Char's heart leapt, and his voice wobbled. "R-really?"

"Look at me, indulging myself when your need is so urgent." Tossing aside the blanket, Rinloo said, "I'll go now. Ask around. Will you be all right?"

He could only shake his head. He didn't want to go back to being alone.

The wolf eased away anyhow. "The other dexes can help. We're the best for this sort of thing, given how many secrets we keep."

Char wanted to know about Seela.

Shouldn't that be the thing he wanted most?

She should be more important than blue stones and black fur and ... and paltry wolves.

Rinloo bent over him, smoothed his hair, and kissed his forehead. "Thank you for your trust, beauty. I'll do everything I can for you."

"Everything?" he echoed, unhappy that gaining one thing still meant losing another.

"All you ask." The wolf brushed his knuckles across Char's cheek and promised, "For as long as you have need of me."

He was gone before Char could argue the point. And he really wanted to. Because Rinloo had made it sound like Char would stop needing him once Seela was found. And that wasn't right. In fact, it felt all wrong.

Char was sure he'd asked about *keeping* a wolf. And keeping meant for always.

Opal would know how to make it happen. Intent on finding the dragon, Char darted out the window.

All at once, howls chorused on every side, and he tried to retreat, but he couldn't see the way back. Char was on the wrong side of Moss's barrier.

Then over the din, a familiar voice cried, "*There* you are!"

IN THE OPEN

Opal perched on a slim branch near Cedar's top. He asked, "Where have you been, maid-boy?"

"Hiding from wolves." Char answered. And because it wasn't entirely true, he quietly added, "From most of the wolves."

"Oho? And where is your hiding place?"

"Not sure. I lost the way."

The dragon eyed him curiously, then beckoned. "Who has been giving you gifts?"

Char drifted closer, but he closed his hand around his new pendant. "I caught a wolf."

Opal blinked. He smiled. "Did you now?"

"It was easy."

"You must have made quite the impression." He laughed over his own joke, then asked, "What pack does your bride hail from?"

Char frowned. "Does that matter?"

"Tell me her name, at least."

Even though he didn't want to, Char felt compelled to answer.

Gaze sliding to the side, he mumbled, "He did not tell me."

Opal blinked. He smiled wider. "Your story has the makings of a ballad."

Char wondered if that meant Opal would sing about him the same way he sang about Seyroo and his courtship.

Leaning nearer, the dragon sniffed lightly. "Have you been trysting with your wolf?"

He plucked at the cords that circled his wrist, then tried to hide them, but that left his necklace exposed. "How should I know?"

"I should think you would notice if … ah. You are not familiar with the term?"

Char nodded once.

Opal's expression shifted toward concern. "Have you any complaints about your bride-to-be?"

"Maybe." But it was hard to think of something. Finally, he said, "He left me alone."

"If that is the *worst* of his failings … hmm." Scanning the area, Opal muttered, "We are entirely too conspicuous here. Cedar, do you know where my young friend belongs?"

The tree appeared on the limb beneath the dragon's. "Hello, Opal. Hello, Char. Why did you leave the den? Are you hungry?"

"Yes!" Char wanted to skim down immediately and see if Pippin had left a spoon on the windowsill for him.

"Hardly advisable," warned Opal. "He is shining like a beacon."

"Moss can fix things," Cedar assured, beckoning to Char. "Moss is really very good."

But before Char could reach the tree, another voice—also familiar—cut across his happiness.

"*You*! You were *here*?"

He dove, weaving through the branches, desperate to reach his wolf's den. But where was it hidden?

Opal and Cedar both shouted, and the howls from below doubled in strength and number. But over it all, the Queen's voice carried sharp and clear. "Wait! You!" She caught up in a trifling. "Char! That is your name, is it not?"

"Leave me alone!" he gasped. "It was an *accident*!"

"That is not …!"

He lunged past a white-haired wolf whose copper eyes widened as he called, "What's wrong, little moonbeam? Do you need help?"

Char did. But not from any other wolf than *his*. He drew breath and shouted for all he was worth. "Paltry wolf! Paltry wolf! Do not let her lock me away!"

WRAPPED IN FUR

Char's distress seared across Rin's senses and spurred him into action. He hadn't even realized he knew his moonbeam's voice, but the call yanked at his soul. What a way to realize he'd been bond-building. And here, he'd thought his moonbeam was naïve. All of Rin's careless promises were going to tear him apart when this festival ended.

Spotting Char's reckless tumble through Cedar's branches, Rin raced to reach him. They collided, and his moonbeam yelped in alarm, then sobbed in relief. Thin arms wound around Rin's neck, and he babbled shakily about cages and queens and captivity.

Two things came through, clear as moonlight.

Char was frightened. And he considered it Rin's fault.

"Hush, beauty. I heard you. I'm here," he soothed, gathering the imp close and rumbling a warning note at those whose curiosity brought them too near. "I've got you, see? You're safe."

Tears splashed against Rin's chest. "I was going to keep you."

"Were you?" He smoothed a hand over silver hair. "Big plans, huh?"

"Opal was supposed to help, but I forgot to ask."

"The dragon bard?" Rin arched his brows at Opal, who'd taken a seat on the nearby staircase. "He does know a great many things."

"Is he the one, maid-boy?" Opal tapped a finger across curved lips. "Highwind pack. And a dex? This is quite the coup."

Rin bared his teeth.

Opal made the sign for peace as he brightly addressed Char. "I *do* know a thing or two about courting and keeping, should you be interested."

"Maybe." Char pressed closer, burying his face against Rin's neck. "Hide me? I do not want to go back to scrubbing. I was not made to scrub."

"You were made to dance," Rin soothed. "I've seen. I know."

"I want custard. And blue stones. And a lake. And ... and a hammock."

He wished he could wrap his moonbeam up in a blanket, hiding him from their increasing audience. One at a time, he shrugged his arms out of his vest and pulled it around Char's slender frame. *That* set off a chorus of wolfsong.

Oh.

Char shuddered. "Are they hunting me?"

"No, beauty." Rin was embarrassed to admit, "They're happy for me."

"*And* awed by her." Opal twirled a finger in the air, drawing attention to a brightness that loomed above and behind Rin's position.

He whirled, putting Cedar at his back and a hand to his sword hilt. But all thought of aggression faded when he made sense of what he was seeing. "Char, is this lady looking for you?"

His mumbled answer was barely audible. But Rinloo caught the words *mean* … and *queen*.

"*She* is your mistress?" he asked faintly.

"Hide me?" With a rebellious glare over his shoulder Char grumpily added, "She can scrub her own floors."

Rinloo glanced between them, then looked to Opal for guidance. "By *queen*, are we talking about …?"

"Oooh, yes." With a flourishing bow to the lady in question, the dragon declared, "The Moon herself has graced this circle with her presence."

HERE IS GOOD

Char did his best to wrap himself around his wolf, legs twisted and fingers knotted, tight as the cords of the necklaces he wore.

"You can let go," Rin said in a low voice.

"I will not."

"This is … probably unnecessary. And a tiny bit undignified."

"Why?"

The wolf, whose nose was mashed in the vicinity of Char's ribs, sighed.

"Release him!" ordered the Queen.

Char glared her way. "You cannot make me."

She hesitated. "I meant *him*. The wolf should let *you* go."

Rinloo held up both hands. "He's caught me, not the other way around."

Cedar tried to intervene. "Come sit on my shoulders, Char. I can keep you safe."

"I *am* safe." Char wasn't about to let go. "This wolf listens. And lets me dance. And … and he might be noble!"

"We must speak," she insisted. "*Now*, Char."

The Queen was so bossy. Char was in no mood for a scolding, so he hid his face against Rinloo's hair.

The squirrel lady showed up then and raised her voice. "Shall we take this discussion to a more private setting?"

"Lead the way, Moss," begged Rinloo. "*Please*."

Char scowled down at him. "What if *this* is the trap?"

"Doesn't matter." His wolf held his gaze. "Even if I must defy the Moon herself, I *will* protect you."

"And let me keep you?"

His brows lifted. "If that's what you really want."

"Promise?"

"Yes, beauty. All you ask, remember?"

He *did* remember and relinquished his hold.

Rinloo adjusted his fur vest around Char's shoulders and pulled him close.

"You wanted to hold me?" asked Char.

"That's one way to put it." His smile was all crooked. "Bear with me?"

"I will allow it." Char rested his head against his wolf's shoulder and turned his attention to the necklaces that he wore. There were still several fine stones to admire. "I will ask for this one next," he confided.

Rinloo huffed. "I'm not sure that's the most important thing, right now."

Char wrinkled his nose at the foolish wolf. What could be more important than blue stones and black fur? Only a trip to the lake could please him more.

Though Rin was poised to defend his moonbeam, he was willing to hear out the Queen. She hardly seemed as stingy and spiteful as Char had implied. More than anything, she looked exasperated by the winsome brat.

Moss led the way toward her kitchen, weaving sigils as she went.

Every onlooker gave way, their posture respectful, their expressions awed.

"This is a night that will be sung about for centuries to come," remarked Opal, who seemed to think his presence was required.

Rinloo asked, "What's your part in this?"

"Witness, I should think. Chronicler, perhaps." The dragon indicated Char. "I thought I saw the beginnings of a ballad in him, but he may end as an epic."

Char grumbled, "I will *not* end."

"But where will you end up?" challenged Opal.

"Here is good." Char sounded totally unconcerned, as if one place was as good as another.

"In the Widelands?" asked the bard. "Or perhaps you are referring to your precious lake?"

"Oh. The lake. I did not think of that."

Rin glanced down. Char seemed caught somewhere between vexed and perplexed.

Opal glided closer. "What *were* you thinking of?"

The moonbeam shot him a rebellious look.

"Tell me where *here* is," urged the dragon.

Though Char thrust out his lower lip and mumbled his answer, Rin caught it.

"With my wolf."

PUT ME DOWN

Pippin turned from the oven at the sudden influx of people. And gaped. Not because it was unusual for Cedar to invite people inside or for Moss to feed them. But because her moonlit lady was among them—stern and dignified. She sat in midair with hands folded, modestly resplendent in swathing moonbeams, as regal as if she sat upon a throne.

"A meeting, my sweet," briskly explained Mother Moss. "It seems your friend has caused some mischief for the Moon, and she wants to have it out. Cedar and I will mediate."

Her friend? She had to mean Char. Yes, there he was. Rinloo had him wrapped in his vest. Pippin had never seen the wolf's tail so puffed, nor his posture so assertive.

Then her foster mother's meaning sank in, and Pippin's attention bounced to her lady. "Did you say ... *the Moon*?"

"And honored we are to have her," Moss murmured. "Help me with some refreshments."

Pippin obeyed, setting out pastries and berries with cream.

Char immediately wriggled from Rinloo's grasp, drifting over to whisper, "Is there custard?"

"I saved you one."

He followed her to the icebox, already hugging a silver spoon.

When she turned to offer his treat, she jumped. Rinloo had followed Char on silent feet and now loomed over them. His posture shifted into apology, and he lightly touched her shoulder, then reeled in Char, whose borrowed vest was dragging on the floor.

"Rinloo, what's happening?" she whispered.

His gaze darted warily, but his tone was calm. "I'm not entirely sure."

Cedar clapped his hands and nodded to the Moon. "You may begin."

For a moment, the queen's gaze met Pippin's. There was wistfulness and apology there. But when she spoke, it was with an authority she'd never displayed when appearing at Pippin's east-facing window.

She said Char was a maid in the queen's court. Little more than a scuttle-shuffler and stardust sweep. "His actions—though accidental—have upended my plans for this festival. I am *trying* to deal with the consequences."

Her plans. Oh, no! She must mean her final gift for Pippin.

Hurrying forward, Pippin reached up to touch her moonbeam's

foot. "Lady? He's my friend. He meant no harm."

The Moon quietly answered, "I know, love."

"He can't gather up what's been lost."

She inclined her head. "I do not expect him to. But if the blessing he stole is traded back to me, all will be well."

"These are mine!" exclaimed Char, who clutched at the necklaces he wore.

"I do not want your stones," soothed the Moon.

His eyes widened in dismay. "Not ... not my wolf!"

The lady sighed. "You misunderstand. I want to give *you* something."

"Why?"

"The bride price you gained by freeing the bounty. I want it back."

Char scowled. "You said you did not want my wolf."

"I do not." With thinning patience, the queen said, "I wish to trade for the right to choose *my* bride. What do you want in exchange?"

Char sucked thoughtfully on his spoon, then asked, "The lake?"

"That is not mine to give."

"Then ... no," Char said softly.

"No?" she echoed, clearly baffled. "But it is no use to you!"

"Not so, Queen of Skies," Opal interjected. "Rinloo-dex is his chosen bride."

Pippin could see dismay cloud her lady's face. "You already squandered it?"

A low growl began, and everyone's attention swung to Rinloo.

Opal stepped between them and lightly asked, "Can any affection truly be squandered?"

"No. Indeed, no." The Moon lifted her hands and murmured, "Pardon my thoughtless words."

Rinloo's warning growl ebbed away, and he stepped forward. "Trade with me, instead."

"You?"

"You want a maiden from these Widelands, and I want a maid from the Luminous Court." The wolf indicated the moonbeam in his arms. "Will that not satisfy the need for balance?"

"Oho! Neatly done!" chimed in Opal. "A maid for a maiden? That has a lovely ring to it. The lyric almost writes itself!"

Pippin felt heat creep into her cheeks. How did Rinloo know about the courtship?

Her gaze fell to her palms, which shone brightly.

Taking an overtly dominant stance, Rinloo said, "You may not be able to release a fresh bounty into the sky, but you could release this moonbeam into my care."

Pippin checked her lady's face and saw the beginnings of hope.

"I can stay?" asked Char.

"If you like," assured Rinloo.

Char shook his head. "But if I stay, someone must go in my place?"

Rinloo said, "Pippin will go."

The boy pushed away from the wolf and darted to her, plucking at her sleeve. "Do you *want* to go?" And more softly, "She might make you scrub floors."

Pippin appreciated his concern. She whispered, "I know how to scrub."

Char's gaze darted to the Moon, as if only now realizing how close he was, and he turned to flee, only to collide with Rinloo's chest. His wolf wasn't letting him out of reach. Pippin liked this quality in wolves, but she was a little miffed that they were treating her lady like a threat.

The Moon frowned. "Char? What do you want?"

He hugged himself. "Besides the lake?"

"Yes. Besides the lake."

"Custard *is* nice," he said, smiling at Pippin. But then he stole a sidelong look at Rinloo. "But blue stones are better."

The lady asked, "Are those gifts?"

"They are mine, now!" Char patted Rinloo's shoulder. "He gave them."

"Gifts freely given," acknowledged the wolf.

"Courting gifts?" asked the Moon.

"Gifts *freely* given," Rinloo repeated with emphasis. "These stones carry no obligation. Ankle and wrist, he can have them all, should he take a fancy. Just as he can have me, if he takes a fancy."

"Ankle?" echoed Char, craning his neck.

The Moon drew herself up. "We should adhere to tradition. Attendants. Tasks. Gifts. Vows."

Pippin touched the Moon's ankle again. "I've already chosen my attendants."

"You ... you have?"

She'd clearly pleased her lady.

"Ankle?" repeated Char, trying to turn himself around in Rinloo's arms. "You had more?"

"They've been there all along," Rinloo said mildly. And to the Moon, "I name Beloor-dex Ambervelte and Ninook-dex Trebellaire as my attendants."

"Imps and dexes!" Opal interjected giddily. "And will there be an exchange of names?"

"Put me down!" demanded Char, who tumbled free.

"W-wait!" gasped Rin.

"Fronds!" exclaimed Cedar.

"Oooh, that's done it," Opal said in worried tones.

Tangled in Rin's fur vest, Char had dropped to the floor.

Getting his limbs under him, he crawled to the stunned wolf's feet and ran a finger along a double-loop of blue beads tied around his ankle. Looking up with a rapturous expression, Char broke the heavy silence. "These are *perfect*!"

GIVING SOMETHING UP

The stones were small, but they looked so pretty, all lined up like dewdrops. There had to be fifty, all told, and Char wondered where his wolf had found so many that were the same size. Why had he not mentioned them before? He should have.

Char was going to scold him, but ... *up* wasn't working.

Since when had *up* ever been difficult? Was the vest too heavy? That must be it. Char was all set to chide his wolf for this fresh inconsideration, but before he could, Rinloo had joined him on the floor.

On the floor?

The *floor*.

His wolf had him by the shoulders, was searching his face, was pulling him close. "Oh, beauty," he groaned. "Please, don't regret this. I'll take responsibility."

"I only wanted ...." Char's voice failed.

"Come with me," his wolf whispered, gathering him up. And addressing the room, he announced, "My offer stands. I await your answer. We won't be far."

And then the strangely weighty world seemed to bend and blur. There was wind and there were footfalls. Char's wolf was running into the night.

"Did you mean to?" he asked gruffly.

Char whispered, "It was an accident."

"Are you perhaps prone to accidents?" There was a smile behind the question.

"Maybe." And lifting his face to see if his wolf was laughing at him, Char quavered, "That is the sort of thing people say."

Rinloo slowed to a stop. "Would you have?"

Char curled tight. "Does it matter?"

"I think it does." His wolf asked another way. "Would you have descended if it meant keeping the lake and the hammock and ... and me?"

"Maybe." But it had happened so fast. Without a thought to anything.

"You look much the same. How do you feel?"

"Heavy ...?" Char wound his arms around his wolf's neck and mumbled, "I cannot find *up*."

"That's because you've left the sky."

"I know," he whined.

"Does it hurt?"

Char shook his head.

Rinloo walked on, growling softly.

"Are you angry with me?"

"I'm only warning off the curious." His wolf nuzzled his hair. "I *am* upset. I'm concerned for you. Is there anything I can do?"

Char didn't know. He could only shake his head again.

Then Rinloo sat. Right on the ground. As if it wasn't at all dangerous. Perhaps it wasn't, anymore.

Sounds filtered through Char's confusion, and he searched for the source. Water lapped softly against the edge of the lake. The rising moon striped its surface, as if it were trying to show him the way home. But Char knew the way was closed to him now. And he knew something else.

"What is it, beauty?" Big hands swiped at the silent tears that fell.

Char blinked at him and bit his trembling lip. It was too terrible to say.

Rinloo pressed their cheeks together and begged, "Talk to me. Tell me what to do."

But there was nothing to be done. "I cannot dance."

CAPTURE THE MOON

With Rinloo's departure, the balance was struck, and the meeting ended. Mother Moss exchanged a long look with Uncle Cedar, who gently shook his head. Pippin wasn't sure if this was the time for introductions between her family and her lady.

To her amazement, Mother Moss asked, "What's your pleasure?"

"Not tonight, Moss," the queen murmured wearily. "There is much to do, and time is fleeting in the Widelands."

Pippin was mystified. Not only did it seem as if her foster parents knew about her moonbeam, she'd have sworn they knew her lady better than she did herself. "You're ... friends?"

Moss glanced between them and shrugged. "More like longtime

acquaintances? This is a Song Circle, my sweet. And she is the one for whom the wolves sing.”

Pippin ventured, “And … you’re a queen?”

“It was appointed to me to rule the night.” With a light kiss for Pippin’s nose, the Moon promised, “I will return at the appointed time.”

And then she was gone.

Turning to her foster parents, Pippin said, “You *did* know.”

“Yes and no.” Mother Moss poured fresh tea for Opal. “We knew you had a secret, and we knew how happy it made you. And … well, moonbeams *can* pass freely through my wards. I had no idea which one guided you here, though. That little detail comes as a surprise to me. Although thinking back, I might have guessed. Our little lost girl needed formidable help.”

“I knew,” confessed Cedar. “I know *everything*.”

“Can’t help himself,” Moss said with a chuckle. “But he never let on.”

Pippin nodded, shook her head, then moved on to something troubling. “Is Char going to be okay?”

Again, the siblings looked to each other for answers, but it was Opal who spoke up.

“That will likely be up to that wolf of his.” The dragon gazed thoughtfully in the direction Rinloo had gone. “While I could not have foreseen this particular outcome, there is a certain poetry to maid-boy’s debacles.”

Cedar said, “Rinloo will protect him. Rinloo loves him.”

“Wolves,” drawled Opal, almost wistfully. “There are worse ways to be smothered.”

Pippin let their words reassure her, but she hoped for a chance to talk to Char for herself. To make sure her friend was all right. To be there if he needed her. Though … she might not be here much longer. Not if Henloo and Kyloora were right about her lady's plans.

It had almost sounded as if she and Char were trading places. For balance. But Char had looked so stricken. And Rinloo's whole posture had communicated alarm over the moonbeam's sudden descent.

Opal was saying, "… as promised! I was able to coax help from an artisan who—like myself—was invited to add a bit of flourish to the Queen's Festival. Her specialty is jewelry. I think you will be pleased."

From an inner pocket, the dragon withdrew a length of silver chain and let it drop. A pale sphere spun out, catching the light as it swayed.

"Fit for a queen," Opal decreed.

Pippin hurried closer. She knew this stone, with its pinkish cast. Spinning, she confirmed it. There was a gap in Mother Moss's calendar. One of the Seven Score Moons had been whisked away and made into a pendant.

Moss claimed the necklace and inspected it closely, then beckoned for Pippin to hold out her hands. The sphere was heavy for its size, lustrous and lovely, and the chain pooled around it. Mother Moss gently closed Pippin's fingers over it, and Uncle Cedar enfolded her hands.

"A fitting gift." He nodded at Opal and repeated, "Fit for a queen."

Pippin laughed and hugged them both. Then hugged Opal for good measure. She would be able to give her lady a fine gift. The perfect gift, really. Because her family had contrived to turn the Pippin Moon into a treasure.

SET A TASK

Rin's heart ached for Char, and he crooned a mournful note in the back of his throat. The sound stirred his moonbeam's interest enough that he looked up.

"What is that?" he demanded snuffily. "What are you doing?"

"I'm sad that you're sad."

"I am not sad. I am *tragic*."

All Rin could think to do was to stand up, walk out over the surface of the lake, and resettle so that he was sitting above the water.

Char shrank against him. "What are you doing? What if I fall in?"

"I have you." Smoothing away the tear tracks on one luminous cheek, he urged, "Look. Your light still dances."

He peeped past Rin's arm and found his reflection waiting.

"Would you have?" Rin repeated. "You called for me. You said you were going to keep me. That dragon called me your chosen bride."

His moonbeam hummed moodily.

At least it wasn't denial.

"If you did want to keep me, we should probably begin. Will you set me a task?"

Char suspiciously asked, "What for?"

"Tradition." Rin shrugged. "You may order me to do things or to find things. In this way, a wolf proves his resolve."

Silvery brows drew together. "You must do as I say?"

"Yes."

"And bring me nice things?"

"Yes."

"Because … you want to stay with me?"

Rin nodded. "All my years would belong to you."

His moonbeam blinked. "How many things?"

"Traditionally, there would be twelve tasks … or twelve gifts … or twelve pledges."

"Like finding Seela?" Char ventured.

"Yes. Shall we make that one of my tasks?"

A small nod. A small frown. Turning his attention back to the lake, the moonbeam reached down to flick the surface of the water. "I know what else."

"Go on, then."

"I want a pitterhind."

"Those little winged critters with green fur?"

Char nodded and mumbled, "I would tame it for Seela. She thinks they are cute. But they are too fast for me to catch."

"Very well. I'll track one down for you."

He looked up then, gaze searching. "You will?"

"If that's one of the tasks you set, I'll do it."

Char pointed down at the water. "This is good, but it could be better."

Rin cautiously said, "I can't give you the lake. It's not mine to give, either."

His moonbeam sighed. "I shine, and that is good. But my light should be *dancing*."

"Oh, beauty," he murmured gruffly. "I cannot give you back the sky."

"Not *that*." Char made a graceful twirl with an arm. "You will have to do it."

Rin suspected that his tail was thoroughly tucked. "You want me to …?"

"Dance. Here. With me."

"Wolves are made to run and to sing. I've never danced before."

Char's gaze turned pitying. But he magnanimously offered, "I will teach you."

NOT ENTIRELY TRADITIONAL

Bartering with his wolf was interesting. Char had never been the one in charge before and handing down orders was nicer than being ordered around. But … *was* it nice?

Not for both of them, surely. Char didn't want to be like a stingy queen. And a wild and free wolf shouldn't be treated like a court maid or garden drudge.

"Why do *I* have to make the rules?" he grumbled. "Where is the balance in that?"

Rinloo nodded thoughtfully. "Tasks are traditional, but it's hardly the only way to show someone that they are treasured."

"Tell me the ways."

"Well … kisses cost nothing, but they can be convincing. Among wolves, it's said that a kiss cannot lie."

"Nobody told me!" Char worked up a glare. "Are you going to kiss me?"

"Not unless you ask it." Rinloo's whole attitude was relaxed. "Did you know that impish kisses can bestow a blessing?"

"Nobody told me that, either." Realization made him gasp. "Do you expect me to kiss you?"

"*Expect*? Nothing about these past few days is something I expected." His wolf petted his hair. "I believe I'll continue to take things as they come."

Char wasn't sure he liked that answer. "You do not want me to kiss you?"

Rinloo hummed. "It's more like … I want to know what you want. And I want your happiness."

He remembered those words. "You said that before."

"Because it's true."

"Like kisses are true?" checked Char.

"That's what they say." The wolf's gaze was so direct. "If you're concerned that you're asking too much of me, set simple tasks. Many do that. Especially if they're eager to be done."

"Is there a prize for finishing quickly?"

Rinloo chuckled. "Maybe so? Until the tasks are completed, a wolf cannot bring their moonbeam into their den."

"I have already been in your den."

"Not … exactly. My room at Cedar's is a *borrowed* den." With downcast eyes, he quietly added, "Some would say we've been trysting."

"We were?"

"No. Not really. Not properly. Or improperly." Clearing his throat, Rinloo repeated, "No."

Char made up his mind that talking to his wolf was *also* interesting. Better than bartering. Although he wasn't sure they'd found a balance here, either. Rinloo did not ask him any questions. Was it possible that he already knew the answers?

Maybe he was glaring. Because the wolf asked, "What's on your mind now?"

"I want to go back to the hammock."

"Sure thing. Not a problem."

They rose so high over the lake, Cedar came into view. And then Rinloo held him tight and raced toward his borrowed den.

"Why so fast?" Char complained.

His wolf didn't answer until they were inside Mother Moss's barrier. "Prying eyes."

"Oh." He plucked at his borrowed vest and asked, "Did this count as one of your tasks?"

"No. This would count as courtesy."

Rinloo set him on the hammock and moved to the basin to dip his hands in the water and splash his face. Char wanted to do the same, but when he tried to get down, the hammock teetered and dumped him on the floor.

"Th-that hurt!"

His wolf's tail tucked. "Do you need help?"

"No," he grumbled, rapping the floorboards before finding his feet. "I walk all the time at home. Walk and walk and walk. It is not new."

Rinloo simply nodded and moved aside, making room for Char at the basin.

While he played with the water, he asked, "Will *you* set tasks for *me*?"

"Why would I?"

Char would have thought it obvious. "For balance."

"I suppose that *would* be fair."

"Not my stones, though," he warned. "I will not give them back."

"They're yours," Rinloo warmly assured. Then more slowly, he asked, "What if I asked for something ... traditional."

"Tell me," he commanded.

His wolf dropped to one knee, sought his gaze, and quietly said, "To be kissed by an imp is a great honor."

"Is that all?"

Rinloo nodded.

Having watched Seyroo—wild things *bore* watching—Char knew how affectionate that wolf was with his moonbeam bride. And how fast Seyroo's tail would wag when his lady reached for him. But that was *simple*. Were wolves actually very simple?

Char nodded. "Give me your hand."

His wolf complied without question. Trusting. Trust was supposed to be good.

"Like ... like this?" Char carefully pressed his lips to the back of Rinloo's hand.

When he withdrew, a little of his light stayed behind. Silver lines swirled across brown skin, creating delicate filigree that made itself at home in the spot he'd kissed. Was that supposed to happen? Char smudged at it with his thumb, and Rinloo gasped.

"Did I hurt you?" Char asked uncertainly.

"It took," whispered his wolf, who seemed to be having trouble breathing.

"Nobody told me about this."

Rinloo's other arm slid around Char, gently pulling him into closer contact. "It *took*," he repeated.

Char searched his face. His wolf seemed happy. "You like it?"

Bowing his head so it rested over Char's heart, Rinloo said,

"I told you it was an honor, didn't I?"

"If you say so." He awkwardly patted his wolf. "Why are you on the floor? There is a hammock."

A short chuckle. A quick squeeze. A low refrain. "It took. I wasn't entirely sure, but … it really did take."

"I did not take anything. I gave something," he muttered.

"You grumbly, clumsy, churlish bundle of impishness," Rinloo said, making every insult an endearment. "It wouldn't have taken if you didn't love me."

"Oh," Char said awkwardly. "That."

CALL TO HER

Pippin needed more time with her lady—to tell, to hear, to plan. She'd always felt as if they understood one another, but now she knew she'd been missing something that had been obvious to everyone else around her. Her moonbeam hadn't simply been indulging a little girl's whim. Pippin was the Moon's whim, as well.

They'd each chosen the other.

Following the Queen's Footpath, Pippin hurried away from Cedar. The wolves in the Circle parted for her. Many dipped their heads in greeting. Some even lowered themselves to their bellies, gazing at her with a little of the admiration that belonged to the Moon.

"Are you near?" she called softly. "Will you come to me if I ask?"

That's what Henloo and Kyloora had recommended. Call to her.

In the deepening darkness, the creek chattered and chuckled over smooth pebbles, barely discernible in the starlight. But then silver streaked its surface, and Pippin looked up with a smile.

Her lady wafted just overhead, a hand pressed to her breast. "I am here."

"You're courting me?"

She nodded.

Pippin sighed. "I wish I'd known. Why didn't you say something?"

"You needed more years—to heal, to thrive, to decide."

"How was I supposed to make a choice if you never presented one?" She wasn't angry, exactly, but she didn't understand why she hadn't been consulted. Sure, she'd been too young at eight or nine or ten. But by the time she was fourteen and fifteen and sixteen, Pippin had been more than a little in love.

Her lady hesitated, as if unsure her answer would be welcomed. "Tradition …?"

One Pippin hadn't been taught. Until now.

"According to that tradition, I can court you, as well."

"True." She drifted nearer, lips parted. "You would do that?"

Pippin drew herself up. "Isn't that my right?"

"Your demands would be my delight."

"Don't switch it back around." With the beginnings of a smile, she countered, "It's *your* demands I'm interested in. Set me a task."

Her moonbeam's lashes fluttered. "You … you truly would do that?"

"Let me make myself clear, even if it will have to be in small ways." Pippin showed her hands. "I don't have much to offer."

"If that is what you wish, there is time." Light fingertips brushed Pippin's hair, then touched her cheek. "I know how to keep what is mine."

She considered that. "So … I can court you even after the bonding ceremony?"

The lady's smile was beautiful. "Yes."

Which posed a conundrum.

"I'm not a wolf, so I can't sing for you. And I don't have a dozen treasures to prove how much I care."

"Not so." Her moonbeam touched the lacy marks left by her kisses. "Here is proof that your heart is true. You are a treasure I seized for myself. Some will say I have stolen you."

Pippin was a little relieved. She didn't have to *do* anything.

But she was also frustrated. Because there was nothing she could do.

"All I really want is more of this. *Time* together. Time to talk … and things."

"And things?" she gently teased.

"Yes. I mean, I want all the parts of … this. Don't you?"

Her lady inclined her head and urged, "Give me a name. That will bind me to you … and you to me. The rest will come in time, for you shall come with me."

"Time is good," Pippin agreed. "Time and things."

Gathering up her hands, the Moon smoothed her thumbs over the filigree that shone upon Pippin's palms. "As the wolves are wont to say, 'All you need, I will be.'"

IMP TO CONSIDER

"You want *my* advice?" Joonta's posture shifted uncertainly. "What makes you think I have any interest in Ephemera? That's kid stuff."

Ignoring his friend's bluster, Laud said, "It's best to work in teams."

Joonta eyed his best friend. "You chase pitterhind?"

"My younger siblings are at that age. Pups like pets."

"I'm not at that age." Joonta pouted. "I've reached my attainment. I'm an adult now!"

"I'm not questioning your maturity," soothed Rin. "I only wondered if you'd seen any during your patrols. They haven't much scent, so they can be difficult to track."

Laud nodded sympathetically. "They're everywhere until you want one."

Joonta sighed deeply. "Fine. I saw some yesterday. I remember the spot."

"Even though they're beneath the notice of adults?" teased Rin.

Tail puffed, Joonta mumbled, "Not entirely. I think Cedar tames them. They'll take seeds right out of your hand."

That was good news. Rin's tail was already wagging.

"Do you want help?" offered Laud.

"Welcome as that would be, I should probably work alone." Rin shrugged. "This is a task Char set for me."

"He asked you to catch Ephemera for him?" asked Ninook, who'd been listening quietly.

"Just the one. He asked for a pitterhind."

"Then a pitterhind he must have," Ninook said warmly. "Will you remain here for the duration of your courtship?"

Rin hesitated. "I would love to stay, but lazing in hammocks and eating Moss's pastries aren't listed among the duties of a dex."

"Perhaps not." Ninook's smile was the knowing sort. "But preserving and protecting all things pertaining to the lost clans *is*. You have an imp to consider."

Entirely true. "This isn't duty."

"I can tell."

Laud shyly asked, "May I see his mark?"

The request dipped into personal territory, but Rin liked the Starmark dex. He beckoned him forward, lifting his hand. Joonta crowded in right beside him, posture pleading. "Go ahead," Rin encouraged. "Maker knows I gawk at it often enough myself."

"What does it mean?" asked Joonta.

Rin's heart was in his throat. It could mean a lot of things, all of them good.

Ninook spared him, suggesting, "Beloor's brother has a mark, just here." He tapped his forehead. "Isn't that right, Laud?"

"Yes. Da has a copper mark, just like a star. And Mother has a silver star. That's why we're Starmarks."

Joonta gazed thoughtfully at the pearly pattern shining on the back of Rinloo's hand. "Will you take a new name?"

"He *has* to," murmured Laud. "They both will. For the bond."

Joonta glanced between them and softly asked, "Does that mean you'll be bondmates?"

Rin wasn't entirely sure. But he did know one thing for certain. "It means that someone wants to share my path."

EASY TO PLEASE

Moss was smiling in a way that made Char grumpy, but he liked the kitchen. So many nice things could be made in a kitchen. Made ... and *eaten*. He was eyeing the line of custards cooling on the counter.

"Are you going to dedicate yourself to Rinloo-dex?" Moss inquired.

Twisting his silver spoon between both hands, Char loftily announced, "Wolves and moonbeams can find happiness together."

"So I've heard. Are you happy with him?"

"I am not happy," he grumbled. "That wolf left me alone."

Moss chuckled. "Only because you sent him away."

"I did not!"

"You did. You gave him a task."

"Oh," he sighed. "That."

The apron-clad lady eased a long-handled thingie through the open door of a deep oven set into one wall. When it came back out, it was covered in small loaves of the crusty bread Rinloo favored.

Char remarked, "Wolves like that sort of thing."

"Rinloo certainly does." She next extracted a pie, which bubbled with berry juices.

"He is a wolf."

"An uncommon one. Your wolf would sooner tear into one of these loaves than a fresh haunch. And he has a sweet tooth to rival your own." Moss spared him a smile. "You're both easy to please."

That was surprising. Char asked, "I could please him?"

"Do you want to try?" she challenged.

"Maybe." He looked longingly toward the custards.

"I could teach you. I'll be losing my apprentice soon, and an extra pair of hands would be welcome in the kitchen."

Char pointed to himself. "I could learn?"

"Oh, you'll probably be a disaster, at first. But you seem the tenacious sort, and you definitely have a taste for finer things." Her gaze was appraising. "You'd need to listen to me."

"I could if I wanted to."

"And ... you'd need to wear an apron."

"Is that a rule? Nobody told me."

"Oh, yes," Moss calmly assured. "An apron protects your clothes from spatters and spills."

Char looked down. "I don't have clothes."

"Clothes are a *very* important Widelands tradition. You'll need some, now that you're staying."

"Maybe my wolf will give me his vest again ...?"

"No need. Cedar and I will provide you with something closer to your size."

"Because I am your apprentice?"

"Yes," Moss agreed, looking pleased that the matter was settled. "You are my apprentice. *Do* please call me Mother Moss."

Char was almost sure he'd been tricked into agreeing to several things at once.

SEE HER OFF

Char didn't want to be anywhere near the ruckus of the Queen's bonding ceremony. Happy wolves were noisy wolves, and the air shivered with their send-off. But he wanted the chance to see Pippin one last time, so he told his wolf to handle the arrangements.

It was important enough to count as one of Rinloo's courting tasks.

Finding things for him to do was getting easier. It was surprising, really, how many things a person could want, given time to think. "Will I have to stop at twelve?"

His wolf turned his attention from the rising moon, which was pink enough to please Opal the Sage, who saw omens everywhere.

"What are we counting?"

"Tasks." Char brushed his foot over the mossy creek bank, then dipped a toe into running water. He'd decided to explore more of the textures offered by the Widelands before submitting to shoes, which were heavy and graceless. Wolves ran barefoot. Why couldn't he?

"*All* you ask, beauty," he reminded. "I won't set a limit."

"Even if I want more blue stones?" Char had wheedled away nearly every one of his wolf's accessories.

"Stones come in more colors than blue, you know."

"Tell me!"

Rinloo said, "Some packs favor white or orange or green. And you've seen the different stones that create Moss's calendar."

"I am learning the Seven Score Moons," Char boasted.

"Ambitious! Shall I quiz you?"

Char hesitated. "Not yet."

Nodding to the east, his wolf softly said, "Here they come."

He hid behind Rinloo and whispered, "Does the Queen look angry?"

"Not even a little bit."

Char risked a peek. "They are riding wolves?"

"Pippin cannot fly on her own, so her attendants will carry them into the sky."

The possibility had never once occurred to him. "I could ride you home?"

Rinloo's tail drooped. "If you asked it, yes. I could take you there, now."

He grabbed the fur vest to hold him back. "You said I could stay."

"Then let's stay."

So simple. Char was glad wolves were simple.

The newly bonded ladies arrived and slid from their mounts. Pippin hurried forward to hug Rinloo, then reached for Char. He shied away.

"It's not a trap," Pippin promised with a laugh.

Char glanced at the hovering Queen, who was toying with a pretty pink pendant, round as the moon that soared overhead. She inclined her head, so he edged out from behind Rinloo and tentatively lifted his arms. Pippin rushed into them and squeezed him tightly. That worried him.

"Are you afraid to go?"

"Not at all." She gently challenged, "Are you afraid to stay?"

"Not at all." With a concerned glance at Rinloo, who'd gone to stand near the Queen, Char carefully patted Pippin's billowing red hair. All those curls were certainly interesting, but he vastly preferred black fur.

She promised, "The balance is good."

"I will tell you something else that is good. If you want a break from scrubbing, run away to Theodora."

Pippin laughed again. "I won't run away."

"She bakes," he whispered. "Ask her to teach you to make rillberry tarts. And ... you can use my blue plate."

"Is Theodora a friend of yours?"

Char blinked. "Maybe ...? Ask Seyroo. He might know."

"Theodora and Seyroo," she repeated. "Did you want me to give them a message?"

He thought he'd already covered that. "Rillberry tarts. Blue plate. And … and this is for you. We made it together, me and my wolf."

It was harder to let go of the gift than he'd expected, for it was especially fine.

They'd turned the entire double-strand of perfect blue beads that had been around Rinloo's ankle into a necklace, from which they'd hung Char's own silver spoon. He fastened it around Pippin's neck, then gently tapped the spoon to say goodbye to it. But he wasn't sure what to say to the girl whose place he was taking.

"Do you want to give me a message?" he ventured.

Pippin leaned close to whisper, "Be good to your wolf."

He puffed out his chest. "I can do that. It is so easy."

And then they were leaving.

Char supposed he should say something to the Queen. But the only thing he could think to say was, "It was an *accident*."

"A happy one." And then she nodded, which was a relief, since it had to mean she *finally* understood.

KEEPING A PROMISE

Two days later, the wide Circle was empty. Well, almost. Three extra wolves, a dog, and a dragon had stayed back. Char was pretty sure they were waiting for him to do something.

Ninook-dex was unfailingly patient.

Beloor-dex was always amused.

Joonta-dex was bafflingly awed.

And Laud, who was and was not a dex, on account of being a

dog, had the good sense to accept seconds—or thirds—of whatever new recipe Moss let Char try.

"Why are you all named *dex*? Is that a clan name?"

"Not quite," said Beloor with a smile. "We're each a tenth child, and our name marks us."

Ninook gestured to each in turn. "Highwind. Ambervelte. Starmark. Trebellaire."

"Rinloo's a dex," said Laud.

Char gripped the big wooden spoon that was for stirring. "Is that important?"

"It is certainly poetic." Opal the Sage, who was laboring over lyrics, set aside his tea. "And undeniably appropriate."

Joonta blurted, "You chose well, since he can protect you."

"You *did* choose well," agreed Beloor. "Since he could not choose for himself."

Ninook's tail swayed. "You chose, even as you've been chosen."

"Choose this one, Char." Laud pointed to the few crumbs remaining on his plate. "Rinloo will like it."

"I will make another!"

But he didn't get very far into the new batch, for his wolf returned then, breathless and bramble-tangled.

Char was afraid something was wrong. He rushed forward, going up on tiptoe and reaching. "Why are you so high?" he grumbled.

Rinloo lowered himself to one knee and bowed his head so Char could check him over.

He smoothed his hands over his wolf's face, looking for injuries and finding small scratches. Char tossed aside twigs and burrs. "Who hurt you?"

"I only have my clumsy self to blame." Rinloo's smile was the same as always. "Unless you want a share? You sent me out, after all."

The wolf brought up his hands, which were clasped around something. Between strong fingers, Char caught a glimpse of green fur. Then a bright eye.

"Oh," he breathed. "Oooh!"

Cedar was suddenly there, nodding and smiling. "A fine young pitterhind. I wonder if he's hungry?"

Char scrambled to the counter and returned with some of the nuts and fruit that Moss had given him for ingredients. Holding a tidbit where the captured creature could see, he asked, "Do you like to eat?"

A tiny paw reached between the fingers, accompanied by a soft *peep*.

Rinloo's tail wagged. "Joonta was right. The Ephemera around here are mostly tame. Will he run if I turn him loose?"

"No," said Cedar. "I am here, and so is Char."

Mother Moss bustled in, a milk can in each arm. "Ephemera may run from predators, but they fly to imps and reavers, alike."

Slowly, Rinloo parted his fingers. The pitterhind sat back on its haunches and spread its wings. Then in a streak of green fur, it launched itself at Char, who cuddled it to his chest and stroked its head, right between its tiny antlers.

"Were you chased by my wolf?" Char asked sympathetically. "He is very big and very wild."

Said wolf sat upon the floor, legs crossed. And then Char was caught and cradled, but he didn't mind so much. Not with a pitterhind of his own to croon over.

"He was careful. See? You are safe. And so am I." Char offered a wedge of fruit and whispered, "My wolf is big and wild, but I think he must be noble."

Around him, the wolves were carrying on their own conversation. About patrols and pups and puddings. Just rambling from one thing to the next, like people with no place to go. Once again, Char got the sense that everyone was waiting for him to do something.

He couldn't imagine what.

Except ... he should probably thank his wolf for accomplishing his task. That was only good manners. So Char turned as much as he could in Rinloo's arms and brushed a kiss against the only place he could reach.

His wolf gasped. So did the others. So they *were* watching!

"What have you gone and done now?" demanded Opal the Sage.

"Accepted my gift, I should think," said Rinloo, his voice all funny.

"More than the gift," said Mother Moss significantly.

"The whole," agreed Ninook.

"Seconded," said Beloor.

"Speak up, maid-boy," said Opal. "This is as good a time as any, since we are all assembled."

Char looked up unsure what the fuss was about, but before he could demand answers of his wolf, he spied the shining filigree swirling across Rinloo's chest, centered over the place Char had kissed. It was very pretty, and it made obeying the dragon simple. "I must be good at kisses. This one turned out very pretty."

Opal said, "You favor your wolf."

"Do I?" Char brushed his fingers across warm skin to see if his mark would stay. "He kept his promise."

"And so you trust him?" prompted Ninook.

It was a foolish question. And only halfway true. "He trusts me, too."

"We are all assembled," repeated Opal the Sage. "This is somewhat less formal than other bonding ceremonies I have witnessed, but all is well. Are you ready to give this wolf a name?"

WORTHY OF BALLADS

Char already *knew* his name. "He is Paltry."

For several seconds, silence reigned. Had he gotten it wrong?

But no, his wolf was smiling.

"I suppose that *is* what you called him earlier." Opal's brows arched. "Well, Rinloo-dex Highwind? Will you answer to Paltry?"

"If he calls, I will answer."

"Well said." The dragon nodded Char's way. "And for the sake of balance … a name?"

"By rights, I should call you Churlish."

Char scowled, but only a little. He could tell his wolf was only teasing. Paltry's wildness was all around him, thick as black fur and just as warm. Char ducked his head and waited to see if his wolf would truly keep him.

Everyone else was listening in, but Paltry spoke directly to him. "You will be cherished, so that will be your name. Cherish."

"Is it a good name?" he whispered.

"Good and true," Paltry assured.

And so, on the floor of Mother Moss's kitchen, very near the spot where he'd made his ungainly descent, a cherished moonbeam looked up in time to bump noses with a noble wolf.

"Are you going to kiss me?" he asked cautiously.

"It could be considered traditional." His wolf's smile was reassuring, his gaze direct. "What are moonbeam traditions, when it comes to bonding?"

"If there are any, nobody said. Are kisses a rule?"

"No." Paltry's arms tightened around him. "This is enough."

Char, who couldn't quite think of himself as Cherish, glanced at the others. They were making little gestures, urging him to do something. Laud was the easiest to understand. He tapped his lips and pointed at Paltry. Were kisses more important than his wolf was letting on?

"Are you sure? I am not sure you are sure." Nodding at their audience, Char added, "These witnesses do not think this is enough."

"They're mostly teasing."

"Only mostly?" Char narrowed his eyes. "Are they partly right, paltry wolf?"

"There are no rules, beauty. Every bond is as different as the two who share it."

"You are sure of me?"

Paltry didn't hesitate. "I am."

Setting down his pitterhind—who immediately flutter-skipped to Cedar—Char turned to face his wolf fully. He haughtily said, "You are so certain. I would like to be certain, as well."

His wolf's own words.

Paltry knew it and laughed. "What else can I say, Cherish?"

Char thought he could get used to his new name if that's how Paltry said it.

"According to wolves, a kiss does not lie."

"That's how the saying goes." His wolf was being so careful. "Are you asking me to kiss you?"

"Nooo. *I* am going to kiss *you*." He proudly reminded, "I am good at them."

"Then claim me with kisses."

And so, on the floor of Mother Moss's kitchen, very near the spot where he'd made his ungainly descent, a cherished moonbeam offered an honest kiss to a noble wolf, who responded in kind ... and at some length.

Char pulled back and summoned up a glare. Nobody had told him that *this* was how wolves kissed. Sort of wild. Sort of hungry. Paltry had *said* enough, but what he'd *meant* was more. It was right there in his kiss.

"Will that do?" Paltry asked, his gaze slanting toward their audience.

"A good beginning," decreed Mother Moss. "Take care of each other."

"We are agreed," said Ninook on behalf of the canines. "May your bond gain in strength and beauty."

Opal the Sage added a flourish to his notes and beamed. "I am thoroughly diverted and wholly inspired. The stars themselves are tuning their voices to your song. But *my* satisfaction is the least of your worries. Are you satisfied with each other?"

Paltry asked, "Are you satisfied, beauty?"

"No." Which sounded bad now that it was out. Char tried to fix it. "Not yet."

"What is this paltry wolf lacking?"

Nothing. But that would make it sound like Char didn't know his own mind. And he was sure now, because kisses didn't lie. Kisses were simple. Just like wolves. *Un*like words.

"What is lacking is ... is ...." He floundered like a moonbeam who has lost his way up. But then the words stopped dancing out of reach, and he could say them. "What is lacking is *balance!*"

Paltry hummed encouragingly.

Char stiffly decreed, "I will only be satisfied when you are satisfied."

Hands were pulling, and Paltry's nose bumped Char's jaw. "You grumbly, clumsy, churlish bundle of impishness."

"That *is* what you called me." His wolf's voice held an interesting rumble. Char didn't think it was bad, but he thought he should check. "Have I done it wrong?"

"All is well." Paltry nuzzled Char's jaw, trailing his nose down his neck. "But what if I am never satisfied? What if I always want more?"

Char couldn't see the problem. "If I am here, there is always more."

"So you will stay with me, and I will stay with you."

"Yes."

"Because I keep my promises, and you'll keep yours."

"Yes." Char patted his wolf's hair, pleased he finally understood the importance of balance.

"Because I am your bonded, and you are mine."

"Yes."

"Because you love me as much as I love you?"

"Oh. That." Char wasn't sure he wanted to say so, not in front of Opal and the rest. He mumbled, "Maybe that."

"Only maybe?" Paltry asked, his tail slowly thumping the floor.

With a sulky peek at those looking on with smiles, Char leaned in closer and quietly corrected his wolf. "Only always."

THE END

FLATTERED BY FLOWERS

because it takes courage to stay open to new things

"Listen up, Ever. This is
important. Mum loves these."
Valor pointed into a shop
next door called The House
of the Noble Chrysanthemum.

"Mum?" Ever sniffed at the air.

"Lady Starmark likes
traditional Japanese sweets?"
Jacques admitted, "I'm surprised."

"They are a sentimental favorite,"
explained Valor. "This shop's
been around for a long time,
and Mum used to frequent it."

LORD METTELBRIGHT'S MAN

A FAMILY TO SUPPORT

Junpei knocked aside a couple of fist-sized stones and wedged his hoe under a larger, more stubborn one. When the call for workers had come in, clearing an overgrown road had sounded straightforward enough, but all these rocks and ruts had slowed down the whole process.

Putting his height to good use, Junpei pressed steadily. He took it slow. If the handle gave before the rock, he'd be in all kinds of trouble. Day laborers generally earned enough to put a meal on the table, but not much more. If he was careless, he'd lose a day or two, and Mother and Sho would go hungry.

"Come on," he coaxed. "Cooome on out of there. Change can be good. The whole world will look different after today. Brighter than ever. With a whole new perspective."

The foreman, who was working near Junpei, chuckled. "Sweet-talking the stones?"

"Whatever works."

"If it does, I'll start in myself. We're running short on time."

"When's the family supposed to move in?"

"Oh, they're here. Seems they arrived late yesterday. Though how they managed that, I couldn't guess."

Junpei straightened and looked along the road into Keishi, still thickly wreathed in morning mist. "It's just this last part that's really bad."

"If we're lucky, the head of the household will focus on the work we've done, not on the section left to do."

"Maybe this is good," suggested Junpei, facing the short jaunt of rough road ahead. "He'll see for himself what state this was in … and appreciate his fine new road all the more."

"Fair-minded folks like that are hard to come by. But if that's how it turns out, I wouldn't complain." Sounds came from the direction of the house, and the foreman pivoted. "Keep at it. Here comes the owner."

"Sure." Junpei kicked at the stubborn stone with his heel, trying to rock it loose, but most of his attention was on the house. He was as curious as the next man. And the next. And the next.

The foreman noticed. "We're paid to labor, you lot. So labor!"

Shouldering his shovel, the foreman strode off to greet the new owner of this creaking and crumbling estate beyond the farthest edge of Keishi. Junpei thought the distance was inconvenient, but the newly-arrived silk merchant must have taken a liking.

Junpei had looked around a little. There were fruit trees in every courtyard, and many were already blooming—plum and quince and cherry. He hoped the newcomers realized what treasures they were and tended them properly.

Once upon a time, this house and the surrounding lands had belonged to a daimyo, so the proportions were generous. In other words, too big to be practical. But according to local gossip, which

Mother attended to with as much care as she lavished on her biwa, the Hoshina household was large enough to fill its rooms to brimming.

Exactly how many wasn't known.

Nor could anyone say where they'd come from.

The family name was new to their area.

All anyone really knew was that the merchant had prospered elsewhere but wanted a fresh start. Mother thought it suspicious. He could be anyone, from anywhere. And why would he choose such a remote and ramshackle house?

Junpei didn't care. What did it matter? All of Keishi would benefit from the addition of a rich family to the community. The Hoshinas had already made his life easier, providing weeks of steady income right at the end of a harsh winter.

That meant rice and fish and miso and pickles. And fresh milk for Sho, who'd hit a growth spurt and was always famished. After so many sparse meals, every evening felt like a feast.

Murmurs rippled through the line of workers, and the reason became clear. Foreman was standing right next to the newcomer, who had to be twice his height! The giant had long, reddish hair, and his voice boomed jovially. But he wasn't speaking a language Junpei had ever heard.

Foreigners. Wouldn't Mother be shocked?

Right beside Junpei, someone spoke, using more foreign words.

Junpei looked into the upturned face of a boy in his early teens, perhaps a little older than Sho. Or maybe not, given the height and girth of the head of the Hoshina household. The boy was strange, but in a comely way. Wavy red hair flowed past his shoulders, and there was a friendly light in his brown eyes.

He spoke again, touching his chest. "Quen ... err. *Ken* Hoshina."

"Good morning, Ken-kun." Placing his hand over his heart, he said, "My name's Junpei."

"Junpei-san?" he checked.

"Yes."

Ken next gestured to the rock that was giving Junpei trouble, and he said something more. The foreign words sounded like nonsense to Junpei.

"We're moving stones." It was probably silly to try to explain. He flattened his hand and waved it over the ground. "Your road is a mess, and that's no good. Wouldn't you rather have a smooth ride when you come into town?"

With a grin, Ken stuck the toe of his boot into the gap Junpei had made for his hoe and lifted. Carefully levering the stubborn stone out, he rolled it aside, exposing a sizeable hole. The rock had been bigger than it looked, which explained why it had been giving Junpei so much trouble. It *didn't* explain how the boy had managed the task so easily.

Finding his voice, Junpei exclaimed, "Thank you, Ken-kun."

The boy answered with a courteous expression, then jogged off to help the next guy.

FOREIGNERS HAVE STRANGE WAYS

Work went much more smoothly after that, because Ken wasn't the only son of House Hoshina. More men emerged, each larger than the next. Conversation was limited to friendly smiles, basic greetings, and the exchange of names … except in the owner's case. He moved from person to person along with one of the town elders, Hisoka Araki.

Maybe it was a foreign custom? Junpei knew from experience that important people only mingled with important people. This wealthy merchant should be taking tea with the leaders of Keishi, not getting to know men who couldn't even boast a reliable source of income.

Junpei's turn came.

"Hello, friend. Please excuse my clumsy words." The greeting was big and broad and strangely accented. He offered an upturned palm. "I'm going by Hoshina."

Araki explained, "The meeting of palms is traditional where Hoshina-dono comes from."

Returning the greeting, he offered his name in return. "Welcome to the area, sir. You chose a good place. Have you seen the trees?"

Which sounded foolish as soon as he'd said it. They were surrounded by woods. You couldn't miss the trees.

The big man looked curiously between him and Araki, who seemed to be acting as translator.

Hisoka Araki was respected and respectable. A town leader certainly didn't mingle with people of Junpei's ilk, but he hadn't balked at addressing any of their crew. He had the poise of a diplomat, the air of a sage, and striking coloring. He seemed too young to be so thoroughly silvered.

After a brief exchange, which included an intriguing number of shifts in posture, Hisoka turned from Hoshina to ask, "Do you mean the trees in his gardens?"

"Yes, sir."

"Are you perhaps a gardener?"

"No, no. Not me."

"I see. My friend is also looking for carpenters. The existing buildings need repair, and he intends to add new walkways and pavilions."

Hoshina was offering additional work? That was certainly good news for some of their crew, but Junpei shook his head. "I'm unskilled. I can dig and carry, but I cannot build."

"I see." They traded a few more words, and Araki smiled with real fondness at the big man. "He wants you to know that he chose this house in part because of the trees. You are welcome to visit his gardens anytime."

"Me?"

"Yes, Junpei-san."

"That is very generous. Thank you, Araki-san."

"Sensei, if you wouldn't mind." He beckoned between them. "I prefer *sensei*."

Was he a doctor? Or a scholar? Junpei had no guesses, but he ducked his head and murmured, "Araki-sensei."

"Hisoka!" interjected the owner, who reeled out words like one who loved conversation. They flowed past Junpei without meaning, but he thought they were perhaps speaking about him.

Finally, Araki said, "My friend has taken a liking to you. If you have no other obligations, he wants to hire you. A day's wage if you'll spend your mornings here, doing odd jobs.

Junpei wasn't sure he'd heard right. "Half days?"

"For a full day's wage." With a faint smile, Araki murmured,

"Did I not say he's taken a liking to you? I'm sure I did."

Bowing low to both of them, Junpei exclaimed, "Thank you so much! I'll be here!"

HOUSE UNDER THE WISTERIA

Junpei shouldered his hoe and began the long walk back into town. Their small house on the north end of Keishi wasn't in the worst district. Kikusawa was a nice neighborhood, entirely respectable, even if they weren't.

When Mother was young, she'd worked in one of those tearooms where a girl's company could be purchased. With her beauty and her talent with the biwa, she'd secured the patronage of more than one admirer. Junpei's father had made a present of their current home, lavishing its interior screens with his artistry. And in its miniscule garden, he'd planted a namesake wisteria.

It wasn't Mother's given name, but the one he'd used for her. Her working name. Sumire.

Mother considered its blooming branches a sign of that man's eternal love and often sat playing in its shade. She made a lovely picture, framed by swaying purple flowers. Junpei had no doubt it was the exact scene his father had envisioned from the outset.

As if they were in one of his paintings.

One he'd lost interest in as soon as it was done.

That man had set Mother up, then walked away. Junpei often wished his father had been more pragmatic in his parting extravagance. A fruit tree would have given them more to eat.

"I'm home!" he called, kicking off his sandals.

Mother answered his greeting, hurrying forward and making him bend so she could kiss his cheek. He was nearly thirty, yet she still treated him like a little boy.

"You're back early, Jun-kun." Her voice was cultured, musical. But also concerned. "Is the job already done?"

"There is more to do," he assured. "We finished early today because Hoshina-dono's sons helped us. But they asked me back. I can still earn more."

Mother relaxed a little. Then smiled her most charming smile. "You saw him? What was Hoshina-dono like?"

"A good man, I think. He has Hisoka Araki's support." Junpei quickly pivoted, asking, "Isn't Sho home from school yet?"

"He went off with friends. You know how he is. Very like his father, in that way."

Junpei had been fourteen when Mother fell pregnant again. She'd been unable to work any longer, so he'd stepped up, doing odd jobs to earn a few coins. Any work. Hard work. Dull work. Just ... work.

Mother relied upon Junpei.

But Sho was indulged.

He wasn't spoiled, exactly, but neither was he expected to dig up stones or labor in fields, even though Sho was nearing the age when Junpei began taking menial jobs. All the money Mother brought in from biwa lessons went toward Sho's schooling. Because he really was very like his father—lively, likeable, and brimming with potential.

Sho attended classes.

Sho learned the biwa.

Sho had private tutors.

And at this hour, Sho should have been seated at their table, attending to his studies. But Junpei wouldn't go find him and remind him of his duties. When it came right down to it, Junpei indulged his little brother, too. Or maybe he was being selfish. A carefree afternoon was something Junpei could appreciate. This was his first in many weeks.

"I'll be in my room," he murmured.

Mother smiled, stepped back, and bowed.

Junpei slid open the door to the cramped room that was his only scrap of privacy. Ducking through, he breathed deeply. Long and narrow, this space allowed him to stretch to his full length when it was time to pull out his futon. But whenever he was here during waking hours, this was his workshop.

A far cry from his father's atelier.

But Junpei pushed aside the wooden shutters that took up half of one wall, leaving only the paper screen between him and the garden. Light suffused the space, and he smiled at the lineup of paper parasols awaiting his brush. He'd only managed to finish two yesterday, and those by lamplight. Daylight was better for this sort of work.

As the sound of Mother's biwa started in the next room, Junpei tied back his sleeves and started mixing his paints.

He sold these parasols to a friend of Mother's who ran a shop. So it counted as work, even if it didn't bring in much money. Because paints were costly, and paper was hard to come by. But he kept at it, perhaps because in some ways, he was very like his own father.

This was the *only* work Junpei ever looked forward to.

No, it was more than that.

The planning, the procurement, the patience required. The meditative calm, the sweeping brush strokes, the bloom of paint. All of it, every part.

Art was the first thing Junpei had ever loved.

FORAGE ON THE SLOPES

Junpei quietly worked his way upward, moving from tree to tree. This time of year, they could gather edible shoots and spring greens to supplement their diet. Mother was originally from a mountain village to the north, and she'd passed along her people's wisdom to Junpei. Many sansai—edible spring plants—flourished on the slopes below Kikusawa Shrine.

Sho was with him today. Mother had insisted, not that his younger brother had resisted. He was twelve and *always* hungry. Even now, he foraged with a hosta shoot between his teeth.

"Find any butterbur, yet?" Junpei asked.

"Plenty!" Sho backtracked to display the contents of his shallow basket, which also included fern fiddlers and mustard greens. "Wish it wasn't too soon for mushrooms. They're more filling."

"We should look for those leeks Mother favors."

"There's a patch higher up."

"There is."

With a grin, Sho announced, "I'm going on ahead."

As he scrambled higher, Junpei shook his head. It hadn't been all that long ago that he'd been teaching his little brother which plants were safe to eat. Now, Sho was acting like the expert.

Junpei angled upward, searching for the spring chrysanthemums he liked while gathering more fiddlers.

They were pretty high here, well above the rooftops of their neighborhood. As far as Junpei could tell, nobody else foraged here. Maybe it was simple ignorance. Maybe it was respect for the shrine grounds. Junpei hadn't ever felt guilty about taking the greens he carried away. If animals could browse these slopes, why not them?

A flutter of movement caught his eye, and he glanced up.

Flower petals drifted down from somewhere atop the hill.

It was beautiful.

Junpei set his back to the nearest tree and watched the silent swirl of white petals. Plum blossoms. He remembered the stand of fruit trees in one of Kikusawa Shrine's many courtyards. And the central courtyard, where an enormous sacred tree flowered.

He wasn't particularly devout, so he didn't climb the long stairs to the hilltop shrine very often. The last time he'd been there in springtime was when he'd gone to pray for a blessing and purchase a charm to ensure a safe pregnancy for Mother.

The shrinekeeper had patiently walked him through the process. Junpei had liked Matsu Miyabe straight away. A good man. They still traded greetings sometimes, though more often in the neighborhood below the shrine than atop the hill.

Maybe Junpei should pay a visit again, soon. He could purchase a charm for Sho, a blessing for his studies.

A subtle fragrance beckoned from above, and Junpei was tempted to climb higher, just to get closer.

He checked to see where Sho had gotten to.

His brother was easy to spot in his yellow half-coat. Sho stood at the very top of the slope, gazing at something—or someone—on the shrine grounds. Junpei doubted that the boy was admiring the gardens. Shrine maidens, maybe? Sho was getting to be that age.

Junpei decided to turn back and worked his way downhill. There was a rock not far from the verge, his favorite spot to sit and wait. He'd always felt a little sneaky there, because it afforded a view of the road, but passersby couldn't see well into the trees.

Since they lived nearby, Junpei knew many of them. Neighbors or notables.

Again, he glanced Sho's way. His brother was on his way down. That was good. They'd have a feast for their midday meal.

Then he looked back at the road, and his breath caught.

A lady was walking past, and her kimono was a masterpiece of springtime. Junpei thrilled at the pattern and stared hard, trying to memorize the bow and bend of each branch and the lavish scattering of plum blossoms.

She stopped short and turned his way.

Her parasol tilted back, and Junpei was looking straight into a pair of wide eyes that were the most remarkable shade of blue. Could she see him? It seemed so. His pulse quickened, and his cheeks heated. He hadn't meant to be rude.

Pressing a hand to his heart, he dragged his gaze away and dipped his head.

When he stole a peek, she touched her own heart, inclined her head, and walked on.

The only thing he could think was that it was a shame her parasol was plain. If Junpei had been carrying his paintbox, he could have adorned it in a matter of minutes and returned it to her hand, a bower of plum blossoms.

Sho reached him, then, and crowded onto the stone seat. "What's the matter? Why're you gawping?"

"There was a woman just now. With a parasol."

"Oh, yeah?" His younger brother leaned forward, looking up and down the road. "Was it one of *your* parasols?"

"No." Junpei would have liked to see that. Very much. "She was beautiful. Like a flower."

Sho elbowed him. "Love at first sight?"

"That would be foolish."

"You didn't deny it!" his brother teased. "You must be in love. I'm going to tell mother."

Junpei dragged Sho into a headlock. "And *that* would be folly."

"Her favorite kind!"

"It's not love. How could it be? I have no idea who she is." He roughed up his brother's light brown hair, which was curly enough to defy combing, then picked out a few flower petals. Most were pink. A few were tiny and red. "What were *you* looking at? Up there?"

Sho hesitated. "There was a man I've never seen before."

Junpei hummed in mild interest. "What did he look like?"

His brother opened his mouth, then hesitated. With a bewildered expression, he said, "I don't remember."

ANOTHER FOREIGNER IN TOWN

Junpei was on his way home from work a few days later when a woman hailed him in the street. Well, not him specifically. The rest scattered before her, but when he stood his ground, she veered his way.

She was a foreigner, and she was *tall*.

He was considered tall by local standards. When neighbors needed to reach something from a high shelf or rescue a cat from a tree branch, they generally sent for Junpei. Others were taller, but they were also surlier. Having a good temper had led to Junpei being considered a neighborhood resource.

This lady surpassed his height by a handsbreadth or more, and she was scowling. She addressed him in commanding tones, but her hands were spread in a peaceable gesture.

"I'm sorry," he offered. "I don't know your words."

She tried a few phrases, but Junpei could only shake his head.

The woman huffed moodily, and he felt bad for her. She needed a translator like Hoshina-dono did. But he wondered if it was wise to lead a stranger all the way out to their estate. And he wasn't sure where to find Hisoka Araki. Someone closer would be better.

Patting his chest, he announced, "Junpei."

She sighed and tapped her own shoulder. "Anna."

"Anna-san." With a respectful bow, he gestured toward the hilltop that dominated Kikusawa. "I'll lead you to our shrinekeeper. He's a vastly more learned man. He may know your words."

She eyed him skeptically.

Hers was a weighty gaze.

Bowing again, he backed toward their destination. "Follow me, Anna-san. Help is this way."

With a harrumph, she fell in step beside him.

Anna wasn't just tall. Her skin was quite light, as was the hair that had been cropped close to her head, and her eyes glinted like green ice. Her clothes were similarly strange, and she carried several weapons. Now that he considered the matter, Junpei wondered if *he* was wise, going off with this stranger.

She met his gaze and arched her brows.

"I'm sorry to stare. It's a bad habit of mine." Gesturing toward the long row of red-painted gates that framed the stairway to Kikusawa Shrine, he said, "We climb. All the way to the top."

Anna's expression turned incredulous.

He could understand why.

Even he had to duck his head under most of the torii. She'd have to stoop the entire way. "I wonder if you'll understand …?" Junpei tapped the top of his head, then lifted a hand before his face to signal apology. Grimacing, he moved a few paces beyond the stairs and parted the shrubbery, saying, "So sorry, Anna-san. I know it's a bother, so I prefer this route. Will it do for you?"

She smirked and waved for him to lead on.

ALWAYS A KIND WORD

Junpei wasn't sure how their ascent turned into a race, but Anna easily outpaced him, despite being in unfamiliar territory. She was smiling by the time they burst out of the greenery and into the courtyard at the top. To think, a little friendly competition had banished her scowl. She was a strange one.

"We're looking for the shrinekeeper now," he explained. "Matsu Miyabe. This is his home."

"Matsu?" she echoed, scanning the gardens.

He wasn't sure how to explain that given names were too personal to use without permission. "Miyabe-san," he corrected. "To be respectful, Miyabe-san."

She simply grunted again. It had the feel of an affirmative.

Junpei wondered where the man would be at this time of day. Aiming for the central shrine, he peered into each little garden they passed. Alleys ran between storehouses as well. And there was a sprawling house, fairly bursting at the seams, Matsu kept it so full.

Another idea struck. If Matsu didn't know Anna's words, Junpei *could* try at his favorite teahouse. But he wasn't sure if the proprietor should be anybody's first impression of Keishi. Perhaps one of Matsu's children could carry a message to Hisoka Araki?

Someone caught his attention. He was standing beside the tree that dominated the hilltop. Full sleeves and billowing hakama. Long, dark hair, left loose. And a crown of flowers as red as the torii gates.

Who could it be?

"Junpei!" hailed a familiar voice.

Relieved, he hurried to meet the man they needed. Matsu Miyabe was known throughout Keishi as a learned man with a love for books. Visitors to their city would come here just to see him, and according to local gossip, of which Mother stayed abreast, Matsu could speak four languages.

"I found a lady," Junpei managed, before Anna barged in to speak for herself.

Matsu's surprise faded into his usual genial expression, and Junpei was nearly as relieved as the lady herself. He'd chosen well.

The shrinekeeper knew her words.

Their conversation left him out, and he was trying to decide if he should just excuse himself when Matsu turned to him.

"Junpei, do you mind helping my boys in the eastern storehouse? Little Kenzou was just telling me that there are cobwebs he can't reach."

With a rueful smile, Junpei said, "If my height can do you some good, I'm happy to lend a hand."

"Sho is with them," Matsu added. "He's here most afternoons."

Junpei's surprise must have shown. His brother was supposed to be *studying* most afternoons. He and mother were working hard to give him the tools to follow in his novelist father's footsteps. Since they were so similar. Since Sho seemed perfectly suited.

"He's welcome, of course. A fine lad." Matsu watched his face with sympathy. "Did you know he's been helping Taiki and Masao with their mathematics? And the little ones beg for him to read."

"I didn't know."

The man stepped closer and gripped his elbow. "Sho is growing into a fine man. Like you."

Junpei tucked his chin and wished—not for the first time—that he'd had a father like Matsu. Was it any wonder Sho lingered here? "Will you be able to help Anna-san?"

"She and I will have tea and talk some more. You did well to bring her to me. Thank you."

"I'll go and find my brother. Since you have a guest. Or … guests? Who was the man I saw earlier?" Junpei looked off toward the tree. "He seemed tall, but not skinny like me. And he dressed like you, but ... differently. Somehow."

Matsu's eyebrows jumped. "Is that so?"

Junpei was beginning to feel foolish. It had just happened, but the memory was already fuzzy. "I think he had long hair, but that would be strange. Did I imagine it?"

"You have good eyes." The shrinekeeper's smile was back. "It's all right, Junpei. You must have spotted Kusunoki. I guess you'd say he's a childhood friend. We grew up together, and even now, he's like a brother to me. He's often hereabouts, but most people don't notice."

"Oh? That must be lonesome." Junpei felt as if he'd trespassed on something private.

"He keeps to himself. Should I pass along your greetings?"

"Please. If it won't trouble him ...?"

Matsu chuckled. "It'll probably amuse him. Really, it's fine, Junpei. Either way."

Confused, he echoed, "Either way?"

"Whether you remember or not. Don't feel bad. He isn't the lonesome sort."

WE ARE THEIR SANCTUARY

Anna Green gazed after the man who'd been her guide. Junpei hadn't quailed before her, and he'd brought her to the best possible sanctuary. Matsu Miyabe was a member of the In-between, and he spoke English. But most heartening, perhaps, was the way he'd called her "daughter."

Just that.

One word.

How had it worked so swiftly into her soul, assuring her that she was safe?

Anna's training since childhood meant she possessed strength, resilience, and the skills to incapacitate human opponents and render most Amaranthine insensate. She was *strong*. The best of her generation. Mentors and members of her allotment boasted on her behalf, and while they meant well, all their praise and pride had only added up to trouble.

"That man," she said, indicating Junpei. "He is not a reaver?"

"No. At least, he wasn't born into the In-between." The shrinekeeper gazed up into her face. "But you were, Miss Green?"

She squared her shoulders. "Battler class."

"Will you be offended if I ask your age?"

"Eighteen." And because he seemed to have guessed, she awkwardly added, "Almost."

"Are you here to attend Ingress Academy?"

Anna hesitated. "There is a school here?"

"You didn't know?"

Any further inquiry was sidetracked by the reappearance of Junpei, who hefted a broom while chasing four children out of one of the nearby buildings. His battle cry was pitiful. Instead of inspiring fear, it sent his prey into shrieks of laughter.

"I cannot tell who is mocking whom," she murmured.

"They're playing," said Matsu, whose smile was indulgent. "Things are different for children in the public sector, but they still crave a mentor's participation and approval."

"And what do they learn from Junpei?"

"Who can say? We all take something from each other, even as we give something back. That is community."

Anna grunted. "Are those your children?"

Matsu seemed surprised by the question, but turning to look at the group, his expression cleared. "They're mine, most by choice rather than by birth. Ah. Except for Sho. That one there is Junpei's younger brother."

The boy stood out, for his smile was the brightest, his laugh the most contagious. A leader, but the sort who carried his allotment into mischief rather than battle. But one thing puzzled her. "You do mean that boy, with the lighter hair?"

Though all the other children had smooth, black hair—including Junpei—Sho's was a rough halo of brown waves.

"Yes, that's Sho."

"There is little resemblance to Junpei."

"They share a mother."

He left it at that. Half-brothers, then. But she wasn't clear on the rest. "Your children are not your own? Are you fostering for other reavers?"

"No. Those I took in are unendowed—either orphans or abandoned. They needed a home, occupation, education. We do what we can to bring them up, then apprentice them to families here in Kikusawa. Or to nearby farms, if that suits them better."

"You run an orphanage?"

"Not officially." Waving off her admiration, he repeated, "We do what we can."

Anna asked, "You hold classes?"

"Certainly."

"May I join?" Her chin lifted. "I need to learn the language. They can be my teachers."

"A fine idea," he agreed amiably enough. "But that's not why you came …?"

"Well … no."

"You would be more at home with other students at the academy. I can introduce you to the administrators, and they would give you a place."

"No. *Miyabe* was the name I was given. You are the holy man I needed to find."

"Again, may I ask why?"

She adjusted her posture to plead with him. "An old friend told me that your home was the only place I would be able to find the information I seek."

"You want books?"

"Lore."

Matsu nodded slowly. "We do have a collection."

Anna boldly added, "And a weapon."

"That's *not* widely known." He considered her solemnly. "I would even say it's unknown."

"I can explain." With a glance in the direction of Junpei and his tagalongs, she lowered her voice. "*Please*, let me explain?"

"Certainly."

Weariness and worries pressed down, and she sagged under their weight. "I am in a difficult position. Pursued by dragons."

"What do they want from you?"

She scowled. "*Friendship* was not their goal."

Matsu looked shocked. "Are they fools to press a battler?"

"It is strangely difficult to refuse a dragon, even when his proposals are entirely unwelcome." Swallowing hard, she admitted, "A truer friend extricated me and sent me on ahead. He gave the name Miyabe. He spoke of the Chrysanthemum Blaze."

Gesturing for secrecy, Matsu quietly demanded, "*What* friend?"

Anna couldn't help smiling a little. Her mentor inspired them, even from afar. "He is called Opal the Sage."

OF PIGMENT AND PAPER

"Jun-kun?" Mother pushed a dish of pickles closer to him. "Do me a favor?"

He'd barely returned from his morning's work at the Hoshina estate, where he'd been little more than an errand boy. Even so, Junpei waited for new orders.

"You like going to his atelier, anyhow … don't you?"

His heart sank as Mother slid a folded letter across the table. All he said was, "It's been a while."

She brightened.

Not until the meal was over and his hands were clean did he touch that letter. And not until he was halfway across the city did he allow himself a twinge of envy over the quality of the paper. Mother must have paid one of her old acquaintances to write it for her. Such things were costly, and coins were dear.

Junpei only allowed himself a little money for paper and pigments. Usually, just enough to complete the next order. It was tempting to spend more, to indulge his passion, but he was strict with himself.

Hobbies were for other, wealthier households. Yes, they paid well for Sho's schooling, and money went into keeping Mother's biwa in good repair. But just like Junpei's artistry, which was considered an extravagance by gossipy neighbors, everything was tied to his family's livelihood.

They existed on the fringes of luxury, the spurned mistress and her mismatched bastards.

By longstanding arrangement, messages to Junpei's father were carried to the back door of his atelier. These days, it was the only reason Junpei ever came here. Back when he was just a kid, Mother had wheedled him an apprenticeship of sorts.

Even then, Junpei had been in awe of the grand screens and wall scrolls for which his artist father was famous. Lavish and lively. They felt like home. And he'd yearned to try his hand.

He'd scrubbed floors and run errands more than anything, but he'd also learned how to mix pigments, grind ink, and hold a brush. And he'd learned what it meant to be a bastard.

Father barely spared him a glance.

He was often away—dining with clients, pandering to patrons, or spending time with his true family. Because the man had legitimate sons, and two of them were properly acknowledged apprentices. Junpei preferred not to meet them, even as they would have preferred that he didn't exist.

For years, Junpei had relied on scraps and stubs and the dregs of paint pots. And somehow, on that meager charity, Junpei found his way.

Early on, he'd wanted to show that man what he'd done, what he could do. A mistake, in hindsight. With no warning, Junpei found himself banished from the atelier—apprenticeship over, lessons ended, access denied. Yet Junpei had gone skulking back. How could he give up, now that he knew what he could do?

Prideful sire.

Jealous heirs.

Desperate son.

Junpei returned to the atelier, a beggar at the back door. And he'd found an ally in one of his father's employees. Yami-san had been a small man with soft eyes, in charge of flower arrangements. At odd hours, when Father wasn't on the premises, Junpei would steal in.

The sympathetic man would bring out odd scraps of paper, unwashed dishes holding remnants of paint, and a pot of tea. Then the fellow would sit across the table from Junpei and watch him work.

They chatted some, usually about art. He recommended places to go—public gardens and parks, flower shops and shows. He'd been the one to suggest visiting the bookseller's booth where Junpei sometimes loitered. And that discovery led to another, since the way home from Naoki's led past the little tearoom Junpei visited whenever he had coin to spare.

He dared to hope that his old friend Yami-san would answer his knock.

But no. It was one of the sons, his expression sour.

Stifling a sigh, Junpei proffered the letter and resigned himself to a long, uncomfortable wait.

WHERE TEA TASTES BEST

Junpei trudged homeward.

Whatever message Mother had sent, it had certainly garnered a response. Father had thrown open the back door, looked Junpei up and down, and slung a knotted bag against his chest. The glitter of annoyance in his eyes contradicted the weight of the purse. The door snapped shut again, without either man saying a word.

It felt like a lot of money.

Last time, she'd wanted enough to repair her biwa. Once, Junpei knew she'd begged for painted silk in which to array herself. Father had indulged that whim with a superior sort of pride. And far more grace than he'd shown today. Junpei rubbed at his breastbone, which still smarted.

He didn't understand their relationship. Honestly, he didn't want to. Junpei could only assume that Mother knew when and how far it was wise to push the man.

Leaving the loftier parts of Keishi behind, he eased into the comfortable familiarity of his own neighborhood ... and paused. Twice recently, his favorite tearoom had come to mind. Today, more than any other day, Junpei deserved a little comfort. So he put off his return home, intent on indulging himself at Moonglade Tearoom.

That's when he spotted her again.

A cascade of plum blossoms and startlingly blue eyes.

She lifted her parasol, and Junpei could see her arranged hair. Such light brown was an unusual color; Sho could attest to that. But Junpei thought it was beautiful … and knew he shouldn't be staring.

With a quizzical smile, the woman walked his way.

He wanted to hide. He wanted to speak. He *needed* to breathe.

"For you," she said, holding out something.

Tongue-tied, Junpei lifted both palms to receive it, then watched her graceful retreat into the shop right next door to Moonglade Tearoom. He knew it well enough. The House of the Noble Chrysanthemum sold traditional sweets. The wrapped block in his hand must have been a sample. Should he follow her inside? Maybe ask for her name?

But then a tall man leaned out of the tearoom door and called, "You coming my way, Junpei? Perfect timing! I need a man of your talents!"

"Good afternoon, Paltry-san." Junpei tucked the sweet into his sleeve, spared the shop a final glance, and crossed to Moonglade's owner. "Most seem to think my only talent is being tall. Yet in this, you have me beat."

Paltry dominated any room, a good head and shoulders taller than every man in Kikusawa, if not all of Keishi. He was clearly a foreigner, though he'd adopted local styles, and his Japanese was flawless. Water lilies decorated today's kimono, and his hairstyle employed a great many combs. Junpei wondered if the man didn't know that he sometimes adopted women's fashion … or if he simply didn't care.

"Just Paltry, please. We're friends, aren't we?"

"As often as I can manage." Junpei only stopped in once or twice a month, barely often enough to be considered a regular, let alone to put them on a first-name basis.

Paltry wrapped an arm around Junpei's shoulders and guided him inside. "I have an unexpected guest. An old friend from my homeland just moved into the area. If you'll practice with him, your tea and snacks will be complementary, today. All you want. No charge."

"Practice?"

"Japanese. He's learning the language. Can you spare him some time? For me?"

Junpei murmured his agreement, hardly believing his good fortune. Moonglade's tea was excellent, and their snacks were unlike anything he'd tasted before. *Pastries*, Churlish called them. And he could eat as much as he wanted?

A chair scraped back, and a man stood to offer a greeting.

He was nearly as tall as Paltry, and Junpei had seen him before. He was part of Hoshina-dono's household and was often in the company of young Ken.

"This is my good friend, Laud."

Junpei nodded, then shook his head. That wasn't the name he'd been given before. Neither did the man look the same. More baffled than anything, Junpei blurted, "Why is your hair white?"

TWO KINDS OF CAKE

"Hold that thought," said Paltry, who firmly guided Junpei toward a chair. "Sit right here, and just … hold on. I have an answer for that, and I'm pretty sure it's a good one. Churlish!"

Junpei stood his ground, unsure he wanted the seat.

The boy who ruled over the tearoom's kitchen arrived, and Junpei gaped at him, too. Had everyone's hair changed color?

"He can see me." Churlish brushed suddenly-silver hair behind an ear, which now came to a point.

"So it seems," agreed Paltry.

With a small shrug, Churlish asked, "Do you still want cake? I made two kinds."

Junpei looked to Paltry for some help in understanding what was going on, only to find that the man's eyes were similarly changed. "Silver?" he whispered.

"You noticed. Well, I'm not entirely surprised. You've always had a bit of shine." Paltry's voice was pitched to soothe. "You're taking all of this rather well."

"Am I?" Half to himself, Junpei asked, "Should I be?"

"Yes. You like new things, don't you?" Paltry promised, "You're one of the bravest men in Kikusawa, if not all of Keishi."

Was he? He didn't see how.

Something moved in Junpei's periphery.

It was a tail. Paltry's tail.

"Peace, friend. We *are* friends, remember?" And raising his voice slightly, Paltry called, "Can *somebody* send for Matsu?"

Churlish must have gone into the kitchen, again, because he now carried a tray. Peering up into Junpei's face, he asked, "Are you afraid of me? That *would* be silly."

"I don't think so ...?"

"Good. Sit here, across from Laud. Or are you afraid of him?"

Another long look, this one chiding. "That would probably make him sad."

Junpei nodded. Then shook his head. He'd lost track of the question he needed to answer. "Your eyes are silver now. So strange."

Churlish frowned. "Where I come from, everyone has silver eyes. Where you come from, everyone has brown eyes. Mostly."

"Do you come from far away?"

"It did not seem so at the time. Do you like lakes?"

"I'm ... not sure ...?"

"You like cake, though." Churlish moved a teapot and cups from his tray to the table, where Laud sat with gaze downcast. "There are two kinds of cake today, but I know how to make lots of other kinds."

Junpei murmured, "I believe you."

"And there are lots more than two kinds of people. I am one kind. Paltry is another kind. And you have always been nice to us." Churlish tugged and pushed, getting Junpei to sit before asking, "Will you stop, now that you know we are a different kind of people?"

"You think I'm nice?"

Rolling his eyes, Churlish said, "You eat my pastries, and you do not mind that they are different. And you talk to Paltry, even though he is big and wild and has a tail. I *like* black fur. Do you?"

"I'm not sure," he repeated.

Churlish poured tea for him and for the one he called Laud. "Do you want me to tell him what you said? He does not know much Japanese, and he is very confused."

"So am I."

"When people are confused, they should talk. I know." And then he spoke to Laud in another language. Not for long. Just a sentence or two. Turning back to Junpei, Churlish said, "I told him you asked about his hair."

Laud was looking at him now. And his eyes were changed.

Junpei leaned across the table, intrigued by the color. "There are stories about people falling in among strange folk. Are you youkai?"

"No. The clans may have inspired your stories, though." Paltry crouched beside the table and relayed, "More people are coming. People you trust. They can explain."

"Or ... I could make him forget," suggested another.

Junpei saw Paltry's tail puff and settle as a stranger strolled into their midst. This one had white hair, too.

"You?" exclaimed Churlish. "What are *you* doing here?"

"Incidental matters have somehow overlapped in a confluence of destinies. Do not scowl so. It gives the wrong impression." And to Junpei, he genially added, "I am an old friend. No need to fear. Neither them, nor me."

As if Junpei ever could. He couldn't imagine being afraid of anyone here.

"Entirely susceptible," remarked the newcomer. "Would you like me to ... unburden him with regards to today's discoveries?"

Junpei hardly knew what to think when Churlish flung slender arms around his shoulders and hugged him tightly. He wasn't alarmed, exactly. But in some distant part of his mind, he knew this was highly unusual.

Scowling, the boy demanded, "Leave him alone! Junpei is our friend!"

Paltry acted so quickly, Junpei didn't see him move. He loomed over the stranger, one hand covering his mouth.

And ... there seemed to be a rumble in the air. Almost like a growling animal. Which probably should have been scary, but Junpei knew there was no need to fear. Somehow.

Gently pushing aside Paltry's hand, the newcomer said, "That will do, maid-boy. Call off your wolf. I will not meddle where I am unneeded." He bowed to Junpei, possibly in apology. "My name is Opulence Windlore, renowned the world over as Opal the Sage."

To Junpei's surprise, Paltry wrapped an arm around the sage's shoulders, pulling him into a rough hug and dropping a kiss atop his head. "How is our favorite bard?"

Quite the change in attitude.

"Passable, though muddling through pressing matters. Have any of you caught wind of a young lady of my acquaintance? She is fair enough to stand out in these parts. Tall. Blonde. Battler-bold."

Junpei whispered, "Anna?"

All eyes swung his way, and he did his best to huddle behind Churlish.

Suddenly, Opal was at his shoulder, and his words were sweet. "Tell me where she is."

"With me!" Matsu leaned against the entry, puffing slightly, as if he'd been running. "Anna Green is safe with me."

"And you are?" inquired the sage.

With a quick glance around the room, Matsu sought Junpei's gaze and promised, "I'm this man's friend."

NOTHING UP THIS SLEEVE

Before any more could be said, another man shouldered into the room, although at this point, Junpei wasn't entirely sure that they *were* men. Had he fallen in among gods or demons?

An already-familiar booming voice, thick with concern, was asking questions. Someone had sent for Hoshina-dono? The silk merchant cut off at the sight of him and hurried to kneel beside Junpei's chair.

"My little brother." He indicated Laud, though his gaze never wavered. "He called for help."

Brothers? Nobody had explained their connection. There was a definite resemblance. They had the same eyes.

"Junpei?" Hoshina-dono touched his arm.

The big man was so gentle, but the claws were such a surprise, Junpei stiffened.

"Him, too," interjected Opal. "Nothing to fear from the likes of Harmonious. Calm yourself, young man. You are among friendly folk."

Reassuring words. Junpei already felt better. Why had he been uneasy, even for a moment?

"None of that," growled Paltry.

"A simple palliative. Would you rather he fainted?" To Hoshina-dono, Opal added, "Every one of our illusions has dropped. He sees you. Quite plainly."

The big man's expression softened. "I'm sorry, Junpei. Are you all right?"

"Yes," he managed.

"My little brother was afraid for you."

Junpei looked to Laud. "I worry about my little brother, too."

Hoshina-dono scanned the room, then switched to his own language.

"He wants to know what happened," relayed Churlish, who lofted a tray as he scooted around Hoshina-dono, setting it between Junpei and Laud. "Cake. You should eat some. It is good.

And I know *everything*."

"What do you claim to know, maid-boy?" inquired Opal the Sage.

"Wolves are simple."

"Granted ...?" Paltry's tail took to swaying.

Churlish stuck his nose in the air. "Dragons are sly."

Opal merely hummed.

"Cats have secrets."

From the direction of the door, another familiar voice remarked, "Quite the crowd, today, Paltry. Has something happened?"

"Hisoka!" called Hoshina-dono. "This lad ...!"

"I was *not* finished," grumbled Churlish.

"We're listening," soothed Paltry. "Go ahead."

"Wolves are simple. Dragons are sly. Cats have secrets." Churlish drew himself up and finished, "Tanuki play pranks."

Hoshina-dono frowned, and Hisoka Araki inquired, "Are you having trouble with tricksters?"

Paltry blinked. "I wouldn't say *trouble*."

"They make good neighbors," said Churlish.

Opal said, "His sleeve, I believe."

Hoshina-dono bent closer. Junpei had never been sniffed before. He looked to Churlish for support.

The boy rolled his eyes and wisely said, "Dogs are even simpler than wolves."

"Harmonious wouldn't hurt a soul," assured Paltry.

Junpei was pretty sure he was calling the head of the Hoshina family by name. The unfamiliar syllables were baffling.

"You're right, Sage," murmured Hoshina-dono. "It's here. Junpei, what do you have up your sleeve?"

SOME BOYS RIDE DOGS

Anna resisted the suggestion that she hide away at Ingress Academy. Opal had been very specific. The things she needed most would be found here, at Kikusawa Shrine. So she stayed, even though its many children shied away from her. All except Sho, who had his older half-brother's courage. Thanks to Sho, Anna was making a little progress with the language.

Simple phrases. Too basic to touch the complexities weighing on her heart and mind.

She could say *please* and *thank you*, and she could apologize. But she could not warn these children to beware of dragons. And though Matsu understood her, she didn't know him well. How could she confide the fears that kept her awake at night? What kind of battler quaked and quailed at every change in the wind?

Frustration drove her to establish routines. Even in unfamiliar territory, she could stick to her training and maintain a boundary. So Anna donned her weapons and patrolled—carefully, quietly, and always out of view, lest her differences cause a panic.

Moving stealthily through the trees that grew thick on the shrine's slopes, she allowed herself to relax into familiar rhythms. Slow steps. Deep breaths. She stretched her senses, searching for any hint of an oncoming threat ... and entirely missed a nearer one.

A massive animal broke cover, and she had it at swordpoint before she registered lustrous red fur and wide copper eyes.

The Kith held quite still.

Anna did, too, and not entirely by choice. There was a staying hand at her wrist and a soft voice coming from the vicinity of her elbow.

"Please, do not hurt Rise."

The moment she relaxed, the boy released her and returned to the Kith, leaping lightly onto his back. A dog. Anna hadn't realized there were any dog clans in this part of the world. Then it registered. The boy spoke English.

"Peace," she offered, sheathing her blade. "And apologies."

He immediately brightened. "Do you live here? We are new."

"I arrived recently, and I am staying here for now." She indicated the shrine. "Your Kith is a dog?"

"Yes. We are Starmarks." Though he didn't go so far as to offer his hands, the boy said, "I am Quen. This is Rise."

"Peace," she repeated, offering a vastly more polite introduction. "Not many people in this city speak English."

"There are more than you might think. Da moved our whole clan here, and we know your language. Others, too."

"What brings a clan of dogs to Keishi?"

"Matchmaking. Mostly." Quen's expression was too solemn for him to be joking.

"Seeking ties?" she ventured, trying to recall which wolf packs were nearby.

"Avoiding them." With a subtle shift in posture, he asked, "What about you, Anna Green? What brings *you* to Keishi?"

"Trouble. Mostly." She quietly admitted, "I have seen no signs of pursuit, but I suppose I am on edge."

"What kind of trouble are you in?"

Anna might not normally have confided in one so young, but Quen had to be several times her own age, despite appearances. And it was so nice to be able to confide at all. "I ran from that trouble, and I sought sanctuary here."

Quen's gaze lingered for a moment on the weapon at her side. "And you think your troubles may have followed you?"

"It would not surprise me."

"Is your trouble the human kind?"

"Amaranthine." She grimaced. "Dragon clan."

The boy didn't even bat an eye. "What are your defenses?"

Anna firmed her posture. "Myself."

Quen shook his head, looking disappointed in her. "That is not enough."

"I am very good with a sword."

"Not enough," he repeated. "You need strong allies. And probably a mediator."

"I *have* one. He promised to meet me here."

The boy asked, "Why rely on one ally when you could have many? My clan has always kept close ties with humans."

Anna softly challenged, "And you speak for your clan?"

"No. But I know Da. If he was here, he would offer, too."

"Very generous, I am sure. But I am already causing trouble for Reaver Miyabe and his family."

"If you will put away your sword, I will introduce you to my uncle. He is visiting an old friend, just there." Quen pointed into the neighborhood below. "Did you know there is a wolf at your very doorstep?"

She hadn't.

"He is another good ally to have. Close enough to call upon." Again, Quen urged, "Put away your sword."

"I am a battler," she protested.

Quen patiently said, "You are not at war with the people of Kikusawa, and your blade will do little good against a dragon."

"I am aware."

"Come with me. I will treat you at that sweet shop down there. It is run by a tanuki clan. Have you ever tasted mochi?"

With a small shake of her head, Anna unbuckled her sword, set it aside, and trailed after the generous boy and his dog. Maybe it was wise to find more allies before Opal arrived. And … Anna liked sweets.

HOUSE OF NOBLE FLOWERS

Anna peered around, unsure if the low ceiling and dim interior was typical of all shops in this country. Given the looming threat of possible pursuit, she hadn't explored the neighborhood below the shrine. From its exterior, Anna never would have guessed this was a sweets shop. Nothing resembled the types she knew.

"Back already, young sir?" inquired the man behind the counter. He certainly looked like a local to Anna, but he spoke in accented English. A welcome surprise that suggested he was more than he seemed.

Quen executed a respectful bow. "We would like to share a pot of tea. And some of that mochi you gave me last time."

"Liked it, did you?" The man began stacking pillowy white rounds into a shallow box. "I'll add some daifuku. You're sure to like it. And your friend?"

She stepped forward and presented her hands. "Anna Green, recently arrived."

"So I'm told. Matsu is an old friend." He dusted his hands and met her palms before inquiring, "Where are you from, Reaver Green?"

"It does not matter. I will not be going back."

He accepted that with a nod and set about filling a teapot.

Quen asked, "Do you mind if I use your garden, again? So Rise can join us?"

"Make yourself at home." And to Anna, he added, "The Wendwood clan bids you welcome. May you find peace among the Amaranthine of Keishi."

With the soft jingle of chimes, another customer entered the shop, and Quen took Anna by the wrist, easily balancing a tray while leading her through an open screen and into a garden that sprawled right up to the forest's edge. The Wendwood clan were a short tumble down a long slope from Matsu's.

Arraying the contents of the tray onto a table situated under a tree with fat red buds, Quen whistled softly, and Rise pushed through the undergrowth. He trundled over, tail wagging. At first. Something must have caught his attention, because he went still, staring fixedly at a point before giving a low *wuff*.

Anna tensed, already wishing her blade was back in her hand.

"It is all right," Quen murmured. And a little louder, "I am sorry if we are intruding."

With a scattering of petals, an illusion dissipated, revealing a lady in a kimono. Mischievous smile. Merry eyes. "I am found out."

"Should we go?" asked the earnest young dog.

"Take your ease," she replied waving toward a bench. "I was hoping for a different visitor, but the wolf next door snatched him up and spoiled my fun."

Belatedly, Anna realized that the lady also spoke in English. "May I know your name?"

"I'm Chika Wendwood, tanuki clan. Shall we be friends, Anna Green?"

NO WISH TO UNSETTLE

"Up my sleeve?" Junpei's questing fingers found the sweet he'd received. Bringing out the block, he displayed it on the palm of his hand. "This?"

Hoshina-dono murmured something, then fumbled for words. "May I touch? Just a little?"

Junpei offered the thing.

To his surprise, the big man brought his hand under Junpei's, copper eyes nearly crossing as he focused. Although he sniffed and muttered, nothing made sense. But then Hisoka Araki placed a hand on Hoshina-dono's shoulder and pointedly met Junpei's gaze.

That hand was clawed. And the man's eyes were orange.

"Allow me to translate? Or better yet, to explain what's happened."

"Thank you, sir?"

"*Sensei*," he reminded. "It's more comfortable."

"Araki-sensei." And because there was no way such a prestigious person should be expected to know, he humbly added, "I'm Junpei."

"I remember." His expression could only be called kind. "As Churlish so aptly put it, we are another kind of people. A peaceful people. Friends, if you're willing."

"But you're … one of Keishi's elders …?"

"A position I'm honored to hold." Hisoka exuded calm. "One that allows me to do some good for both our peoples."

"And mine," interrupted Churlish, who sashayed up with another tray. "I matter, too."

Junpei could see how Churlish stood out, even amidst this strange company. A shining beauty. And yet, his manner hadn't changed one bit.

"Aren't you going to eat?" Churlish pushed a plate closer to Laud, who was hiding his hands behind his back, and set another dish in front of Hoshina-dono, who still knelt beside the table. "Junpei, tell them to try my cakes. They are good, are they not?"

"Very good. The best. More people should know how good your baking is."

"They would if they could," Churlish boasted. "But most people do not notice our shop."

"How could they miss it?"

With a superior smile, he asked, "Before now, did you notice Paltry's tail?"

"N-no."

"Like that," said Churlish. As if the matter was both explained and settled.

Hisoka spoke up. "I *am* curious how you found your way here."

"The first time?" Junpei looked to Paltry. "Something smelled good, and I was hungry. And I had a little extra coin ...?"

"He's unregistered, of course," Paltry said. "Gets it from his mother's side, I'd wager. Since his younger half-brother's got a glimmer."

Junpei hadn't realized Paltry knew about his family. Then again, people did talk. But *shine*?

Matsu spoke up again. "Agreed. Sho has potential. Kusunoki took an immediate liking to him."

Junpei had no idea what that meant, and turning from them, he met Laud's gaze again. The big, white-haired fellow still sat quietly, hands tucked. Clearing his throat, Junpei nudged the plate of cakes closer to him. "It's okay. I already saw your claws."

Laud's head tipped to the side.

Junpei felt so helpless, being unable to make himself understood. "Sensei? Tell him it's okay?"

Hisoka Araki smoothly stepped in, bridging the gap.

With a cautious nod, Laud slid his hands across the table, palm up.

"A customary greeting," said Hisoka. "If you have the courage to meet his palms, it will surely put Laud more at ease. He has no wish to unsettle you."

Junpei carefully reclaimed his hand from Hoshina-dono.

The big man smiled crookedly. "It's all right, lad. Make peace with my brother. But save some peace for me," he said in amiable tones.

Hisoka translated.

Setting aside the sweet that seemed to be at the heart of this kerfuffle, Junpei surrendered his hands. "Good to meet you. Again …? I guess."

It wasn't much, but he guessed Hisoka could smooth things over.

"My name is Laud." He spoke with painstaking care. It was probably one of the only phrases he'd learned so far.

With an encouraging nod, Junpei slowly returned the greeting. "My name is Junpei."

The big guy ducked his head and retreated to his side of the table before slowly reaching for food.

"I'll bring more," Churlish promised, practically skipping back to the kitchen.

Hoshina-dono presented his own hands, saying something to Hisoka.

Sensei chuckled. "Harmonious wants to make sure you understand. He would gladly offer you a place in his pack, but he cannot trespass upon a prior claim."

"Claim?" Junpei asked as he met palms with the silk merchant whose name had changed.

"Someone has favored you with a gift. And pranks are a sign of preference among members of the tanuki clan." With the barest of smiles, Hisoka added, "You have an admirer."

Recalling the blue-eyed lady in the plum blossom kimono, Junpei stammered and blushed.

This set off a fresh conference between Hisoka and Harmonious.

Meanwhile, Churlish returned with a heaped tray, and Junpei showed him the block. "Is there something strange about this?"

"I know what this is!" he exclaimed. "This is chocolate!"

"Is that good?"

"*So* good! I have not had any in so long. They do not have any here. Officially."

"Where does it come from?"

"Far away. Across the sea. We used to go everywhere, but we made a friend and decided to stay. Even though there is no lake."

Junpei wasn't sure these details were any help to his current confusion. "Do you want it? Or you, Hoshina-dono?"

"No, no!" quickly answered the silk merchant. "Keep it, lad. Someone made a present of it, and I wouldn't want to meddle.

There are too many meddlers in the world."

Again, Hisoka translated.

Churlish gave the sweet a longing look, but agreed, "It is yours."

Hoshina-dono, who seemed to answer to Harmonious while among others of his kind, carefully closed Junpei's fingers over the gift. With a soft light in his eyes, he murmured something, giving his hands a pat.

Once more, Hisoka translated. "Good for you."

YOU WILL BE FINE

"Are you sad?" asked Churlish. "Or upset? Or dissatisfied? *I* get dissatisfied, so I know how dreadful that can be."

Junpei hummed vaguely. The others—even Laud—had moved to a table across the room, where Opal the Sage held court, his voice rising and falling in some dramatic tale. Or so it seemed. Maybe later, he'd ask Matsu what language they'd all been speaking.

Not that knowing a word for their words would unlock them. He murmured, "I can read and write, you know."

"And that makes you sad?"

Usually, it was a thing he was proud of. In his early days at the atelier, there'd been lessons with Yami-san in the back room— brush strokes and books, syllabaries and signatures. Yami-san really had been patient. And probably too generous, given how much Sho's tutelage cost.

"What I mean is that ... I didn't realize how much I don't know."

Churlish patted his shoulder. "Not everyone can know everything."

"But you do?"

"I know everything that is important for me to know." He hesitated. "Except one thing. And it *does* make me sad. But I know something that is good for sad days. Wait."

He was gone in a twirl and returned in a twinkling.

"This." He pressed a warm clay cup into Junpei's palm. "I make good custard. I am good at custard. I am also good to my wolf, and I am good to my friends. Taste."

Junpei accepted the small silver spoon Churlish wiggled under his nose.

Propping his hip against the table, he looked ready to oversee every last bite, though his attention strayed to the conversation in the opposite corner.

"Am I in trouble?" whispered Junpei.

"Do you like tails?"

"I ... I do not dislike tails ...?"

"Then you will be fine. I was fine." Nodding toward the cabal, he said, "Talking is good. Sharing ideas and sharing puddings is good. That is peace."

So simple. Maybe too simplistic. But Churlish's confidence was reassuring.

"I'm glad you're here."

Twisting a strand of blue beads at his wrist, he murmured, "So am I."

"I heard that!" called Paltry, all smiles.

"I meant *maybe*," grumbled his partner, who whisked off to the kitchen. "Only maybe."

Separating from the others, Paltry switched to Japanese.

"Harmonious says you've been working at his estate?"

"I do odd jobs."

"Like …?"

Junpei wasn't sure what his friend was after. "Normal stuff. Cleaning and carrying. I lent the gardener a hand this morning."

Paltry waggled a finger at him, then lifted down one of the many paper lanterns that decorated the tearoom. "What do you think of this, Harmonious? You, too, Hisoka. Wouldn't you say this is beyond lovely?"

To Junpei's embarrassment, the pair not only studied his handiwork, they rose from the table in order to inspect the other lanterns in the room. All his. He always saved his best pieces for Paltry.

"Yours?" inquired Hisoka.

"Yes."

Paltry jostled Harmonious with an elbow. "Why is my friend grubbing in your garden when he could be ornamenting your screens?"

"We could commission you?" asked Hisoka.

Junpei floundered for an appropriate answer. "Most go to the Eitoku atelier for such things."

"Are you refusing?" Hisoka quietly advised, "Don't."

Harmonious seemed taken with the idea. "I am familiar with chrysanthemums, and here are cherry blossoms, of course. Ah, these are orchids, yes? But what about these small, red ones. Are they native to the area?"

Hisoka patiently translated.

Junpei ventured, "Red flowers have always been associated with Kikusawa."

"Why?" asked Harmonious, clearly interested.

There was a reason. Something to do with the shrine. He looked to Matsu for help in answering.

"You should visit our gardens," the shrinekeeper smoothly suggested. "Come summertime, they will be filled with chrysanthemums. If you see them for yourself, you will understand."

He spoke in Japanese, probably to include Junpei.

While Hisoka translated for the sake of Harmonious and Laud, Opal eased to Junpei's side. "Do me a favor."

Of course he would. "Anything."

"Keep the truth of our existence a secret."

As if he'd ever breathe a word. "I will. I promise."

"Also, we need a few hours privacy. Perhaps more. You should spend the rest of the afternoon in a place you enjoy. Somewhere safe. Somewhere that makes you happy."

What a magnificent idea! Junpei murmured his thanks and moved to leave.

Churlish caught his wrist. "But you *can* return. Whenever you want."

"Yes, yes," soothed Opal. "I would never banish you from the company of friends."

Junpei was glad. Paltry made him feel safe, and Churlish's sass made him smile. "I will gladly visit again."

Just then, the door slid open, and there was Hoshina-dono's young son. "Hello, Ken-kun. Did you know you look very like your father?"

"Junpei-san?"

And seeing the tall lady behind Ken, he added, "Hello, Anna-san. I have to go. I must do Opal a favor. There's somewhere I must go. I'm always happy there."

Her eyes narrowed. "Opal?" she called in warning tones.

"A harmless necessity!" retorted the sage.

Anna scowled, but her tone gentled. "I understand why you must go, Junpei-san. Perhaps we will meet again." Her glare cut across the room. "*Will* you be able to return?"

"A few hours. Another day," said Junpei. "If I can find the coin."

Paltry eased over and gripped his shoulder.

"I must go," said Junpei. The need to do so was gaining in urgency.

"I know, friend." Paltry pressed a coin into his hand. "Churlish will save you one of his custards."

Junpei didn't like to take coin that he hadn't earned, but somewhere deep down, he also didn't want to leave. *This* was the place where he felt safest and happiest. But there was another place he sometimes went. "I must go to Naoki."

Paltry's tail wagged. "You have a knack for finding good company."

Still, Junpei lingered, clutching that coin.

Bending to meet his gaze, Paltry said, "Come by later. Use the back door. Churlish can feed you, and we can talk more. If you can."

Junpei managed a nod before need forced him away. Hurrying along the street, he wondered how one slim coin could make him feel so much richer.

QUESTIONABLE TASTE IN BALLADS

Anna quickly assessed the tearoom and its occupants. To her surprise, the place was furnished with sturdy benches and proper tables with wide chairs. High ceilings encouraged her to stand straight, and for the first time in many days, she didn't tower over everyone in the vicinity.

Once more taking her by the wrist, Quen said, "It will be fine. They are all Da's friends."

She had no trouble deciding which of the males was Quen's father, but she'd no sooner singled him out when he dropped into a crouch. Then sat on the floor.

Tugging her in another direction, Quen introduced her to a wolf called Paltry, who summoned his partner. They made a strange duo—a kimono-clad man with baubles in his hair and a sulky boy with bobbed black hair. But they welcomed her without hesitation and offered their aid even before knowing why she needed it.

Necessary niceties were exchanged, and they presented her to a feline who wished to be called Sensei. As it happened, he was a teacher at Ingress Academy, so he quizzed her in some detail about her own schooling.

Anna had intended to be discreet, but the cat pried little tidbits of information into the open. Before she knew it, she'd admitted to her age, her familial branch, her ranking in the last battler tournament, and the aptitude that had landed her a place in Opulence Windlore's service.

"Singing lessons!" boasted Opal. "They are universally effective. The more abysmal the student, the stronger the urge to resist the vocal rigors I inflict."

"How very … you," said Matsu, showing dimples.

"And it works?" asked Quen, entirely fascinated.

"Like a charm," said Paltry, not even trying to keep a straight face.

Churlish thrust out his lower lip. "I do not remember singing lessons."

"Ah, but *would* you?" inquired the dragon.

The boy turned to Paltry, aghast. "Did he make me sing?"

"If memory serves, it was more of a duet. But I'd had a lot of star wine …."

All throughout the lively discussion, Anna's attention kept straying to Quen's father, whose fidgets reminded her of a restless child. He rolled to his knees. He sat back on his heels, He sat with legs crossed, hands gripping his ankles. And every time her gaze flicked his way, he was looking at her with a hopeful expression.

"So you gave Anna singing lessons to inure her to dragon sway?" surmised Quen.

"My sympathies," murmured Paltry.

Matsu nodded. "His taste in ballads is often … questionable."

Anna really wished Opal didn't enjoy telling this story so much.

"I'm not sure I understand the problem," said Hisoka.

The dragon spread his hands wide. "She failed."

Quen's glance was sympathetic. "You can't sing?"

"Not. Quite," Anna gritted out.

"Oho! She took to singing like a lark. Anna's voice is a treasure!" Opal coyly confided, "She enjoyed her lessons so much, she never learned to resist me. So when I offered her a part in my cortege …!"

Anna blushed. "I am a battler, not a bard."

"And I maintain that *both* makes you doubly formidable." Opal sighed happily. "Our duets reach into the heavens, coaxing descants from the very stars."

Quen's eyes were wide. "You've sung with dragons?"

"Just the one."

"And was it wonderful?"

Anna hadn't sought Opal's patronage, but neither had she tried to escape it. His raptures were not her style, but she couldn't deny a certain fondness for her mentor. "As wonderful as you would expect. Until it was terrible."

"Ah. Yes." The dragon winced. "Things took a bad turn. But here we are! Safe."

"For the moment," she allowed.

Quen craned his neck. "Da? Don't you want to meet Anna?"

"I would," he said, casting a pleading look in Hisoka-sensei's direction.

The cat courteously mediated. "Harmonious Starmark recently joined our community, bringing his entire den from overseas. His progeny are here in force—Kith and Kindred." Hisoka's expression gentled, and he touched her arm before quietly adding, "My good friend came to escape the machinations of Wardenclave's matchmakers. For many decades now, he has been bereft of a bondmate. You would call him a widower."

Most Amaranthine introductions came with personal information attached. So she accepted this detail with a nod and crisply declared, "Anna Green."

"Anna," he murmured.

By rights, he should have declared what name she should use for him. "Why are you on your knees, Harmonious Starmark?"

"I have no wish to overwhelm you by ... looming?"

Ridiculous. "Are you questioning my courage?"

Quen said, "She is a battler, Da! And see? Paltry is just as tall."

"So he is," Harmonious said awkwardly. And still, he made no effort to stand.

Pulling Quen against her side and thumping his shoulder, Anna took charge. "Your son suggested I make allies in Keishi."

"I am willing." Eyes widening, Harmonious looked like a dog begging for scraps. "Choose me."

"Choose *us*," corrected Quen. "Our den is strong."

Anna challenged, "Strong enough to stand?"

Never breaking eye contact, Harmonious rose to his full height, which *was* impressive.

"I will grant you are tall." Squaring her shoulders, she staunchly added, "But I am no waif."

His gaze went from her face to that of his son, who still leaned into her side. "She is strong, this lady," he said seriously.

Quen grinned. "Rise likes her, too."

His father's lips quirked into a pleased smile.

Anna wanted to move on, and if taking charge accomplished that, she'd do it. "Is English fine? There is much I need to know, and there is much you all must learn."

But Harmonious eased closer and asked, "May I touch?"

So he wouldn't curtail the courtesies? Anna offered her palms in a perfunctory manner.

Without haste, he covered them with his own before sliding his hands beneath in a silent pledge of support. It was subtle, the shift. Somehow, he managed to cradle her hands between his, and he took long, slow breaths. He was searching her scent as intently as he was searching her face. What did he hope to find?

When she pulled back, he let her go with a tentative smile.

So restrained. So respectful. So different from the dragons who'd tried to force a claim.

I SEE HER EVERYWHERE

Junpei knew he needed to get to Naoki's place, but his steps slowed when he caught a glimpse of plum blossoms beneath the pleats of a parasol. He was almost positive he saw her again—on a bridge, in a garden, upon a bench. But each time, urgency pressed him onward, right into the part of town that catered to people who had money for more than basics.

Finer things.

Little luxuries.

The first time Junpei visited Naoki's book stall, his attention was immediately caught by a display of floral prints. He'd ducked inside for a closer look, since the flowering trees weren't like any he'd ever seen. Noticing his fascination, Naoki had brought over a book with botanical illustrations.

"I can't afford this," Junpei confessed. Surely the man could see how shabby he was.

But Naoki had guided him to a small table, invited him to sit, and said, "Look your fill."

So Junpei had. And still did. Because Naoki was the sort of shopkeeper who didn't mind if a careful man with clean hands paged through his wares. In fact, they'd struck up a polite sort of friendship. Junpei had been invited to call Naoki by his given name, and the man had begun searching for and setting aside things he knew Junpei would appreciate.

Foreign books with fancy art plates.

Scrolls with illustrated poetry.

Novels with lavishly painted flyleaves.

Pausing on the threshold, Junpei looked back the way he'd come.

"What has you craning about? Did you lose Sho?" Naoki came to stand with him. He was the sort of man who seemed interested in everything. Small in stature, he wore round spectacles that hooked behind his ears, and there were unusual bracelets on both his wrists, like prayer beads cut from translucent stone. Junpei was used to the soft clatter they made whenever Naoki spoke, for while his smiles were the quiet sort, his hands had a lot to say.

"Not Sho. But there was a lady. Did you see where she went?"

"What sort of lady are you looking for?"

"There is this lady with a plain parasol. I've been seeing her everywhere."

Junpei shook his head and went inside, breathing a sigh of relief now that he'd done as Opal said. He loved the smell of this shop. All his favorite things had been steeped into the very air—paper, ink, and flowers.

Naoki's shop was long and narrow, fit between a candlemaker's stall and a place that displayed hairpins and combs. Junpei usually moved straight to his spot at the table in the back, but today he pondered Naoki's seat behind the low counter where he made sales.

Two chairs filled the space, along with a slender cushioned bench for propping one's feet. Junpei had never seen someone use the chair on the left, though two lap blankets draped there, and the foot cushion showed signs of equal wear on both sides.

Between customers, Naoki sat here, reading.

Had there always been two chairs? Junpei couldn't recall.

The faint rustle of cloth and a tiny *ting* made him turn his head. Junpei quickly lowered his gaze, since he didn't like to interrupt when Naoki was with his real customers. A single red flower petal drifted to the floor, drawing Junpei's eyes to the man's geta. They were angled away, so he risked a peek … and blinked.

Naoki pushed past Junpei, reaching for a book under the counter. "I found something unusual. You'll love this one."

Junpei cautiously said, "I do like new things."

Something must have shown on his face, because Naoki asked, "Are you well? How is your family?"

"Well enough," he answered, though he shook his head.

Frowning now, Naoki asked, "What brings you here today?"

"This place makes me feel happy. And … you make me feel safe." He lowered his gaze again. "I *do* like it here. Even if things have to change."

Coming out from behind the counter, Naoki murmured, "Pardon me." He touched Junpei's cheek and searched his eyes. "You are not quite yourself, today."

"I think so, too." Junpei risked a peek to one side, where two more petals had joined the first on the floor. "Let me stay? I need to stay in a safe and happy place for a few hours."

"Why?"

Junpei struggled for words. "It's what he said."

Naoki's expression changed, becoming fierce … maybe even angry. But his tone was calm when he asked, "Who told you to go to a safe and happy place?"

"I'm not sure I should say." Junpei swallowed hard. "I'm … not sure I can."

"Relax," urged Naoki. "There are truths along the edges of disobedience, and they can't hurt you. Let's start over. Did you meet someone new today?"

"Yes."

"Were you afraid today?"

"A little. At first …?"

"Did they send you to me?"

"No. Yes. No." Junpei hunched his shoulders. "Not exactly. I chose you."

Naoki nodded. "Thank you for that. You *are* safe. I can promise this. Understand?"

"Less than I'd like. Today's been … unusual."

After a few moments' consideration, Naoki asked, "If I make you feel safe and happy, would it be okay if we went somewhere together?"

He pondered that, then nodded. "I can do that."

Pitching his voice differently, Naoki announced, "We're going to Kikusawa Shrine."

Junpei nodded again, but there was a clack of wooden sandals and a fragrant breeze as the other man preceded them outside. It seemed the three of them were going together.

SAFE AND HAPPY PLACE

As they walked, Naoki occasionally plied Junpei with more questions. "Why do you need a *safe* and happy place, I wonder. Is safety a concern?"

Junpei searched to find words along the edges of the whole truth. Now that he knew where to look, they came more easily. "To put me at ease. I think it was meant as a kindness."

Naoki hummed. "What sort of person was kind to you?"

"A sage."

"From what faith?"

Junpei smiled uneasily. "I don't think he was that kind of sage."

They climbed the long stairs to the shrine. Matsu was nowhere to be found, which made sense, since he was probably still at the tearoom. Even with its keeper gone, Kikusawa was a good, safe place. But Junpei wouldn't have called his current state of mind *happy*.

Sho was here, playing with the orphans instead of his classmates.

"Again?" sighed Junpei.

"Surely, the shrine isn't out of bounds for the boy," said Naoki.

Junpei was uncomfortable with the truth. "Mother wants him to get along with boys from the kinds of families who could help him along. He could, too. Everyone likes Sho."

"But Sho doesn't like everyone?"

"That's not entirely true. But ... he has his favorites."

Naoki chuckled. "Don't most people?"

Junpei knew it was only the truth, so he wouldn't chase down his brother or deliver a scolding. Instead, he ventured, "May I ask an awkward question?"

His companion's expression brightened. "That might be interesting."

"Why are red flowers associated with Kikusawa Shrine?"

With a subtle shift of posture, Naoki said, "Most people would say it's the chrysanthemums."

"Is that what *you* think?"

The man looked away, looked back, and smiled faintly. "No."

Junpei drew a deep breath and got to the awkward part. "Does it have anything to do with the man I saw here recently? He had red flowers in his hair."

"Hmm?" Naoki traded a look with the person who'd accompanied them. "That's singular. Why don't you ask Matsu?"

"I did. He was surprised." Junpei tried to remember details about that conversation, but his recollection had gone all fuzzy at the edges.

While he fumbled for another question, the man in geta touched Naoki's shoulder and quietly said, "There is a boy who has never been here before. Kusunoki is concerned."

"That was it!" Junpei exclaimed, grateful to have his memory jogged. "Matsu's childhood friend. His name is Kusunoki."

Ignoring him, the man in geta quietly said, "When it is convenient, could we speak? I believe Kusunoki has good reason to be worried."

It dawned on Junpei, then. Neither Naoki nor his companion realized that Junpei could see him. Another upshot of the prank, no doubt. Raising a hand in apology, Junpei said, "If it's something urgent, it's all right."

They blinked at him.

Naoki asked, "Since when do you notice things that are supposed to be secret?"

"Since today …? Today has been … unusual."

"Tell me what you see," Naoki prompted, his expression guarded.

Meeting a red-eyed gaze, Junpei offered a respectful nod. "I see another man with long, black hair and a lavish crown of red flowers. You are similar to Kusunoki, but Matsu's friend has more height and girth and wears hakama."

With a heavy sigh, Naoki said, "Junpei, meet my longtime companion, Hajime."

Junpei presented his hands, and Hajime asked, "Are you a reaver, then?"

"A what?"

"No, I think not," said Naoki. "But what's this about a boy?"

Hajime pointed. "Kusunoki is restless, but he does not know why. He does not remember ... before."

Naoki stiffened and muttered, "Are we found?"

"I cannot deny that possibility."

Junpei glanced between them and the boy, who happened to be standing with Sho. They were of similar height, so they were probably similar in age. From this distance, Junpei couldn't see anything amiss. But Naoki and Hajime wore matching expressions of ... fear.

"What is it?" Junpei asked, already striding toward his brother. "I'm getting Sho."

Hajime was suddenly in front of him, arms spread wide. "Wait," he begged. "It is not safe."

All the more reason to reach Sho. "I'm getting my little brother."

"Brother ...?" Hajime echoed weakly. And he winked out, appearing beside the two boys.

The stranger ran, and Sho called after him, hand outstretched.

Junpei arrived a moment later, pulling Sho close.

His brother thanked him with an elbow to the ribs. "What gives? Let go, Jun-nii!"

"Is everyone all right?" asked Naoki, who next reached them.

"Fine," breathed Junpei.

Sho wrangled free and straightened his clothes, still looking in the direction the other boy had fled. Junpei gripped his shoulder, though, unsettled by the sudden turn of events. His brother glared up at him, then froze, his gaze drifting to Hajime.

In his usual, undaunted way, Sho asked, "Should I be worried about the red eyes?"

"Whose?" asked Hajime, indicating himself. "Mine?"

"Nope," said Sho, pointing off. "His. The boy with purple hair."

ENTERING THE BACK WAY

Junpei escorted Sho home, stayed long enough to satisfy Mother, and excused himself. *For a walk*, he'd said. Twilight was descending, and those *few hours* had finally ticked down somewhere in the back of his mind. Now that he was in the clear, Paltry's invitation was all Junpei could think about.

The noren was down at Moonglade Tearoom, but Paltry had said something about a back door. An unobtrusive side alley led away from the familiar and into shadow. Was it a garden wall? He shuffled cautiously along until he reached a turning that should put him behind the shop.

To his relief, a soft light beckoned him onward. He thought at first that Paltry must have left a light for him atop the stout gatepost, but the glow wasn't coming from a paper lantern. Churlish sat there, silvery as moonlight, hugging his knees as he gazed into the sky.

"Good evening," Junpei quietly called.

"You came! I knew you would." Churlish held out his hands

to be lifted down. "Come and meet the dexes. They want a better introduction than they could make with Opal meddling."

"He's not here?"

"Are you glad?"

Junpei admitted, "A little."

Churlish solemnly said, "Me, too. Dragons are tricky."

Junpei frowned. "Opal is a dragon?"

"And a bard. If he likes you, he might put you in a song."

"Are you in a song?"

"Maybe." His face brightened, and he mumbled, "There must be something *else* you want to know. Ask that, instead."

"Alright. What are dexes?"

"Just another secret." Silver eyes turned searching. "Are you afraid of secrets?"

"Should I be?"

"Not ours." Churlish exuded confidence. "We are the good kind."

"I don't think I'm afraid. Would I be here if I was?"

"I *knew* you would be fine." Waving for him to follow, Churlish assured, "I know *everything*."

As it happened, Junpei already knew these dexes. Paltry, Laud, and Quen were waiting, as was an impossibly large dog with silky red fur. Staying behind Churlish, Junpei stammered, "Th-this is a dex?"

Quen hurried forward. "Rise is a Kith. *I* am a dex. Or the doggish equivalent."

"Churlish, what have you been telling him?" chided Paltry.

"Only the truth. He wanted to know."

"We should tell it in order," Paltry grumbled, stalking in his partner's wake toward the kitchen. Over his shoulder, he called,

"You first, Quen. Ease him into the place he belongs."

Junpei offered the boy a small smile. "Your name isn't Ken Hoshina. Not really."

Standing straight and offering both hands, he spoke in words Junpei could understand. He must have been practicing. "I am Eloquence Starmark. My friends call me Quen. I would be pleased if there can be peace between us."

And then Laud was there, palms extended. And Junpei met the dog as well. And Paltry was back, hustling everyone into the tearoom, where Churlish had crammed one of the small tables with bowls, baskets, and crockery. While they ate, they sat so close, Junpei's shoulders would bump Paltry's or Laud's. By the fourth time, he stopped apologizing for it.

Churlish advocated the liberal use of butter and kept passing slathered wedges of bread.

Quen ate with surprising appetite for such a skinny kid, as if he were trying to keep up with—or catch up to—the rest of them.

For the most part, Junpei simply listened, because Paltry had a lot to say—about clans, about cooperation, about starry souls, and about a secret society to which Junpei could belong.

"When an unregistered reaver is found, if the circumstances are right, they can be brought in. That's what we're doing now. Inducting you into the In-between."

"Why me?" asked Junpei.

"Bloodline is part of it. Always is," he answered vaguely.

"You've known me since I was ... fourteen? Why now?" pressed Junpei.

"In a way, we're bringing you in because we consider you a

friend. And in a related way, we want you closer for your protection. But ...."

When Paltry trailed off, Laud pointed Junpei's way. Or more specifically, at his sleeve, where the block of sweet had remained. He spoke, but his words were lost on Junpei.

"Yeah, I know." Paltry shrugged broad shoulders. "That little trick forced the issue. We had no choice."

Retrieving the chocolate and holding it up, Junpei asked, "This?"

"That," Paltry acknowledged. "Which brings us to the next topic of discussion."

Junpei wasn't sure why his friend looked so amused, why Laud seemed to be blushing. Quen asked something in swift, eager tones, and Churlish stuck his nose in the air, saying, "I will tell if you will not."

"No, no. I'll do it," Paltry said. And to Junpei. "It's nothing bad. In fact, many a male would be flattered by such a token."

"Which means ...?"

With a gentle expression, Paltry explained, "We may have called her sigil a prank, but Harmonious was right about the claim. It's safe to say she has ... intentions. Perhaps a better word would be ... well...."

Churlish cut in and cut to the chase. "Courtship."

LOVE AT FIRST SIGHT

Although it was late when Junpei finally returned home, he left his futon in its cupboard, moving instead to light enough lamps to paint by. He arranged his supplies, but in the process of tying back his sleeves, he re-encountered the swinging weight of the blue-eyed lady's gift.

He brought it out and set it on the table.

Sitting before it, Junpei ran his fingers over the paper, which was thick and white and sparsely flecked with blue. He'd never seen the like. Inside was a fresh mystery, for a second layer of paper was waxy to the touch and cleverly folded. Easing this back, he uncovered a sweet that was dark and waxy. He sniffed but couldn't place the scent. The spot where his thumb made contact turned slippery, for the stuff had melted at his touch.

Junpei licked it. *Different.*

Not in a bad way. Just … new.

Nothing to be afraid of.

He nipped the corner off, rewrapped the block in the inner paper, and licked his fingers clean before turning his attention to the thick paper of the outer layer. Its weight fascinated him, and he found a small mark on one corner, the impression of a moth. Junpei could only assume it was a kind of maker's mark, for such fine paper must have a craftsman.

Junpei flattened and pressed it, and when inspiration struck, he reached for his collection of brushes, finding the two tiniest. Pulling the box where he kept his paints closer, he hesitated over what palette to prepare.

Plum blossoms, surely. Like the pattern on his lady's kimono.

Wouldn't that be the most appropriate answer?

For he owed one. The dexes had explained that it was both custom and courtesy.

Paltry had assured him that it was safe to refuse. A simple rebuff would stop everything. But before his friend had finished with explanations, Junpei had already decided that his answer would be a favorable one.

Water and a wash of palest blue.

Junpei watched in fascination as the paint traveled and bloomed. This paper was a wonder, finer than any scrap he'd ever foraged from the atelier. So he proceeded patiently, almost teasing himself. He could see how it should look, but he wouldn't rush. This was a message without words, and he wanted it to be perfect.

He would give her this answer, and the flowers would speak for him.

They would let her know that he thought the chocolate was good ... and that she wore springtime beautifully ... and that he had probably been hers since the first time their eyes met.

ADDRESS HER WITH RESPECT

Paltry and Matsu escorted Anna to the home of Harmonious Starmark, who'd offered to play host to a conference of local Amaranthine. The compound was some distance from the city center, but the choice made sense to Anna. Privacy was paramount, which made the lack of barriers and wards confusing.

Introductions took the entire morning, for Harmonious seemed to think it important that Anna meet *every* member of his household. From his youngest—Quen and Rise—right on up through his other nine sons and daughters, many of whom had bondmates and children of their own.

"Reaver Anna Green," he said, again and again.

"Just Anna," she finally grumbled.

Harmonious hesitated. "In this country, given names are only used by one's intimate friends."

"In this country, my given name is pronounceable." The children of Kikusawa shrine had struggled with her surname, trying to fit the letters into their own syllabary. "Anna is simpler."

"Hisoka," he called. "Will Reaver Green be needing a local name? Like Hoshina?"

The feline mildly inquired, "You're offering to share your name?"

"What? Oh! I only meant …!" And raising both hands, Harmonious dithered through explanations and apologies.

As if she might've misunderstood. Which she hadn't.

Harmonious finally trailed off with a rueful glance and a soft, "Not that I'd mind."

Now, that … that was harder to understand.

"Midori," Hisoka suggested. "It's the local word for the color green. Let those who wish to show respect call you Midori-san."

And so Harmonious changed his tune. "Midori Anna," he said, again and again. Making sure the young ones knew how to address her respectfully.

Anna was having difficulty reconciling his grandfatherly status with all his hopeful enthusiasm. He was like a boy, showing off his best treasures, eager for her to be amazed.

His daughter Rampant remarked, "You have him charmed."

Looking down at little Sonnet, who snuggled against her shoulder, happily crooning, Anna said, "Your son is beautiful."

Copper eyes held the sparkle of amusement. "Oh, him, too."

Anna wasn't sure how to take that.

Caressing her little one's silky hair, Rampant murmured,

"I think Da is trying to impress you."

"I hardly think so." She glanced over to where Harmonious stood with his eldest son, Merit, and the Elderbough tracker who'd cheerfully butted in, suggesting she also call his best friend Penny.

Harmonious turned her way and just sort of … stalled. Why was he staring?

Anna scanned the room, hoping for context, only to realize that most members of the Starmark clan were on the alert, and they were watching Harmonious watch her.

Rampant eased into her father's line of sight, hiding Anna from view. She arched her brows and asked, "Are you being pursued?"

"Probably." It was the whole reason for this meeting, if they ever got to it.

"Hmm? That's not necessarily a bad thing." Rampant held out her hands, and Sonnet went to her. "Give Da a reason, and he'll outpace all comers."

Anna wanted clarification, because it almost sounded as though Rampant thought her father was ….

"Midori-san," interrupted Harmonious, who'd stolen up behind his daughter. "Hisoka thinks we should begin."

"Begin *what*, exactly?" she asked testily.

"Uhh. Convening. In the next room." He gestured with both hands. "Sentinel and Laud have warded it for privacy."

"Oh." And because the name was still strange to her ears, she said, "My name is Anna."

"Yes, my dear. I know."

"I told you to call me *Anna*."

"If you're sure …?"

"You will find me quite decisive."

Eyes alight, he said, "Thank you."

"And … how would you like to be called?" For though he'd guided her through numerous introductions, their own exchange of names had been rushed and scanty.

"By name. By any name. And often."

His tone was easy, but the undercurrent remained. Something hopeful and wistful and willing.

She didn't like it.

She wouldn't address it.

"Thank you, Harmonious," she said, keeping her tone and her posture entirely neutral.

His smile dimmed somewhat, but he remained courteous to a fault.

ALWAYS IN THE AUDIENCE

For reasons of his own, Opal stubbornly refused to explain matters, so Anna would have to speak for herself.

It was fine. The facts were simple.

She would not shrink from obligation.

Seated upon a floor cushion, with a tea tray before her and Quen at her side, she strove to keep her story brief.

"Two dragons approached me at a Song Circle. They were very … complimentary." It had happened during one of the rare moments when Opal wasn't at her side. They'd timed it just right. "This same pair was at the next Song Circle. And the next. Always in the audience."

Opal grimly interjected, "Always with a kind word."

She winced.

Quen whined softly.

"This past Dichotomy Day, one of them offered to make me his bride. I declined." Anna fidgeted. "They grew increasingly persuasive."

She had several gaps in her memory. Stolen moments.

Shame burned through her, for she'd been weak. Helpless to resist. Not their suggestions. Nor the liberties they took—body and soul.

Tails puffed and began to switch, for a handful of wolves had been included in the conference. Adoonah-soh Elderbough and her bondmate Ninook. Merit's best friend turned out to be one of their sons, a tracker who'd asked to be called Boon. Joonta and Karoo were from the Ambervelte pack, and there was Paltry, of course.

"Sway?" Harmonious looked stunned.

"I *am* susceptible." Anna's jaw tightened. "If not for Opal ...."

Her mentor's expression was pensive. "Had the stars been aligned any differently, the fiends would have absconded with her. And may yet try, since they have followed Anna here."

They had? This was the first she'd heard, and her stomach plunged.

"To what end?" asked Harmonious. "Their offer was declined. Their interest was rebuffed."

Hisoka spoke kindly. "Not every soul is as guileless as yours, old friend."

"Acquisition. Capture. Confinement," Opal said bluntly. "They still want Anna. They mean to have her."

"Unwilling?" Harmonious croaked.

His innocent befuddlement in that moment was almost endearing. He sought her gaze, and he seemed to be pleading with her. Begging her to deny it? She wished she could. But then Quen touched her elbow.

"Ask it," he urged. "Now that we understand, ask."

The first words out of Anna's mouth weren't a question. "I do not like their offer."

"You would mince words *now*?" Opal drawled.

"I ... I *hate* their offer. And them."

Tails thumped the floor in silent approval. It gave Anna the courage to go on.

"I am not helpless, but ... I need help." Another statement.

Quen smiled up at her and whispered, "Ask it, Anna. How else can we answer?"

So she squared her shoulders and glared determinedly at Harmonious Starmark. "Do not let them take me. Please?"

Barely a question. Almost an order, given her tone. Yet he lunged across the room, toppling teacups in his haste.

Kneeling before her, he reached out, only to tuck his hands behind his back. "I will stand with you against them. You will be safe. I swear it."

Anna blinked hard.

Harmonious sealed his pledge with a soft kiss to her forehead and whispered, "Will you trust me?"

She gave the only answer that was honest. "I will try."

TAKES AFTER HER MOTHER

Junpei ducked under the fluttering noren outside the House of the Noble Chrysanthemum. He hadn't been inside for years, but he'd been a regular once, because Mother had craved strawberry daifuku when she was pregnant with Sho.

The man behind the counter hadn't changed much in the intervening years. "Hello, Uncle," Junpei said cautiously.

"Giving up already?" Dark eyes twinkled. "Come now, Jun-kun. Give it a guess."

It was just like old times, this game. Brothers owned the shop, and Junpei had never been able to tell them apart.

"Uhh ... Uncle Haruka?"

The man smiled impishly. "Not I!"

"Uncle Haruki," Junpei sheepishly amended. "Do you know where I might find a lady in a plum blossom kimono? She has blue eyes."

"Takes after her mother," the man said mildly. "Did my girl cause you some mischief?"

"A little." And belatedly, "She's your daughter?"

"My youngest."

Junpei wasn't sure if there was some protocol he should follow. Shuffling forward, he offered his palms. "Is she here? May I speak with her?"

"I have no objections."

Taking one of Junpei's hands into his own, Haruki lightly traced a pattern on his palm. The lines shimmered slightly, and by the time he finished, Junpei was staring at the tip of a neat claw against his skin. When he dragged his gaze to Haruki's, his eyes were a soft gold, though just as prone to twinkling.

"Do *you* have any objections?" asked the shopkeeper, who looked so much younger now.

Junpei simply shook his head.

Haruki pulled both of Junpei's hands into his own, gently squeezed them, and leaned back to call through the door behind him. "Chika? Your young man is here!"

Then holding a finger to his lips, Haruki vanished.

Further proof that tanuki were fond of tricks.

Curtains fluttered, and his lady emerged, arrayed in a creamy kimono decorated by a thicket of windblown bamboo. It was exquisite. Recalling himself, Junpei fished in his sleeve and brought out his gift, presenting it with both hands.

Her brows arched, but she brushed back her sleeves and reached across the counter to receive the pressed paper that now bore a delicate spray of plum blossoms.

She peered at his painting closely, flipped it, sniffed it, and even found the watermark. "Is this from …?"

Junpei nodded.

"Did you enjoy …?"

Still tongue-tied, he pressed a hand to his heart and bowed his head.

"Again," she ordered.

His gaze jumped to hers.

She held out a new block of chocolate, wrapped in the same luxurious paper. Showing dimples, she urged, "Bring me another. Flatter me with flowers."

"I will. Gladly." Junpei was relieved to have found his voice. "Is something like this enough for something so important?"

"What more are you willing to give?"

He blushed at her tone, but he carried through with the second half of his plan. "If it's all right, may I borrow your parasol?"

She blinked, and laughter bubbled up. Not the mocking sort, though. She seemed pleased to be asked.

A minute later, Chika came around the counter and pressed her paper parasol into his hands. Junpei's thoughts were already on the colors he'd choose and the flowers she might favor, so he wasn't prepared for her nose to bump his. How had she gotten so close? Or so high, for that matter.

"Junpei," she purred. "You have pleased me."

Her nearness left him cross-eyed. "Ah … well … good?"

She startled him further by rubbing her cheek against his, then switching sides to rub the other. "My people are affectionate."

"O-oooh." His heart was skipping, and a sweet scent made his cheeks warm.

"This is how I will welcome your gifts."

Junpei eased back and whispered, "Are you teasing me, Chika-sama?"

She shook her head. "Even a trickster knows the value of trust. Give me a chance to win yours."

"I will." And because it was true, he repeated, "Gladly."

THEY FOUND EACH OTHER

The wolves called for another meeting at the Starmark compound, and Anna was obliged to attend. During the long walk there, Matsu explained that the Elderbough trackers had been trying to confirm rumors of strangers in Keishi. "They must have found something," he said, without any trace of concern.

Anna looked to Paltry, who'd insisted on escorting them. "I haven't heard. So it can't be *too* urgent."

"Why gather if there is nothing to report?" she asked.

"Friends do," said the wolf vaguely.

Matsu chuckled … but Anna couldn't see why.

Harmonious was waiting at the entrance and came striding their way, but as far as she could tell, his only concern was playing the good host. Meeting her palms, he quickly shifted so that his were supporting hers. "Have you been well?"

"As you can see," she said stiffly.

"Thank goodness," he murmured, moving on to greet Matsu in kind.

Quen arrived to pull her inside, softly reminding her of his denmates' names as so many siblings, cousins, nieces, and nephews greeted her in passing. Opal was already there, ensconced upon a cushioned bench, surrounded by an eager audience. As usual. People were always begging for stories from him.

Anna recognized his tale. He told "The Queen's Footpath" often and well. Unlike many of the more traditional romantic ballads, this one sparkled with humor, for the moon maid was silly and clumsy by turns.

Paltry came up behind her and sighed. "Is he still spinning this old yarn?"

"This is one of his favorites." She shook her head. "I cannot understand it."

"Which part?"

"The moon maid … she is *nothing* but trouble. Why would the wolf invite so much disaster into his den?"

Paltry laughed.

Anna's confusion doubled.

"I'm sure he had reason enough." Nodding toward the bard, Paltry asked, "It's a love story, isn't it?"

"I suppose."

The wolf's smile gentled. "Opal pretties it up a fair bit, but the long and the short of it is … they found each other."

"I suppose," she grudgingly repeated. "Since the story is about a wolf."

"Everyone knows how canines are about bonds," Paltry agreed amiably. "We're protective of those we cherish. And attentive in small ways. See? Harmonious has seen to our comfort."

He nodded toward the room beyond, where rugs and cushions surrounded low tables laden with teapots and covered dishes.

"We make good allies and better friends." Paltry urged her forward with a touch. "Take heart, Midori-san, and take the seat Quen is saving for you."

Eloquence beckoned, and she accepted his invitation, first greeting Rise before settling against his bulk. There were more wolves today, and she spotted crests from horse and moth clans. Hisoka had returned, and he spoke in low tones with Matsu. Opal finished his tale to a smattering of applause and sauntered in ahead of Laud, who closed the doors and added sigils.

"Merit, Boon, you boys may begin." Harmonious scanned the room, nodded to himself, then came to sit at Anna's other side.

She decided to ignore him in favor of the trackers' report.

Merit rambled though opening courtesies in his father's stead—polite and to-the-point. Anna was favorably impressed with Harmonious' heir. He was sensible without being tiresome about it. By contrast, his friend Boon adopted a deceptively easy-going manner.

"No dragons have settled in this part of the world. The closest harems are on the continent, and the nearest heights are even farther afield." Merit looked toward Opal, and his smile made him look even more like his father. "However, we Starmarks cannot discount the songs of stars."

Anna wasn't sure what he meant by that, and she missed any explanation, because Harmonious leaned over to murmur, "More tea, Anna?"

She didn't wish to be impolite. "Thank you," she said crisply, before pointedly turning her attention back to Merit.

Harmonious filled her cup.

Midway through Merit's list of Amaranthine on staff at Ingress Academy, Harmonious interrupted again.

"Another cushion?"

Anna whispered, "Do not trouble yourself."

Introductions followed. One of their guests was Mare Rilka Withershanks, a healer from the horse clans. And the Nightbide clan had sent a scribe.

Again, Harmonious distracted Anna with questions.

"Have you tasted these?" Lifting the cover off a serving dish, he revealed rows of small cakes. "Churlish borrowed our kitchen earlier. He has a gift for pastries."

"Or these," murmured Quen, indicating a bamboo tray of daifuku. "They're from the House of the Noble Chrysanthemum."

She perked up.

Quen beamed and secured two for her.

Harmonious snagged one for himself and cautiously tested his fangs on it. The mochi gummed and stretched and became unwieldy. His brows buckled in bewilderment, and he muffled his grunt of surprise by cramming the whole thing in his mouth.

Quen plastered both hands over his, stifling giggles.

"Whu–?" Harmonious tried around the glom. "Whuh iff vish?"

Anna only knew because she'd asked Chika the same question. "Pounded, sweetened rice … folded around mashed, sweetened beans."

He grunted again. And choked a little.

Anna passed him her tea, which he gratefully downed. To Quen, she said, "I do not think it is to his taste."

"More for me," exulted the boy.

"For us," she corrected, taking a dainty bite of her new favorite.

Harmonious refilled Anna's teacup and gulped and scowled. But there was a shine in his eyes, and she thought that if he'd had a tail, it would be thumping tatami.

He ranged outward to find more tea, having drained their pot.

Quen leaned into Anna, and she glanced down in surprise. She wasn't used to these sorts of affections. What had Paltry said? *Good allies and better friends.* This certainly had the feel of camaraderie to it, though the boy's gaze was fixed with awe upon his father.

"What?" she whispered.

He looked from her to him and back again before whispering, "Da is *smiling.*"

Anna tried to think back. Yes, she was sure. "He smiles often enough."

"He does," Quen slowly agreed. "When *you* are here."

THROUGH THE GARDEN DOOR

Junpei was setting out his paints when his brother eased open the sliding screen to the garden and crawled through. The sneak. He'd been pulling this trick ever since he was little, because Mother couldn't scold him for interrupting Junpei if she didn't know he was trespassing.

Even though it was an intrusion, Junpei had never turned Sho away. He didn't do it often. Only when something was bothering him. Or when he needed to talk.

"Good evening," Junpei murmured, fishing a second cushion out from under his table.

Sho sat upon it and quietly asked, "What're you doing?"

"I have this new paper. The paint loves it, so I've been making flowers bloom."

His brother hummed uncertainly, smiled tentatively. "Looks like you're having fun ...?"

"I am."

"You really like flowers, huh?"

"I suppose I do."

"Nobody ever teases you?" Sho ventured.

"Usually, nobody ever finds out." Junpei wondered if someone had been making fun of Sho for one of his pastimes. "I did get asked if I was a gardener, recently. Had to tell them *no*. I wasn't qualified for the job."

"Hmm?"

Junpei slid a painting he'd begun last night across the table. A stone lantern like the ones at Kikusawa Shrine, with a scattering of tiny red flower petals carried on a playful breeze. He said, "Did you want to talk about what happened the other day?"

It was only a guess.

"Hmm?" Sho kept his gaze on the painting. "Which thing do you mean?"

"Well, you met some of my friends while we were up top. The two men who were with me."

"Oh? Oooh." Sho seemed genuinely bewildered. "Did something like that happen?"

Junpei thought a lot had happened. "The bookseller with glasses? The boy with purple hair? The man with red eyes?"

His little brother rolled his eyes. "Maybe *you* should be the novelist."

He didn't remember? Is this what Matsu had meant? Junpei forced a laugh. "I guess it does sound pretty fanciful."

Sliding back the painting, Sho asked, "Who's this one for?"

"Do you remember the girl I saw?"

"I didn't see her." His brother squinted. "You weren't making her up?"

"She's real, and she's ... interested in me. I guess." Lowering his voice, Junpei begged, "It's too soon to tell Mother, though. Okay?"

"You've got a girl?"

"Yes." He tried to sound casual. He probably flubbed it.

Sho hummed again. "What do you like about her?"

Junpei ventured, "Everything ...?"

His brother snorted. "That's the kind of answer that doesn't say anything. You better come up with a better reason before Mother catches wind."

"Probably." Junpei shyly confessed, "She has brown hair. It's even lighter than yours."

"You don't mind?"

"Mmm ... nope. She's lovely."

Sho said, "So she'll actually kinda look like my sister?"

"She'll *be* your sister."

"You sound pretty confident." His teasing smile fell away. "Can you afford a bride?"

Junpei didn't want Sho to worry about money. "It'll be fine. One of the town elders and the new silk merchant found out about my painting. They commissioned some work, and they've offered to be my patrons."

"They'll pay you to paint?"

"Yes."

"That's ... really good, isn't it?"

"It's all been amazing. I've never had such an exciting week in my life." Junpei lightly touched the red flower petals in his tiny painting. He was worried for Naoki and Hajime. "You really can't remember the boy who was talking to you at the Shrine?"

"Please don't ask," whispered Sho.

Junpei was suddenly, horribly worried. Something about his brother's expression brought Opal the Sage to mind. "I won't. I don't have to." He borrowed a page from Naoki's book. "There are truths along the edges, and those are safe to say."

Sho's gaze turned pleading.

"Did you meet someone new the other day?"

"Yes."

"And I suppose they've been back?"

"Mm-hmm."

"New things can be pretty amazing. Just because someone is different, doesn't mean they're bad." Junpei gently tweaked a lock of his brother's hair. "There are all kinds of people in the world."

"If you say so." Sho gave the tiniest shake of his head.

Junpei was almost afraid to ask. "Did your new friend … scare you?"

Sho swallowed hard. "Not at first."

It hardly took any coaxing for Sho to agree to stay the night in Junpei's room. And it took even less time for Junpei to make up his mind to tell Paltry. Tomorrow. Right after work. Well, after work *and* after a brief visit to the House of the Noble Chrysanthemum.

WE SHOULD TALK MORE

Junpei wasn't sure how often he was meant to call upon Chika, so he'd gone with his own impulse and dropped by her family's shop every day. The visits were brief. All he really did was present her with his latest painting on the paper sleeves from the chocolates she'd given.

Orchids touched with pink, nodding in a spring breeze.

They'd earned him a smile, and she urged, "More."

Bamboo against a sunlit haze, green and gold with the promise of summer.

She'd filled his hands with more chocolates and kissed his cheek before murmuring, "More."

The papers from *those* sweets were back in Junpei's room, being flattened between the pages of a book. Except for the one he'd shown to Sho last night. That one probably counted as a personal piece. Because ... hmm. Why was that again? Naoki would remember, surely.

For today, Junpei was ready to return Chika's parasol.

She beckoned for him to follow her into the garden behind the shop, where he placed the newly embellished accessory upon her outstretched palms.

She opened it, admiring the cascades of plum blossoms he'd added. Propping it over her shoulder, she twirled merrily and asked, "Will there be chrysanthemums, next?"

Junpei was honestly amazed. "How did you guess?"

"That my gentleman knows the Four Gentlemen?" Chika's gaze softened. "I'm very good at guessing, but I'd rather know things because you *tell* me."

"That would be good." He tucked his hands into his sleeves and admitted, "There's so much I don't know."

"Walk with me," Chika invited, indicating the door. "Talk with me."

She gathered a small drawstring bag and her wrap, since evening was nearing. Pride stirred when she brought the parasol as well.

"Where do you want to go?" he asked.

Chika hummed. "Somewhere you are drawn to."

"The shrine?" he suggested.

"All right. I haven't been up there since returning." She indicated that he should lead.

Contrary to custom, he stayed by her side. "You've been away?"

"For quite some time." Chika eyed him thoughtfully. "You know about the difference between Amaranthine and human life spans?"

"Paltry explained. It must be wonderful to have such a full life." She smiled tentatively. "You're not bothered?"

"A little, I suppose. It makes me want to paint a thousand pictures and then a thousand more. So you'll have beautiful things to remember me by." Junpei lowered his gaze. "Is that too presumptuous?"

"No. I'm presuming all over the place, myself. Or did you not notice that I claimed you before we were introduced."

"I noticed. I did wonder," he admitted. "But I've never questioned it."

"Maybe you should ask more questions."

Junpei ventured, "If you're newly returned, where did you go?"

"A faraway land across the sea. They had chocolate there. And new songs. And strange customs. And many secrets." She favored him with another smile. "While I was there, I made up my mind to find a man with a beautiful soul once I returned, and here you were."

"Am I here now because of a song … or a custom … or a secret?" he asked, half-joking.

Chika slipped her hand into his and coyly asked, "Why not all three?"

Junpei hardly minded having to stoop under torii gates all the way up the long stair, but he did straighten and unobtrusively stretch once he was in the open again. Only to lose his breath with a startled, "*Oof,*" as Chika shoved the length of her closed parasol into his midriff.

"Hold this," she ordered in an urgent undertone … and vanished.

HELP WILL FIND YOU

Anna's restlessness drove her to patrol the boundaries of Kikusawa Shrine several times throughout the day, even though the Elderbough pack knew their business. She needed *some* occupation.

Sunset hues were streaking the sky when Matsu scolded her for neglecting her lessons with the children. "Let them distract you in useful ways."

She accepted this as she would an order, but she murmured, "Something is bothering me."

"Have you seen anything?"

Anna hated to speak the possibility aloud. "Even if I had, would I remember?"

Matsu frowned. "The wards have been refreshed, and we have friends close at hand."

"Yes, but …."

The children crowded around, and greetings rose on every side, since they'd lost their trepidation. Although Matsu had encouraged them to call her Midori-san, most had come up with slightly different versions of her name. They called her big sister or lady, angel or saint.

She hardly minded, since they did the same for Matsu. With honorifics, they claimed a connection to him, and in accepting their many nicknames, diminutives, and endearments, Matsu let them know they belonged.

Anna appreciated the subtleties, even as she despaired of unraveling them all. There was so much to learn. Not just the words, but their nuances.

"What shall we teach Midori-san today?" asked Matsu, once everyone was seated.

Suggestions rang out, and she tried not to chafe at their childishness. She had learned the names of colors and seasons and numbers and so many different animals. But these weren't the kinds of words she needed most.

"May I ask for some words I want to know?"

Matsu smiled encouragingly. "Let us hear them."

"Run," she said.

He translated, and the children helped her practice.

Next, she asked, "Hide?"

They taught her the word, and they talked of running games and hiding games.

"Danger," she said.

Matsu grew solemn, but he calmly provided the word she wanted.

"What about ... find help?" Anna asked. "Or ... bring Paltry?"

The shrine keeper didn't translate her request for the children. "He and his shop are not easy for ordinary children to find. But if you speak your need aloud, there are ears to hear. Call out, and if your need is great, you will be answered."

"By whom?" she asked skeptically. "I know a wolf's ears are good, but ...!"

Matsu lifted a hand and said, "Kusunoki."

As one, the children turned toward the tree that dominated

the courtyard. Two of the little girls clapped their hands twice and bowed their heads.

Anna asked, "You pray to the tree?"

"Kusunoki is a friend to all who live under his branches," Matsu said mildly. "If you need help, it will find you."

So cryptic. Anna wanted more particulars, but she could wait for a private conversation.

"Oh, no!" complained one of the boys. "It's him. He's back."

In the deepening shadows near the treeline, a boy peered at them from around a stone lantern. He gestured imperiously, and Sho slowly stood.

"Have you made a new friend?" asked Matsu.

"No," whispered one of the girls.

"I don't like him," said another.

"And why is that?" quizzed Matsu.

"He's bossy. And sneaky."

"Shisoku is ... different," said Sho, shuffling toward the other boy. "He scares me."

Matsu translated for her, and Anna jumped to her feet, grabbing his arm. "Where are you going?"

Sho tried to shrug his way free, saying something more.

Again, Matsu translated. "He says he *has* to go. That he's that boy's favorite."

"Did he not say the boy frightens him?"

After a brief exchange, Matsu's eyes widened. "I believe he's being compelled. And by more than threats to the littler children."

She dearly wished for her sword. "I will go with him."

Matsu whispered something to Sho, who looked up at her.

"Thank you, Saint Midori."

Anna kept her hand where it was and let Sho lead her toward the pale Amaranthine boy whose sneer filled her with dread. The closer they came, the surer she was that his hair wasn't just dark … it was dark purple. And those eyes. She knew those eyes.

"Dragon," she whispered.

The Amaranthine boy's chin came up. "I do not need you. Only him. Go away."

Anna turned around and walked away, even though some part of her soul screamed against leaving Sho behind. But the dragon had only said to go … not *where* she must go. So Anna strode swiftly toward the room where her sword waited.

Except she didn't get that far. Someone sideswiped her, carrying her upward.

It was still *away*, so it was fine. "Chika?" she managed. "There is a dragon."

Leaves and branches smacked Anna about her head and shoulders as Chika carried her up into the courtyard's tree. When they arrived upon a sturdy limb, Anna latched on, holding tight. To her astonishment, a few of the children were already seated among the nearest branches. How had Chika brought them so swiftly?

Her new friend grimly promised, "I can help. So can he."

Suddenly, she was facing a thickset young man with flowers in his long, black hair. Craggy features. Glittering green eyes. Urgent tones. "Stay quiet. I will bring Paltry."

Anna wanted to argue. She was a battler. This was her fault. Sho was still in danger. But the stranger was gone, and the only thing she managed to ask was, "Who was that?"

Chika pressed her finger to Anna's lips. "Hush," she insisted. "That was Kusunoki."

THERE IS A DRAGON

Junpei wavered at the top of the stairs. Chika may have been fond of surprises, but her disappearance hadn't felt like a silly prank. Something was wrong, but where? Leaning the parasol behind a stone lantern, he took a few steps, listening hard.

Too quiet.

So tense.

Junpei rubbed at the palm of his hand, where Uncle Haruki had drawn a mark. If things were happening, he *should* be able to see them. Right?

Maybe not. So Junpei asked the emptiness, "Is something wrong? Can I help?"

A man appeared—big and sturdy and strange. Just ... blinked into existence and loomed over him.

"*Ehyahhh...!*" Junpei's exclamation wavered to an end as recognition dawned. This had to be the childhood friend Matsu had mentioned, although he looked much younger than the shrinekeeper. And why was he crowned with red flowers? They were certainly striking ... and vaguely familiar. "S-sorry. Hello. I'm Junpei ...?"

"I know. Come with me."

Junpei stepped forward, asking, "Where ...?"

The question was barely begun when strong hands closed around Junpei's upper arms, and the world went dark. Or ... dim?

Junpei peered around—walls, ceiling beams, cabinets, boxes. "Where is this?"

"One of the storehouses. It should be safe."

"Safe from ...?"

"Mmm, dragons."

Junpei didn't like the sound of that. "Where's Chika?"

"Helping to hide the children."

Uncertainty veered into dread. "Is my brother out there?"

A jerky nod. "Sho is in danger."

"Where?" Junpei caught the fullness of the man's sleeve. "I need to get to him."

He hesitated. "Chika wants you hidden."

"Sho is my brother!" Junpei's eyes were adjusting, and he frantically searched the dim, this time for a door. "He needs me!"

"Mmm, true." The man's gaze went soft with sympathy. "I understand."

"Take me to him!"

"*Near* him," he promised. "But not too close. This dragon is dangerous."

And then Junpei was in a different part of the twilit courtyard, where Sho stood with another boy.

"Play with me!" demanded the dark-haired boy who had Sho by the front of his half-coat. "Do it right!"

"Sho!" called Junpei. "Time to go. It'll be dinnertime soon. Mother will be waiting."

"Who are you?" asked the strange boy, head tipping to one side as he considered him.

"My brother," said Sho, whose gaze pleaded with Junpei.

Stepping forward, Junpei asked, "What game are you playing? Could I join?"

"You feel nice," said the boy, who crooked the fingers of his free hand. "Even nicer than this one. Why is that? Come closer."

It was like Opal all over again. Junpei *needed* to take a step, but he found that one was enough.

"I said come closer," grumbled the boy, whose hold on Sho slipped enough to show tears in the yellow cloth.

"What game are we playing?" asked Junpei, who slid forward another half-step.

The boy released Sho.

In the same instant, Matsu's flower-crowned friend appeared behind Sho, pulled him close, and vanished. Safe!

A hiss of surprise. A narrowing of red eyes. "You *tricked* me!"

Junpei watched in horror as the boy's balled fists uncurled, revealing wicked claws. He crouched, coiling to spring, but before the attack came, someone intervened, scooping Junpei off his feet and carrying him away.

"Good evening, Junpei," Paltry rumbled. "Thank you for your help. We'll handle it from here."

The world righted itself, and they were overlooking Kikusawa's central courtyard from atop the main shrine. Junpei heaved a shuddering breath. Maybe the *between* place that the dexes had brought him into wasn't all teacakes and tail-wagging.

A howl sounded in the distance, and Paltry turned toward the sound. His smile showed a hint of fang. And then, "Kusunoki?"

That was it! The name of Matsu's friend. He'd somehow forgotten.

Kusunoki popped into existence at Paltry's side, arms open to receive Junpei.

"Sho ...?" he managed, wanting to be sure his brother was safe.

But Kusunoki only begged, "Hurry!"

Paltry snarled and dove as the screams of children came from below.

LEND ME THE SWORD

Anna didn't want to frighten the children huddled among the branches around her, but she needed answers. Now.

"Chika," she called. "What's going on? Where is Matsu? Why are his children crying?"

But the voice that answered wasn't Chika.

"Opal stashed you in a tree? He shall find you plucked."

"Look at this tree, brother," urged a second voice. "Look closely!"

"Is this *really* the time for specimens?" And raising his voice for her benefit, "I have had a long journey, beauty. Reward me well!"

Beneath her feet, power swelled, and in the fading light, she thought she caught the ripple and twist of scales. At least one of her pursuers had taken truest form.

"Come away, dear child," came a new voice in accented English.

She found herself cradled by a man whose size belied his strength.

"Good evening, Anna Green. The name's Haruka Wendwood."

"I remember." Over the tanuki's shoulder, she saw Chika sweep two little ones from the lower branches.

"My niece sent word. We'll do what we can until ... ah. Here they are." Haruka glided to the tile roof of one of the shrine's storehouses and steadied Anna on her feet.

She crouched low as an enormous dog hit the central courtyard with enough force to crater flagstone.

Haruka clucked his tongue. "Hardly subtle, but a good distraction. Stay safe."

And Anna was alone again, only stranded on a roof this time. "Kusunoki!" she whispered, not wanting to attract the twin dragons.

An instant later, the young man stood beside her and generously helped her to her feet. His gaze was patient, though slightly unsettling. The green of his eyes seemed to be faceted, and they gleamed unnaturally in the fading light.

"There is a weapon here. I know about it from Opal."

He simply nodded.

"Give it to me, so I can fight." When he didn't answer, she shook his arm. "I have trained for this! Yield the Chrysanthemum Blaze to me!"

"Anna Green," he finally said. "Matsu trusts you. I will trust you."

Kusunoki's large hands gripped her shoulders, and the hush of indoors closed around her—still, silent, and smelling of incense. She shifted her weight, and her hip jostled something in the utter blackness. "I cannot see."

"Wait a moment."

He was gone. She felt him go and knew she was alone. But then he was simply *there* again, holding a painted lantern at the end of a stick. Lifting it toward the far corner, he indicated an ornate cupboard.

If it held a fabled treasure, no hint of its presence reached her.

However, once Kusunoki fiddled with the tricky catches and the doors swung wide, the resonance of potent stones called.

"He is willing. Wield him well," murmured her companion.

Lanternlight glinted off red facets as she lifted the Chrysanthemum Blaze from its stand. The blade was heavy for its size, but Anna was confident in her strength. "Out," she ordered.

Gently pulling her into his side, Kusunoki effortlessly transferred Anna to the field of battle.

YOU ARE SAFE NOW

Junpei stumbled off-balance when Kusunoki abandoned him in the dark. Unsure if it was the same room as last time, Junpei chose a direction and shuffled forward, arms outstretched. His fingers bumped wood paneling. Orienting himself to the wall, he moved to one side, seeking the door, which he hauled open on its hinges by a big ring handle.

"Thank you, Junpei," said Hisoka Araki. "Your timing could not be better."

He squinted into the light of a familiar chrysanthemum-flourished lantern, which seemed to kindle flames in Hisoka's orange eyes. The city elder dropped his gaze and pivoted, bringing Junpei's attention to the limp child draped over his arm.

"Akemi!" Junpei quickly relieved Hisoka of his burden. There was blood on the girl's torn clothing.

"Coming through," said Paltry, who carried two more children. "Posy, can you manage more lights?"

Hisoka moved to the lamps arranged throughout the room, and

as illumination spread, Junpei guessed that this building was used to store and maintain clothing. Kimono stands took up much of the floor space, and neat piles of folded cloth occupied a long table. Hushed. Safe. But the scent of blood jarred Junpei into action. Surely Matsu wouldn't mind if he used something here for bandages.

Paltry set down one of his small passengers, and the boy burst into tears.

"It's okay, Kenzou." Junpei beckoned. "You and Taiki are safe now."

While he tried to calm the frightened child, Junpei looked to Paltry, who was patting Taiki's ashen cheek. The wolf inhaled deeply, and his tail tucked. "Posy, there's poison."

Hisoka grimaced. "Warn the others."

"Done."

Already moving for the door, Hisoka said, "I'll bring Rilka."

"*Hurry.*" To Junpei, Paltry added, "One of our healers."

Kusunoki reappeared with a child in each arm, both uninjured, and immediately vanished. And Uncle Haruka—or possibly Haruki—skidded through the door with a youngster clutching a bloodied shoulder. And then Quen hustled Sho through the door. Both boys carried clingy little ones.

"Sho!" Junpei called.

His little brother wasted no time getting to his side. "Jun-nii, he ... he was so angry with me. Is it my fault?"

"This isn't on you, kid." Paltry's voice rumbled with authority. "Do what you can here. You'll be okay. Wendwood illusions are keeping this place under wraps."

The wolf drew a sword as he strode out, his tail puffed double.

Junpei counted heads and knew there were children missing.

Three more boys. One of Matsu's daughters. Matsu himself. He started for the door.

Quen caught his arm. "Stay here."

The boy wore armor, and a sword rode at his waist. He looked far more equipped for the confusion outside.

"Can't we do anything?" He gestured, hoping to get his meaning across.

Quen smiled grimly and spoke in simple terms. "Uncle Laud told me to guard this door. That is what I can do."

Junpei wryly admitted, "That's probably more than I can do."

Hisoka landed on the flagstones in front of them, followed by a woman who merely nodded in passing. She must be the healer. Junpei wasn't sure if he should be more amazed by the speed of their arrival … or that they'd seemingly dropped from the sky. He leaned out, scanning the emerging stars.

Sho returned to his side, pale and tense as he peered into the courtyard.

Junpei couldn't help checking him over, needing to reassure himself. To his dismay, the front of his brother's half-coat was soaked with blood. "Were you cut? Or … scratched?"

"No. Not me," said Sho.

He was relieved, and then he was astonished. "Look!" Junpei breathed.

One by one, lights bloomed in the stone lanterns, but they couldn't have been lit by normal lamps. Soft colors pooled on the ground—pink, blue, green, gold. *Beautiful.* But as more lights rose into the air, twinkling and spinning, they illuminated a nightmare scene. Scales writhed as a serpentine creature curled upward, winding its body around the sacred tree's trunk.

Junpei glanced at Quen, whose jaw was set, and then at Sho.

Tears streaked his little brother's face. Sho brokenly relayed, "It's Matsu's blood."

WRITHING SCALES OF PURPLE

Anna stalked across the courtyard, gathering her ire so that the crystal sword hummed in her hands. Boon whipped around, gaze wary, but she lifted a hand, signaling for forces to rally. In a heartbeat, Boon, Paltry, and Laud formed ranks around her, ready to defend.

Harmonious found his way to her, but he looked both awkward and unarmed. "Anna, are you well?"

"I am imperiled," she countered. "As you can see."

"I ... well, yes." His gaze dropped to the weapon in her hands. "But not acquired, captured, or confined. Which is heartening."

"Get behind us, Harmonious Starmark."

He glanced toward the dragon, which had begun to unwind from the tree. "I would feel better if you didn't have to fa–"

"I am a *battler*," she growled. "I know what I am about!"

Harmonious simply crouched so they were eye-to-eye and patiently finished his sentence. "If you didn't have to face them alone. I may not have my brother's skill with weaponry, but I can support you."

She shook her head. She didn't need shielding. He was in the way!

"Ride me," he invited. "Where I come from, battlers ride dogs."

"It's true enough," said Paltry.

"Trick riding requires training," warned Boon. "And trust."

Anna hesitated.

"Let me keep my promise," pleaded Harmonious. "They cannot take you if I have you."

"Speed. Mobility," said Laud.

Boon grinned and added, "All those big, sharp teeth."

"Yes," she snapped. "All right. Yes."

Harmonious turned to crouch, and Anna gaped at him.

Laud snapped, "Get *on*."

Oh! Anna scrambled to comply and was barely astride his broad shoulders when Harmonious leapt skyward, narrowly missing the lash of a scaled tail. Then she was scrambling for a handhold when her companion diffused into a dazzling shift that she'd only ever seen from a safe distance. Power and personality clashed against her senses, and then there was fur between her fingers and a howl in her ears.

Anna rode what looked like a great red wolf, and he galloped in a tight circle above the shrine, giving her an unparalleled view. Channeling her considerable fury into red crystal that seemed to lap it up and look for more, she smiled grimly as the Chrysanthemum Blaze bloomed with a lurid glow. She tuned her soul to its song and laughed.

Two dragons twisted their heads to find her in the sky. Together they launched from the courtyard, helpless to resist, drawn toward their deaths.

"Higher," Anna ordered her mount. And to the hissing dragons, "Come to me! My answer is ready!"

DRIFT OF FLOWER PETALS

Howls and a shrill fluting sent a shiver down Junpei's spine, and he eased back into the shelter of the doorway, even as Quen stepped into the open, craning his neck to see what was happening.

"Da took truest form," he reported.

Junpei edged out, peering into the dark. "I don't see anything."

"They took flight." Quen's gaze followed some point overhead. "The dragons are chasing him."

"Not entirely true," said a voice that made Junpei flinch. Opal the Sage was ushering a small group of people to their shelter. The dragon winced and clamped his hands over his ears. "Anna is luring them with the Blaze."

Paltry rushed to the dragon and hauled him into his arms. "What do you need?" he rumbled.

"Wards. Several." With a brittle laugh, Opal complained, "What a racket."

They bustled him inside, and Junpei whispered, "I don't hear anything."

Quen shook his head and shrugged.

"So ... are they leading the dragons away?" asked Junpei.

"Nooo," the boy said, his gaze jumping from one point to another. "I do not think that is Anna's plan."

Hisoka Araki called for attention. "While the way is clear, we need to move everyone from Matsu's household. Please, move the uninjured to the archive, which must also be preserved. Scribe Nightbide is waiting to receive us there."

Paltry asked, "Haruka, Haruki, how much of this place can you shield?"

"Not the whole property. You'll need to pick and choose."

Hisoka turned to Matsu's kin. "Guide our choices."

Matsu's two younger brothers and their families also served as shrinekeepers. Matsu's wife stood with them, and Junpei was relieved to see their missing daughter safely tucked against her side. They exchanged looks and murmured among themselves before Matsu's aged mother gave their decision. "The main shrine. The archive. The treasure room."

"We'll do all we can," Hisoka promised.

More people arrived—wolves, if their tails were anything to go by—and they quickly escorted everyone away. Sho went with them, but Junpei hung back. A hand slipped into his, and he glanced down to find Chika at his side.

"What about the injured?" asked a lady wolf.

"Rilka?" inquired Hisoka.

She offered a sad smile and a small headshake.

Junpei saw every tail in the room tuck.

Chika slipped from his side. "I can help, Mare Withershanks. Entrust their dreams to me, and they will be sweet."

What did they mean? Junpei couldn't bring himself to ask.

Quen sniffled and turned away.

"Are they ... dying?" he whispered, heartbroken. Akemi, Taiki, Masao, and Hina.

Again, a hand found his, but when he looked to see who it was, a finger pressed to his lips. He stared into red eyes for a startled moment before Hajime stole him away.

"Will you come?" he asked.

Junpei was already gone, standing among the softly glowing lights in one of the side gardens. "Is Naoki here?" he ventured.

Trembling fingertips touched his lips again. "Do not say our names. Please."

He simply nodded.

"Come and hold Kusunoki's hand."

Junpei nodded, but he whispered, "Why?"

"My son needs a friend. That is how we are." Hajime sadly added, "He asked for you."

"Kusunoki did?"

Hajime's headshake scattered flower petals. "Matsu did."

ONE OF FOUR STORMS

Anna was getting a feel for the way Harmonious moved. With a fistful of fur and curt orders, she guided him higher, staying beyond the dragons' reach. The twins twisted and snapped, eyes gleaming with an unnatural light. She shuddered to think how such reprehensible creatures had gained the sky.

When she unleashed a greater measure of her soul, her mount's stride faltered.

"Do not lose trust now, Harmonious Starmark!" she called challengingly.

He wheeled and snarled at the oncoming dragons.

One hesitated, but the other leapt for her, and she flung all her outrage into a swing of the Chrysanthemum Blaze. Though styled as a blade, the crystals served as a conduit for her brutal intent.

Arcs of brilliance span away, slashing through purple scales and eliciting a shrilling bellow.

The air went still, not a breath stirred, as if the wind itself let the dragon fall.

"Follow!" she cried, sending another slash after the tumbling dragon.

Harmonious dropped, and they bore down, pressing the attack. Focused power sliced, clipping a wing. The dragon wailed, and his twin plunged squalling after him, attempting to cushion his landing. They careened toward the shrine, flipped off a barrier, and skewed down the slope in a disastrous tumble that turned the long line of torii arches into kindling.

Harmonious landed in the street below, and Anna slid from his shoulders, stepping through shattered wood and strewn branches. In the light cast by the Blaze, she noted the dark spatter of blood as the dragons floundered apart.

Shifting into speaking form, the shorter brother stumbled back, heaving for air and clutching at his side. "One of the Storms," he hissed, eyes wide and wild. "Come away, brother."

Claws scrabbled at the ground, and coils shuddered.

Spears of wood jutted from wet scales, and wings dragged.

Anna's gaze flicked to the ruined slope. Wolves watched from different points along the hilltop, bearing mute witness. No one moved to stop her. No one questioned her actions. And in their silence, they condemned these dragons.

Lights swirled through the treetops, small and erratic, and a fragrance hung heavy in the air—floral, pleasant. It eased her rancor, and she lowered the Blaze until its tip touched the ground.

Suddenly, a boy darted from the trees and flung his arms around the waist of the dragon in speaking form. "Go away!" the child shrieked. "You, go! Now!"

Anna grit her teeth. Why was a child here?

"Make her go, Father!" begged the pale child. "Tell her to leave us alone!"

"Shisoku, I will deal with you, later," promised the dragon. "Go, now. Get clear of here."

The boy shrank from the threat in his father's tone, skittering away.

That one's gaze never strayed from Anna's face as he stepped to his twin's side and asked, "Can you rise, Brother?"

Curving claws made another bid for purchase, and poison hissed as it seeped to the ground.

Anna didn't wait for him to fling it her way. With grim authority, she loosed a pulse of power that drove both dragons flat.

Her would-be suitor twisted and shifted. Huddled on the street, clutching at injuries, he resorted to words. "That is *enough* from you. Stop, woman."

"No." Anna lifted her chin. "You cannot stop me. Not anymore. Not ever."

With the Chrysanthemum Blaze in her hands, his words were nothing. She could resist. He was powerless.

He must have realized it as well, for his gaze swung past her. Sucking in air, he raised his voice. "Stop her, dog."

Anna stiffened when arms enfolded her from behind. She turned slightly and muttered, "This is hardly helpful."

Harmonious' brows were tight-knit, his gaze troubled.

She tried to push him back with an elbow.

He hid his face against her neck. "Anna," he managed. "Anna."

"Forget, dog." The dragon sneered and demanded, "Forget her."

A growl vibrated through Anna's whole body, and Harmonious snarled, "Why does everyone think I should forget? I will not let go of those I love! Never!"

Anna reached up to yank a handful of auburn hair. "I *forbid* you to forget. So take heed."

And because it was the only thing she could think to do, Anna initiated tending. It was a rough thing, for she was no more a cosset than a bard, and her soul was riled.

He grunted, and his hold on her tightened.

"You cannot forget someone once they are a part of you. Take in my scent, dog. Learn the shape of my soul, though its song is far from gentle."

"A-anna," he said gruffly. He breathed in, and she felt the drag on her soul, as if he were drinking deeply.

"Hardly the time," she warned.

With a murmured apology, he pressed his lips to her shoulder and ... tried to put back what he'd taken. At least, that's what it felt like. Strength rushed into Anna, doubling her resources, then doubling them again. Headier than strong drink, surer than steel.

"You make a good ally, Harmonious Starmark." And gathering all he'd given, Anna channeled it through the Blaze and struck her tormentor, knocking him back.

"Brother!" squealed the other, who returned to truest form, gathering up his twin and taking to the sky in a limping, listing flight.

Far from satisfied, Anna pushed more into the Blaze and commanded, "After them!"

Harmonious remained in speaking form, catching her up and swiftly gaining height. But in that moment, the night sky shattered, and brilliance blinded them. A voice thundered with urgency, almost too loud to hear, and it begged Anna for mercy.

Not for the fleeing dragons, but for one much dearer and closer to hand.

"Opal!" she gasped.

A HAND TO HOLD

Because Hajime brought him around from a series of paths he'd never used before, Junpei felt a little lost. But he was grateful for a better look at the mysterious lights that had appeared all around the shrine. It was as if someone had stolen stars from the sky. Or gathered up the scattered shards of a rainbow.

Up close, he could see that they were crystals, though he couldn't imagine who had strung them in midair. He was still trying to think how to capture their luminescence in a painting when something fluttered past.

Wings? Not a moth, surely. It had felt larger than that. Had sleepy birds fled their roosts?

Another series of short wingbeats descended, and something caught in his hair, chittering as it clung. He balked, pulling Hajime up short, and whispered, "What is it?"

"You are attracting Ephemera. Calm yourself. These are both harmless and adorable."

"Get it off?" he begged, bending so his companion could reach.

Hajime made hushing sounds. Maybe they were for the animal. Maybe they were for him. And when he stepped back, he had a strange creature in his hands. A teensy, winged monkey with pale fur that glowed in much the same way Churlish did.

"Nothing to fear," soothed Hajime. "Not from innocents such as these."

"Why have I never seen one before?"

"Perhaps because you *could* not. You have gained, I think. Bonds have a way of building." He passed the little animal to Junpei and smiled sadly. "Bring this one. Kusunoki dotes on them. Perhaps it will be a comfort."

Junpei almost asked why. But he knew, even before they arrived at the base of the big tree.

Kusunoki sat among its roots, stroking Matsu's hair and pleading with him in teary undertones. Naoki knelt at his side.

"He was like a brother to me," Kusunoki said in pleading tones.

"I know," soothed Naoki. "The best of brothers."

"I needed a brother. I ... I do not have one. Even though I should ...?"

"That's my fault, probably. But it couldn't be helped, the way you were sprigged. Your other parent ... well .... It was an unusual combination. And yours was the only seed that sprouted."

"It is only natural for a tree to long for a grove," Hajime murmured. "But look. Here is Junpei."

Kusunoki lifted his face, and his lips trembled. "I am not a medicinal tree. I could not save him."

"It isn't your fault," soothed Naoki. "Dragon poison is vicious."

Tears trickled down Kusunoki's face. "He tried to stop the dragon's boy from hurting our children. Matsu … he hugged him."

That did sound like something Matsu would do. Junpei crouched on Kusunoki's other side. "Look what I found."

"A quisp. They do not stir so much anymore." Looking to Naoki, Kusunoki mumbled, "Usually only for you."

Naoki lifted his wrists, showing off the heavy beads. "Not I. Not since your sapling days, when this was a roadside shrine."

"That woman is to blame," said Hajime. "She is a frightening one."

"Mmm." Kusunoki went back to stroking Matsu's hair. "She drove away the dragons. Are you safe now?"

"I will make sure of it," vowed Hajime.

"There are other wolves than Paltry," Kusunoki fretted. "They saw me."

"Unavoidable," sighed Naoki. "But not insurmountable. Trust us. And … if you can, trust Junpei."

Kusunoki frowned. "I do not want another friend."

"You know that's not true. Matsu knew as well. That's why he sent for Junpei."

Hajime urged, "Take his hand, leafling. The others will forget, but he can be company for you."

With a stony expression, Kusunoki lifted a trembling hand.

Junpei released the quisp, which scampered onto his shoulder, and folded both his hands around Kusunoki's larger one. Nothing more was said, but flower petals filled the air, as if every bloom in the tree overhead was falling along with Kusunoki's tears.

The fragrance was unlike anything Junpei had ever smelled. But he decided it was … nice.

WHEN A HEART BREAKS

Harmonious returned to the street, which wasn't where Anna wanted to be at all. "Where is Opulence?" she demanded.

"Above," said one of the nearby wolves. "In the archive."

Anna swung around, intent on reaching her mentor, but the wreckage of red-painted wood barred the way. She would need to cut through the woods. But before she could redirect her steps, Harmonious spoke.

"Anna? If you will permit …?"

Why wouldn't she? "Hurry!"

Harmonious gathered her up again, took flight, and set her before the doors to Matsu's archive. Its extensive collection of lore had occupied Opal for much of the visit—both reading and contributing.

"Opulence?" She eased through the narrow door and scanned the crowded room. Huddled children. Members of Matsu's family. One of the Nightbide moths. Hisoka-sensei and the she-wolf who led the Elderbough pack. "Opal?" Anna called more softly.

One of the tanuki beckoned from the far corner, and she worked her way past crowded shelves. Out of habit, she noted who was present … and who was missing.

But she reached the turning of a narrow aisle. There she found her mentor with his hands over his ears, rocking in place.

"Opal?" she whispered.

Red-rimmed eyes lifted, and the dragon summoned up a meager smile. "I am sorry to have missed the battle. Was it worthy of ballads?"

"Are you …?" She could feel that something was wrong, but she wasn't sure what. He seemed diminished somehow. "Did I hurt you?"

He tried to wave off her concern. "I have weathered the storm. I am only slightly broken."

"Shattered," corrected the tanuki, who went right on layering sigils over the dragon, as if he needed armoring.

She was aghast.

"Now, Anna," Opal chided. "I have always known it was a possibility. Just one of the many perils of taking on a prodigy."

"Is the mare still here?"

"She has her hands full, brewing calming teas."

"You are more important than a hot drink!" she countered.

Opal raised a quelling hand, which only shook a little. "Not to those who are very recently bereft of their kindred."

Anna flinched. The gaps. She knew who should have been here. "Taiki ... Akemi ... Hina ... Masao ...?"

"We shall sing for them once I can manage," Opal wearily vowed.

"Junpei," she gasped, thinking of Chika's beloved.

Paltry spoke up from beside Harmonious, who'd followed. "Junpei made it through."

"Is he with Matsu?" When Paltry flinched, she begged, "Where is Matsu?"

The wolf wearily shook his head.

Anna's horror redoubled. "I ... how can I ever atone? I should not have come!"

Arms wrapped around her from behind. "Do not wish us away," murmured Harmonious. "Your need was ours to match and meet."

Opal fluttered his fingers at him. "I take it you did not rebuff the old dog?"

She jabbed Harmonious with an elbow, admittedly weak as rebuffs went.

He grunted and grumbled, "My concern does not mean I think you helpless. Alliances such as ours are formed between equals."

"That one's been bond-building," remarked Opal.

Paltry quietly said, "It's a good thing, too. I *did* see the battle, and they might not have managed otherwise."

Anna didn't want to consider that too closely. "But what can I do, Opal? You know I am no good with people. And I know so little of their language."

Her mentor smiled sweetly, and his next words were lightly laced with sway. "Fear not, child. All you need to do is show them how you feel. They will understand."

Tears immediately spilled.

Harmonious whined softly.

Hisoka-sensei took over, then, and time passed in a blur as he lent words to her regrets and her grief and her resolve to honor Matsu's memory ... somehow.

When Sensei returned her to Opal's side, the dragon stirred enough to murmur, "Will you sing me a lullaby, Anna? I need to sleep, and I cannot hear the stars from here."

They were not compelling words, but Anna could not refuse him.

So she took a steadying breath and sang a song of trees.

SOMEBODY HAS TO REMEMBER

A few days later, Junpei sat through the strangest dinner conver-sation. Because Keishi was abuzz over the devastation at

Kikusawa Shrine.

"I heard from the apothecary, who heard it from the Nakamuras, who live right up against the slopes, that there was a dreadful noise that night—howling and screeching and the sound of a flute."

Junpei supposed a dragon's call might sound a little like a flute. "Is that so?"

"It was dragons," said Sho, who only picked at his food.

Mother gasped. "You're not the first to say so! My old friends at the Camelia Palace told me that two of their guests were bragging about seeing dragons in the sky. But they weren't sure how much credence to give their tale, since the gentlemen were on their third bottle."

"There were *three* dragons," mumbled Sho.

Junpei was surprised his younger brother remembered. Everyone who'd been close to Kikusawa Shrine during the dragon attack had hazy recollections of the events. All these rumors were coming from people who'd seen something from a safe distance, but nobody could confirm anything.

Except Sho.

After the meal was over, Junpei pulled his brother aside. "You remember?"

"Somebody has to," he grumbled.

"But how ...?"

"I wrote it out. It's a good story, but it's more than a story. It happened." His brother looked ready to pick a fight.

Junpei chose a soft answer. "Yes, it did. I'll never forget."

Sho searched his face and confessed, "I told the other boys in my class that the city was saved by Saint Midori."

"She was amazing," Junpei agreed.

His brother gaped at him. "You … you really do remember?"

Junpei understood then. His brother didn't actually remember the events. All he had was his account, which was limited to the things he'd seen that night. The secrets were safe, but … Sho was suffering because of them.

"Do you want to talk about it?"

"You'd listen?" he asked in a small voice.

Junpei could do better than that. "Tell me on the way."

His brother's gaze turned suspicious. "On the way *where*?"

"To meet some friends of mine." And taking his brother by the hand, he led the way to Moonglade Tearoom.

CAN THIS BE LOVE

The moment Paltry spotted Sho at Junpei's side, his expression softened, and he dropped to one knee. "Hey, there, Sho. Remember me at all?"

"Probably not." Junpei put an arm around his brother's shoulders. "Someday, people will be calling my brother Sho the Sage. He wrote an account of Saint Midori and the Dragons."

"A budding bard, are you?" Paltry lapsed into an easy smile. "Maybe you can help a friend of mine? He's still learning Japanese. Practice with him, and tonight's snacks are on the house."

Sho looked to Junpei, who'd noticed who was sitting with Churlish at the corner table. He advised, "Take Paltry up on it. You barely touched dinner."

With a very polite bow, Sho said, "Thank you very much."

"Come meet Quen," urged Paltry, beckoning for Sho to follow.

Junpei waved him off. "Go make friends. My boss is here, and I want to say hello."

Because Harmonious and Hisoka were at a table in the opposite corner.

Sho's gaze flitted around the room, and he mumbled, "Thanks, Jun-nii."

Junpei watched his brother greet Quen, wondering if his brother saw brown eyes or copper. Maybe it didn't matter. He'd let the dexes decide.

Striding back, Paltry clapped Junpei's shoulder. "Sho's in good hands. Quen is a gentle soul."

"Yes." And because he couldn't think of a tactful way to ask, Junpei blurted, "Have you forgotten anything?"

"Would I know if I had?" countered Paltry, whose smile went lopsided.

"You haven't."

"I haven't," confirmed the wolf. "Let's just say I'm not susceptible. Churlish and I have been here a long time, so we've built up a resistance to ... well .... How much do *you* remember?"

"Everything." Junpei eased closer and lowered his voice. "Naoki's a friend, and ... his longtime companion fixed things so Kusunoki would have a friend. After Matsu ...."

"Got it. And that's good." Nodding toward the table where Harmonious and Hisoka were set up, he urged, "I'll bring you a cup so you can help them drain the rest of his cask of star wine."

Hisoka Araki turned their way and smiled, hand extended.

Junpei hurried over, murmuring a *good evening* and accepting a seat.

Harmonious blinked at him, then leaned closer. "Did you notice how strong she is? Authority in her bearing. She would lead well."

At a loss, Junpei looked to Hisoka for a translation.

With a patient smile, Hisoka answered in simple Japanese. "Yes, yes. Anna is a fine woman. Anyone can see this."

Harmonious narrowed his eyes, as if sorting through the words, then nodded. "Fine. Very fine. Very, very fine. Such a lady would bring honor to her pack."

"Yes," Hisoka calmly agreed. And to Junpei, "My old friend has always been fond of star wine."

"Here, here," Harmonious beckoned for Junpei's cup.

"Oh! Umm." Junpei turned toward the kitchen.

Paltry strode out and set a cup before Junpei before scolding, "You've gone past tipsy and straight to drunk, Harmonious. Leave some for the rest of us."

"I share. Star wine is for sharing!" Harmonious frowned in concentration. "Do you think she would like a glass?"

"Anna isn't here," said Hisoka. "But you may fill Junpei's cup."

Harmonious took the sake bowl, only to gaze lovingly into its depths. "This is the exact color of her eyes."

Paltry snorted.

Hisoka chuckled.

Junpei ventured, "You miss Anna-san?"

"Anna," Harmonious breathed. "I want her to look my way."

"You're difficult to ignore," said Paltry, pausing to translate for Junpei.

"But am I difficult to love?"

Hisoka's gaze turned fond. "I have never found it so."

Paltry leaned over and tousled Harmonious' hair. "You're certainly my second favorite pooch. Right after Laud."

Harmonious blinked, then buried his face on his arms. "I'm being foolish."

"Don't dismiss love so lightly," said Paltry.

Copper eyes peeped mournfully. "Is it love then?"

"Only you can say for certain," Hisoka said smilingly.

"What do you think, Junpei?" asked Paltry. "Does this poor sot have any hope?"

Junpei guessed that was up to Anna, but he wasn't sure it was his place to say.

Hisoka mildly said, "Junpei is in a similar circumstance. Don't you recall the claim? He's courting a Wendwood."

Harmonious sat up straight. "Does he know?"

"He wants to know if you're aware you're courting a lady of the clans," relayed Hisoka.

"Yes. Tanuki clan. She made sure I understood."

"You're in love?" Harmonious asked cautiously.

People didn't usually talk about this kind of stuff, but Junpei kind of wanted to laugh. "So are you," he pointed out. "Is it really so rare?"

"I don't see that rarity matters," said Paltry. "Isn't it enough that you found each other?"

Harmonious covered his face with both hands. "But ... even if she .... Maker have mercy, I'm not sure I can lose another ...!"

"Ah." Paltry rubbed the back of his neck. "Life span."

Hisoka filled in for Junpei. "He has loved and lost before."

Junpei grabbed for Harmonious and fumbled for words. "Hoshina-dono … Harmonious-sama … sir! I understand. I mean, I *don't* but … how do I explain?"

Harmonious tipped his head to the side and sniffed, as if Junpei's scent made more sense than his words. "Say it your own way, lad. Hisoka will make things clear."

"It's about life span." Junpei looked to Hisoka and Paltry first, wanting to be sure his message made it through. Then he shyly met Harmonious Starmark's waiting gaze. "If you're worried about *keeping* Anna, I think Chika could help."

TANUKI MAKE GOOD NEIGHBORS

"I have an *enormous* favor to ask."

Anna automatically shifted into a receptive pose. "Is something amiss, Chika?"

"Oh, there's mischief involved, and all of it's mine. Can you come with me for a while?"

"How far? And for how long?" Anna indicated the door at her back. "I must stand guard while Opal sleeps."

Chika dimpled. "I thought of that. Laud will do it."

At her wave, one of the Starmark dogs stepped into view. The white-haired one who spoke little and carried at least seven concealed weapons. Not that she was counting.

"He volunteered," Chika hurried on. "And your mentor won't mind a bit. They're old friends."

Laud quietly promised, "Upon my word and the name of my

clan, he will rest secure."

"That's a Starmark for you!" Hooking Anna's arm, Chika hurried her along the path toward the trees. "Now then, let's have a lovely tramp along a pretty little lane that wends through a wood."

Anna had no trouble keeping up with the light-footed tanuki. "Is the play on words intentional? Wending through woods. Wendwood."

"Tanuki do love to play, and words are fair game. Which brings me to our purposes today." Chika opened a gate that sang with stones and sigilcraft, gesturing for Anna to precede her. "There's an old tanuki tradition, and I've decided to embrace it. Starting today."

The entrance was very near the garden behind The House of the Noble Chrysanthemum. Surely this bamboo-lined lane belonged to the Wendwood clan. Lush and green, with just enough room for two to walk side-by-side, Anna could hear nothing of the busy neighborhood they left behind. No doubt the clan employed many wards and barriers to protect this sanctuary.

"Lovely, isn't it?" Chika inquired.

"Completely." Still, Anna couldn't completely relax. "Why are we here?"

"Straight to business. I approve." And with a twirl of her parasol, she announced, "In human terms, I want you to help me elope!"

Anna listened with growing mystification. "Is that not hasty?"

"Oooh, not really. We're a small community. Most of us have already sorted out our preferred partners from among our playmates. But the real fun is keeping everything a secret. A pair chooses two trusted friends to act as witnesses. Vows are exchanged in a place like this, over the course of a set number of days. In our case, four."

"Only four?" Anna felt a little silly, repeating, "Is that not … hasty?"

"It's *symbolic*," Chika countered. "Four promises for four seasons, for my gentleman artist is enamored of the Junzi. He has flattered me with flowers, and I am well pleased. Now, he'll claim me with kisses."

"And all I have to do is watch?"

Chika's eyes sparkled, "And hunt Junpei down if he gets cold feet."

Anna chuckled. "My tracking skills are up to the task."

"Then we're all set. They're waiting just around the next bend."

Only then did Anna wonder who Junpei had chosen as his witness. "Who …?"

Chicka interrupted with a laugh. "Which of them looks more nervous to you?"

No response was needed, for Junpei stood straight and serene, gazing up through the shifting bamboo leaves with a half-smile on his face. By contrast, his companion paced and pulled at his hair, fiddled with his sleeves, and muttered to himself.

Harmonious Starmark.

"He does not know we are here?" Anna whispered.

Chika murmured, "I couldn't resist a peek."

With a snap of her fingers, whatever illusion that had covered their approach vanished, and Harmonious started violently. But he rallied enough to smile and shuffle forward to greet her with an almost reverent, "Anna."

CLAIM ME WITH KISSES

Junpei joined Chika on a bench set into a bow in the lane. She offered a hand, and he took it in both of his. Curious, he asked, "Did you tell him what he needed to know?"

"I did. And better yet, we'll demonstrate."

He glanced toward Harmonious and Anna, who stood a little ways off. "They're going to be watching?"

"They're our witnesses," Chika pointed out.

Junpei hummed uncertainly. "I don't think it's going well. They're not even talking."

Harmonious started guiltily and glanced at the stoic woman at his side.

"Did he hear me?" Junpei whispered.

"Many a keen ear in the clans." Chika glibly asked, "Didn't you give him any advice?"

"Well, no. I mean … I don't know his language."

"He is learning ours quickly. Otherwise, how would he know to be sheepish?"

Junpei darted another look at Harmonious. "I don't think he needs help. Just courage."

"Anna is a formidable woman. But I believe that is part of her appeal." Chika took a sing-song tone. "Catch if catch can, good sir. The trail is before you, and it may yet lead to a good den."

Across the way, Harmonious shuffled his feet, dipped his head, and turned toward Anna.

"Now!" murmured Chika. "Do you plan to speak only of them? Or shall we seek our own happiness?"

Junpei smiled crookedly. "I only wanted to be sure your plan was working."

"It's all up to him now. No more meddling." Scooting a little closer, she searched his face. "Shall we look to our own bond?"

"Yes. What do I need to do? Or ... say?"

"Promise to love me?"

That inspired a straighter smile. "I cannot even imagine stopping."

"An attitude I shall encourage by all my wiles." More seriously, Chika said, "Let's share all our days?"

"Through every season," he agreed.

"Ah, yes. That was to be our theme. My gentleman for all seasons." Her hand came up to caress his cheek. "Trust your future to me. This will be pleasant for both of us. Even pleasurable, once we can continue in privacy. But for now, just a taste."

Junpei's heart beat harder, and his face heated. "I don't know what to do."

"We're going to begin a bond that will link your life to mine." Chika's calm was soothing. "Over time, we'll tend it, and as you and I gain from it, time will fade in importance, though not in beauty."

"All right. Yes, please."

"There's nothing to fear. It's simple, really." She scooted a little closer. "I'll guide you."

"My life is in your hands."

"And mine in yours." She drew him down until their foreheads touched. "My people call this tending. It's a kind of give and take. Close your eyes and find me."

Which wasn't much to go on, but it turned out to be all Junpei needed.

Chika bloomed across his senses like paint across paper, bringing new color and beauty, inspiring awe and eagerness. She made him want to linger here, just like this, basking in the swirl of new sensations. But she also made him want to reach for his brushes. To capture this moment in some tangible way. Already, he was imagining the palette he would need, the way light and dark would mingle and blend.

"What are you imagining?" she whispered. "Because I like how it feels."

Junpei hummed. "I think that if I am your gentleman artist, then you must be my muse."

Chika giggled. Then teased him with whispery little kisses until he groaned.

When he tugged her snug against him and pressed more firmly, she went pliant and pulled him in, and Junpei no longer needed guiding. He was right where he'd always belonged.

HE FINDS HER DECISIVE

"You can hear them?" Anna quizzed.

"Ah. Yes. Of course. But my grasp of the language isn't what it needs to be."

She scrutinized Harmonious, then looked at the hand-holding couple across the way. "Why did they choose witnesses who cannot speak their language?"

"Do we need an exact translation? They're certainly taken with each other. That's clear enough by posture and ... ah, tone."

Anna wasn't sure why Harmonious radiated so much awkwardness. "Sometimes, posture and tone are at odds. Or confusing."

"Oh?"

"Yours, for example." Anna searched his face. "Quen did say matchmakers made you uncomfortable. Do you not approve?"

Harmonious gaped. "I want nothing but Junpei's happiness! Miss Wendwood is his choice, just as he is hers! As to the matter of matchmakers .... Quen was referring to my father, who repeatedly encouraged me to take a new bondmate. It was wearying. I left."

"If you prefer to remain alone, that is your right."

"No!" Harmonious looked even more discombobulated. "I mean, yes. But that's not it at all!"

"I was there when you said you did not wish to forget the one you loved." She couldn't help but feel they were talking in circles. "Were you not referring to your bondmate?"

"Aurora. Yes. She is dear to me, still." He rubbed at the side of his face. "This is going poorly."

Anna looked across the way. "I disagree. Everything seems amicable, over there. Although, I am not certain how closely I am meant to watch."

"Our duty as conspirators is to pay close enough attention to confirm the stages of their courtship while affording them as much privacy as is polite."

"So vague."

"Please." Harmonious held up his hands and begged, "May I begin again?"

She hadn't realized he was attempting to start something. "They seem in no hurry."

"Anna," was as far as he got for several moments. "Anna, I'm not opposed to taking a new bondmate. But she'd have to be *my* choice. Mine."

"I understand your aversion to being coerced."

He winced. "Which is why I have been reluctant to press the matter."

If she was supposed to know what he was referring to, he was mistaken. But she had nowhere else to be. He'd probably get around to a point eventually.

Harmonious sighed and took a cautious posture, as if he didn't want to offend. "When I asked about their match, I was *referring* to a human accepting an Amaranthine partner."

"I have never heard of it before. Well, not outside of ballads."

"Would *you* ever consider such a match?"

"It would depend entirely upon who ...." She caught on then and frowned.

Harmonious nodded. "If it was *me*?"

"I am hardly a sensible choice."

He looked utterly baffled. "Isn't that for me to decide?"

Anna reviewed their acquaintance, and her consternation grew. Friendly overtures. Hopeful postures. Attentiveness. Is this what Quen had meant about his Da's smile? Blades and blows, no wonder Opal had been silently laughing at her.

And suddenly, her mentor's words came back to her. *You did not rebuff the old dog.* And something more. "Opal said you'd been bond-building."

"He was correct. I'm not sure what I was thinking at that moment, but … I accept any blame you wish to lay." Harmonious lowered his gaze. "The tending rather went to my head."

She knew when he meant. During battle. "But I initiated."

"Your trust pleased me. And when the tides turned, you were glorious." Admiration shone in his eyes.

"It was all backward," she recalled. "Your strength flowing into me."

"You … you felt that?"

Silly question. She waved it off. "It went to my head as well. I was able to draw on your power, then channel it through the Blaze."

His expression clouded. "You remember that part, too?"

"I would hardly forget."

"But … they have. My clan. Our allies. What's left of the Miyabe family. They only have the vaguest sense of what happened that night."

"Why?" Anna shook her head. "It cannot have been dragon sway. We routed them."

"We did." And more softly, pleadingly, he added, "We make a good team."

"Even so, I am a poor choice."

Harmonious firmly said, "That's for *me* to decide. *You* must decide if I have the makings of a good bondmate."

Anna snorted. "Your entire clan is a testament to that."

He hung his head and groaned. "My dear, I am not speaking in generalities."

Head on then.

"You were right. This *is* going poorly." Anna preferred direct orders, a clear objective. "May *I* pose some questions?"

Harmonious swiftly took a receptive posture.

"I am your choice?"

"Yes."

"Based on ...?"

"Love."

Anna's eyebrows lifted. "Is that not rather hasty?"

"Quite sudden," he cheerfully agreed. "You took me entirely by surprise."

"And having chosen in haste, you wish to marry in haste?" She gestured toward Junpei and Chika. "To elope?"

"I'd leap at the chance," he admitted. "But I can be patient. I'm willing to court your favor, especially since ... I seem to have been beneath your notice."

"Hardly. You've been looming large since our introduction."

His shoulders squared, but his smile didn't lose its self-deprecating twist.

She posed her next question. "Why a human?"

"Because ... you're human ...?"

"And as ephemeral as nippets in the eyes of an ancient."

"I am ... old ... *ish*." He looked abashed. "You find my years off-putting?"

Anna chided herself for being too vague. Clarity was needed. The more direct she was, the better. "In a matter of decades, I will die. Sooner, if the tide of some future battle turns against me."

Harmonious smiled a little. "You'd refuse me because you don't want me to be sad?"

Grimly going back to her first point, she repeated, "I am hardly a sensible choice."

"Look. There, now. They've begun." He nodded toward the bench. "Can you tell from here?"

The couple were as close as they could be without Chika piling onto Junpei's lap, and their foreheads were touching. Chika's happiness was palpable, and Junpei exuded so much serenity. "Is tending a part of tanuki courtship?"

There was a gruff edge to Harmonious' undertone. "Chika is tending Junpei."

"*He* is the reaver," Anna pointed out. "He must be tending her."

"Those who take can give, or so Miss Wendwood tells me. And by cultivating a mutual bond, an Amaranthine is able to share their years with their human partner."

"Is that really possible?"

"Granted, it's not widely known or even discussed in this part of the world, but I don't think she was teasing when she shared the secret with me. So that I could share it with you."

They were kissing now. Anna lowered her gaze.

Harmonious cleared his throat. "She may have also offered to … reciprocate. Should you be favorably inclined."

"I dearly wish you would stop trying to put things so delicately."

He blinked. "Having seen the … ah … *force* of your rebuffs firsthand, I have no wish to incur one."

Anna may have smiled.

Harmonious may have brightened. "If my pursuit pleases you, here are two witnesses. Junpei and Chika would watch over our beginnings, even as we watch over theirs."

"How convenient."

"For once, I do not mind the meddling." Harmonious gestured between them and asked, "Share my years?"

"You would invite danger into your den?" Anna reminded, "I have made enemies."

"Without hesitation. And my pledge remains, even if you have no wish to lead my clan."

That gave her pause. "When you say *lead* …?"

"You would be Lady Starmark."

Anna prided herself on being decisive. She struck an authoritative pose. "They need three more days like this one?"

"That's how it was explained to me."

"Then you have three more days in which to persuade me."

Harmonious rubbed at his jaw with a shaky hand. "What form of persuasion …?"

"I leave that to you. But be warned, these interludes are brief. And my patience for niceties is severely limited." She nodded toward the beaming couple. "See? They are already finished."

"Then … it is our turn?" Harmonious asked, his gaze on Chika.

She fluttered her fingers at them, then whispered to Junpei, who looked relieved.

Harmonious ventured, "Three more days … *and* today?"

Anna tilted her chin challengingly. "If our negotiations thus far did not satisfy you."

"Maker bless, that was almost a *yes*." And more formally, "Before these witnesses, I will say it plainly. You are my choice. And … I would like very much to try tending you, again. Since words are failing me, let my heart speak?"

A reasonable tactic.

Perhaps even wise.

"Is that how it works?" she asked.

Harmonious eased closer. "May I touch?"

She eyed him warily. "Within reason."

All he did was offer his palms. She covered them, and he carefully moved his hands into a supporting position. "This should do." And closing his eyes, he murmured, "Whenever you are ready."

Interest piqued, Anna lifted her chin, shut her eyes, and welcomed Harmonious into the sort of communion that fostered tending. Such an exchange was always honest. Her trust for Opulence Windlore was largely due to the person he revealed himself to be during tending. Anna was only giving Harmonious the same opportunity.

But it wasn't even remotely similar.

Because Opal's affections were so aloof as to be grandfatherly, for his heart belonged to another, brighter soul than hers. But Harmonious was carefully holding back a vast storehouse of pent-up feelings. Yearning and protectiveness and hope and attraction. And the fear that he would be too much for her.

"Are you underestimating me, again?" she inquired.

He huffed, and his strength washed over her, then—warm and worried. It was too much a part of his nature for him to do otherwise. An inclination toward peace. Honesty in every dealing. Respect for humankind.

Little by little, he surrendered more to her, and she took everything. Far too soon, he was easing back, and she clung to him, wanting more. He had to know it, too. Well, she wouldn't be ashamed. It had been good.

"Do you understand?" he softly begged.

Oh, she did.

That he was boundless.

And she was beloved.

Both truths were daunting in their way, but Anna would face them like the battler she was. Searching his gaze, she found it impossible to withhold an answer that was more than *almost*. "Yes."

LET ME GO DEEP

"You are bonded to Chika?" Kusunoki asked.

"Yes. Everything's settled. Mother adores her, and Sho doesn't mind. Neighbors think we're living with her parents until I can set us up in a house. But there's a cluster of thatched huts at the end of a secret lane, and one of them is ours now."

"The tanuki hideaway? Mmm… I know it." His fingers tightened around Junpei's hand. "You are close by."

"Close enough for you to reach? Naoki said that was important."

Kusunoki looked away. "I do not think it matters."

Junpei was seriously concerned for his friend, who was apparently this tree. "Has something changed? I know the dragons twisted all around your limbs. Were you damaged?"

"I am glad you remember. Nobody else does. The children do not even pray to me anymore, without Matsu to remind them."

"Hajime did say that people would forget. Was that the right choice?"

"For his safety and for Naoki's … yes. They do not like dragons. This place has become their hideaway."

"It's good, isn't it? Having them close."

"If they left, I would be even more alone. But they are each other's, and no one is mine."

Junpei had suspected as much. "I won't do?"

"I did try."

"What about Matsu's children? Could you befriend one of them?"

Kusunoki took his time answering. "I could. I have done it before. Every few generations, one of the Miyabe children would find me, and it would be *almost* enough. Why does it always have to end?"

"Human lives are short compared to a tree's. But … there may be a way. With the right sort of bond." Junpei tapped his chest. "Like mine with Chika."

"Mmm."

"Or what if you found someone who already shares a tree's years? An Amaranthine partner?"

Kusunoki wearily shook his head.

"What can I do?" Junpei brought his other hand up in the supportive gesture he'd learned.

Slowly, sadly, Kusunoki said, "Bring Father. And Naoki."

Junpei returned to Kusunoki's side, keeping his promise even though Kusunoki clearly needed more than he was able to offer. Naoki caught up, pulling Hajime along behind him.

The breeze scattered red petals onto the pavers, reminding Junpei that Kusunoki's branches had been bare of flowers since Matsu's death.

Naoki asked questions, sounding very like a doctor.

Hajime's gaze darted from one face to the next, looking as if he might have something to say … but didn't want to say it.

"I am so tired of this," Kusunoki complained. "So tired."

Naoki looked close to tears when he turned to Hajime. "What recourse do we have?"

With a sigh, Hajime crouched before his son and offered a hand. "Sleep, leafling. You should be able to do it. I think you have already begun. Go deep for a time. Sleep like a stone."

"What if …?" Kusunoki's protest trailed off uncertainly.

Naoki said, "We'll stay in the area. Watch over you when we can."

"And I'm near," offered Junpei. "I'll visit. And watch for your return."

Kusunoki's gaze turned inward. "I think I can. Mmm… I will."

He vanished without saying goodbye. But Junpei guessed that in the long run, it wasn't.

UNDER THE CAMPHOR TREE

Anna allowed the daughters of the Starmark clan to array her for the bonding ceremony. Chika had encouraged it, much as she'd urged Anna to adhere to a lengthy canine courtship. All the phases and gifts had allowed Harmonious' family to participate in welcoming a new Lady Starmark into their den.

Personally, Anna thought Chika was being hypocritical. The tanuki had merrily eloped, with her kin none the wiser.

Anna's four days as a witness—and Harmonious' attendant persuasion—had served as a sort of betrothal. He'd kept his pledges simple and his tending sessions brief. After consulting with Chika, Anna had negotiated a few terms.

He brought her a star-etched comb and told her the story of his clan.

She demanded the right to defend his clan whenever a threat arose.

He commissioned Junpei to paint the screens in the pavilion they'd share.

She asked that Opulence Windlore sing a blessing over their bonding.

He presented a map showing his lands ... and the portion allotted for an orphanage.

She requested measures to put off pregnancy, since Chika warned of complications.

Although she thought it pained him, Harmonious agreed. It was for her protection, in the end, and he respected her wishes in every regard.

And so, twelve moons later, Reaver Anna Green, arrayed in Starmark colors, stood under Kikusawa Shrine's sacred tree, ready for a final exchange of vows.

"Is this a camphor tree?" she asked, for her Japanese was vastly improved.

Junpei looked up from where he was painting a delicate chrysanthemum upon the new flagstones. So many had to be replaced after last year's attack. Little by little, the evidence was disappearing.

"This is Kusunoki," he answered.

"I know," she said slowly. "I had not realized you remembered."

Junpei sat upon the ground, slowly twirling the paintbrush between his fingers. "Chika has forgotten, but I didn't. Kusunoki and I shared a promise. Maybe that mattered."

"Harmonious and I remember everything."

"Good. It's less lonely, that way." His gaze turned thoughtful. "You flew pretty far, that night. The air's probably really clear from way up high."

"Has Chika never taken you flying?"

Junpei shook his head. "I'll have to ask. Might be fun. But this needs finishing first."

"Are chrysanthemums your signature?"

"Not really, no. But they suit you. And Kusunoki didn't bloom this year. So ... consider this a gift from the two of us. Congratulations on your bonding, Saint Midori. You are sure to be a tribute to your den."

And because she'd since learned the traditional response to such compliments, the soon-to-be Lady Starmark used it to thank him. "For now and for ever."

THE END

never more than
FORTHRIGHT

a teller of tales who began as a fandom ficcer. (Which basically means that no one in RL knows about her anime habit, her manga collection, or her penchant for serial storytelling.) Kinda sorta almost famous for gently-paced, WAFFy adventures that might inadvertently overturn your OTP, forthy will forever adore drabble challenges, surprise fanart, and twinkles (which are rumored to keep well in jars). As always... be nice, play fair, have fun! ::twinkle::

FORTHWRITES.COM

Abundant thanks to all who lend their support by reading, rating, and reviewing my stories, wherever they may be found. ::twinkle::

ALSO BY FORTHRIGHT

AMARANTHINE SAGA

Tsumiko and the Enslaved Fox

Kimiko and the Accidental Proposal

Tamiko and the Two Janitors

Mikoto and the Reaver Village

Fumiko and the Finicky Nestmate

Pimiko and the Uncharted Island

SONGS OF THE AMARANTHINE

Marked by Stars

Followed by Thunder

Dragged through Hedgerows

Governed by Whimsy

Hemmed in Silver

Captured on Film

Bathed in Moonlight

Flattered by Flowers

AMARANTHINE INTERLUDES

Lord Mettlebright's Man

PATREON EXCLUSIVES

Bard & Barbarian

Kimiko and the Cycle of Moons

When I reach 400 patrons, I'll begin publishing a new subscription-based storyline on Patreon. Loosely based on the old Amaranthine tale, "The Wolf and the Moon Maiden," this serial will involve three sisters, twelve pledges, and the long-awaited stirring of a sleeping landmark. Become a patron at https://www.patreon.com/forthrightly

Readers have often asked for more of Kimiko Miyabe's courtship of Eloquence Starmark. Their grand cycle is a tale I'm eager to tell. **Once I reach my posted community goal over on Patreon**, I'll begin a serialized account that ranges from fittings in the seamstress's workroom at the Starmark compound to the forming of fresh triads at New Saga High School. And of course, all the drama at Kikusawa Shrine: three sisters, twelve kisses, and the long-awaited stirring of a sleeping landmark.

Become a patron at https://www.patreon.com/forthrightly

Bard & Barbarian

BY FORTHRIGHT

*Imber was only a boy when he met the divine beast
who would one day share his adventures.*

A serialized fantasy that's currently a Patreon exclusive. Access to the ongoing adventure is available at all tiers of support. Now with bi-weekly audio installments, narrated by Travis Baldree. Become a patron in order to read along.

https://www.patreon.com/forthrightly

www.ingramcontent.com/pod-product-compliance
Lightning Source LLC
Chambersburg PA
CBHW060300100726
47907CB00002B/226